Liz Byrski was born and broug... ... Western Australia since 1981. She is the author of a number of non-fiction books, and has worked as a staff and freelance journalist, a broadcaster with ABC Radio and an adviser to a minister in the WA Government. Liz now lectures in professional writing at Curtin University. She is also the author of *Gang of Four*.

www.lizbyrski.com.au

Also by Liz Byrski

Gang of Four

Liz Byrski

FOOD, SEX & MONEY

PAN
Pan Macmillan Australia

First published 2005 in Macmillan by Pan Macmillan Australia Pty Limited
This Pan edition published in 2006 by Pan Macmillan Australia
1 Market Street, Sydney

Reprinted 2006

A CIP catalogue record for this book is available from
the National Library of Australia

ISBN-13: 978 0 330 42265 9
ISBN-10: 0 330 42265 0

The characters and events in this book are fictitious and any resemblance to
real persons, living or dead, is purely coincidental.

Typeset in Palatino by Post Pre-press Group
Printed in Australia by McPherson's Printing Group

Papers used by Pan Macmillan Australia Pty Ltd are natural, recyclable
products made from wood grown in sustainable forests. The manufacturing
processes conform to the environmental regulations of the country of origin.

Author photograph: Murray Simon

ACKNOWLEDGMENTS

Sheila and Don Drummond gave me the best ever crash course on Melbourne and its suburbs, driving me everywhere, feeding me, and making me welcome and extremely comfortable in gorgeous, snowy Woodend.

Lorraine Haw provided me with information on emergency treatment and other medical issues.

The wonderful team at Pan Macmillan – Cate Paterson, Sarina Rowell and Jo Jarrah – kept me on track and comprehensible, and dealt with my work with professionalism and respect.

My family and my women friends are a source of constant support and great inspiration.

I thank you all.

Thanks too to Jenny Joseph for permission to use extracts from her poem 'Warning', © Jenny Joseph, *Selected Poems*, Bloodaxe, 1992.

Information on the Red Hat Society can be found at www.redhatsociety.com and there are several groups in Australia.

ONE

Once, a long time ago when she was very much younger, Bonnie had had sex for money. In fact, it wasn't just once, it was quite a few times – but she preferred to think of it, the whole episode, as once. It wasn't anything sordid, of course: no soliciting, no kerb-crawling punters, no cash on the dressing table of some grubby motel, nothing like that. It was more of an investment strategy, and at the time it seemed perfectly reasonable. She was young, single, a newly qualified accountant and she had grown up with money; now she wanted financial independence. He was older, married, a banker and very rich.

'You should get yourself a share portfolio, Bonnie,' he told her a few times. 'I'd be happy to advise you.' And he slid his hand down the side of her skirt and it settled on the curve of her rather shapely bottom and stayed there.

Bonnie, always a realist, understood that a comparatively short-term investment of her body could be the key to a lifetime of financial security. 'After all, it's not as though he's revolting,' she told her flatmate. 'And – well, he'll be getting something he really wants, so I might as well get something I want. He's not totally unfanciable; in fact, he's quite sweet. Sex is the seed capital for my security.'

The flatmate, who had just completed an arts degree with a double major in philosophy and ethics, rolled her eyes and suggested that Bonnie invest in some condoms.

It proved to be a highly satisfactory joint venture. The banker deposited his seed, and Bonnie's assets in blue-chip shares grew, until the awkward moment when even the prospect of adding a few shares in a West Australian gold mine no longer seemed sufficiently attractive and she cut out of the deal and began banking elsewhere. These days Bonnie rarely gave it a thought, unless it was to contrast her first pragmatic sexual encounters with the subsequent thirty-plus years of satisfactory monogamy with Jeff. The only two men she had ever slept with were bankers, the first for investment purposes, the second when she fell in love and married; the irony was not lost on her and doubtless some feminist therapist could come up with an interesting theory about this, but Bonnie preferred not to know. There was, she thought, a bit too much interest in finding out about oneself these days and a person could easily overload on insight.

But that first adventure in investment did run through her mind now, as she sat at the dressing table putting on her mascara and wondering if she had dressed up too much for this reunion with her old school friends. It bounced back into her consciousness because the last time she met them she had been building that investment portfolio one night a week in a very comfortable city apartment, which was the banker's weekday residence. Not that she'd mentioned it to Fran and Sylvia at the time, of course. They had stopped sharing all their secrets three years earlier when they graduated from the convent. Since that day the ties of sisterhood, forged in the shadowy corners of the locker room and the bleak alcove at the back of the hockey hut, had been strained by distance and the discovery of the wider world outside.

The mascara wand slipped and one eye suddenly acquired a Dusty Springfield look. Bonnie leaned back surveying her face from all angles and decided that she'd put on too much make-up anyway. Here in Australia her face seemed different, the features too small and neat; she'd always wished for fuller lips, and now they seemed thinner than ever. She'd considered collagen injections, and those permanent tattoos that built a firm but unobtrusive lip outline like permanent lipstick, but she feared ending up with an obtrusive pout from the former and the agonising pain that would certainly be attached to the latter.

She peered again – perhaps it was just that her face was thinner? She had lost about five kilos since Jeff died. She began removing the make-up with a cleansing pad designed for mature skin. Less make-up seemed to be the thing here: in the three months she'd been back she'd noticed that older women seemed to favour a more natural look than European women. Bonnie didn't want to look false, or dated; on the other hand, she didn't want to turn up looking older than the other two. They would all turn fifty-six this year, but you just couldn't tell with women. These days, fifty-five year olds could look like forty or seventy.

She stared at her now half-naked face in the mirror, wishing she hadn't organised the reunion, wishing she'd never discovered the wretched website where you could contact your old school friends. They'd left St Theresa's convent in 1964, gone their separate ways, staying in touch but at a distance, until two years later there had been the invitation to Sylvia's wedding. What a surprise that had been. Bonnie and Fran had been at a total loss to understand how it had happened; how confident, self-contained Sylvia, destined for a brilliant career in fashion design, had suddenly decided to marry a handsome but poverty-stricken PhD theology student whose ambition was to become a minister of religion. It hadn't become any clearer at the wedding, when Colin, despite his good looks, appeared to be a well-meaning but tedious young man, prone to sulks and lacking in humour. A year later they had met again for a farewell drink before Fran set off for London with a backpack and not much else. And now it was thirty-seven years, almost to the day, since they had sat in the St Kilda bar where the music was too loud and some oaf spilled his beer all over Bonnie's new blouse.

She looked at the blouse she was wearing now, adjusting the collar, turning side-on to the mirror. She looked like a corporate wife, a corporate European wife, which was, after all, what she had been for more than thirty years. Now she was a new widow – is that how one described it? 'Recently widowed' sounded better – a recently widowed woman in her mid-fifties, back in Australia again, alone, displaced, confused . . . Bonnie stopped herself. This was not what she needed. Meeting the others again she needed to look chipper, that's what Jeff would have said – chipper. Silly word, really, but it used to sound all right when he said it.

Bonnie got up from the dressing-table stool and took off the Chanel suit. Even in Zurich she had sometimes thought it made too much of a statement, but it had cost a bomb so it was almost criminal to get rid of it. She dropped the skirt on the bed; maybe there was a recycling shop nearby. Something casual might be better, linen perhaps; it was surprisingly warm for April. Yes, the cream linen top and skirt would be more suitable, and very flattering. They made her look taller, stretched her out a bit; she could do with that.

Bonnie was in good physical shape, especially since she had lost those few kilos, but she'd always battled the solid frame inherited from her father. It translated into a tendency to look chunky, and she'd become skilled at countering it with carefully chosen clothes. She stepped into the skirt, smoothing it over her hips, taking a deep breath to calm the butterflies. She was home but it felt like a foreign country. On previous trips back over the years, Jeff had been with her, but this was different: Jeff was gone and she had turned her back on the comfortable life in Switzerland, sold everything and come home to Melbourne for good. She'd thought it would feel better, that she couldn't live on in the places they had shared, but it seemed that when Jeff died Bonnie's confidence had died with him, and here she was, alone, feeling like a stranger – and it was very scary.

She twisted around in front of the mirror checking her appearance. What would the other two be like now? Fran apparently had some chaotic freelance food writing work, which sounded totally in character. She had always seemed to lurch from one drama to the next, rushing everywhere at the last minute, doing more than anyone else and somehow staying cheerful about it. And Sylvia? Neat probably, neat as ever. Miss Understated, they'd called her, until they'd changed it to Miss-understood when she'd married Colin. Bonnie reapplied the mascara, very lightly this time, and then a bronze-toned lipstick; better, definitely better and, satisfied with the way she looked, she picked up her bag and ran down the stairs.

'I'm off now, Mum,' she said, popping her head around the door of the living room. 'Lunch with Sylvia and Fran, remember?'

Her mother looked up from the newspaper. 'Yes, dear, I do remember, you've already told me where you're going, three times at least.'

'There's some of that quiche left in the fridge . . .' Bonnie began, 'it only needs to go in the microwave.'

Irene put down the paper and took off her glasses. 'Bonita dear, it's wonderful to have you home but your arrival hasn't rendered me incapable of looking after myself. For heaven's sake, stop fussing, enjoy your lunch and give those girls my love.'

'Right then,' said Bonnie with a weak smile, 'right . . . well, I'll go then.'

'Yes, dear. You look very nice, by the way, and stop worrying; they're your friends, not the Spanish Inquisition.'

Fran was running late. Nothing unusual in that, but it was the last thing she needed. She had wanted time to prepare, to make sure she looked her best, and that meant getting dressed and undressed at least half a dozen times until she found something that made her look thinner. A waste of energy because nothing really made her look thinner; just sometimes she would discover the odd garment that made her look a little less fat. For the last month, in anticipation of this reunion, Fran had redoubled her efforts at the gym in the hope of doing one of those Catherine Zeta-Jones–Renée Zellweger sudden weight loss things and ending up ten kilos lighter in four weeks. She knew it was hopeless but panic compelled her. She had just completed an agonising forty minutes on the treadmill, *with* an incline factor of two-point-five, and an even worse fifteen minutes of torture on the cross-trainer. Fran hated the cross-trainer, and often mused that it would be nice if, at her funeral, there could be a ritual burning of the cross-trainer, which she was pretty sure would be the cause of her death.

Still sweating and beetroot-faced from the gym, she pulled into the driveway and stopped behind a yellow VW Beetle, which meant Caro was here. That was the last thing she needed with only two hours between her and this wonderful, intriguing, terrifying reunion with her school friends. Caro was lying on the sofa talking on her mobile phone when Fran let herself in through the back door; she waved a hand and a foot in unison at her mother and mouthed a smiling 'hello'. Fran waved, kicking off her shoes and heading for the shower.

The last four weeks at the gym didn't seem to have had much effect, she thought, standing naked in front of the bathroom mirror; maybe because she invariably came straight home and tucked into a huge plate of something delicious to reward herself for surviving the workout. Was it actually possible to be a food writer and not be fat? Even Nigella was comfortably rounded – voluptuous, actually, and statuesque. Of course, voluptuous and statuesque would be fine, wonderful. Podgy was not. Podgy with great hair would have been better, but Fran had been allocated very fine, silky, pale hair which defied any colour definition. Ah well, she thought, stepping into the shower, at least they'd easily recognise her; she'd always been podgy, now she was just older and podgy. It was what they used to call her: Podge, Podge Whittaker. 'I may have to kill the first one of them who calls me Podge,' she sighed, turning on the taps.

When Fran came out, Caro was lying sprawled across her bed. 'Wear that rust-coloured silk shirt!' she said.

'Does it make me look thinner?' Fran asked.

'Well, you're not exactly a thin person, are you, Mum?' Caro said. 'But it *is* very flattering and it suits you. I would say it certainly makes you look *younger*, especially with the black linen three-quarter pants. And with those chunky black sandals – good!'

'You're sure?'

'I'm sure. What're you so worried about, anyway? It's only a couple of old school friends. They won't care what you wear. Nobody cares what friends wear these days.'

Fran slipped her arms into the sleeves of the shirt. 'You wouldn't understand,' she said. 'We're a different generation. They'll be sizing me up, working out what my life's been like, how I'm doing now.'

'You mean *you'll* be sizing *them* up,' Caro said with disturbing insight. 'No one's as neurotic about how they look as you are, Mum, honestly.'

Fran straightened her shoulders and buttoned up the shirt. 'You've no idea what it's like,' she said. 'How could someone of twenty-eight, with a taut midriff and a ring in her navel, have any idea what it's like to be fifty-five, short, and twenty kilos overweight? You know nothing, Caro, so shut up!'

'Well, I won't have a taut midriff much longer,' Caro said, smiling and smoothing her hand across the area in question.

'What d'you mean?' Fran asked, searching now for a particular pair of gold hoop earrings. 'What did you come for, anyway? I can't hang around for long or I'll be late.'

'I came to tell you,' Caro said, stretching out among her mother's discarded clothes with an infuriating air of satisfaction, 'that I won't have a taut midriff much longer because I'm pregnant. Mike and I are having a baby.'

In the restaurant car park Fran stared at herself in the driving mirror. Her face was still essence of beetroot; the gym, the unseasonal heat, her own bad timing and Caro's news had all conspired to ensure that she would arrive looking like one of those rosy-cheeked Russian dolls that were as broad as they were tall and contained two other dolls within them. Surely the air conditioning would be good here? She'd reviewed this place once years ago for *Eating Out* magazine, and remembered saying it was pretentious and overpriced, but did that also mean cool?

Fran felt a mix of excitement and anxiety. It wasn't that she didn't want to be a grandmother, but it had come as such a surprise – a shock, really. And while part of her was thrilled at the prospect of a baby, she couldn't help wondering if her daughter was really ready for motherhood; maturity seemed to be a long time coming. Caro and Mike had met ten years ago when they were both eighteen, and they'd been together ever since. Fran was constantly surprised that the relationship had survived the residual streak of adolescence that was a particularly annoying

7

aspect of Caro's personality. She foresaw chaos, more chaos than usual, and that was really saying something.

She pressed a cooling Wet One on her forehead and glowing cheeks, wondering if she had arrived last or if she'd wait a bit longer in the car before going in, wondering what Sylvia would be wearing; something tailored probably, subtle colours, and not new. Even at school she'd had just a few carefully chosen and well-cared-for outfits that never seemed to crease. She'd never had any money to spare but her mother had been a dressmaker, and Sylvia had started designing and making her own clothes at the age of thirteen and had always looked good. As for Bonnie, she'd probably be wearing one of those classic suits, with an edge-to-edge jacket, very European and costing a fortune. Ah well, that was Bonnie, the rich widow now, which was probably why she picked this restaurant, with no idea how ill-equipped she and Sylvia were to pay for it.

A silver grey BMW slid into the shade in the far corner of the car park and Fran's heartbeat quickened. This was the sort of car that Bonnie would have, not a middle-aged Camry stuffed with old issues of *Gourmet Traveller* and *Eating Out* and *Eating In* and a bin bag full of clothes she ought to drop off to the Salvos. A man in a dark business suit got out of the BMW and strolled into the restaurant. So it wasn't Bonnie's, after all. A trickle of sweat crept down the middle of Fran's back. It was too hot to stay in the car. She swung the door open and stepped out, looking anxiously towards the restaurant. There was still time to pop into the toilets to check her appearance. And at least she'd have exciting news, something more interesting than the usual sagas about the agonies of freelancing, attempts at weight loss, and buying clothes that might one day fit but never actually did. She wondered if Sylvia was a grandmother yet. A grandmother! Now, that was dignified. No reasonable woman would refer to a grandmother as Podge. Fran locked the car and headed up the steps into the restaurant.

Sylvia had arrived at the restaurant twenty minutes early and was relieved to have time to sit alone at the window table that

Bonnie had reserved, gazing out over the river, trying to calm herself. The morning had been so appalling that she had barely given a thought to meeting the others again. She had thrown on her black linen dress and stormed out of the house, leaving Colin standing open mouthed in the bedroom, almost white with shock. Sylvia could see it all in her mind like a scene from a movie; she was in the bedroom searching for something to wear and Colin had wandered in to change for the Dean's lunch.

'We should leave at twelve,' he said, stepping into his black trousers and watching himself in the mirror as he did up his fly.

'I told you last week,' Sylvia said, 'I'm not going. I've got other plans.'

He looked up in alarm. 'But whatever will they think? After all, Bill *is* the Dean and this lunch is especially for the senior clergy and their wives.'

'I'm sure they'll understand,' Sylvia had said, containing her impatience by brushing her hair vigorously, twisting it up and fixing it at the back of her head with a large tortoiseshell clip. 'Just explain that I've a previous arrangement for lunch with friends whom I haven't seen for thirty-seven years.'

'But they're expecting you.'

'They're only expecting me because *you* accepted the invitation on my behalf *after* I'd told you that I was meeting Bonnie and Fran. This reunion has been arranged for four weeks, it's been marked on the kitchen calendar and the one in your study, but you ignored it thinking you could pressure me into going to this thing at the Deanery. Well, you can't!'

Colin, struggling to fix the stud on a clean dog collar, adopted the injured, sulky look that he had perfected for occasions when he wanted to pressure her into doing something he considered was the province of a Canon's wife. 'That thing in your hair looks like a giant bulldog clip,' he grunted. 'You are so unreasonable, Syl. Why can't you come to lunch today and meet your friends another time? Surely it's not too much to ask?'

It was at this point that the mind movie went into slow motion and Sylvia saw herself swing round, grab the Lladro shepherdess and hurl it across the room so that it hit the door frame and smashed onto the floor. She had never actually thrown anything before, although frustration had often taken her dangerously close to it. She wasn't sure now whether she had meant just to throw it, or to throw it at Colin. The moment, thirty-two years earlier, when he had given it to her for their fifth wedding anniversary, flashed briefly before her eyes as they both gazed at the shards of pale blue, grey and white porcelain scattered across the polished floorboards.

'Yes, it is!' she said in a low and dangerous voice. 'It *is* too much to ask. I spend every damn day being Mrs Reverend Canon Colin Fleming. Well, today's different; today I'm Sylvia, Sylvia Lowry, and I'm doing something I want to do, so you can just stuff the Dean's lunch wherever you wish to stuff it.' And reaching out for the string of amber beads, she slipped them over her head. 'I'll be back late this afternoon, and you can tell the Dean and his apostles that it's your own stupid fault that led them to expect me in the first place.' And, grabbing her bag from the bedpost, she swept out of the bedroom.

'What about the Lladro?' Colin called lamely. 'I bought you that.'

'Yes, and you can clear it up,' she said, slamming the front door behind her.

The restaurant was deliciously cool with pristine white linen, sparkling crystal and deferential waitstaff who kept refilling her glass with iced water. It was much more formal and expensive than the sort of place that Sylvia usually went to eat, either with Colin or with friends, and the calm elegance was just what she needed. Trust Bonnie to book somewhere like this. Normally Sylvia would have balked at the price but this was a special occasion, more special, actually, since the Lladro incident. Bonnie had probably given little thought to the cost, anyway; she had doubtless spent much of her life in expensive European restaurants while Jeff was alive.

Sylvia wondered briefly what it felt like to be a widow and flushed at the realisation that the only emotion she could summon at the prospect was one of relief. Surely she didn't wish Colin dead? No! No, of course not, she just wished that she wasn't married to him and to the tedious, seemingly endless responsibilities of a clergy wife. Smashing the Lladro was a reaction to more than three decades of faithful, albeit resentful, service to his career choice – or vocation, as he liked to call it. The waiter filled Sylvia's glass again and she smiled her thanks, sipped the icy water, and then took a long deep breath and exhaled slowly, trying to breathe away her tension and concentrate on the occasion.

Bonnie and Fran, what would they look like? She often read Fran's column in the newspaper and it had a small, grainy portrait at the top. A few times Sylvia had considered calling her or sending a note to her at the newspaper but had always backed off. Fran was obviously successful and busy and probably wouldn't want to be bothered, and Sylvia dreaded the prospect of being ignored or getting a dismissive response. But she'd really longed to make contact. They'd been best friends, after all, and that was why she'd registered with the website; maybe, she thought, one of them would go online and register too. It took almost two years and she'd forgotten about it until a few weeks earlier, when there'd been a message from Bonnie.

Bonnie – elegant as ever, no doubt, oozing European chic. Jeff had made a fortune and his death in January had been all over the business pages, alongside incomprehensible graphs showing what effect it was having on the share prices of the international merchant bank he had headed. And now here was Bonnie, a widow, presumably a very rich widow, home in Australia, living with her mother in that lovely old house in Gardenvale, where the three of them used to sit in the apple tree and speculate about which one would be the first to get a proper tongue kiss.

Sylvia leaned back in her chair feeling a little more relaxed. It was twelve-thirty, they'd be here any minute – well, no, not Fran of course, she would be late. Fran was always late. And as she glanced up, Sylvia saw a woman hesitate at the entrance to the restaurant; a woman of medium height, with short, beautifully cut dark hair, dressed in cream linen. Sylvia gasped in shock because the woman was in her fifties and she had been expecting someone in her twenties. She stood to greet her and saw the same time-lapse surprise cross Bonnie's face as she made her way to the table.

Irene Masters sat in the living room in her favourite chair, listening as her daughter started the car, reversed down the drive and out into the street. She sat tense and upright, waiting for the pause as Bonnie changed gear and accelerated up the hill, then, with a sigh of relief, Irene leaned back and closed her eyes, relishing the stillness of the house. She had the place to herself at last, for – what? Three hours at least, maybe more. It seemed like the greatest luxury. Irene thought ruefully of the selfishly peaceful years she had spent alone in this house, reading, sewing, pottering around doing jobs, listening to music, playing the piano, entertaining her friends, without ever fully appreciating the joys of solitude. But in the three months that Bonnie had been home Irene never seemed to get any time to herself.

It wasn't that she didn't love her daughter, and she was delighted to have her back after all those years on the other side of the world. It just seemed that Jeff's death had led Bonnie to embark on a mission of looking after her mother. Perhaps it was to be expected, Irene reflected; for years Bonnie had focused her efforts on looking after Jeff, providing the sort of home where staff, business associates and clients could always expect a warm and gracious welcome. Now that he was gone she clearly needed another target for her energy. Once the funeral was over she had put the apartment in the hands of an agent and announced she was coming home to live.

Bonnie hadn't actually asked if she could come home but that, Irene thought, was understandable; it had been the family home for decades. She and Dennis had inherited it from his parents, their children had been born and lived here until Simon left at twenty-one, and two years later, Bonnie, by then also twenty-one, graduated from her accountancy training and moved into a shared apartment. The two of them had always treated it as home, coming and going when it suited them, until Bonnie married Jeff and went to Hong Kong and then to Europe. Simon had moved back when his marriage broke up and he had to sell his house. He was in his forties and ended up staying a couple of years. So it was natural for Bonnie to assume she could come back, and Irene had not been averse to the idea of their living together while Bonnie sorted out her future. But in the last few weeks it had become clear that Bonnie was home to stay.

Irene got up, found her favourite CD, and skipped to the second movement of Rachmaninov's second piano concerto. It always sent a shiver down her spine, transporting her back to the first time she heard it with Dennis, in the cinema when they went to see *Brief Encounter*. The trouble with Bonnie, Irene thought, was that she had never learned to love classical music. She treated it as background sound, turning the volume low and then talking over it. Sacrilege as far as Irene was concerned, and she turned the volume up now, letting the music take control of her, letting it blot out everything else until the concerto finished.

What was she to do about Bonnie? Irene knew it made sense for them to share the house; she was, after all, eighty now and before long she might actually need to be looked after. But this wasn't right, she wasn't ready for it yet, and it wasn't right for Bonnie either. She needed a life of her own. Irene knew several women of Bonnie's age who were dreading the day when they might have to take on the care of one or both parents. But here was Bonnie hurling herself into it well before it was necessary. If Bonnie could live her own life while sharing the house Irene would have been delighted to have her there, but not like this; not this uneasy, unnecessary care relationship that Bonnie had established as soon as she set foot in the place.

'It's driving me right round the bend,' Irene had told her friend Marjorie the previous day on the way home from their art class. 'She won't leave me alone, wants to cook for me, keeps asking me if I'm all right, wants me to go shopping with her. She's never out of the house for more than an hour at a time and when she gets back she looks at me as though she's wondering if I contracted some fatal disease while she was out. I just don't know what I'm going to do.'

'It's early days yet,' Marjorie said, pulling into the café car park. 'Let's go and have a cuppa. Sounds like she's displacing the loss of Jeff onto you.'

Irene nodded. 'Yes, no more Jeff to look after so she'll look after me instead.'

'More than that,' Marjorie said thoughtfully, locking the car door. 'She's lonely and frightened. Jeff's been ripped away from her, now she's worried that you'll be next. Fairly natural, really, if you think about it. Simon's dead, and Dennis, and . . . and she doesn't have children of her own. And now Jeff. But the over-protectiveness must be a nightmare for you.'

'It is, and I do understand the reasons,' Irene said. 'But you're the analyst, what's the answer? What am I to do?'

'I *was* the analyst,' Marjorie corrected her. 'I'm retired now.'

'You're a Jungian, they never retire. Tell me what to do.'

'We don't tell our clients what to do, we encourage them to find their own solutions.'

'Encourage me, then.'

'Well,' said Marjorie, selecting a corner table, 'I think the answer could be in the Greek tour.'

'The Greek tour?'

'Yes, it's twelve weeks and it is something you've always wanted to do. In fact, you only cried off because Bonnie was coming back and you weren't sure how she'd be.'

'You mean go on the tour after all and leave her in the house alone?'

'Exactly. Come with us as planned. It's enough time for her to feel the pinch and kick-start herself into something else, but not so long that she'll get depressed.'

'It seems a bit unkind,' Irene said, 'bearing in mind what you said just now. I am her mother, after all, maybe she needs me right now. Especially if she's lonely.'

'By the time we leave for Athens, Jeff will have been dead for five months, time enough for her to start to get a grip on her own life. This is not healthy, Irene, not healthy at all. You're not geriatric yet, and you've been wanting to do this trip for years.

It was your idea in the first place. Give yourself this chance, and you'll be giving Bonnie a chance to find her own way too.'

Irene hit repeat on the remote control and the concerto began again. Maybe Marjorie was right. Time alone might well be just what Bonnie needed, and the tour was certainly what she needed for herself. She had suggested it to the historical society and it had been planned at the pleasant meandering pace that would suit her perfectly. No one else had stepped up to fill the place she'd relinquished when Bonnie had called to say she was coming home. Maybe tomorrow she'd call the secretary and pop in with her deposit. Meanwhile, though, she'd make the most of having the house to herself for another couple of hours, make something for supper without Bonnie looking over her shoulder, trying to take over.

Outside the window she could see the apple tree where Dennis had built the platform for them to sit and they had draped the surrounding branches with old curtains. Sylvia and Fran – such nice girls. Maybe they'd get Bonnie involved in something if Irene wasn't around. The more she thought about it, the more Irene felt that the Greek tour might be the answer to her present delicate situation.

'I'm home, Mum,' Bonnie called. 'Sorry to be so late . . .' Her voice faded away as she popped her head around the living room door.

'Mum! Mum? I'm home, where are you?'

The house was incredibly still. The red light flashing on the CD player indicated that Irene had been listening to music and the frame that held her tapestry was pulled close to her chair. Bonnie felt the anxiety grip her as she ran through the dining room to the kitchen, and then up the stairs. She paused outside her mother's bedroom door, wondering if she might be asleep, and then tapped gently. There was no sound. Bonnie opened the door slightly to find the room empty, the bed smooth and unruffled. She called out again, but as she ran back down the stairs, past the window on the half-landing, she noticed movement in the garden. Irene was picking her way over the stepping stones through the rose bed to the herb patch at the rear. Bonnie sighed with relief. Of course she was fine, just look at her now. Thank goodness she hadn't rushed out there in a panic calling her – that wouldn't have gone down at all well. She went on down the stairs and into the kitchen to switch on the kettle.

'So, how was your lunch?' Irene asked, putting some parsley and a few sprigs of rosemary on the kitchen table.

'Wonderful,' Bonnie said, not turning around, concentrating on pouring tea. 'It was great to see them again, hard to believe it's been so long. I thought it might be awkward at first but after the first glass of wine we were well away, just like old times.'

Irene nodded, reaching out for the cup Bonnie handed her. 'Good, that's splendid. You must have enjoyed it, you've been gone for ages.'

'Yes, I'm sorry, but after lunch we went to the kiosk,' Bonnie said, sitting across from her mother. 'You know, the grotty little place at the boatshed we used to go to for hot chips when we were kids. It hasn't changed much. Now that the boatshed's not used any longer I don't suppose it'll be able to keep going. But we had a lovely walk along the beach. Sorry I was gone so long. Were you all right?'

Irene gave herself a mental kick for referring to the length of Bonnie's absence. 'I was fine, Bonnie dear,' she said, reaching across the table to pat her daughter's hand. 'Absolutely fine. You must stop fussing about me. I'm used to living alone and not seeing people for ages.'

Bonnie looked down into her tea and nodded. 'Of course; yes, of course. Well, I thought I'd make us some pasta for tonight . . .'

'No need,' Irene said. 'I've made some leek and potato soup, I was just out in the garden getting some parsley to pop in it. I'm in charge tonight, Bonnie. Go and put your feet up and watch the news.'

TWO

Bonnie lay in bed watching the patterns on the ceiling. There was a full moon and the night breeze sent clusters of cloud scudding across its face, shifting in shadowy shapes above her. So, she had done it, actually reached out and done it, arranged the lunch, turned up, behaved as though she was a normal person. She had hugged, talked, laughed, eaten three courses, drunk too much wine, and now it was over. All three of them had been nervous at first, feeling their way, but by the time dessert was served it felt almost as though they had picked up where they left off. But it hadn't solved anything and she had been foolish to think that it could.

Bonnie had felt a flash of shock as Sylvia got up from the table to greet her. She looked so much the same and yet so different. The once dark hair, now silver grey, was loosely caught on top of her head, a few escaping strands softening the line of her face and neck. She was always slim but that now seemed like lean strength, and while her face was lined, it simply added to her beauty. Elegance was in her DNA and Bonnie, who felt she always had to struggle to achieve it, felt a familiar flash of envy.

Sylvia looked her age, perhaps a little less, but the most striking thing about her was her self-assurance. Sylvia measured her words while still sounding spontaneous. Even after they had knocked back a couple of bottles of wine, and walked along the beach in the late afternoon breeze, Sylvia had remained serene. She had told them about a row with Colin that morning and how

17

she had smashed a precious ornament, but she seemed to tell it with detachment, as though talking about someone else. Obviously she found much of what was expected of a minister's wife tedious. Even so, she was clearly in remarkable control of her life. Bonnie was impressed.

And then there was Fran, who had sailed out of the ladies' room and into the restaurant a few minutes later. She was still big of course, but that was Fran, it was impossible to imagine her any other way. Bonnie had thought she looked remarkably youthful; her fair complexion was fresh and glowing, and those striking hazel eyes and her smile drew attention to her face and away from her body. Bonnie had almost forgotten Fran's curiosity and the way she would draw together the most unlikely fragments and make interesting connections. Being a person who tended to think in straight lines, she envied Fran's ability to crisscross, to duck and weave, with ideas and language.

Bonnie stretched her arms above her head feeling, as she had so often felt as a teenager, that intellectually both Fran and Sylvia left her standing. She closed her eyes against the shifting moon-light wondering what they were thinking. They were both so clever, so competent, so complete. There had been a brief period in Bonnie and Jeff's marriage when they had weathered a terrible crisis and, as they clung together in their grief, their relationship had become the most important thing in Bonnie's life. Jeff had urged her so often to find something of her own, but she had always resisted.

'Suppose anything happened to me, Bon,' he'd say. 'What would you do? You need something for yourself. It's not as though we're hard up, after all; you could do more or less whatever you want. A little business, perhaps? Some charity work? Learn the piano? Travel, anything.'

'But I'm happy as I am,' she'd reply. 'I like doing odd bits of work for you, running the house, and entertaining, playing tennis, going to the book group.'

But to please him she had made an effort to learn French, and then some German. She'd been proud of her efforts, but they weren't much use to her now. Languages, entertaining, tennis and reading did nothing to fill the gap Jeff had left. His death had robbed her of part of herself, leaving a terrible emptiness and the sense that she, Bonnie Logan, was not a woman at all, but just an empty shell.

Fran sat on the sofa in the dark, wearing her pyjamas, watching the late movie and eating her way through a packet of Custard Creams. She had told herself she would just have two and then stop, and when she'd said it she had, fleetingly, believed it, the same way she believed that each one she ate would be the last; but at the same time she knew that the whole packet was destined for consumption and that this would be followed by a stodgy and painful period of self-disgust and massive guilt. Fran often felt she was like a madwoman in her desperation to find something sweet to eat. She had been known to get the car out and go down to the petrol station at midnight to buy a Mars Bar, a Twix or a Fry's Turkish Delight, or all three, or possibly two of each. It wasn't even as though she particularly liked Custard Creams, she had bought these in preference to Tim Tams or Kingstons on the basis that she was less likely to binge on them. It was a plan with a long history of failure and always, when she was left facing the empty packet, she wished that she had, after all, bought the biscuits she really loved. It wasn't even as though she was hungry. Lunch had been adequate and really delicious, and after coffee at the kiosk they'd bought large chocolate ice creams and scoffed them as they walked. She hadn't needed a meal but, as always, once she had eaten anything sweet the craving for more simply grew and grew until she succumbed, and then she ended up hating herself and vowing never to do it again.

Fran tried to visualise Sylvia munching her way through a packet of biscuits, but it was impossible to imagine her doing anything so undignified. What a stunning woman Sylvia had become, and she didn't even seem to realise it. She looked like a skin care advertisement for mature women. Fran thought she had rarely seen a woman who seemed so composed, so at peace with her life, so centred. Was it something to do with God? She didn't seem all that keen on the churchy stuff but maybe she'd found some sort of relationship with God, like the nuns at St Theresa's.

Fran had wanted to interrogate her about it but managed to restrain her unfortunate habit of informally interviewing interesting people. It had got her into trouble in the past. Although she appeared confident and outgoing she was actually shy and self-conscious, and dealt with it on social occasions by pinning people against the wall and interviewing them until they began to make desperate eye signals at their friends to rescue them. Well, she'd restrained herself on this occasion, but her desire to discover Sylvia's secret and bottle it was still there. Now they were in touch again, Fran certainly wasn't going to let her go.

Bonnie was something else. Smart – who wouldn't be with that sort of money to spend? Not beautiful but handsome and, Fran thought, close to the emotional edge; a stitched-up woman starting to come apart at the seams. She'd talked a lot about Jeff, which was understandable given he hadn't been gone long, but her sudden decision to sell everything in Switzerland and run back to Melbourne seemed a bit odd. Fran sampled a corner of the last Custard Cream and considered the fact that if you had lived more than thirty years in a place, surely it must seem like home. Bonnie must have had friends in Zurich but here she was living with her mother in the old family home.

Fran took a deep breath and offered a fleeting arrow prayer of thanks to the developers who had established the retirement centre where her own mother was happily installed in her one-bedroom unit. Lila was fit and lively but her memory was increasingly unreliable, and a broken ankle the previous year had confined her to the house and dented her confidence. Finding the unit had eliminated one of Fran's worst recurring dreams: having to look after her mother while still working and trying to pay off her mortgage and save for her own old age. She crumpled the empty biscuit packet. There was no way now that she would be able to sleep having scoffed all that sugar.

Charade was almost finished; Cary Grant and Audrey Hepburn were gazing into each other's eyes outside the American Embassy in Paris. The plot had seemed really thin and Audrey Hepburn's character irritatingly dippy. Fran's eyes filled with tears as Cary took Audrey in his arms. She was never going to be sinking into some hero's arms again, that was for sure – that part of her life was definitely over. There had been a couple of robust sexual encounters about ten years ago but other than that there had been no one since she and Tony split up seventeen years earlier. No self-respecting man fell in love with a whale, and she had proved herself incapable of losing weight, only of getting fatter. Besides, the older she got the more she felt men were a strange species with whom she had little in common. Having a relationship with one seemed incredibly complicated and overrated. Being with Bonnie and Sylvia had been both wonderful and agonising, more agonising than in the past, for much as she loved them – and she realised, with surprise, that it *was* love that she still felt for these sisters of her childhood – she was always going to be the fat, breathless one who could never match their style and sophistication. In her youth there had been the hope of change, the prospect that it might really just be puppy fat that she would grow out of, that one day a fully fledged greyhound might suddenly emerge from this puppy: slim, graceful and elegant. That was clearly not going to happen, and Fran wondered just how she could balance her desire to reconnect fully with her friends with this haunting sense of failure.

Sylvia sat alone in the small bedroom she had converted to a sewing room. On the table sections of a skirt pattern lay pinned to a length of fine, silver grey wool. She had intended to cut it out this evening but instead she sat there in the half-light, in the old armchair she had rescued from a second-hand shop, too distracted even to consider the skirt. By the time she'd got home to Box Hill, Colin had already returned from the Deanery lunch and gone out again to a meeting. She was thankful to have the house to herself, not to have to talk about what had happened, not to have to prepare a meal.

Heading straight up the stairs to the sewing room she had glanced through the open door of his study. The broken pieces of the Lladro were spread out on a sheet of newspaper, a new tube of glue on sentry duty beside them. Sylvia stared at them for a while before going on up the stairs, wondering what Colin had thought he was doing when he collected up the pieces. Was he simply mending something she had broken in what he probably saw as a burst of irrational anger? Sylvia thought about the shepherdess's partner, the lonely shepherd still whole on the dressing table. Did Colin realise that the shepherdess was simply a sign of more profound and irreparable damage?

Sylvia leaned back in her chair and closed her eyes. She had almost told Bonnie and Fran when they were down on the beach, walking along the waterline as they had done so often as teenagers. Well, of course she *had* told them about the incident that morning, but what she hadn't told them was the context. She hadn't used any of the words – like boredom, resentment, disappointment, frustration, hurt, emptiness – that really described how she felt. Oh, and she'd forgotten one – anger – but then, convent girls always knew that anger was an unmentionable emotion, because nice women got hurt instead of getting angry. How deeply ran the rivers of the past. Over the years Sylvia had developed a patina of serenity and composure, had perfected myriad little ways of making it all look right. Today, of course, she had sanitised the Lladro incident in the telling, used a whimsical tone, and made it sound like a commonplace marital tiff. Had Fran and Bonnie sensed the turbulence raging beneath her calm exterior?

Alone in the softly lit room that she had made so essentially hers, Sylvia flushed with embarrassment recalling her own well-concealed response to Bonnie's newly widowed state. There was the restless envy of her sudden and complete freedom and independence and, alongside it, fierce jealousy of a marriage that had so completely fulfilled Bonnie's dreams and desires; the love that lasted through time, that changed and grew and matured, becoming richer with each passing year. Trapped as she was in the grief of losing Jeff, the possibilities of her situation were lost on Bonnie: freedom and independence only meant loss. Clearly she had built her life around Jeff and everything else had been incidental to that, and while Sylvia was uncomfortably aware that she too had allowed her marriage to dictate her life, she thought her own situation was a far more complex mix of responsibility and duty than Bonnie's, which had been fuelled by love.

'I know I've been incredibly lucky,' Bonnie had said, sipping her second glass of wine. 'I was twenty-four when I met Jeff, and that was that. I had a perfect husband, a perfect life. Now he's dead and it's as though everything's died with him.'

'Well, at least you're not hard up, Bon,' Fran had cut in. 'Imagine if you had to struggle financially. That would make it a whole lot worse.'

'I don't know, really,' Bonnie had said with that vague, rather unworldly look she got sometimes. 'Something to worry about might take my mind off what's happened.'

'Take it from me,' Fran had said in a surprisingly crisp tone, manoeuvring her fish off the bone. 'It's better as it is; everything is easier if you don't have to worry about where the next mortgage payment is coming from.'

Sylvia bit her lip trying to stop the tears. Bonnie may have shelved her accountancy career but she had made a success of her marriage; she, on the other hand, had failed to live up to any expectations, her own included. How willingly she had turned down the coveted design apprenticeship in the fashion house and taken a job behind the counter in David Jones, selling what she had once hoped to create. The job had supported them in minimal comfort while Colin finished his PhD. And, having given up her career, she had also turned her back on her Roman Catholic upbringing to marry this ambitious embryonic Anglican priest. At the time love was all that mattered, and love inevitably seemed to involve sacrifices for Colin's ambitions. So she had devoted herself to supporting his work and being the perfect clergy wife, and later the perfect mother.

Colin was a good clergyman, and he tried to be a good husband and father, so long as it didn't interfere with his commitment to God and to the church. For a time Sylvia had found his dependence endearing but eventually it had turned around to bite her. She felt she had no one to blame but herself. She had allowed herself to be subsumed by the man and his job, and now she resented her captivity and yearned for escape, for freedom – something so simple but so utterly impossible.

Sylvia thought about Fran leaving Tony, seventeen years earlier.

'Boring, boring, boring,' she'd said, 'and he never got beyond expecting me to accept his views, his priorities, his way of doing things. I just couldn't hack it any longer.'

Now Tony lived with a small and beautiful biologist from Japan, who lectured at the university where he was a history professor. Fran had been single ever since; and however hard she might be struggling financially Sylvia envied her chaotic life of interviews, recipe and menu planning, of knocking up beautiful dishes in demonstration kitchens, and standing by to spray them with mists of oil or water to keep them glossy while the photographers changed their lenses and experimented with angles. Of all of them, Sylvia thought, Fran was a woman of the times, strong, independent, outspoken and confident. The weight that worried her so much seemed unimportant – she needed a big body to accommodate that big, warm, vibrant personality. Beside her Sylvia felt like a ghost, a wraith inhabiting a sham of a life in which she no longer believed.

She had come so close to confiding in them – it would have been such a relief to talk about it – but it was too soon, this first meeting after so many years apart. Her mother had died twenty years earlier and the only other women she knew well were so involved with Colin and the church that such confidences would create conflicting loyalties, and Sylvia would be the villain of the piece. Bonnie and Fran were different, they were hers alone; they seemed to offer change, new possibilities. But despite the pleasure of restoring their precious friendship, Sylvia was not at all sure that she would ever be able to muster the energy or resources to change anything.

THREE

'So how soon will it start to show?' Caro asked, flinging herself on the couch. 'How long before people look at me and think, that woman's having a baby?'

Fran, struggling with her tax return, looked up from the stack of receipts and bank slips. She shrugged, trying to remember. 'Four to five months, I think, certainly by five. But you'll feel it on your waistband before that.'

'I think I can already,' Caro said, staring down at her stomach. 'I wish it would hurry up. I don't think I can bear to wait, I want it now.'

'Everyone feels like that once they know,' Fran said. 'And the last three months are the worst. Every day seems like an eternity.'

'I haven't had any morning sickness, and twelve weeks is up so probably I won't,' Caro said.

'Lucky you.'

'Did you, Mum?'

'I threw up regularly every morning until sixteen weeks with David, and on and off all day for almost nine months with you.'

'Yuk! Gross!' Caro said with the sort of self-righteousness that implied her mother had not managed her pregnancies as efficiently as she herself was doing. Fran stared at her daughter, and wondered when Caro was going to stop behaving like a teenager and act her age.

'Pregnancies don't always go according to plan,' she said, quietly turning back to the receipts.

'Mine will,' Caro said with irritating smugness. 'Mine will be a textbook pregnancy and delivery, Mike's convinced of that.'

Mike would certainly expect the pregnancy to go by the book, Fran thought, staring at a receipt for $45 from the local bookshop and wondering if she'd actually read whatever book it was she'd bought. Recently emerged from medical school, Mike was only a few months into an internship in emergency. Fran, who was very fond of Mike but irritated by his belief that the clinical trial was a metaphor for life itself, secretly thought that a few months in emergency, closely followed by fatherhood, might be just what he needed to help him come to terms with the unutterable chaos and unpredictability of human life.

'How was your lunch the other day?' Caro asked, getting up and wandering to the kitchen to put the kettle on. 'The old girls' reunion?'

Fran took off her glasses, abandoning the tax return. 'Lovely, actually, just like old times. I'm thinking of organising another lunch, two weeks on Sunday. It's Mother's Day, so I'll ask Bonnie and her mother, and Sylvia and Colin. Their daughter's in England so she won't be around for it. Then there's you and Mike, obviously, and Granny Lila.'

Caro shook her head, unable to speak through a blueberry muffin. 'Sorry, Mum,' she mumbled thickly after a pause, 'we won't be here then. You won't mind, will you? It's Mike's week-end off so we're going for a luxury weekend getaway. It's a surprise, somewhere gorgeous. He says I have to be made a fuss of now I'm going to be a mother.' She scooped coffee into the plunger, tilting her head to one side. 'After all, we've never really done Mother's Day, have we!'

It was a statement not a question, which was fortunate. Had it required an answer Fran would have been hard pressed not to point out that not doing Mother's Day had not been her choice, simply a default situation created largely by Caro herself.

'Anyway,' Caro said, handing her mother a mug of coffee, 'David'll be here, so at least you'll have one of us around.'

'David?'

'Yes, he'll be back Tuesday, won't he?'

'He hasn't said anything to me,' Fran said. 'I haven't heard from him for a few weeks now.'

Caro flushed and clapped her hand across her mouth. 'Oh my god! I forgot to tell you.' She put her cup down. 'He phoned a couple of weeks ago. He'd rung here but you were out so he didn't bother leaving a message, just rang me instead and asked me to tell you he'd be home on the third. He's sick of Qatar so he's coming home for a while. Then he's got something up in Japan starting . . . oh, I can't remember when. Shit, Mum, I'm really sorry. Being pregnant is supposed to make you forgetful, isn't it? Well, there you are!'

Fran was torn between wanting to smack Caro, and delight at the prospect of seeing her son. 'So where's he staying?'

Caro looked surprised. 'Here, of course.'

'Here?'

'Yes, with you, you *are* his mother. He said to let him know if it wasn't okay, but I knew it would be, so I said not to worry, it would be fine, it's just that, whoops, I forgot to tell you.'

Fran sat on the deck contemplating the fading light and wondering where she had failed. Was it her fault for leaving Tony? Caro was eleven at the time – maybe it was the divorce that had made her so self-centred, caused a sort of arrested development. Pregnancy might be a godsend; at last, perhaps, she would start to behave like someone of twenty-eight.

The job probably didn't help. The record company where Caro worked seemed full of fifty-year-old men who all dressed and behaved like teenagers. Fran thought them pathetic, with their paunches bulging over tight jeans, four-letter words on their t-shirts, and their thinning grey hair tied back in straggly pony-tails. They favoured motorbikes by day and white stretch limos by night, when they dressed either all in black, or in white suits with black shirts. It was rather sad, Fran thought, to see them attempting to cling so desperately and unsuccessfully to youth. Caro hardly stood a chance of growing up as long as she worked in that environment.

When Caro left, Fran phoned David. He was indeed due back

in three days' time and was mightily uncomfortable that this was the first she had heard of it.

'I should've called again and spoken to you,' he said. 'After all, I know what she's like. Sorry, Mum, is it okay if I stay with you for a while?'

'Of course,' she said. 'It'll be lovely, but now that I know I'll clear the stack of old files and stuff out of your room. I've been using it for storage.'

'Great, thanks. I'm going up to Sydney for a job interview on the tenth so I might stay for the weekend and catch up with a few people.'

So much for having David around on Mother's Day. Out there in Qatar he wouldn't have any idea of the date, anyhow.

Fran felt her spirits drop. It hit her from time to time, this feeling of being entirely incidental in her children's lives. It was, she supposed, just the way things were these days; the old rituals and celebrations meant nothing anymore. Mother's Day was just a chance for Kmart to sell more fluffy slippers, and David Jones to have special offers on perfume, not to mention getting all those catalogues of white goods – who'd want a washing machine for Mother's Day, anyway?

David had once brought home a jam jar of sand, dyed different colours and layered like a rainbow. It had stood for years on the kitchen windowsill, alongside the large tomato knitted in red wool, stuffed with old tights and topped with four strands of green wool that Caro had made. And she remembered a green felt pot holder embroidered with the words 'Hot Pots' in black wool that she herself had made for Lila. She'd given it to her the year of the picnic.

The picnic! They'd have been eleven that year or maybe twelve, she, Bonnie and Sylvia. Lila had organised it, Sylvia and her mother, Bonnie and hers, and Bonnie's brother Simon, and a couple of other mothers and children, whose names she couldn't remember now. They'd gone together on the bus to Sorrento, and spread their rugs and picnic baskets on the sand. It was autumn, of course, and quite chilly but they'd gone swimming while the mothers sat talking on the rugs. The three of them had stayed in the water long after the others, until they were blue with cold, and then run shivering up the beach to change back into their clothes under cover of their towels. Simon, who was a few years older, had made up a game that had them running around to get warm, and finally they'd collapsed exhausted on the grass alongside the mothers and drunk sweet tea with the distinctive stewed flavour acquired from standing for hours in a Thermos.

Fran thought about it now with nostalgia, the itch of salt on her skin as she dragged off her bathers, the ham sandwiches, lamingtons, lemonade, the dozy contentment of the ride home in the bus, the gentle murmur of the mothers' voices. Perhaps they could do it again. Sylvia's mother was dead, as was Simon, killed in his forties by a drunk driver, but Bonnie's mother, and her own, were very much alive. Fran smiled to herself, and went to the phone to call Bonnie.

'What a lovely idea,' Irene said, taking off her glasses and putting down the paper. 'I do remember that picnic, we had such a good time. Yes, tell Fran it's a wonderful idea. I'd love to do it again.'

'Are you sure it wouldn't be too much for you, not too energetic and noisy?' Bonnie asked, two little furrows forming between her eyebrows.

'Oh, don't be so ridiculous,' Irene said irritably. 'It'll be lovely to see those girls again, and it's years since I saw Lila. Why would it be noisy? Lila's grandchildren are adults and I don't have any.' She could have bitten her tongue for saying it. It wasn't as though she thought about it much these days, and she wouldn't have hurt Bonnie for the world. She flushed. 'Sorry, dear, I didn't mean . . . I was just saying . . . stating a fact, you know children get noisy and then . . .' but she realised she was just making it worse. 'Bonnie, I –'

'It's all right, Mum, I know what you meant,' Bonnie said with a tight smile. 'Well, it will be nice, won't it? How clever of Fran to think of it. Her two will be away so there'll be Lila and you, Fran and me, and she's ringing Sylvia. I wonder if Colin will come. We haven't had a look at him since their wedding.'

'Well, no,' said Colin, 'obviously we can't go. There's the Mother's Day service, and then at two o'clock the tea and the children's art exhibition, so of course we can't go. Nice of Ann to think of us, though.'

'Fran.'

'Huh?'

'Her name is Fran,' Sylvia said, 'and I'm going. If you don't want to come and you need the car I can get a lift with Fran and her mother.'

Colin looked up from the broccoli soup that Sylvia had just put in front of him. 'It's not about the car, it's the service, and the tea.'

'I shall skip the service. And I can make my contribution to the tea the day before. I just won't be there to serve it.' Colin would be wearing his sulky face and Sylvia decided not to look at it because it would instantly convert her annoyance into red-hot anger. 'There are always heaps of volunteers for dishing out the tea, it won't be a problem.'

'It certainly *will* be a problem – what will people say? They'll think there's something wrong if you're not there.'

'Maybe there is.'

'Maybe there is what?'

'Maybe there is something wrong.'

'Well, is there? What's wrong?'

Sylvia put down her spoon. 'Maybe I'm just totally pissed off with spending every Mother's Day doing things for other people. Have you ever thought of that?'

'But I thought you enjoyed it.'

'Colin, be honest, you never even gave it a thought. So, this year I'm going to go out and do something I'd like to do for myself.' It was fortunate, she thought, that the lonely porcelain shepherd was well out of reach.

*

'Is it the weekend after next? So soon?' Lila said. 'I thought Christmas was just a couple of weeks ago, or haven't we had Christmas yet? Anyway – yes, love, that'd be grand. Fancy Bonnie's mother being eighty.'

'Yes,' said Fran. 'Time flies, doesn't it? But you're eighty-four, Mum.'

'Am I really?' Lila said in amazement. 'I thought I was younger than that, but now you mention it, Fran, I think I do remember having an eightieth birthday. Well, that'll be lovely. I must remember to tell them at the centre that I won't be going to the lunch. They always do a very good lunch here on special days, but a picnic will be much nicer. I remember that day very well, you were sick in the bus on the way home.'

'Was I?' said Fran in surprise. 'I don't remember that.'

'I do because you threw up all over my new skirt,' her mother said. 'Your memory must be going, Fran. I can remember it as clearly as if it was yesterday.'

Fran restrained herself from mentioning that her mother couldn't remember yesterday and made an arrangement to pick her up at eleven. 'I'll call that morning to remind you,' she said.

'Oh, I won't need reminding,' Lila said. 'Nothing wrong with my memory, Fran, it's you who can't remember being sick in the bus.'

Fran put down the phone thinking that what with Caro and her mother she had had enough reminders of vomiting to last her for a very long time. Memory was such a tease, some bits so vivid, others so elusive you weren't sure if they were real or something you'd dreamed.

She wondered what it must be like for Lila to live with those bewildering gaps about really important and recent things while still having such vivid memories of the distant past. She swallowed the lump that rose in her throat – at least Lila would enjoy the picnic; old age had endowed her with the capacity simply to enjoy things that in the past would have been overlaid with complex and conflicting emotions and anxiety. Fran wondered if this would happen to her as she aged; whether, as she hit sixty or seventy, she too would find that sort of simplicity and let go of the anxieties that so exhausted her. It would, she thought, be easier to do with money in the bank.

Grabbing a pad and pencil from the benchtop, she went back to the deck and began to plan the best picnic food. She would kill two birds with one stone. Her column this week would be food for a Mother's Day picnic.

FOUR

Sylvia locked the back door behind her and walked across to the church. She was wearing sunglasses and a cotton hat with the floppy brim turned down, hoping it would make it easier for her to avoid speaking to anyone she met on the way. It was ten o'clock and the church would, most likely, be empty. Colin had taken early communion and then gone to a meeting on the other side of the city; after that, he was going to a lecture. Some visiting theologian was speaking at the university about the challenge to ecumenism in the twenty-first century. He had seemed quite excited as he tucked into his toast .

'He's got some radical views, this man,' he'd said. 'Should be stimulating stuff. Can you manage without the car today?'

Sylvia watched his jaws moving rhythmically up and down, his hand lifting his coffee cup to his mouth at regular intervals, his eyes scanning the front page of the *Age*, back and forth, back and forth.

'Yes. So you'll be back late this afternoon?'

He nodded without looking up. 'Early evening – sixish, I should think. By the way, Veronica is going to take over the tea and the art exhibition. She didn't seem to mind, seemed quite pleased, in fact, so you don't need to worry about it.'

'That's good, then,' said Sylvia, who hadn't been worrying. There were always enough willing hands to take on whatever she chose to unload and she liked Veronica Waters more than most. 'You see, you didn't need me after all.'

She knew it was a stupid remark. It wasn't about need, it was about expectation, and it was those expectations over so many years that had brought her to this crisis. A crisis of which Colin, despite her various recent outbursts, still seemed blissfully unaware. Perhaps she should just tell him, try to make him understand how she felt, see if they could sort it out together, but Colin would never be able to understand. He would see her complaining about things that had been part of their marriage since day one. She remembered once, about ten years ago, telling him that the way he read his sermon in bed on Saturday nights, not silently and not aloud, but in that stagey whisper which was supposed not to disturb her, was driving her mad.

'Good gracious, Syl,' he'd said in absolute amazement. 'I've been doing it every Saturday night for more than twenty years, and now suddenly it's driving you mad?'

'Not suddenly,' she'd said. 'It always has, it's just that I'm telling you about it now.'

'Well, then,' he'd said good-naturedly, patting her hip through the quilt, 'it can't have been too bad if it took you all this time to mention it. I think you're just feeling a bit off colour. Anyway, I've finished now, all ready for tomorrow.' And he'd put out the light and slid down under the covers, and the next Saturday night, and every Saturday night since then, he'd gone on whispering his sermon.

Sylvia knew she had been her own worst enemy. For years she had gone on pretending that everything was all right, not mentioning trivial things like the sermon whisper for fear of seeming petty, thinking she could put up with it, until it had built into a mountain of resentment that she could no longer contain. 'If you behave like a doormat they'll wipe their feet on you,' her mother had once told her, long before Colin appeared on the scene. It was a message illustrated by her parents' relationship and by the way the nuns at the convent behaved when the priests turned up. Those wise, strong, intelligent women changed into fluttering, fawning ciphers, as though the priests were Jesus himself, and their reward was to be treated with disdain. It was an example that was hard to ignore. Sylvia had not been a doormat, and Colin certainly hadn't walked on her, but she hadn't carved out anything for herself and he had made the most of the situation.

Sylvia let herself in to the church, pausing just inside the door to absorb the atmosphere. She had always loved being in church, any church, when it was empty; the services and the rituals had never worked for her, but alone in the stillness she could feel herself connected to God. It wasn't the God of the convent, or an angry, vengeful God, but a strong and comforting divine presence that had been with her most of her adult life and that now, in this time of greatest need, seemed strangely elusive. Selecting a pew halfway up the church, Sylvia sat down and closed her eyes, leaning her head on her hands. Lost in thought she didn't hear the door open, so that when someone slid into the pew beside her and spoke her name, her heart thumped in shock.

'I'm so sorry, Sylvia,' Veronica Waters said. 'I didn't mean to startle you.'

'Oh, Veronica, it's all right. I just didn't know there was anyone else in the church.'

Veronica smiled, putting a hand on her arm and then withdrawing it. 'Look, I hope I'm not prying, it's just that I saw you here and . . . well . . . you haven't been looking too good lately, and then Colin said you wouldn't be able to do the exhibition this year. I wondered . . . is there anything wrong?'

Sylvia paused. She wanted so much to talk to someone, and she trusted Veronica, but it was too close to home. She would be forcing Veronica to divide her loyalties, not just between herself and Colin, but with that blurry third party made up of God and the church, the boundaries of which were always so unclear.

'Things aren't too good at the moment,' she said, breaking contact with Veronica's steady gaze. 'I suppose everyone goes through bad patches from time to time, but I guess we'll get over it.' She looked up and in Veronica's eyes she saw something she couldn't quite fathom. Sylvia flushed and looked away again.

Veronica was older by perhaps ten or more years, but Sylvia always felt that in her presence she was in the company of a much older wisdom. 'It's just that I've got the chance to go on a picnic with some school friends and their mothers, like we did years ago.' She paused, feeling as though she sounded trivial. 'I haven't had a Mother's Day off from the church for years . . .'

Veronica put her hand on Sylvia's arm with reassuring firmness. 'You make sure you have a splendid time. And, Sylvia . . . any time you feel like a chat, just pop round.' She paused, waiting until Sylvia's eyes met hers once again. 'Just between us, of course,' she said, 'just between you and me.' And with a smile she got up. 'Enjoy your Mother's Day, you deserve it. Don't give it up, not under any circumstances. Well, I must get on. There are some accounts in the vestry I need to sort out. Goodbye, my dear, take care.'

The phone was ringing when Sylvia got back to the house and she let the answering machine pick it up. For a moment she didn't recognise the rather tentative voice and then she realised it was Bonnie. This was the first time she had heard from her since their reunion lunch. The only other contact had been the call from Fran to organise the picnic.

'Bonnie, Bonnie, I'm here,' Sylvia said, intercepting the answering machine. 'It's lovely to hear from you.'

'Really?' Bonnie said, sounding surprised. 'I thought – oh dear, I hope you don't mind me calling. I just – well, I wondered – would you fancy meeting for a coffee?'

Irene was sorting out her wardrobe in an attempt to decide what she should take with her on the trip. Travel light, Marjorie had said, messing about with luggage could destroy the pleasure of travelling; cotton pants and shirts, a couple of jumpers and a raincoat, because you can't trust European summers. Sandals and comfortable walking shoes. Irene inspected her walking shoes. Not that they'd be doing that much walking – none of them was under seventy-five, and they weren't going in for lengthy treks – but just the same they'd probably be on their feet a lot. Tomorrow she would go out for some shoes; maybe Bonnie would like to go with her.

Irene sighed and sat down on the edge of the bed. Bonnie had gone off in a huff, or at least it was supposed to look like a huff, but Irene knew it was hurt or fear or both. She hadn't been happy at all about the Greek trip.

'But suppose something happened to you?' she'd said, looking at her mother in horror. 'Suppose you were ill or had an accident?'

'I won't be alone, I'm sure my friends will look out for me,' Irene had said, 'and I shall be insured. They do have doctors and hospitals in Greece, you know.'

'Yes,' said Bonnie, twitching her shoulders nervously, 'yes, but not like Australian hospitals. Heavens, you don't know where you might end up.'

'If it makes you feel better, dear, I'll ensure that Marjorie calls you straight away and you can do a mercy dash to rescue me. But I really don't think there's any need to worry.'

Bonnie paused and Irene's heart went out to her as she saw her battling with the complex set of emotions that had flared at the prospect of being left alone. 'But it's such a long time – twelve weeks. Where will you stay?'

'Part of the time – the first month, in fact – in a very luxurious villa with seven bedrooms and three bathrooms, serviced by friendly staff who all speak English. Marjorie and I will share a room. And then there's a bit of travelling around, island hopping, staying in small comfortable hotels, and then back to the villa for the last month.' She tried to make it sound as well managed and unthreatening as possible in the hope of reassuring Bonnie, but it didn't work.

'Island hopping! In small unsafe boats, I suppose, or, worse still, light aircraft. Whatever are you thinking? It's quite ridiculous,' she said, drawing herself up to her full height. 'It's just irresponsible, a lot of old people setting off like that, goodness knows what will happen. And how do you think I feel? I've only just come home after all these years and now you're gadding off with your friends for months on end.' Bonnie's lips were trembling, and her eyes were bright with the start of tears.

Irene took her daughter's hand and drew her down beside her on the bed. 'Bonnie, listen to me, please,' she said firmly. 'I appreciate that you're concerned for me and I promise to behave responsibly. The tour is very carefully arranged and planned for senior citizens. We're all in control of our faculties or we wouldn't be going. I've been looking forward to it for a long time, dear. I think if I had told you I was doing this while Jeff was alive and you were in Switzerland you would have been thrilled for me, maybe even proud of me. It just feels different for you because Jeff is gone and you're living here.'

'What do you mean?' Bonnie asked.

'I mean, it's like when children grow up. As long as they live at home you're parenting, trying to make sure they eat properly, every time they go out you worry if they'll have an accident, you panic if they're late home, or if you think they're mixing with the wrong people, taking drugs or drinking too much. Then they move out and all that switches off.'

'Out of sight out of mind, you mean?'

'No, that's not what I mean. It's just different when your children aren't living with you. While there's this overall concern about them, you somehow don't feel you have to be vigilant all the time. When you lived in Zurich, you weren't worrying about my welfare and safety all the time, nor should you have been. It's only now, because you're here and we're living together, you've started treating me as though you're the parent and I'm the child.'

Bonnie kept staring out of the window. 'Were you worrying about Simon like that when he lived here after the divorce?'

'Yes,' Irene nodded, 'and a lot of good that did. He was forty-two years old, living with me, and he went out one night and that wretched drunk woman in the other car killed him. So much for my efforts to keep him safe. I worried like that when you and Jeff were here on holidays, but not when you were back in Zurich. I worry like that about you now that you're here again. But the people you love have to be allowed to live their own lives and take their own risks.'

There was a long silence. 'I suppose so,' Bonnie said eventually, the hostility gone now though Irene could still hear the fear. 'But I'll miss you.'

'And that might not be a bad thing,' Irene said, knowing that she was swimming into very dangerous waters. 'You need to think about the future, a new life for yourself. I love having you here but you can't fill the gap by looking after me. If I'm suddenly struck down and need constant care I might have to eat my words, but you're young, Bonnie, you have a lot of years ahead. They can be wonderful for you, but only if you're prepared to see the challenge and the possibilities.'

'I can't think of any possibilities at the moment,' Bonnie said, looking down at her hands clasped in her lap. 'I feel completely lost without him. I don't know what to do.'

Irene put her arms around her daughter and hugged her. 'I know, but you won't find out while you've got me to focus on. This is tough love, Bonnie dear. I'm not saying you shouldn't still be grieving, that will take a long time, but you need to take care of yourself now, not be concentrating on me, and not poor Jeff either. He wouldn't want it. He loved you so much, Bonnie, he'd want you to recover and have a good life.'

Irene sighed as she went over it all again. Was she right or was she just being selfish? Had she pushed Bonnie too far too soon? It had, she realised, been easier for her when Dennis died. Simon was gone, but Bonnie was still alive and well, albeit in Europe, and Irene had always crammed her life with activities, her painting and tapestry, the historical society, her love of music, plenty of women friends, the Save the Children Fund, and then the Save the Forests campaign – they were like a bunch of keys to a new start.

Irene picked up her battered walking shoes and carried them downstairs. Shortly after their conversation, Bonnie had made a phone call and then called up the stairs that she was going out for coffee. She hadn't said where or with whom, and Irene hoped that was a good sign. Her daughter was keeping something to herself for a change. Perhaps Marjorie was right; leaving Bonnie alone in the house for a while might make her take off the training wheels and ride confidently towards the future.

'This is a lovely surprise,' Sylvia said, sitting down at the table. 'I can't remember when I last came to Carlton. It's not that far but I just never seem to come to this part of town.'

'I hope you didn't mind me calling . . .' Bonnie said.

'I was delighted. I really needed something good to happen today. And I'm so looking forward to the picnic. Wasn't that a great idea of Fran's?'

Bonnie nodded. 'Yes, we're both looking forward to it, Mum and I. Is Colin coming?'

Sylvia shook her head. 'No, the call of duty. I decided to shirk mine. I haven't had a good Mother's Day since Kim went to England. You never had children, Bonnie?' As soon as the words were out, Sylvia wished she hadn't asked. It was too intimate a question after so many years of distance.

Bonnie hesitated.

'Sorry,' Sylvia added, blushing. 'That was thoughtless of me, I shouldn't have asked. None of my business.'

'No,' Bonnie said. 'It's just . . . well, I don't usually talk about it.'

Sylvia waited, uncertain whether or not to persist.

'We did have a child,' Bonnie said. 'A little girl, Lucy. She died, a problem with her lungs, and there were other problems too. She was four months old.'

'Bonnie, I'm so sorry, what a terrible thing . . .'

'They put it down to a drug I was given for morning sickness, Debendox. You might have heard about it.'

Sylvia nodded. 'Yes, I remember reading about an action by some parents. I'm so sorry, Bonnie.'

'Well . . . all in the past now,' Bonnie said in an unusually brittle tone. 'It's a bit like it never happened.'

Sylvia put her hand on Bonnie's arm. 'I wish we'd stayed in touch, then Fran and I would have been there for you. I thought about you, Bonnie, you and Fran. I've always missed what we had.'

'Me too,' Bonnie said, swallowing hard. 'That's why I called today. I needed someone to talk to. It's about Mum.'

Sylvia raised her eyebrows. 'Feisty and independent as ever?'

'Yes, and that's the thing, really. Today we had a bit of a blue because she told me she's going to Greece next month, a twelve-week tour.'

'Oh, what a terrific thing to be doing at her age,' Sylvia said. 'I hope I've got the energy when the time comes, and the friends to do it with. Perhaps we should book in advance, Bonnie!'

Bonnie smiled awkwardly. 'Yes, I can see that's what I'd think if it was someone else's mother, but . . . I'm so afraid something will happen to her. She thinks I'm compensating for losing Jeff by looking after her . . .' She paused. 'You think that too, don't you? I can see from your expression.'

Sylvia put down her coffee cup. 'It did cross my mind the other day when you told us what you were doing now. Irene's trip might be a good thing. Maybe you need some time on your own.'

'She might die,' Bonnie said bluntly, her eyes filling up with tears, 'then there'd be no one left.'

Sylvia leaned across the table and gripped her hand. 'And she might die if she stays home with you, Bonnie. She's eighty, but she's also used to being alone and doing what she wants. You can't start wrapping her in cotton wool, it's not fair.'

Bonnie pulled some tissues from her bag and dried her eyes. 'Oh Lord, I'm being so ridiculous,' she groaned. 'I'm sorry, she's right, you're right, I know that. Jeff warned me about this and I never took it seriously. I have no life of my own, no idea how to be alone.'

Sylvia walked up from the coffee shop to the corner of Lygon Street and paused at the traffic lights, wishing there was somewhere to go other than home. It was ironic, she thought, that she had sat in Brunetti's with Bonnie, dishing out advice about change, about creating a life for herself, when her own life was such a mess. Why hadn't she been brave enough to confide her own troubles? Loyalty, she supposed. Much as she longed to talk about how she felt, it just didn't seem fair to do so behind Colin's back, but it was a trap because in her heart Sylvia knew that any conversation with Colin would be akin to banging her head against a brick wall. He had mended the shepherdess and put it back on the dressing table. Neither of them had mentioned it, just the same way that neither of them had mentioned the fact that they had stopped having sex. That hadn't been discussed at all. She didn't think it was a deliberate decision by either of them, it had just stopped two or three years ago, perhaps more.

Sylvia shrugged and glanced at her watch. Almost four o'clock. She could get the bus home or go to the bookshop and to that wonderful fabric shop further down – was it on Palmerston or Lytton Street? It was so long since she'd been there she couldn't quite remember. She crossed the street and walked down towards the bookshop as the audience from the two o'clock screening began to spill out of Cinema Nova onto the pavement. And there Sylvia stopped dead in her tracks. Just ahead of her among the cinema crowd was Colin, his close-cropped head instantly recognisable as he bent to listen to the woman whose hand he was holding. And as Sylvia watched, he straightened up, laughing, and the two of them set off hand-in-hand in the direction of the university. She stood blinking in disbelief. Not only was Colin emerging from the cinema in broad daylight, with another, considerably younger, woman, he hadn't even bothered to remove his clerical collar.

FIVE

'You don't have to do anything at all about the food, Bonnie,' Fran said, hitching herself onto the high stool in Irene's kitchen. 'That's what I called by to say. I was almost passing, on my way to St Kilda for a photo shoot for a pamphlet I'm doing for an olive grower. So I thought I'd just drop by.'

'It's lovely to see you, Fran, after all these years,' Irene said, joining her on the other stool while Bonnie filled the kettle. 'I often read your reviews and use lots of your recipes. The zucchini and parmesan soup is one of my special favourites, and the dried fruits with rose and almond cream.'

'Oh, that's one of my favourites too,' Fran said. 'Daren't make it too often because I just scoff the lot and it's roaring with calories, but I'll bring some along to the picnic.'

Bonnie poured water into the teapot and sat down opposite them. 'You must let us bring something or it won't be quite the same,' she said. 'We should all bring a picnic basket and pool the food. I'm sure that's what we did before.'

'That would be fairer,' Irene said. 'Yes, Fran, let's all bring something, as long as I get to have some of yours!' She laughed. 'One of the compensations of age is that one can get away with outrageous greed!'

'Well, no sandwiches of sliced bread and tinned ham this time,' Bonnie said.

'I wouldn't rely on it,' Fran said with a grin. 'As far as my mother's concerned, a picnic is not a picnic without ham sandwiches, and preferably tinned ham. I can double bake a beautiful ham on the bone but she never reckons it's as good as the tinned stuff. Our only hope is that she'll forget to make them. Her memory's not what it used to be.'

'I shall certainly eat some if she makes them,' Irene said. 'I'm so looking forward to seeing Lila again, and you're going to be a grandmother, I hear, Fran?'

Fran nodded, picking up one of Bonnie's almond biscuits. 'Yes, if we all survive the pregnancy. Caro's turning out to be the expectant mother from hell. But there was another reason I called by, Bonnie, I wanted a favour. It's my tax. I'm a couple of years behind and I've got it in a really awful mess. I wondered if you'd come round some time and help me sort it out. I've been struggling for years doing it alone but now with the GST I'm totally confused.'

Bonnie pulled a face. 'I'm really not up to date with Australian tax, but I'm sure all the information we'd need is on the Tax Office website so, yes, I could certainly have a look at it.'

Fran grinned. 'At least you might be able to understand the instructions, which is more than I can do. One day next week, perhaps? Oh – and do you mind if David comes to the picnic? He's home again, just got back from Qatar. He was planning to go to Sydney for the weekend but he decided to postpone it to be here for Mother's Day.'

Bonnie stared at herself in the mirror and smiled. It was silly, probably, but she felt quite thrilled that Fran had asked her to help with her tax returns; it was odd that such a little thing could suddenly lift her spirits. And the conversation with Sylvia had helped. Perhaps fixing the reunion had been the right thing, after all. She'd had fun with her women friends in Zurich, organising dinners, playing tennis, commiserating over the men's obsessions with their work, but somehow they lacked the forthrightness and the intimacy that she thought she might rediscover with Sylvia and Fran. She'd liked the way that Fran had called by that afternoon, and how she'd plunged into a conversation with Irene as though they'd last seen each other three weeks, rather than over three decades, ago.

Bonnie slipped out of her clothes and reached for her dressing gown, catching sight of her body in the mirror. It was showing signs of wear and tear. The tiny lines on her skin had once been almost imperceptible, but now she didn't have to struggle to see them – the smoothness of youth, even the smoothness of her forties and early fifties, had gone. She stared at her breasts: not bad, really. Certainly there had been a shift downward but it could have been worse. The frightful thing, and she couldn't avoid looking, was the way her pubic hair had faded. Faded or gone grey? Both, she realised with a sigh. She had been dying the hair on her head for so long that she had lost touch with how much grey there must be up there, but if this was any indicator she might be almost as grey as Sylvia. Sylvia didn't attempt to hide her grey and it looked so elegant. Bonnie parted her hair, which had been coloured four weeks earlier: there it was, the natural colour – actually, the natural grey – trying to take over again. Maybe growing it out was the thing, but how would she live for months with a wide grey parting? The idea didn't have a lot going for it.

Bonnie wondered how she would look to anyone, specifically a man, seeing her body for the first time. It was all academic anyway because she couldn't imagine ever being naked, ever making love, with anyone else ever. At the same time, she couldn't imagine spending the rest of her life without a man. A little shiver ran through her as she thought about never having sex again. She certainly didn't want it now, but the idea that the door was closed forever was quite scary.

She wondered if Fran had a lover. Maybe lots of sex was what accounted for her wonderful complexion, or was that just the English genes? Yes, Bonnie thought, Fran almost certainly had a lover – maybe it was the olive grower. She imagined a stocky, olive-skinned Italian, with dark hair greying at the temples, successful, earthy but sophisticated, passionate and adoring, who would send Fran flowers, take her for wonderful meals, appreciate her abundance, talk to her of love and romance. And she imagined Fran and the olive grower romping around the bedroom, laughing together at their pleasure in their own ageing but still sensuous bodies.

And what about Sylvia and Colin? It was difficult to imagine as it was so long since she'd seen him but Colin, as Sylvia spoke of him, seemed a distant, shadowy figure. Probably not a lot of romping around, perhaps a rather quiet, dignified sex life, frequent but gentle, affectionate, with the comfort of people who have grown to know each other's likes and dislikes over the years.

She sighed and wrapped the dressing gown around her, remembering making love with Jeff, the last time just the night before he died. Strange – cruel, really – how you never knew that you were making love for the last time. She swallowed the start of a sob. While she was thankful not to be troubled by sexual urges now, what if they did return? How would she cope with it? How would she cope without being unfaithful to Jeff's memory? If that time ever came, she thought, she would probably feel able to ask Fran's advice. Seventeen years as a single woman probably provided lots of useful experience, mature assertive strategies for every situation.

At the other end of the house she heard the water running in Irene's bathroom and suddenly Bonnie wondered if her mother had been celibate since she was widowed at the age of sixty-two. Even *considering* the alternative was so shocking that Bonnie blushed deeply and turned out the light. Surely not! Could she have? That was something she certainly didn't want to think about. She climbed into bed in the dark and closed her eyes tightly.

David lay on the bed in his old bedroom staring at the nail in the ceiling that his father had put there years earlier, to hold a model plane. His father. He'd have to go and see him soon. David's stomach lurched at the thought. So far he'd escaped with a phone call because Tony and Lee were both so busy. Even so, he couldn't put it off much longer. But not this weekend anyway; he really wanted to go to that picnic. The thought of his mother and her friends and their mothers was strangely comforting. On Monday, perhaps, he'd face his father, late in the day when Tony got home from work, which would mean he could keep it short.

Everyone thought Tony was easygoing but David always found his father hard work. He had such high expectations that didn't relate to anything David wanted for himself. There'd be an interrogation for sure. Why hadn't he completed the contract in Qatar? Another wasted opportunity. What was he going to do now? Tony would almost certainly deliver the old lecture on how, in his day, people got a job and stuck with it, didn't chop and change all over the place. David had tried many times to explain that he'd taken up teaching English as a second language simply so that he *could* chop and change, move around, live in different countries, different cities, experience different cultures. David wondered if Tony would ever let go of the academic aspirations he'd had for him since the day he was born.

He sighed and got up from the bed wondering if his pliers were still in the top drawer of the desk. There they were, just where he'd left them. He stood on the bed, reached up, pulled the irritating nail from the ceiling and tossed it in the bin, thinking about his mother. She'd been disappointed that he hadn't been able to tuck into her food with his old enthusiasm, and he hadn't yet summoned the courage to explain. He'd have to tell her, and tell her soon, tell both his parents. Fran would be okay – upset, of course – but she'd understand. There wouldn't be any third degree with her but Tony was not going to be easy.

He wondered briefly if he'd tell Fran first and then maybe she'd help him tell his father, but no, he was thirty-two, for heaven's sake; he had to deal with this himself. The first thing was to tell her, get that out of the way. Perhaps he'd wait until after the picnic. But the more he thought about it the more it seemed that he was compounding the crime of not having come clean as soon as he got back. Okay, he'd tell her before the picnic. Then tell his father, and then reorganise the Japan interview. He was pretty sure he'd get the job; he'd already had two extensive phone interviews. They didn't want him to start until July, so he had time for all the other stuff he'd come home to do.

The car door slammed outside David's bedroom window, and

he heard Fran's key in the front door. She was back from the olive pressing – well, this time was as good as any other. He took a deep breath and wandered down to the kitchen as Fran came in, carrying four large cans of olive oil.

'Hi, darl, look at all this oil he gave me. Such a nice man, and it's beautiful quality.'

David looked at the cans of oil, imagined a lot of very glossy olives floating in a glistening pool of oil, and struggled to force down the nausea.

'Good stuff,' he said. 'Tea?'

'Please,' Fran said, putting the cans away in the cupboard. 'I called in to see Bonnie and Irene too, about the picnic. And Bonnie's going to help me sort out the tax thing. She's an accountant, or at least she was, but I'm hoping it's like riding a bike, you know – you never forget how to do it. There's some of that lasagna left we could have tonight if that's –'

'Mum,' David cut in, jiggling the tea bag in the mug and not looking up, 'look, about food, I'm not having a very good relationship with it at the moment, as you've probably noticed.'

Fran nodded vigorously as she transferred her notebook and file of slides from the benchtop to the dining table. 'Yes, I had noticed. Change of climate, probably.'

'No, actually it's more than that,' David said, and his heart began thumping so loudly that he was surprised she didn't ask where the noise was coming from.

'It's fine,' she said, only half paying attention, sorting through the transparencies of the olives. 'You're old enough to make up your own mind what you want to eat –'

'Mum, can you stop that a minute and listen, please?'

Fran looked up at him and took off her glasses. 'What?'

David leaned against the sink, mug in hand, and looked down at his feet. 'It's not the food, it's me. I'm . . . well . . . I'm sick.'

'Sick? Some gastro thing?'

'No, sort of seriously sick . . .' He paused. 'I've got Hepatitis C, Mum. It makes me nauseous a lot of the time. I know you were so pleased when I told you I don't drink anymore – it's because I had to stop . . . this just fucks up your liver and . . .' The words that had been pouring out evaporated suddenly. The shock on her face was so clear that he didn't know what to say.

David put his cup on the draining board and when he looked up again there were tears in her eyes, and she looked like she had at the airport the first time he'd gone overseas to work. Suddenly all the fear and panic he'd bottled up threatened to overwhelm him. She walked around the bench, into the kitchen, and put her arms around him. They clung together without speaking, and for the first time since he'd got the diagnosis in the hospital in Qatar, David was able to cry.

SIX

Sylvia lay flat on her back on Fran's tartan rug staring up at the pale, cloudless sky, and holding out her glass to David, who promptly topped it up with champagne. It was, she thought, warmer than the other Mother's Day picnic, when her fingers had turned blue and wrinkled from staying so long in the icy water. She sat up, crossing her legs and looking around her; surprisingly little had changed about the place. She hadn't been to this beach, to any beach, for years; she'd forgotten how good it felt to be watching the water, to smell the salt breeze and the seaweed. A seagull dived and swooped towards the picnic baskets and she watched David shoo it away. How lucky Fran was to have at least one of her children here, and how sweet David was, so much at ease with this group of women.

On Friday a parcel had arrived from England with a card and a long letter, and in silver tissue paper was a beautiful nightdress: very pale pink satin trimmed with silver grey lace. Sylvia had taken it from the tissue paper and stood in front of the mirror in her jeans and jumper, holding the nightdress against her. It was perfect, Kim had got it absolutely right, but she knew she couldn't wear it, couldn't get into bed beside Colin wearing this beautiful nightdress, feeling as she did. She had rewrapped it in the tissue and tucked it away in the cupboard, wondering if or when, and under what circumstances, she might feel able to put it on.

'Your husband couldn't come then, dear?' Lila asked, perched above her on a canvas chair. 'Fran said he had to work. Was it a serious operation? It must be very difficult for doctors having to rush off at all hours. I have a very nice young doctor, his name is Ahmed. I don't suppose your husband would know him?'

'No, Mrs Whittaker,' Sylvia said, turning to her with a smile. 'No, my husband's not a doctor, he's a clergyman, a Canon.'

'Oh, for goodness sake, don't call me Mrs Whittaker. It's Lila, you know that. A Canon, really – that's nice, although I can't imagine why Fran told me he was a doctor.' Lila took a sip of her champagne and waved across to Fran, who was sitting on the other rug with Bonnie. 'Fran, Fran! Sylvia's husband is a Canon, he's a vicar, not a doctor at all; you got it all wrong.'

Fran rolled her eyes, smiling conspiratorially at Sylvia. 'Sorry, Mum, silly old me.'

Sylvia rested her elbows on her knees and thought about Colin, about the affectionate, considerate way he had bent to listen when the woman spoke to him outside the cinema, and then steered her across the street. She was still numb with shock, not just that he was deceiving her but that he was doing it so blatantly. That afternoon she had caught the bus home and walked back to the house feeling not hurt, not angry, just numb and confused.

When Colin arrived home around six-thirty, self-assured, smiling, looking just as he always did after meetings or lectures or services, she had watched closely for signs of guilt or insecurity. Not the obvious lipstick-on-the-collar signs, but the more subtle ones: elation, nervousness, overcompensation. There were none. He looked totally relaxed and she wondered if this was because it was the first time and he thought he'd got away with it, or because he'd been doing it for so long that he *knew* he could get away with it.

'Fascinating,' he said with a smile when she asked him about the lecture. 'Absolutely fascinating, lots to think about. It's part of a series – I'm going again next week.'

'Really, that's nice,' she said, curious to see if he would detect the insincerity in her tone. 'And the meeting?'

'Oh, fine,' he said, thumbing through the mail. 'Boring, you know what these things are like.'

'No,' she said, 'I don't. Tell me.'

He looked up instantly then. A sliver of insecurity flickered across his face and was rapidly replaced by a reassuring smile. 'Just the usual community stuff – how to stretch the social welfare dollars.'

'Oh that,' she said, and he'd nodded and wandered off into the study, from where she heard the sound of his paperknife slicing through envelopes.

Because it was impossible for her to define how she *felt*, Sylvia had thought at length about what she wanted to *do*, and had decided that first she needed to know more. No action was the best solution until she knew just what she was dealing with, and the first step in that direction was to find out if the lecture series was real and, if not, to see what happened on the day of the next 'lecture'. Meanwhile, she wondered how many past lectures, meetings, and pastoral visits might have served as cover for similar encounters. There were so many committees and fundraising projects, meetings and talks, that she had never queried, and why would she? And of course there were also the retreats, retreats that lasted a weekend, sometimes a whole week, during which there was no contact, no phone calls because it was time spent in thoughtful, prayerful solitude, communicating with oneself, and with God – or perhaps not.

And so, just the day before yesterday, having phoned the university and learned that there was no lecture series, Sylvia had set out, rather earlier than the previous week, to see if the two o'clock screening was a regular date. She had felt perfectly ridiculous in her hat and sunglasses, and was overwhelmed with anger at Colin for making her behave like a cliché. She hovered for a while near the front of the bookshop, picking up and putting down books and then, concerned that the staff might think her a potential shoplifter, found a seat in the nearby coffee shop, masked, she hoped, by a veranda post.

The audience from the two o'clock screening straggled out and dispersed and there was no sign of them, but as Sylvia was about to pay for the three cups of coffee that had left her hyper and twitchy, she saw them. They were walking along on the other side of Lygon Street, Colin, on this occasion, wearing a blue shirt that he usually kept in the car for those pastoral visits with people he thought might be a little intimidated by 'the uniform'. Sylvia stared hard at the woman. She was probably in her thirties, attractive but no great beauty, with an athletic build and short blonde hair cut in layers. She was wearing a navy blue sweater and faded jeans; they were holding hands again, but this time as they paused at the lights waiting to cross the road, Colin did the most extraordinary thing. He let go of her hand and put his arm around her shoulders. He was the taller by at least six inches and he drew her closer to his side and kissed the top of her head, and with that intimate gesture he thrust a knife into Sylvia's heart, slicing through the numbness. A gasp burst from her throat and she put a hand on the table to steady herself. The woman looked up at him and smiled and, as the lights changed, they strolled across the street, arms around each other, and turned into a side street.

Sylvia's original intention had been to follow them if she saw them but now, reeling with shock and hurt, she left the café and wandered blindly back towards the bus stop, dredging the recesses of her memory for a time, any time, when Colin had ever demonstrated such spontaneous affection towards her. She found she had to rewind more than thirty years to recall one. He had always been acutely embarrassed by the slightest gesture of affection in public, and now here he was strolling down the street with his arm around an unknown young woman, seemingly entirely at ease with something that, even as a young man, he had always shunned. And most extraordinary of all was the fact that he was doing this openly. He knew so many people that the odds of being recognised were high. Even if he wasn't worried that she would find out, he would surely realise that this could get back to the Dean or the Bishop. Sylvia couldn't avoid feeling that it was somehow deliberate, as though he was challenging all of them – her, the church hierarchy, the community, everyone. Maybe even God?

Numbness had been replaced by hurt and anger, furious anger, and resentment, but Colin's clandestine affair had also relieved her of the burden of guilt she had felt at her own disaffection. It released her from the responsibilities that had imprisoned her for years, leaving her free to act for herself, and although she didn't yet know what she was going to do, she was absolutely sure that she was going to do something very soon. Sylvia uncrossed her legs and stretched them out in front of her, listening to Irene and David praising Lila's ham sandwiches and, further off, to Fran and Bonnie puzzling over the long forgotten names of the others who had been at the first picnic.

'To mothers, grandmothers and daughters!' David said, holding up his glass of mineral water in a toast.

'And sons,' Irene smiled, raising hers towards him.

And fleetingly Sylvia remembered Simon, who had been at the first picnic and whom Irene had lost. 'And sons!' she added, raising her glass, and the others chorused the full toast, and broke into joyful, sentimental laughter.

Fran stood up, flexing her legs to get rid of the pins and needles, transferred herself to the chair that Lila had just vacated, and watched as her mother and her son wandered towards the water's edge. Lila was hanging on to David's arm, telling him some long and involved story about the dances she used to go to as a young girl. They moved slowly, David guiding her across the uneven sand, his head bent to hear what she was saying, and Fran thought Lila looked smaller, as though she had shrunk. Was she actually smaller or was it simply the effect of seeing David's youth and height alongside her? Lila was wearing a pair of purple cotton trousers, a lavender blouse, and leather pumps in a different shade of purple.

One Christmas a few years earlier, Fran had bought her mother a framed print of a poem called 'Warning'. Lila had unwrapped the print and studied the poem for a few moments in silence and then began to read it aloud.

When I am an old woman I shall wear purple,
With a red hat that doesn't go and doesn't suit me
And I shall spend my pension on brandy and summer gloves
And satin sandals, and say we've no money for butter . . .

Lila had paused and looked at Fran. 'I like this,' she said. 'Thank you, Fran, I like it very much,' and she read on, intermittently aloud: '*I shall sit down on the pavement when I'm tired . . . And make up for the sobriety of my youth . . .* Who wrote this poem?' she asked, turning the frame in her hands and reading the poet's name at the bottom. 'Jenny Joseph, I see. Is she a friend of yours, Fran? I'd like to meet her.'

Fran shook her head. 'She's English. The poem was written in the sixties.'

'Pity,' Lila said. 'She knows a thing or two, this Jenny Joseph. '*I shall go out in my slippers in the rain, And pick the flowers in other people's gardens . . .*' And Lila read softly on to the end of the poem and sat for a moment staring at it as a tear rolled down her cheek and splashed onto the glass. Then she pulled down the sleeve of her cardigan and wiped the tear away. 'I think this is one of the nicest presents I've had in my whole life, Fran,' Lila said, crossing the room to kiss her.

A couple of weeks later, Lila had called and asked Fran to drop by and pick up a bag of old clothes to deliver to the charity shop. Fran was on her way home after interviewing a famous visiting gourmet chef and was not far away, so she made the detour.

'It's me, Mum,' she called, letting herself in through Lila's back door. 'Oh, a new dress! What a lovely colour.'

'Yes,' Lila said, twirling slowly for Fran to admire the purple and lilac print. 'I spent my whole pension on some new things, come and look.' And she drew Fran into the bedroom where a variety of different outfits in various shades of purple, lilac and lavender were spread out for inspection. And on the wall above Lila's bed, replacing the Mediterranean seascape, was the poem. Since then Lila had purpled her life, a little at a time, from her wardrobe, to her bed linen, to the cotton mats she crocheted for her dressing table, to the purple mugs she bought to replace her old china.

'I left it a little late, really,' she said thoughtfully when Fran commented on the newly acquired purple bathmats and crocheted toilet roll cover, 'so I have to make up for lost time.'

Fran thought she was lucky that so far Lila had not chosen to splash out on the red hat, or experimented with spitting, both of which were options considered in the poem.

Taking a couple of surprisingly lively steps back from the water's edge, Lila appeared to be showing David a dance step, and Fran watched in fascination as David put his right arm around Lila's waist and took her right hand in his left, and the two of them began a stately dance. She held her breath trying to stifle the sob that rose in her throat. Silhouetted against the late afternoon sky she could see David's new fragility. It was spiritual more than physical, although he was also thinner than when he had gone away. But since he had broken his news she had noticed other things; the slight discolouration in the whites of his eyes, the shadows beneath them which she had, at first, attributed to jet lag, the sudden onset of fatigue; things apparent only to a mother now searching constantly for signs.

David turned Lila gently, swaying to and fro and laughing, throwing back his head, the soft fair hair, so like Fran's own, catching the last gold of the sun's rays. Did he really understand what this meant? Did he understand what it meant for relationships, for his work? Late that night, after they had sat for hours talking, crying, hugging or holding hands, each trying to comfort and reassure the other, David had eventually drifted off to bed and Fran, whose response to most crises was first to acquire as much information as possible, had done some research on the Internet. She had to assume that he knew as much as she did, probably more, and she wanted to ask him, but he seemed to prefer to let it rest and now she was trapped, the victim of her own restless knowledge.

'Look at those two,' Sylvia said, sitting down beside her, nodding towards the pair dancing by the water. 'Aren't they beautiful? Don't you wish you had a camera?'

Bonnie sneaked a look at her mother, who had turned her chair to capture the last of the sun's rays on her face. She breathed a sigh of relief that she had managed to stop herself from pointing out that Irene wasn't wearing sunscreen. Since the conversation about Greece and then her talk with Sylvia, she had been shocked at the number of times she'd had the urge to organise Irene, or say something relating to her safety. The effort of restraining herself was enormous and she had begun to wonder if she had been as neurotic with Jeff. Probably not. He'd certainly have told her if it had annoyed him and, anyway, men just loved to be the centre of attention, to feel they were being looked after. In a couple of weeks' time Irene would be on her way to Greece and Bonnie would be alone again; the prospect of the empty house hovered threateningly like the entrance to a cave.

She wondered how her mother had coped with her first months as a widow and realised that when she and Jeff had returned to Zurich, three weeks after her father's funeral, she had given little thought to the huge burden of grief and adjustment that Irene was facing alone. Bonnie felt a deep sense of shame that she could have been so insensitive.

'Brushing up your tan before you head off to Italy, Irene?' Lila said as David led her back to her chair. 'I hope you're going to send me a postcard.'

'It's Greece, Lila,' Irene said, opening her eyes and turning towards her. 'And of course I'll send you a card. I'm certainly not going to lose touch with you again. And when I get back I'm going to bore you to death with my photographs.'

'Oh, I'll enjoy that,' Lila said. 'And, Bonnie, you're to come and see me while your mum's away. I want to show you my unit. I'm changing everything to purple, like the poem. I want you to see it.'

'Another bottle of champagne, I think,' Bonnie said several hours later, struggling out of her chair and making her way, somewhat unsteadily, to the fridge.

'I don't think I'd better,' Sylvia said. 'I'm supposed to be driving.'

'You're already past it,' Fran cut in. 'You'd better leave the car here and we'll share a cab. So, let's just have one more?'

'No, no!' Bonnie said, steadying herself against the fridge door. 'You can't possibly go home. It has to be a sleepover, like in the old days. Go on, say you'll stay.'

It was well after nine, and David had taken Lila home, leaving Fran free to spend the evening with Sylvia and Bonnie at Irene's house.

'A good idea,' Irene said, getting up from her chair. 'Neither of you should drive. I'm off to bed now but all the beds are made up, and you're welcome to stay.'

'See,' said Bonnie, weaving her way triumphantly back across the room with the champagne. 'You must stay or Mum'll be disappointed.'

Sylvia looked at Fran and raised her eyebrows. 'Okay with you?'

'Fine – I'll phone David and let him know. But what about you, will Colin mind?'

'Stuff Colin,' Sylvia said, and Bonnie's eyebrows almost shot off the top of her head. 'He'll be out but I'll leave a message on the machine.'

Bonnie took extra care refilling the glasses and then sank back into her chair, kicking off her shoes and tucking her legs under her. 'I am extremely drunk,' she announced. 'I can't remember when I was ever as drunk as this. Here's to meeting again.' They raised their glasses and chorused the toast.

'This is so nice,' Sylvia said, resting her bare feet on the edge of the coffee table. 'Just like old times, except we used to be sharing secrets in the bedroom while the adults were in the lounge. Now it's the other way around.'

Bonnie grinned. 'Secrets, yes . . .' She paused, trying to make sure the words came out right, and held up her hand as they began to laugh at her. 'Stop laughing at once, both of you. If we're saring shecrets – I mean, sharing secrets – I have a very serious question to ask Fran.'

'Ask away, Bon,' Fran said, shaking with laughter, swinging her legs up onto the couch and settling back against the cushions. 'Ask away.'

'I can only ask while seriously under the influence, so you have to forgive me in advance.'

'I forgive you in advance,' Fran said, trying to keep her face straight.

'The olive grower,' Bonnie said. 'Is the olive grower your lover?'

Fran spluttered into her champagne. 'Ah,' she said, getting her breath back, 'wouldn't that be nice. But actually, Bon, the olive grower and his partner are the two most gorgeous gay men I've ever met in my life. So, unfortunately, no. There hasn't been a lover in my life for the last ten years at least.'

Bonnie looked crestfallen. 'Amazing,' she sighed. 'I was so sure. I thought if I ever needed advice on that score you'd be the one.'

'Not me, darl, certainly not me. For enormously fat women in their fifties, lovers, like really nice clothes, are not on the radar.'

'Such a shame,' Bonnie said. 'I'd constructed such a sexy scenario for you. And anyway, you're not enormously fat. I'm sorry about the lover, though.'

'Me too,' said Sylvia, 'although frankly I think celibacy may have a lot going for it. Men are not my favourite species at present. But I could help with the clothes, Fran. If you draw what you want I could make it up for you, or we could design it together. I am a demon with the sewing machine.'

Fran sat forward. 'Really, Syl? That would be fantastic. I can never get anything nice in my size. If you're big you're supposed to be broad shouldered and tall as well. All we big women aren't like Maggie T, and I always end up with shoulders near my elbows and waistlines round my knees.'

'I could make you some lovely things,' Sylvia said. 'We can work out the patterns and then we could go together to that fabric shop just off Lygon Street. They have gorgeous materials from Europe, really unusual.'

'Me too,' Bonnie said. 'Can I come? I know that shop, I used to go with Mum years ago – the one not far from where we had coffee, Syl?'

'That's it,' Sylvia said. 'I nearly went there that day but something stopped me. Something amazing stopped me.' She paused, her heart suddenly beating faster as she realised that speaking it would make it real, and then there could be no going back. After this she could no longer pretend to herself, to Colin, or to anyone else, that nothing was happening.

'I saw Colin with another woman, a younger woman, holding hands, and then I saw them a second time and he was kissing her.'

'I can't believe it,' Caro said, dumping herself on the sofa and kicking off her shoes. 'You mean she's not coming home tonight?'

David shook his head and handed his sister a cup of coffee. 'That's right. I took Grandma home and Mum's staying at Bonnie's place. She phoned about half an hour ago. D'you take milk, Mike?'

'I'll just have a beer, thanks, Dave,' Mike said, helping himself to a can from the fridge. 'We came back early to surprise Fran. Caro said she was having a Mother's Day lunch, but there was no one here, so we hung about for ages, then we went home and came back again.'

'She even had her mobile switched off,' Caro said irritably. 'I can't believe she didn't tell me it was a picnic instead.'

'Why would you need to know?' David said, sitting down with his coffee. 'You'd opted out of Mother's Day and were having a romantic weekend.'

'Is that what she said?' Caro asked, putting down her mug and slopping coffee in the process, 'that I'd opted out of Mother's Day?'

David shook his head. 'No, that's what I said. Mum said you were going away for the weekend to celebrate the baby.'

Caro, slightly mollified, got up and went to the kitchen to collect a dishcloth. David had annoyed her immensely ever since he got back from Qatar. He'd seemed pleased about the idea of being an uncle but also vague and distracted, and she'd always been jealous of the way he and Fran got on. It went back to the divorce, and David being four years older, suddenly becoming the man in charge of things, or at least that was how it had seemed at the time. In her heart, Caro knew she was probably being unfair, but knowing something and getting rid of the feelings attached to it were worlds apart. Resenting David and competing with him had become part of who she was, and it was easier when he was away.

'So much for trying to do the right thing,' she said, mopping up the spilled coffee. 'Well, I suppose she was pleased to have you there. Was it deadly boring?'

'On the contrary,' David said in a tone that got right up Caro's nose. 'It was great – sort of old-fashioned and nice. I like those women, wish I'd met them before. Strange how they all lost touch. Anyway, they've clearly stitched up the gaps and are making up for lost time. Did you two have a good weekend?'

'Terrific,' Mike said. 'We went to this gorgeous boutique bed and breakfast place. Wonderful food, lovely scenery, and it's attached to a vineyard – superb wine.'

David raised his eyebrows at Caro. 'Should you be drinking wine?'

'A glass now and again won't hurt,' Mike said, smiling at her and reaching out for her hand. 'Not now she's past the first trimester.'

Caro moved closer to him. Mike was such a great ally in her struggle to be as good as David. 'Just because you're on the wagon it doesn't mean everyone else has to be,' she said.

'Of course not. But sometimes there are very good reasons,' David said. 'I just thought it was supposed to be bad for pregnant women –'

'So what's your very good reason?' Caro cut in sharply. 'Did you join AA or something? I seem to remember that a night getting wrecked used to be one of your favourite regular pastimes.'

David paused, drawing in his breath. He hadn't anticipated this but they would have to know sometime. 'Mmm, it sure was,' he said. 'But I had to give it away. You might as well know, I've got Hep C.' He looked across at Mike. 'You'd know what that means – stuffed liver, nausea, all the rest of that crap. I had to come home to see a doctor here, organise medication . . .'

'Oh, my god!' Caro said, putting both hands protectively on her stomach. 'It's not catching, is it? I mean, you won't give it to the baby?'

SEVEN

Sylvia let herself in through the front door pausing briefly to ensure that Colin had, as usual on a Monday morning, left to do his hospital visits. She dropped her handbag on the bottom step of the stairs and wandered through to the kitchen, where the smell of burnt toast and cold coffee hung in the air. Evidence of Colin's breakfast was distributed across the benchtop and the table; a multigrain loaf surrounded by breadcrumbs, the toaster with one blackened slice standing to attention, the coffee plunger with the still-warm grounds in the bottom, plate, knife and cup on the table alongside the butter dish and his favourite Oxford marmalade minus the lid. Even his chair stood as he had left it, pushed back from the table, jutting out into the centre of the room.

Sighing, Sylvia covered the butter and the marmalade and put them in the fridge. She was about to move the plate and cup to the sink when she stopped herself. He could find it as he had left it. She imagined his shock when he returned at lunchtime and a tiny but satisfactory sliver of revenge was shaved from her dense store of anger and resentment.

A fluorescent orange Post-it slip glared at her from the corkboard where they left messages for each other. 'YOU MISSED KIM'S MOTHER'S DAY CALL!!!' it shouted. Colin was a purist when it came to punctuation so the extra exclamation marks were clearly intended to be guilt-inducing. Sylvia sat down at her usual place at the table, taking in the clumsy domestic reproaches. It was, she thought, all pretty crass for a man who espoused sharing the domestic load and had, at times, even laid claim to feminist views generally. Was this the best he could do to punish her for her absence? Not very creative. She was sure she could do a lot better when the time came for dishing out punishment. But punishment wasn't really what she had in mind – turning her back on the whole bloody lot of it was far nearer the mark. Now that she had told Bonnie and Fran about Colin's infidelity, she would have to act, but she was still no nearer knowing how to handle it.

'No,' Bonnie had said, shaking her head and reaching over to refill their glasses. 'No way, you must have got it wrong, Syl. Not Colin, he's a minister, and . . . they just don't –'

'Bastard,' Fran cut in, 'the absolute bastard. Of course she hasn't got it wrong. She saw them together twice, for heaven's sake. What would you have thought if you'd seen Jeff –'

Bonnie gasped and clapped her hand across her mouth. 'He wouldn't have, he just wouldn't . . . Fran, how could you suggest . . . ?'

'Sorry.' Fran flushed. 'Sorry, that was stupid and insensitive, of course not, but you see what I mean? Of course Sylvia hasn't got it wrong.' She turned to Sylvia. 'So what are you going to do?'

Sylvia shrugged and shook her head. 'I don't know. Packing a bag and leaving is looking very attractive but it's not that easy – nowhere to go, no income, nothing belongs to me. The week I got married my mother gave me advice about keeping a separate bank account and I was shocked at the idea. Wish I'd taken her advice.'

Fran nodded. 'I know what you mean. It would have been like you expected something to go wrong. Anyway, you have got somewhere to go, you can come to me. Even with David home I've got plenty of space.'

'Or you could come here, ' Bonnie volunteered. 'I know Mum wouldn't mind, and she'll be away for ages.'

Sylvia looked around the kitchen and wondered what Colin had been thinking when he left the note and the breakfast mess. Had he intended her to feel guilty about staying away overnight? Did *he* feel guilt about his infidelity, his dishonesty, his deception? In view of his own misdemeanours, discretion and generosity might have been a more diplomatic response to her unscheduled absence. She was still overwhelmed with the longing just to get up and walk away, to avoid painful discussions and arguments about what had happened and why. Independence beckoned enticingly but it was a mirage that evaporated each time she tried to focus on it.

Independence demanded things she hadn't got. Everything they had both earned in their lifetime was in shared accounts and investments. It had been Colin's planning but she had not objected. When Kim was born, Sylvia, by then a departmental manager at David Jones, had given up her job, slowly taking on more of the parish responsibilities, and so the church acquired two employees for the price of one. Knowledge of her skills as a needlewoman had spread and she had been in regular demand organising costumes for school plays, parish pantomimes, and confirmation dresses for the children whose mothers paled at the sight of a needle. Slowly and inexorably the work of maintaining and restoring the fabrics for the diocese had found its way to her, and while she was paid a small fee for reworking the gold thread on the stoles, or the crimson embroidery on the bishop's cloak and the antique lace on the altar cloths, it all went into the shared income.

'Take up thy sewing machine and walk, Sylvia,' she murmured grimly into the silent kitchen, 'because that's about what you'll have if you just walk away.'

The phone rang suddenly, startling her, and she swung around to answer it and then stopped herself. Let the answering machine pick it up. There was something else she needed to know before she faced Colin, and she got up from the table, let herself out through the kitchen door and made her way through the garden and behind the vestry into the quiet cul-de-sac of Church Close and knocked on the door of number three.

'Sylvia! This is a nice surprise,' Veronica said, stepping back to open the door wider. 'Do come in. Did you enjoy your picnic?' She was wearing a pale grey velour tracksuit piped with white and her black-framed glasses were perched on top of her head. 'Would you like some coffee or perhaps you'd prefer tea?'

It was a small townhouse with a galley-style kitchen overlooking a sunlit living room. Timber-framed French windows opened to a small paved backyard crammed with well-tended pot plants and hanging baskets. Sylvia suddenly saw it through new eyes: this was what it was like for a woman living alone; it looked peaceful, pleasant, remarkably desirable.

'You do have milk, don't you?' Veronica asked, bringing in a tray of coffee. 'This is delightful. I was just writing a little note about the children's art exhibition for the local paper. It all went very well but we did miss you . . .' She faltered seeing Sylvia's face as she handed her the cup. 'Oh dear,' she said, 'is something . . . ?'

'You know, don't you?' Sylvia said. 'You know about what's going on with Colin.'

Veronica paused and put down the cup. 'Yes, dear, I do know. Not formally, not sort of officially, you understand, but I've heard, and clearly now you've heard too.'

'I saw them together,' Sylvia said. 'Twice. Do you know her?'

'No.' Veronica shook her head. 'I only know that she's a social worker and a lot younger than Colin.'

Sylvia swallowed hard. 'Does everyone know? Are they all talking about it?'

'Not everyone, Sylvia, a few.'

'They say the wife is always the last to know?'

'Well, you're not the last, but you're not the first either. And, of course, when a few people know that means a few more soon will.'

Sylvia bit her lip, wishing that she could have controlled the tears that were sliding down her face. 'Why didn't you tell me?'

Veronica reached across the table and took her hand. 'Sylvia dear, I like and respect you very much, but we are hardly close friends. I didn't want to be the nosy old neighbour spying on the vicar. When I saw you in the church last week I felt so bad I almost said something, but then you said you were going through a rough patch, and I thought that meant you knew and were dealing with it.'

Sylvia brushed the tears away and took a gulp of her coffee. 'Do you know how long it's been going on?'

'I heard about it a few weeks ago,' Veronica said, 'but the person who told me said it was a longish time, a year or more. Apparently, the Dean knows and spoke to Colin about it . . . some time ago. That's . . . that's all I really know.'

Ice entered Sylvia's veins, freezing her blood and arresting the tears. So there was not just Colin's infidelity and deception to cope with, there was the public side – even the Dean knew. She remembered lunches and sundowners at the Deanery, and Bill, his kindly hand on her arm, steering her into a quiet corner to chat about how hard it must be to have her only daughter and grandchildren far away in England; complimenting her on the exquisite embroidery repairs to the cathedral tapestry. Pity! Pity for her blindness, her stupid inability to see what was going on around her, her total ignorance of something that everyone there knew but her. How pitiful she must seem.

'I'm so sorry, Sylvia,' Veronica began. 'Perhaps I should have said something earlier . . .'

Sylvia shook her head. 'No, you did what you thought was right. I can't believe I didn't know. He's always been very detached, you see – distant, really – and more so over the years. I just thought . . . I hardly know what I thought.' She shook her head. 'You know, Veronica, I would never have credited Colin with the imagination to do something like this.'

'Huh!' Veronica said, pouring her own coffee. 'Imagination? In my experience, most men's imagination is located between their legs. And since I heard what Colin was up to I can tell you that there have been many occasions when I have come close to kicking him right in his imagination.'

David walked up the street from the tram stop to the house, his backpack over his shoulder, wishing he had never given up smoking. The last four hours had been peppered with moments of intense longing for a habit he'd abandoned three years earlier. He should have been ecstatic, and he should still have been in Sydney, meeting up with old friends. He'd planned an evening of celebration, envisaging himself walking through the streets of

Kyoto to work, occupying his office, meeting the staff of teachers for whom, as director of studies, he'd be responsible. He'd got the job, he'd even managed to push up the salary and get them to pay for business-class travel. They were delighted with him and wanted him there by the end of June.

'Just one thing,' the director had said, 'merely a formality, but we need you to have a medical.'

David's eyes had glazed over as the man went on about how the contract would be mailed to him as soon as the medical clearance was received. He was framing a question about the appropriateness, even the legality, of the request but the director had foreseen it and was explaining that it was a requirement not of this school, but of the Japanese company itself for whom they were merely managing the recruitment. Better to get it done here than have to go through all the palaver once he got there – after all, the director had said, smiling again, he was obviously fit so there shouldn't be any problems.

The irony was sickening. He'd worked in seven different countries over the last twelve years and never before had his contract been subject to a medical. In the early days as a rookie teacher he'd just turn up at the door of a language school and pick up a few classes the same day. But now he was really good, good enough to be a director of studies in a school that taught English to Japanese executives, and his medical condition was going to stuff up absolutely everything. He had left the interview, wandered out into Oxford Street in a daze and stood briefly contemplating the possibilities.

He could probably get away with postponing the medical until his arrival, in the hope that it would simply be forgotten. The risk was that if it wasn't forgotten and he was sent home on medical grounds, they might refuse to pay his fare, and want him to repay the cost of the outbound trip as well. Stupid ideas raced through his mind: getting someone else to attend the medical in his place, bribing a doctor to lie for him, asking Mike to fill out the form for him. It would be a waste of time, though; he'd got the job, but there was no way he'd be going to Japan.

He was suddenly overwhelmed with loneliness and the threat

of the depression that had haunted his last weeks in Qatar hovered just behind his shoulder. He wanted to be home, just as he had wanted to be home once he'd got the diagnosis; suddenly, stupidly perhaps, anywhere else seemed threatening and hostile. He pulled out his mobile and cancelled his arrangements for the rest of the day, then he flagged down a taxi and headed out to the airport, hoping he could pick up a seat on the next flight back to Melbourne. A few hours later he was home again.

'But you don't know for sure that they would knock you back on the strength of the medical,' Fran said, moving a pile of files off the couch, where she had been looking for her last tax return. 'I mean, if the employer was worried about medical costs you could have your own insurance.'

David smiled, sipping the cup of tea she'd given him.

'And who do you think would insure me, Mum? An insurer would only give me coverage from which the existing condition would be exempt.'

'Would you two like me to leave?' Bonnie asked from her seat at the computer where she was working on Fran's tax. 'I can come back at a better time if you need to discuss this more.'

David shook his head. 'It's fine, Bonnie. Don't leave because of me. It's not as if you didn't already know. If I can borrow the car, Mum, I think I'll go and face the music with Dad and Lee. It's got to be done sometime and today can't get much worse.'

Fran followed him out to the car, concern forming creases between her eyebrows. 'Are you sure you want to do this now? Another day or two won't hurt.'

He shook his head. 'Might as well get it done with, then it won't be hanging over me.' He paused at the car door. 'Can I stay on a bit longer with you?'

'Of course, as long as you like.'

'I'm thinking it might be time to settle down here for a bit. See how I go, stick with the treatment, and there's always plenty of language teaching jobs. I'll buy a car, find somewhere to live –'

'You can live here,' Fran cut in.

'Just till I find somewhere,' he smiled. 'I'm too old to live with my mum. Besides, I don't want you knowing what I'm up to all the time.'

She nodded. 'Whatever. But it's a good idea, staying in Melbourne . . .'

David saw the relief in her face. It was the same look she'd had when he'd walked away unharmed from a horrible car accident, and when the police constable searching his room hadn't found the expected stash of marijuana. The look almost made him want to cry again and he gave her a quick hug before climbing into the car, wondering briefly how it really felt to be a parent and to care so desperately about what happened to someone whom you could no longer pop into a highchair for safety.

'He says he's going to stay on in Melbourne,' Fran said, resuming her place amid the files on the couch. 'So at least I'll be able to keep an eye on him.'

'That's good,' Bonnie said somewhat distractedly, her eyes still on the screen. 'You won't worry so much if he's nearby. Fran, what have you actually *done* with all the GST you've collected over the last two years?'

'I haven't done anything with it because I couldn't work out the stupid forms,' Fran said. 'I just paid it into the account with the other money until I could sort it out.'

'And the receipts for things you've bought for your work?'

Fran waved a file tray in the air. 'Yes, I've got some of those. Haven't kept all of them, of course.'

'So, you haven't got all the receipts and you haven't filed an income tax or a GST return, or paid any tax, for the last two years?'

'No, but I've put a bit aside to cover it.'

'How much exactly?' Bonnie asked, jotting some figures on a pad beside her.

'Just over three thousand – it's in my savings account.'

'I see,' Bonnie said, taking off her glasses and rubbing the bridge of her nose.

'I could probably rustle up another five hundred if necessary,' Fran said, feeling the stirrings of unease. 'I used to just whiz everything over to the accountant but he retired and I haven't got around to finding a new one. I'm not really sure how much I've earned over the last couple of years, but it's always a struggle so it's probably around the same as the preceding years. I just haven't been very good at keeping records.'

'You haven't actually kept *any* records,' Bonnie said, clearing her throat. 'Just a few receipts and, fortunately, your invoices.'

Fran pulled a face. 'I know, I know. For a self-employed person I'm useless at it but he always did it for me, you see, and there's always so much else to do. I just sort of, well . . . ignored it.'

'Yes,' said Bonnie warily, 'I can see that. The thing is, Fran, what you owe is a good bit more than you've got saved.'

'How much is a good bit more?' Fran asked, her heart suddenly starting to beat very much faster.

'Quite a lot, actually.' Bonnie glanced down at the figures and then looked up at her again. 'Your income tax and GST together come to over fourteen thousand, and there'll also be some interest charged on top of that.'

Caro was on her way back to her desk from the toilets when she tripped up two steps and staggered, steadying herself against the wall. She stood there a moment, heart pounding furiously, fear flooding her body and making her head spin. She had just vomited for the fifth time that day and was already weak and light-headed; now the fear made her feel as though she was trembling inside. She couldn't have hurt the baby, could she? After all, she hadn't really fallen, just tripped and staggered. People did all sorts of things when they were pregnant, rode horses, played netball, and this was really nothing.

She made her way carefully back to her desk and sank into her chair, hoping that no one would notice the greenish pallor she had just seen in the mirror. How could she know that it was all right? The whole pregnancy thing was terrifying. She'd thought it would be a breeze, that was what Mike had promised. She was young, healthy, ate well, didn't smoke and only had an occasional glass of wine. But it was the responsibility. It hadn't really hit her until she'd started telling people, her mother, David, her Gran, then the phone call to Mike's parents in Singapore. Suddenly it was all terrifyingly real: she was responsible for getting this whole other person into the world, a baby, a child, when she actually still felt like a child herself.

Caro felt the nausea rising again. It was ironic that just a week after she had boasted to Fran that she had graduated into the vomit-free zone, she actually started throwing up every day, and not just in the mornings but, like her mother had said, on and off all day, every day, relentlessly. She took a deep breath and sipped some water and then she felt a slight twinge around the area of her disappearing waist. Was it a serious twinge? What did it mean?

She picked up the phone to call Mike and then put it down. She couldn't call him at work again. Last time she'd had a twinge she'd called him and he had been in the middle of deciding if an elderly man with impacted faecal matter was at risk of a burst bowel. He'd been lovely, of course, very patient, that was Mike – but he'd told her firmly that twinges were perfectly normal, her body was going through dramatic changes and there would be lots of strange twinges and other things over the coming months.

'Ring Fran,' he told her. 'You need to talk to a woman. Your mother's had two kids, for heaven's sake, ring her now.'

But Caro couldn't. She just couldn't let her mother see how vulnerable and scared she felt. For the last seventeen years starting with the divorce, Caro had fashioned herself into the iron woman, tough, sassy and together. While David had traversed the war zone between Fran and Tony, calming them down, relaying messages the language of which he invariably tempered, Caro had remained aloof. She had always been a bright child, not intellectual but street smart, and she had wrapped herself in that bright, hard smartness and built a snazzy little wall around herself so none of the gross, embarrassing drama or intense pain of it all could penetrate. She'd actually drawn a picture of it at the time. One night, lying on her bed with her radio turned up to drown the sound of the raised voices, she'd drawn herself surrounded by this neat cerise wall with ramparts along the top. It had fixed in her mind that night and she could still see it firmly in place, the neatly drawn black portcullis designed to resist marauding invaders, keeping everyone out and her safe inside. Caro had never quite worked out how Mike had made it over the ramparts; from time to time she had pushed him out and raised the drawbridge, but he always knew the way back in and somehow, she thought, now that she was having their baby, she would be keeping Mike locked firmly inside.

Caro drummed her fingers on her desk and then picked up the phone and dialled her grandmother's number.

'You weren't at the picnic, Caro dear,' Lila said. 'That wasn't nice, you know. I think you could have been there for your mother.'

Caro rolled her eyes at the telephone and wondered why it was that her grandmother forgot so much but was always on the ball over things that would be best forgotten or ignored.

'And how's Nick?'

'Mike, Gran, his name is Mike.'

'Ah yes, he's a lovely boy, Caro, you're very lucky. Did I tell you I got my best chair reupholstered? Purple, you know, very nice deep purple velvet. It cost me rather a lot but it was worth it. When can you pop round and see it?'

'I'll come at the weekend, Gran,' Caro said. 'Sunday, Mike and I'll come and take you out for afternoon tea. But I just wanted to ask you something.'

'I'm writing it down,' Lila said. 'Sunday, that'll be nice. I have to write things down these days. I don't suppose you've noticed but I'm getting a bit forgetful.'

'Really, Gran?' Caro's face softened to a smile. Sometimes she felt Lila brought out the best in her. 'No, I hadn't noticed. But I wanted to ask you . . . well, you remember about me being pregnant?'

'Of course, dear, now I wouldn't forget that – my first great grandchild. I hope you're taking care.'

'Yes, yes, I am but . . . do you remember – did you get funny sort of twinges when you were pregnant?'

Lila laughed. 'Twinges, of course, twinges, horrible stretchy feelings, nasty tightening-up feelings when you think you'll explode or your eyes will bulge out of your head, pressure on the bladder, backache, nerves in your legs going dead, indigestion, swollen ankles. It's pretty awful, really. I don't go along with all the stuff they tell you these days about how wonderful having babies is. It's a ghastly business if you ask me, the whole pregnancy thing, and as for the birth itself –'

'Thanks, Gran,' Caro cut in, feeling the fear prickling the back of her neck. 'Just wanted to check, that's all. I'll get you to tell me the rest of it at the weekend. Better go now – I'm at work.'

'It's the worry that's the worst, of course,' Lila continued, 'thinking that the baby might be dead and you wouldn't even know. Happened to a woman I knew, she walked about with a dead baby inside her for weeks before they found out. Anyway, dear, I won't hold you up if you're busy. Thanks for ringing. Give my love to Mike.'

Caro put down the phone and rested her head in her hands. The phone call hadn't been such a good idea after all. Maybe she should slip downstairs and talk to Sarah in accounts; she had a two year old. She stood up, swaying slightly as another wave of nausea assaulted her. The trouble was, she knew nothing at all about pregnancy or babies, and despite his reassurances she didn't think Mike knew much either; she wasn't too sure of the extent of the midwifery part of medical training. She'd start with Sarah and go from there but first of all she thought she might just take the rest of the week off.

EIGHT

Bonnie sat on the deck outside the scruffy boatshed kiosk watching the seagulls duck and weave and realising that it was probably the worst spot she could have chosen. A real estate agent's board fixed to the boardwalk announced that the kiosk was closing and alongside it, on the wall of the boatshed itself, another announced that the building was for sale with permission for certain commercial developments. The end of an era, she thought sadly. So many teenage dreams had been built around the boatshed; here they had loitered shyly, hoping to catch the eye of some dazzling young man on a yacht, and fantasised about what they'd wear as they relaxed on deck, sipping cocktails at sunset.

Bonnie drew her coat more tightly around her and wound her scarf around her neck. She needed to be out in the air, with the smell of the sea and the harsh cries of the seagulls wheeling in the distance. She wasn't sure why she'd walked up here, only that she had to get out of the empty house.

'No, I really don't want you to take me to the airport, Bonnie,' Irene had insisted. 'It would just complicate things. The minibus is picking up all twelve of us and they'll organise all our luggage. There's a special arrangement for us to check in away from the other passengers so we don't have to queue. They must think we're really decrepit but never mind, it's an excellent arrangement.'

Bonnie, who had been awake since five, tortured with apprehension and anxiety, had lugged Irene's bags down the stairs and placed them just inside the front door. 'Are you sure you've got everything? Tickets, passport, glasses, money, credit card, mobile phone?'

Irene checked everything and looked up smiling. 'All present and correct.' A horn sounded outside and Irene opened the front door and waved towards the elderly faces peering from the windows of the bus.

'There they are, perfect timing. Look at them all in there, see – there's Marjorie! Goodness, it's just like being a teenager going to school camp – so exciting.' She supervised the driver putting her bags into the bus and then turned back to Bonnie, reaching out to hug her. 'Well, darling, here I go! I promise I'll take care and I'll phone you once a week and you have to promise not to worry.'

Bonnie hung on to the hug and then stood back with a watery smile. 'I promise to try. Have a really wonderful time and, Mum . . .'

'Yes?'

'I really love you and I'll miss you.'

Irene hugged her again. 'I love you too, darling, and I always miss you, but I'll be back in no time at all, boring you silly with my geriatric adventures.'

The bus pulled out of the drive and disappeared down the road and Bonnie's composure, which had been under tight rein, immediately evaporated. The empty stillness of the house settled on her and as she walked back into the kitchen she began to weep with the same desperate intensity as she had during the weeks following Jeff's death. It was two hours before she could get her head together and compose herself to cope with the weeks of isolation ahead. Knowing she needed some fresh air, she'd washed her face, grabbed her coat and sunglasses and made her way straight to the kiosk, hoping for . . . hoping for what? She didn't even know.

A few weeks ago things had seemed to be on an upward curve. The Mother's Day picnic and the evening with Fran and Sylvia had made her feel she was going to be okay. She sensed promise. They were like lifebuoys and with them around she felt she might, somehow, do what her mother kept telling her to do – get a life – but since then things had stalled. She hadn't heard from Sylvia and in a way that wasn't surprising. Sylvia had gone home to confront Colin about his affair; coping with that was obviously her first priority, but somehow Bonnie had expected that Sylvia would be in touch to talk, even to take up her offer to stay with her, but she'd heard nothing.

And then there was the business with Fran, and Bonnie knew she'd stuffed that up herself. She'd loved sorting out the tax, it made her feel useful, competent, and they'd laughed their way through most of that day until she'd had to deliver the news about Fran's tax liability. Bonnie could see now how badly she had dealt with it. Fran was devastated at the size of her debt and Bonnie had only wanted to help when she'd told her not to worry, that it was only a small amount and she'd be happy to settle it for her. Fran's face, at first white with shock, had flushed crimson with embarrassment, but Bonnie had failed to recognise that look and had gone on to make it worse.

'Really, Fran,' she'd said, 'it's easy, a drop in the ocean, honestly.' And as Fran opened her mouth and shut it again, Bonnie realised the insensitivity of what she had said. Money had never been an issue for her. Even when she was bonking the banker she wasn't hard up, it was just a part of the financial planning that would free her from her parents' loving but irritating protection. But for Fran it had all been so different. While Bonnie had been a fee payer at St Theresa's, Fran and Sylvia had been scholarship girls, and they had both struggled to hold their own against the taunts of the girls whose families reeked of old money. And when Fran and Tony had split up, the division of the spoils had been more like a division of the debt. What Fran now owned – a decent house with a mortgage, its contents, a solid six-year-old car and a bit of cash – was the result of years of hard work and financial struggle as a single parent.

Bonnie cursed herself for not fully registering what Fran had said that first day at lunch about struggling with her mortgage. Money meant nothing to Bonnie and she was irritated when people referred to their financial status, good or bad; she knew nothing about life on the financial edge and, even now, despite the time she had spent cursing herself for her insensitivity, she still couldn't quite comprehend the reality. She could pay Fran's tax bill without even noticing it, so it had seemed the obvious solution. The fact that her offer would embarrass Fran and trap her between the rock of potential rescue and the hard place of humiliation had simply never dawned on her.

'I couldn't possibly let you do that, Bonnie,' Fran had said, her face crimson, eyes dangerously bright as she battled her pride. 'I'd feel . . . it would feel . . . I don't know, just terrible.'

'Then let me lend it to you,' Bonnie had persisted. 'It's attracting interest all the time.' Fran shook her head. 'I can't, you see, I don't know how or when I could pay you back.'

'It doesn't matter, Fran. You will or you won't, it just doesn't matter. Think about it,' she'd said again as she left, 'but not for too long. Call me.'

Fran nodded, trying to look her in the eye. 'Honestly, I do appreciate your offer but . . .' And her voice had faded away and she ended up with a bleak forced smile on her face as Bonnie backed the car out of the drive. It was ten days now and she still hadn't called.

Bonnie pushed aside her empty coffee cup and shivered as a cloud drifted across the sun. The temperature didn't change, it just *seemed* colder, bleaker, like the house, like the weeks ahead.

Further down the beach a woman with short grey hair was walking slowly. She was wearing old jeans, a sweater and sneakers and she walked confidently across the sea wall and down to the water's edge where the three of them had walked that first day. The woman looked as though she knew who she was and where she was going. Bonnie longed to be like that; why was it that she was on the edge of everything and involved in nothing, while her friends' lives were complex, intense, involved, painful? Was that harder, she wondered, than this terrifying emptiness?

The sun emerged again and Bonnie sighed and stood up, taking a last look at the boatshed before turning back to the car park. She had to face the house again sometime. Maybe she could just call one of them, like she'd called Sylvia once before. Could it be as easy as that?

*

'I got you an almond croissant from the French bakery,' Caro said, putting the bakery package down on the coffee table. 'You look nice in that top.'

Fran, confused by the unexpected visit, the thoughtfulness of the croissant and the unsolicited compliment, chose to ignore the note of surprise that accompanied the latter.

'Yum, thanks,' she said, tearing open the white paper bag. 'Ten o'clock on a Friday morning, how come you're not at work?'

'Mental health day,' Caro said.

Fran raised her eyebrows. 'Didn't you have a couple of those the week before last?'

'Yep. I had a whole mental health week, actually. They owe me. I worked three weekends on the trot helping with the launch of that Scrawny Boys album, and never got paid for it.'

Fran put down the tray with the croissants, coffee plunger, mugs and milk.

'They're both for you,' Caro said, staring at the croissants. 'I don't really fancy one today.'

Fran looked up sharply. 'Really? Are you okay? You do look a bit pale.'

'I'm fine, just not hungry. Were you off out somewhere?'

'A celebrity chef interview, a feature for *Gourmet Traveller*,' Fran said. 'But I don't need to leave till ten-thirty. I hear you went to inspect Gran's chair.'

Caro nodded, swinging her legs up to rest her feet on the table. 'We went to take her out for tea, but we did the admiring the chair bit too. I don't think she can go much further with the purple thing, do you? There's not much left.'

'Don't kid yourself,' Fran sighed. 'She hasn't started on the paintwork, the kitchen cupboards or the bathroom tiles yet, and next week I'm taking her to get new glasses – purple, of course. I suppose we should be thankful that the poem is about purple, not fluorescent lime or mission brown.'

'Chair looked good, though,' Caro said, investigating the worn fabric on the arm of the sofa to avoid watching Fran start on her croissant. 'You should get this suite recovered, Mum, it's getting a bit scruffy.'

Fran brushed pastry flakes from her lips. 'Oh well, sometime, I suppose, but it's not a priority.'

'Or get something new, why don't you? You've had this for donkey's years.'

'It was the first thing I bought on my own after your father and I split up,' Fran said. 'I'm really rather attached to it.' She certainly wasn't going to give Caro any inkling that a new suite was beyond the realms of financial probability for the foreseeable future. She had never, ever, let either of the kids know the precarious nature of her finances since the divorce. Guilt over their pain had made her determined never to burden them with any of her worries. As she had lurched from one financial crisis to another it was an act of faith to continue to shell out for school trips, new clothes, holiday spending money and college and HECS debts as though she could afford it. Having Bonnie know her present situation was bad enough; having David or Caro know was too horrible to contemplate.

Fran knew she was entirely the wrong sort of person to be self-employed. It was feast or famine, no work at all or so much that she was snowed under but scared to turn anything down. She should really have been working somewhere structured, where she knew what she'd be earning that week, that month, that year, and with tax and superannuation deducted before it ever reached her. But she had never been good at fitting into institutions and had clung to the apparent freedom of freelancing despite the prison of stress it created, and the constant struggle to keep all the balls in the air.

'More coffee?' she asked, pushing the plunger across the table.

Caro shook her head. 'I think I'll just have a glass of water, thanks. Where's Davo?'

'House hunting, or flat hunting really. He's gone to see something in Collingwood. He's got a job over there starting next week, so it would be really convenient. Have you decided to have the baby at home or in hospital?'

'Not sure yet,' Caro said, pouring herself a glass of water. 'Mike says hospital, but I'd like to stay at home, or go to that new birthing centre. What d'you reckon?'

Fran was so surprised to be asked her opinion she almost choked on the second croissant. 'Home is a nice *idea* but it's a big upheaval and I think you want to be somewhere where you're sure of being looked after. The birthing centre's supposed to be lovely, everything you need. I'd go for that.'

Caro nodded. 'That's what I think. That's why I'm on my way to meet a midwife.' She put her glass on the table and sat down again. 'There's a woman at work who's pregnant,' she said, carefully avoiding eye contact. 'She's about as far gone as me and she's throwing up all the time. Didn't start till the fourth month.'

'Well, there you are,' Fran said. 'Just shows how lucky you are.'

'Mmm . . . Not only that, she's terrified all the time that she might damage it. Keeps thinking she might have hurt the baby, or it might be dead.'

'Has she felt it move yet?'

Caro paused. 'Probably not. What does it feel like?'

'Just like nudging or twitching, it's reassuring at first. Later it's weird to feel this large thing moving around inside you.'

'Really?'

'Yes . . . except that when first you feel it move you sometimes don't feel it again for several days. Then you start worrying that something awful's happened to it. She might find that a bit worrying.' She got up and carried the tray to the kitchen. 'I'm so proud of you, Caro, coping so well. I was a gibbering wreck when I was pregnant. Perhaps it helps having a doctor in the house.'

'Oh yeah,' Caro said awkwardly. 'I suppose.'

It was after two when Fran escaped from the celebrity chef, his rather overheated restaurant and his obsession with dousing everything in raspberry coulis. She wasn't far from Bonnie's place and she'd planned to call in there on the way home. In fact, she'd picked up the phone to call her a couple of days earlier and then, remembering that Irene was off in two days' time, decided to leave them in peace. She felt better now that she'd had time to think out her options, and she needed to let Bonnie know that, despite her embarrassment, she'd really appreciated her offer to pay the tax bill.

After Bonnie had left that night, Fran spent several agonising hours crying, pacing back and forth across the lounge and eating a tub of Connoisseur double chocolate ice cream, followed by a container of almond and coffee biscotti she'd made as a prelude to using the recipe in her column. She was, essentially, a realistic person; uncertainty was her worst enemy but once she knew the facts she could usually decide a course of action and come to terms with it. There was only one solution: she must sell the house. What did she need a big four-bedroom family home for, anyway? It had been ideal when she and Tony had bought it and when they split up she'd kept it and taken over the home loan. Not only taken it over but increased it by getting people in to do, in six weeks, the renovations she and Tony had planned to do over a period of years.

Getting the kitchen refitted had been the biggest expense but as cooking and writing about cooking were to provide her with a living, the kitchen was a top priority, and while they were messing around with plumbing it made sense to fix the bathroom and add on another small bathroom off the main bedroom. Fran was fond of the house, it had served her well, but she felt no powerful sentimental attachment to it. If she sold it she could pay off the home loan, settle up with the Tax Office and still have enough to buy herself a nice little unit or townhouse without a mortgage. She'd always fancied St Kilda or Balaclava. After all, she only needed a small place, as long as it had a kitchen that could cope with her work needs.

The more she thought about it the more she wondered why she hadn't done it years ago, when David and Caro left home. There'd be less housework and no guilt-inducing garden to die of neglect. She would accept Bonnie's offer of a loan to pay off the tax, and then repay her in full when the house was sold. She inhaled deeply and sat up straighter; the prospect shifted a huge burden. She'd wait until David had found a place and moved out, then she'd put the house on the market straight away. Maybe Bonnie or Sylvia, or both of them, would go house hunting with her.

As Fran reached Irene's house she saw Bonnie walking towards her. Her shoulders were hunched, her head was down and her hands pressed deep into her pockets. She didn't even seem to notice that Fran had pulled up at the gate.

'Bon, hi!' she called, opening the car door. 'Have you got a minute or am I intruding?'

Bonnie looked up suddenly as though jolted from some painful reverie and her face broke into a smile of relief and delight. 'Intruding? No, Fran, no way,' she said. 'I can't think of anyone I'd rather see right now. Come on in and I'll put the kettle on.'

'So you see,' Fran said, 'it's an excellent plan in every respect.'

Bonnie nodded. 'It is if you're sure that's what you want.'

'I'm sure. The idea of getting rid of that home loan, and having a smaller place, somewhere that's entirely my own, no debts, a new start, it's exciting.'

'Yes,' Bonnie said thoughtfully, 'yes, I can see that. Well, that's good. But have you done the sums? Worked it out carefully? You need to get a valuation on the house and work out what the sale and purchase costs will be, and then see if you could get something you're happy to live in with what you've got left.'

'Oh yes, I know that. What d'you think those costs would come to?'

'Look, I'm out of touch but there was a real estate talkback program on the radio the other day, and I think they were saying that people should allow up to thirty thousand dollars to cover the costs of buying and selling. You know, agents' fees, stamp duty, removals.'

'Thirty thousand?' Fran flinched. 'I've lived in one place so long I'd no idea. But still, it's a big house and a big block. Richmond's becoming quite trendy. I think I'd have enough left for somewhere decent. Of course, this all hangs on you still being prepared to lend me the money for the tax bill, despite the fact that I refused it the other day.'

'It's done,' Bonnie said, 'don't give it another thought, and I'm sorry for being so tactless.' She paused, a big grin spreading across her face. 'I've still got the weekend papers – shall we have a look in the real estate section?'

They spread the papers across the dining room table searching the real estate listings to get an idea of what Fran might ask for her place, and then for what she could afford.

'The boatshed is up for sale,' Bonnie said, pointing to a large display ad at the foot of the page. 'I was there this morning. Even the kiosk is closing.'

'Remember how romantic we thought it was,' Fran said, running her finger down the list of townhouses and apartments in St Kilda. 'I dreamed of marrying someone with one of those big yachts. Wouldn't give you a thank you for it now, the bloke or the yacht, rather be on solid ground.'

'And single?' Bonnie asked as the phone rang.

'And definitely single.'

Bonnie took off her glasses and padded in her socks to the kitchen to answer the phone. Fran read on, her spirits lifting every minute. Property prices in Richmond had rocketed; it looked as though she could ask quite a bit more than she'd thought and even with the associated costs she could still get somewhere nice and have money left over.

'Fran!'

She jumped and swung round to see Bonnie in the doorway, pulling on her shoes. 'Get your coat,' she said. 'It's Sylvia, she's leaving Colin. We're going to pick her up.'

NINE

Sylvia sat by the window on the staircase from where she would be able to see Bonnie's car coming up the street. She felt as though she had been carved in stone, rigid, incapable of moving and cold, very cold. The house wasn't warm at the best of times but this feeling was nothing to do with the temperature. For about the millionth time she wondered how she felt, why she wasn't crying or shouting, slamming doors and breaking more porcelain. Maybe it was simply that the undercurrent of relief was dominant now.

Colin's infidelity had legitimated her longing to walk away from her marriage and that almost outweighed the humiliation of knowing it was the talk of the church community. For several days after her conversation with Veronica she hadn't found the words or the energy to kick-start the action and she had wondered why Colin seemed not to notice her tension, or the fact that she was barely being civil to him.

On the Thursday evening she was sitting in her sewing room, contemplating what this said, not only about his lack of sensitivity, but about their entire relationship over the decades, when Colin, just returned from officiating at a funeral, popped his head around the door.

'Just wondering about dinner?' he said, and she desperately wanted to punch the pleasant but tentative smile off his face.

'Yes,' she said, getting up. 'It only needs reheating.' And she passed him in the doorway, taking care to ensure that no part of her body touched any part of his.

'Funeral went off well,' he said, following her down the stairs. 'Lot of people turned up. I'd no idea old Ted Watson had so many friends.'

Sylvia ignored him, slipped the lasagna into the microwave and set the dial to reheat.

'Now, I won't be in for dinner tomorrow evening,' Colin said, pouring two glasses of red wine and putting them beside the place settings on the table. 'In fact, I'll be out most of the day – meeting in the morning, then the lecture series, then the old social welfare stuff in the afternoon, could go on for a long time so I might have a beer and a sandwich with the others when it's finished.'

'Really?' Sylvia said, feeling strangely giddy. 'That's odd. I thought tomorrow was the day you usually met your girlfriend.'

The words rolled unexpectedly off her tongue and drummed into the silence. She moved to sit down, feeling her legs turning to jelly, but recognised in an instant that she had more authority while standing, so she leaned back against the sink.

The colour had drained from Colin's face. Sylvia had read books in which that happened to people but she had never really thought it could happen quite so fast. He went from a healthy colour to deathly pallor in seconds.

'I . . . er . . . I don't know what you mean,' he said, looking down at the table, starting to fiddle with the cutlery. 'Lecture series . . . you know, I did tell you . . .'

'Don't do this, Colin,' she said softly. 'At least do me the courtesy of not telling me any more lies.'

'So you know?' he said, looking up. She thought she knew him so well and now she realised that she was seeing an emotion she had not seen in him before – fear. 'Who told you?'

'No one,' she said. 'I saw you, two weeks running, the first time by accident, the second time by design. How long has this been going on?'

'Does it matter?' he said, defensive now. 'You saw us twice – does time make me more or less unfaithful?'

'Don't play games!' Sylvia snapped. 'How long?'

'Two years, maybe more.'

'Two years! And everyone knows, not surprisingly as you don't seem concerned about walking hand in hand down the road and kissing her in a city where a hell of a lot of people know just who you are. The first time you were even wearing your dog collar.'

He stared at her, his defensiveness crumbling, and he seemed to shrink into the chair. 'I'm sorry,' he said. 'I'm so sorry, Syl. It must sound ridiculous, but I never wanted to hurt you. I was lonely, I started to feel lonely and lost, as though I didn't fit anywhere.'

'You're right,' she cut in sharply, 'it does sound ridiculous. You always fit, you've tailored yourself to an exact fit with the church's cloth; it's your life, it's your skin. Don't tell me you don't fit anywhere.'

'But that was it, you see,' Colin said, looking up at her with a new and unfamiliar desolation in his eyes. 'It doesn't fit me anymore, or I don't fit it. The faith – it isn't working anymore. I'm a sham. After all these years I no longer know what it's all been about, and then –'

'Just a minute,' Sylvia cut in. 'Are you telling me that you've . . . you've lost your faith?'

Colin nodded, his expression bleak and exhausted. 'Yes, I was at my wits' end. I'd dedicated my life to my faith and then I found it was ebbing away. There was doubt, more doubt, and then . . . nothing . . . I battled it for ages, found a spiritual director . . . but I was getting nowhere.'

'You didn't tell me,' she began. 'You never said a thing.'

'I didn't want to worry you,' he said. 'You seemed quite content with things so I . . .' He paused. 'We didn't talk much about that sort of thing.'

Sylvia's anger exploded. 'That sort of thing? No, we didn't much discuss that *sort of thing*, why would we? How could we if you didn't even tell me?'

He shrugged. 'I didn't know how to tell you, and then, when I met . . . when I met Jenny, I started to feel different, as though there was hope . . . you know?'

'What do you mean *you know*?' Sylvia said, feeling as though she was trapped in a nightmare. 'Know what? What do you mean, hope? Hope of what, finding your faith?'

'No,' Colin said, shaking his head. 'No, not that, just hope of . . . of something different to believe in.'

The microwave stopped with three loud pings that startled them both and digital letters flashed the word 'Enjoy!'. They stared at each other, shocked first by the noise and then confused by the sudden silence.

'I know there's no excuse,' Colin said. 'No excuse for deceiving you, but it's a *reason*, don't you see? Can you imagine what it's like to devote all your life to your faith and then find it gone?'

Sylvia closed her eyes, took a deep breath and sat down at the table. 'Yes, I can imagine that,' she said. 'Actually, I can feel it. I also dedicated my life to faith. For almost forty years my life has revolved around *your faith*. I gave up everything to support you in what you believed was being asked of you. How long has this been going on?'

Colin rubbed his eyes. 'I told you –'

'Not the affair, your apostasy.'

'Oh! I see, longer, much longer, four years, perhaps a bit longer. It was after we went to the ecumenical conference in London, when we stayed with Kim.'

Sylvia gasped. 'Four years! And you didn't even tell me? Don't you think I had a right to know? Don't you understand what your faith and your ministry demanded of me?' He looked confused, as though he couldn't fully comprehend what she was saying. 'How could you, Colin? How could you go on with the ministry, go on with all of it . . . pretending? I don't understand.'

'I've lost everything,' he said, and she suddenly despised the childish whine of his voice.

She slammed her hand on the table. 'No you haven't,' she shouted, peering more closely into his face. 'You've given up on God and replaced him with a woman who's young enough to be your daughter. And you don't even understand what this means to me.' She paused. 'Do you love her?'

He looked up confused. 'I think so.'

'You *think* so? You *think* so! Well, you'd better make up your mind because now you can have her. Her or God, neither or both, you can be an adulterous apostate or a monk, whatever you damn well like, but you'd better sort this out with the Dean or the Bishop or whoever you need to, because tomorrow I'm going to find a divorce lawyer.'

That night she left him sitting in the kitchen, went straight up to the bedroom and, consumed with manic energy, moved all her things into the spare room. The days that followed were a cold war, hostile, calm and terrifying. She didn't go to a lawyer because she simply hadn't the energy; the shock paralysed her.

As the next week passed, there were conversations about the future. Colin went to see the Dean and the Bishop; he tried to tell her about the discussions, about the processes that he must now go through to determine his own position before finally deciding to relinquish the ministry. But Sylvia couldn't listen, she didn't want to know. She no longer cared, she could no longer consider him and she wasn't interested in the other woman. She didn't hate him but she could not forgive him and to be in the same house was torture.

'Let's be sensible about it,' Colin said a couple of days later. 'Don't rush into anything. You can't just move out – anyway, there's nowhere to go. We need to sort out our assets, all that business. The best thing is if you stay here for a while.'

But a week later to the day, Sylvia knew that she couldn't spend another night in the house: the church's house, the house that had existed for Colin to be who and what he had so desperately wanted to be. In all the stilted conversations of the last week neither of them had suggested trying again; they both knew that the time for that was long past. It was over and there was no going back.

She pulled out a suitcase from the cupboard under the stairs, packed it, disconnected her sewing machine and put it into its case, put her sewing things into some fabric bags, and dialled Bonnie's number.

'On the third day she rose again from the dead,' Bonnie said as Sylvia came downstairs fully dressed and with her hair swept up in its customary roll. 'Oh sorry, is that blasphemous? It wasn't meant to be.'

Sylvia smiled. 'It's okay. It does feel like that, actually. I do seem to have spent the last few days suspended in some awful sort of tomb.'

Fran, who had just arrived carrying a large cake tin, put the tin down and hugged her.

'You look heaps better. When we brought you back here you looked like a basket case. I couldn't believe you hadn't even cried.'

'She's made up for it since,' Bonnie said and Sylvia nodded in agreement.

'Absolutely, I've cried most of the time since. But this morning I woke up feeling different, as though it had lifted. Now I just feel fragile, like I'm getting over a long illness, but recovery is in sight.'

'Excellent,' Fran said, opening the cake tin. 'Coffee and walnut. I've been experimenting – it's got mascarpone and a dash of Baileys so I've brought it along for the expert tasting team. How about you, Bon? You look really good.'

Bonnie lifted the cake from the tin and cut into it. 'This is really appalling, but looking after Sylvia has made me feel better. There's been a lot of organising, I've had to fend off Colin, the Bishop and the Dean, who all say they have to talk to her, and then I've had to sort out a solicitor. We're going to see her this afternoon. I haven't had time to feel lonely or panic about Mum. So much for the great lesson of being alone in the house and not looking after people.'

'Taking care of someone who desperately needs it isn't the same as compulsively looking after someone who's perfectly capable of looking after themselves,' Fran said.

'Exactly,' Sylvia added. 'Bonnie's been fantastic; I've been waited on hand and foot, she's listened to me for hours on end and fought off intruders with a whip and chair. I don't know how she managed it.'

Fran leaned over and took a piece of cake. 'Have you talked to your daughter?'

'Yes, a couple of times,' Sylvia said. 'And I know she's spoken to Colin. It's a wee bit awkward because a few years ago Brendan, her husband, had an affair and Kim was on the point of leaving. I was the one who persuaded her to stay and give it another go. She hasn't actually said anything but I've got this feeling that she thinks I'm a bit of a hypocrite.'

'That was different,' Bonnie said. 'They had a baby of six months and a three year old, and from what you said he was full of remorse and desperate for her to stay.'

'And Colin?' Fran asked. 'Is *he* full of remorse and wanting you to stay?'

'Absolutely not. Colin is caught up in his own self-pity. He's suitably guilt-ridden over his infidelity but he sees himself as the victim in all this. Don't you think, Bonnie?'

'Yes, I spoke to him a couple of times. All he seems to see is his dilemma with the church, the fact that he won't have a job, and he'll have to get out of the house.'

'He could hardly go on ministering or canoning or whatever if he doesn't believe in it anymore,' Fran said with a laugh.

'It's a mystery to me that he kept up the pretence for so long,' Sylvia said. 'He won't know how to cope. I suppose this woman replaces God, and certainly replaces me, but there's nothing to replace the responsibilities and the status and the framework of the church. He's never done anything else.'

'How will *you* cope without the church, Syl?' Fran asked.

Sylvia shrugged. 'I've resented it for years. I know you two gave it all away when we left school, but I've hung on to my faith – just crossed the floor, so to speak. I don't have a problem with God, and I've struggled to separate that from the resentment I feel about the church. That hasn't been easy. Now I guess I'm free to work out what I really feel.'

'Weird, isn't it,' Fran said, 'how quite suddenly we're all in this transition. It's like limbo.' She laughed, raising her coffee cup. 'Must be your fault, Bonnie. It all began with you coming back here and organising that lunch. In the last few weeks everything's changed for all of us.'

'I thought it was you two who'd changed everything for me,' Bonnie said in amazement. 'Anyway, I like it. Here's to change. More cake?'

TEN

David put the box of books down in the middle of the polished floor and looked around. He liked the way the ceiling beams cast intersecting lines of shadow through the shafts of light that slanted in through the tall windows. Behind him he heard Matt struggling up the stairs with more books and he went back to help.

'So what d'you think?' he asked.

Matt straightened up, nodding slowly, taking in everything from the newly polished floor to the cedar blinds and the Japanese rice-paper screens that separated the living and sleeping areas. He let out a long, slow whistle. 'Tasty, very tasty.'

David grinned. 'Suitable bachelor pad?'

'Perfect! I'm almost jealous.'

'Go easy, mate, I'm only renting it. You own yours.'

Matt shrugged. 'Yeah, well, whatever. But it's great. I love these warehouse conversions, so much character. Are you going to have enough stuff?'

David sat down on one of the boxes. 'Mum's giving me some things – she's decided to sell the house – but I'll have to buy some stuff too.'

Matt ran his hands through his hair and wandered over to the window. 'Better let me come with you. You always had lousy taste in furniture.'

David grinned again. 'The orange chair?'

'An inadequate description, your honour: the fluorescent orange, synthetic fur chair with bald patches and the reek of cat's piss.'

'Mmm!' David nodded. 'I think I'd had a couple of spliffs the day I went to that garage sale.'

'That would also account for the lime-green lava lamp, and an almost life-size statue of Jesus with most of the paint flaking off?'

'I guess so, but you must admit the chair was very comfortable.'

'Only after being doused with a whole can of lemon air-freshener and hidden under a blanket. Anyway, this place is brilliant. Women will fall at your feet when you bring them here.'

David said wryly, 'Not a good idea under the circumstances.'

Matt swung round to face him. 'You don't have to be a monk, you know. Just take care of yourself, eat properly, exercise, and decide with your doctor what treatment you'll have.'

David, smiling, said, 'You sound like the blurb on the support group website.'

Matt looked awkward. 'Yeah, well, just wanted to find out a bit more.'

'You forgot the bit that says no screwing around.'

Matt shrugged. 'It doesn't say no sex, it says safe sex and . . . anyway, you know all about it. But take it easy, mate, you've got to get better – you're my oldest friend.'

David smiled at him again and swallowed down the flood of emotion that suddenly welled. He nodded.

'So,' Matt said, 'get some cool gear in here. Then you can get back into it all again, the old party animal.'

David shook his head. 'A quiet life, I think.'

'You! I doubt it.' He paused, looking up, the cheerful mask suddenly dropped. 'It seems so fucking unfair. All those years we were messing around with drugs, popping stuff up our noses, down our throats and in our veins and I'm healthy as an ox and you're . . . well . . .'

David said, 'Luck of the draw, I suppose. Only myself to blame. Just be thankful you didn't share that particular needle. We're both lucky to be alive, really, when you think about the way we were in that flat in Brunswick.'

Matt nodded. 'Our parents must have been shitting themselves. Now look at us. Respectable professionals. No drugs, no fags and only the occasional bottle of red. Gee, it's bloody good to have you back, mate, shonky liver or not. Best to be near friends and family when you're not too hot healthwise.'

David nodded, sitting down on one of the boxes. 'I know. It makes sense, especially while I make up my mind about treatment. Trouble is, though, I'm stuck with it for life.'

Matt looked awkwardly at the floor, rubbing the toe of his shoe around a polished knot in the timber. 'But you can have a life, a normal life. It says so. Lots of people do.'

'If I decide on the treatment the best it can do is stop it getting worse. I'm stuck with this. What woman would have a relationship with me? I can't even drown my sorrows in drink. I'm thirty-two and I feel like I'm fucking sixty, like my future's been ripped away, and the worst thing is I've only myself to blame.'

Irene swam slowly back and forth along the length of the villa's small pool. She thought it must be fifteen years since she'd been swimming and as she felt the pleasant tug of her muscles in the sparkling water, she wondered why she'd ever stopped. She turned over onto her back, hooking her hands over the rail, and let her body float out in front of her as she gazed up at the fleet of small white clouds skidding across the sky. Perfect, she thought, cooler than summer at home but delightful, and she sniffed to catch the scent of the pines and olive trees that spread in neat rows up the hill behind the villa. Looking down again at the surface of the water she contemplated her body, a wavy blur in the navy blue bathers, her legs, white by contrast, looking quite acceptable under the sparkling surface of the water. Such a shame that when she relinquished its flattering distortions age and gravity would once again take their toll. Not for the first time Irene was confronted by the strange contradiction that she could still feel so young in so many ways, but was living in the body of an old woman.

Beside the pool, Marjorie, wearing bathers under a cotton shirt, was stretched out on a banana lounge under the umbrella, book in hand. 'Gin time!' she called imperiously, waving a glass at Irene.

'Costas just brought the drinks. Lunch is in twenty minutes.'

Irene turned over onto her stomach, swam slowly back to the end of the pool, pulled herself up the steps and picked her way cautiously across the wet stone paving.

'This is the life!' she said, picking up her towel and drying off her hair. 'They'll all be freezing back home and look at us. I feel like Joan Collins.'

Marjorie raised her eyebrows. 'I'll refrain from commenting on that. Here's your drink, have an olive.'

Irene spread her towel over the banana lounge and settled herself back on it. 'How old do you feel, Marje?'

Marjorie peered at her over the top of her glasses. 'At what particular moment in time?'

'Oh, don't be so pedantic, for heaven's sake. Any time – how old do you feel?'

'Sometimes I really feel my age,' Marjorie said thoughtfully. 'Like while we were trudging around Athens in the heat and dust. I felt about a hundred then, and when we landed after that long flight. But most of the time I feel quite young in myself. I think the essential me is still somewhere around thirty – it's just my body that gets in the way. Why?'

'Just wondered. I feel much the same. In some ways I like being old, feeling I'm wiser and it's okay to do what I want to do. But you're right, although I feel young in my head there's stuff I just don't have the stamina for anymore.' She paused, contemplating the view across the sparkling water. 'Do you think it's different here?'

'What?'

'Being old. Europeans treat their old people differently. I don't feel so past it here as I do at home. Anyway, I'm glad we didn't go on the trip today. It's been a bit hectic so far – temples, carvings, vineyards, ruins, traditional dancing – all perfectly wonderful but so exhausting. So much for the leisurely pace. I don't know how the others can cope.'

'They're just the same but they're too proud to admit it,' Marjorie said. 'Tomorrow they'll be wiped out and we'll be fresh and rested. Anyhow, when you phone Bonnie, don't tell her we're exhausted or she'll send the Red Cross in to airlift you back to Melbourne.'

'Actually,' Irene said, sipping her drink, 'I think Bonnie's got her hands full at the moment. She's helping Fran to sell her house and look for something new, and Sylvia's been staying there for the last couple of weeks. She's left her husband.'

'Sounds good,' Marjorie said. 'Still doing the looking after but at least it's justifiable. So, what's going on with you and Hamish?'

'Hamish? What do you mean?'

Marjorie closed her book and put it on the table, turning to face Irene. 'Hamish. He's following you everywhere like a devoted labrador.'

'Don't be ridiculous,' Irene said. 'He's doing nothing of the sort, and he certainly hasn't followed me today. He's gone off on the fishing boat with the others.'

'Only because George shamed him into it. He wouldn't let up on him at breakfast about how Hamish had said going on the fishing boat was one of the things he most wanted to do.'

'Well, I'm sure he'll enjoy it,' Irene said, picking the slice of lemon from her gin and tonic and sucking it.

'Maybe, but every time I see him he's either pulling out your chair, getting you a drink, or casting you furtive longing glances across a crowded minibus.'

'Don't be silly,' Irene said. 'Hamish and I have known each other for years. He was Dennis's closest friend.'

'What's that got to do with it? Heavens, Irene, haven't you noticed? He's flirting with you.'

Irene laughed out loud. 'Is he? Oh well, so what? He's hardly going to race me off into the cabana for a moonlit night of passion – then Bonnie really would need to mount the rescue mission.'

'I wouldn't be so sure,' Marjorie said speculatively. 'Hamish is very fond of you. Always has been. I think it would be lovely. Wouldn't you like to have a bit of a fling again, Irene?'

'For goodness sake, Marjorie,' Irene said. 'That Jungian stuff has gone to your head. I'm eighty and Hamish is eighty-one. I've enough to do getting myself from place to place. Come on, time for lunch, Costas is waving to us and I'm starving.' She got up, pulled the cotton beach wrap around her and headed for the table on the patio.

'Methinks she doth protest too much,' Marjorie said, picking up her glass and following Irene to the table. 'You're never too old for love. That's vintage Marjorie, by the way, nothing at all to do with Jung.'

ELEVEN

Fran stood on the stool in Irene's dining room thinking about very rich, very short, blue cheese pastry with fresh raspberries and mascarpone, while Sylvia crawled around on the floor pinning the flared hem of the long sable brown velvet skirt.

'Stand straight, please, Fran,' she mumbled through a mouthful of pins. 'You're lurching.'

'Sorry,' Fran said, straightening up and looking longingly at the dish of pistachios and dried apricots that Bonnie had put on the table just out of reach. Since she'd put her house on the market her eating was more out of control than ever. It was the mix of anxiety and excitement that did it, that and the fact that she had a lot of work on. It had always been a fatal combination which resulted in her stuffing herself in an effort to feel calm and safe, and as though she could cope.

'You look beautiful, Fran,' Bonnie said. 'That colour is great for you and the cut of the jacket and skirt are so flattering, very slimming.'

'Really?' Fran said, looking down at the skirt and bending slightly.

'Don't *do* that!' Sylvia said. 'I'll never get this hem right.'

'You're brilliant, Syl, designing it and making it. I wouldn't know where to begin.'

Sylvia put in the final three pins, and then got to her feet and stepped back, looking critically at her work. 'Yes, that'll be okay. You can take it off now, Fran. That tin is full of buttons – see if you like any of them. If not, we might need to get some.'

'It feels lovely,' Fran said, peeling off the jacket. 'I could never have found anything so nice ready made. Everyone at the dinner will think it cost a fortune and wonder where I got it.'

'Have you sorted out your talk yet?' Bonnie asked.

Fran shrugged. 'More or less.'

'I hope they're paying you a good fee,' Sylvia said, taking the skirt from Fran and spreading it out on the table to check the pins.

'Oh, they don't pay. That's what makes it such a pain. All the preparation, then the anxiety, then sitting through dinner being polite to people you don't know. Then just as the dessert appears, I have to speak. You can't believe how agonising it is to watch everyone tucking in to their crème brûlée while you stand up to speak.'

'You mean you're not being paid?' Bonnie said in disbelief. 'So how long does all this take and how often do you do it?'

'I get asked quite a lot,' Fran said, stepping back into her black trousers. 'But I often say no because it takes about a day to work out the talk, and another half to worry about it, and then, of course, the whole evening at the thing itself. I get very anxious about it because all these people have turned up, paid a bomb for the evening and I'm the entertainment.'

Bonnie and Sylvia exchanged a glance. 'Well, who are these people? Have you asked to be paid?'

Fran shook her head. 'Oh no . . . they just assume you'll do it. Sometimes people actually invite you as though they're doing you a favour.'

'That's ridiculous,' Bonnie said. 'People get paid hundreds of dollars for public speaking. Why are you doing it for nothing?'

'Famous people get paid,' Fran said. 'Not people like me.'

'Yes they do,' Sylvia cut in. 'I often organised speakers for some of the church groups and for the diocesan dinners, and people charged anything from three to five hundred dollars a time. People like you.'

'I organised some international people for Jeff sometimes,' Bonnie said. 'They sometimes got several thousand, plus first-class accommodation. I know it's not quite the same but you should be getting a sensible fee, Fran.'

Fran looked from one to the other, feeling a flush of inadequacy creep up her neck.

'I couldn't. Some of them are just clubs, you know, like Rotary or –'

'So what?' Bonnie said. 'Sylvia's stuff was for the church but they paid. You're a local celebrity, Fran, you're an expert, you have a weekly cookery page in the paper and that column in *Eating In*, you do recipes and restaurant reviews. I bet that celebrity chef you interviewed would charge and he's just a chef, you're a writer as well . . . it's ridiculous.'

'Oh well,' Fran said, helping herself to a handful of pistachios. 'If they offered I'd take it but I couldn't just ask.'

'Rubbish,' Bonnie said. 'If you can't do it you need an agent who can.' She paused and swung round to face her. 'I could do it. I could be your agent.'

Sylvia clapped her hands. 'Brilliant, Bon, of course you could.'

Fran stared at them in amazement. 'But I couldn't . . . Bonnie, why should you . . . ?'

'Because I can and because I want to,' Bonnie said, her eyes bright with enthusiasm. 'You're so talented, Fran, and hardworking. Honestly, you might be pissed off when I say this but when I was looking at your invoices I was horrified. You work so hard and what you do is so popular, you should be earning at least twice what you're getting at present. But you're not very businesslike.'

'And you're too modest,' Sylvia added. 'You don't realise how many people read your articles and use your recipes. Bonnie's right, let her be your agent – your business manager.'

'But it's just me, it isn't really a business . . .'

'*But it is*,' Bonnie insisted. 'It *could* be a really profitable business if you'd take that side of it seriously. Having the ideas and being a terrific writer and a wonderful creative gourmet cook isn't enough. You need to deal with the business side to make it work for you.'

Fran stared at them, battling with a part of herself that was so deeply ingrained it felt unchangeable. It wasn't just that she hated bookkeeping and found the tax system confusing and frustrating, it was a resistance based on childhood hurt and resentment. She was back in the kitchen standing behind her father's chair as he did his record keeping, entering neat columns of figures into a book, checking orders and planning calls.

'Not just now, Fran,' he'd say, 'no time tonight. Another day, Saturday maybe. I'll take you and your mother on a picnic.' But however long she stood there, shifting impatiently from one foot to the other, twisting her hair, tugging at her socks, sighing noisily to attract his attention, he never found the time for her. Even if he finished his work before her bedtime, he would be out of the door and down to the pub.

'Your dad's very busy, dear,' Lila would explain, sitting on the end of Fran's bed. 'He's got a lot on – we just have to be patient.'

Fran looked at Bonnie and swallowed hard. 'You already helped me with the tax and you're lending me money. And you, Syl, at the worst time of your life you're making clothes for me, and you're both helping me find a house. It doesn't seem fair.'

'But I want to,' Sylvia said with a smile. 'Fran, doing this with you is helping me.'

'Yes but –'

'Yes but nothing,' Bonnie cut in. 'Sylvia's right. Doing your tax made me feel useful. It needed doing, it wasn't something I made up to occupy myself, like terrorising Mum by taking over her life. You're so good at what you do, Fran, and Sylvia's such a great designer and dressmaker and an organiser, I felt absolutely useless. But you've helped me realise there are things I'm good at.'

Fran looked at Bonnie. She certainly looked very different from the day they'd first met. Now she was more like the Bonnie of the old days, confident, energetic.

'Okay,' Fran nodded. 'Thanks, Bonnie, let's see how it goes.'

'Yes!' Bonnie cried, punching the air.

'Good decision,' Sylvia said. 'The lesson for this week is learning to accept help. Next week's lesson will be actually asking for it.' She hugged Fran. 'You'll look gorgeous at that dinner.'

'Yes,' Bonnie said. 'You will and, Sylvia, you and I are going to go along. I want to take a good look at the talent I'm marketing. Meanwhile, let's go house hunting.'

*

Caro let herself in through the front door, looked around at the immaculately tidy living room and wandered through to the equally tidy and gleaming kitchen. The kitchen was usually a work-in-progress, cluttered with lists, recipe ideas, or ingredients waiting to be lashed into the service of some new culinary creation, but since she'd put the house up for sale Fran had done a massive clear-up and a ruthless rationalisation of her possessions. Recipes had been filed, ingredients stored in cupboards, and old magazines, non-matching cushions, ornaments, pictures and other things accrued over the years had been loaded into boxes and moved outside. A monster garage sale was threatening and meanwhile the house was to be immaculate at all times in case of sudden visits from the real estate agent accompanied by prospective buyers. Caro dropped her keys and bag on the empty coffee table and wandered down to the bedrooms and the sound of David's CD player.

'Hi,' she yelled, opening the door.

'Oh! Hi!' he said, dumping a pile of t-shirts into a suitcase that lay open on the bed. He leaned over to turn down the volume. 'Didn't hear you come in.'

'Not surprised,' Caro said, sitting on his bed. 'You're still playing Elvis Costello – he's so yesterday. I could get you some really cool stuff from work if you like.'

'Thanks but no thanks. I'm not into elevator music.'

'You sound like Dad,' Caro said, curling her legs underneath her. 'By the way, I keep forgetting to ask how he was about the . . . you know . . . your stuff.'

'Christ, that's weeks ago now. He's been okay, actually. Bit shaken, and I think he was going to give me the lecture about my misspent youth, but Lee cut him off. She was lovely and he sort of softened up and managed to say all the right things. I think the prospect of being a grandfather has had an effect on him. He's very warm and fuzzy about that.'

Caro nodded. 'Where's Mum?'

'Gone with her friends to look at a house.'

'She seems to be spending a lot of time with those women these days,' Caro said, unable to keep the edge from her voice.

'Good, isn't it? Good for her, I mean.'

Caro shrugged. 'Don't you mind this?' she asked, nodding towards the suitcases.

'Why should I mind? I was moving out anyway. You and Mike'll have to come and see this place I've got.'

'But don't you mind the house being sold?'

David shook his head. 'No, I think it's a great idea. Makes much more sense for Mum – less work, new start, and I think she's been a bit worried about money. This'll sort it out.'

Caro shrugged again. 'Suppose so. When are you moving?'

'Day after tomorrow. You should call round at the weekend.'

'Yeah,' she nodded. 'Okay, Mike's off on Saturday evening, we'll come over and we can get takeaway – or will you be out raging somewhere?'

He turned towards her, eyebrows raised. 'Hardly. My raging days were over long ago. Mum says to take anything you want and then put everything else in boxes for the garage sale.'

Caro went along to her old room with butterflies fluttering inexplicably in her stomach. As she reached the door her heart started to beat quite fast and she stood for a moment, her hand on the knob, trying to calm herself. Just inside the door was the faded strip of pink ribbon that she had tacked across the carpet years earlier. She stood on the outside of it where anyone wanting to speak to her had had to stand until she actually invited them to cross the ribbon wall. Caro bent down and ran her fingers over the ribbon; faded and grubby, it was otherwise still in good condition. Once, during their first few months together, she had walked out on Mike and stormed back home with her backpack and headed straight for this room.

'Fine,' Fran had said, standing in the open doorway on the outside of the ribbon. 'Your room is always there for you.' And later that evening when Caro was lying on the bed crying her eyes out, her mother had tapped on the door, opened it slightly, and waited again to be invited in.

Caro smiled to herself and straightened up, looking around her. There had been so many times when, as a teenager, she'd hidden here, nursing her anger and her hurt, her terrible sense of impotence, hiding behind her ribbon. Well, it wouldn't be here much longer, she was an adult now, and soon there would be a baby to look after. Caro broke into a cold sweat at the prospect, and flopped down onto the bed. A very young Michael Hutchence smiled at her from the wall, and on the dressing table a pink fur teddy bear sat leaning against the triple mirror. It was still the bedroom of a teenage girl, the bedroom of the person Caro felt she still was.

She rubbed her eyes and lay down clutching a heart-shaped pink velvet cushion to her chest. She had held babies a few times, but never for long, and now a baby was living off her blood and organs, planning shortly to move out of her body and occupy her life in a different sort of way. She struggled to her feet, tossed aside the cushion and dived out of the door across the passage to the bathroom, where she sank onto her knees alongside the lavatory bowl.

Minutes later, David was tapping on the bathroom door. 'Caro? Caro, are you okay?'

She staggered to her feet, splashed her face with water and opened the door, her face half buried in a towel. 'Yep, fine. Morning sickness late in the afternoon!'

'Poor thing,' David said, putting his arm around her shoulders. 'Come on into the kitchen and I'll make you some tea. Then, if you like, you can sit on your bed like a princess and I'll pack your stuff for you.'

Caro leaned against him, unable to control the sobs. He pulled her closer.

'Whatever's the matter, darl?'

'You said that before,' Caro sobbed.

'Huh?'

'When Dad left, the first time we had to go and stay with him and Lee for a weekend.'

'I don't remember.'

'I didn't want to go but Mum said I had to and I cried and you said, "Sit on your bed like a princess and I'll pack your stuff for you".'

'Really? I said that? That was an extraordinarily nice thing to say to a younger sister who was being a vile brat.'

'Yes,' Caro said. 'You *were* nice then.'

'And not now?'

'I don't know,' she said, swallowing another sob. 'It all went a bit funny after that.'

'The pink ribbon time? Yes, I do remember now. You wouldn't let me in to pack the stuff and insisted on going just with what you were wearing. You wore the same stuff, including those awful pink clogs, all weekend, even in bed.'

Caro nodded. 'It seemed a good idea at the time.'

'And now?'

'This is harder. I'm scared – the baby, Mum moving, you being sick . . . everything.'

'Come on,' David said, steering her towards the kitchen. 'I'll make the tea and you spill the beans, and *then* I'll pack your stuff. Sisters – honestly! Can't live with 'em, can't live without 'em.'

TWELVE

Bonnie thought she was late. She'd had trouble parking and had run from the car park, up the escalators to the arrivals area, and reached the gate uncomfortably hot and breathless, to find that the flight was fifteen minutes late and was just landing. She breathed a huge sigh of relief and flopped down in a seat from where she would be able to see the aircraft taxiing towards the terminal. Slipping her fingers inside the polo neck of her black sweater she pulled the wool away from her skin. The airport, like most public buildings, was not designed with the comfort of constantly overheated middle-aged women in mind. Not only was she hot but her neck itched with the tiny hairs that had escaped the hairdresser's neck brush.

She fidgeted slightly and caught a glimpse of her reflection in the window glass. She thought she might look okay but who could tell when the image was so elusive, disappearing instantly as a blast of light emerged from behind some clouds and hit the window? Bonnie took a Wet One from the packet inside her bag and, holding out the polo neck, wiped the cloth around her neck and inspected the tiny hairs attached to it. Then, ignoring the stony gaze of a man sitting nearby, she tossed it in the bin. Maybe she looked a complete freak and that was why he was staring. She ran her hand over the remains of her hair and was struck by the thought that she might look like a prison escapee.

Two hours earlier, enveloped in a voluminous black nylon cape, Bonnie had sat staring in the mirror watching as the final strands of her dyed mahogany brown hair fluttered to her shoulders and then to the floor.

'Don't look so worried,' Vincent, the stylist, had said, seeing the terror on her face. 'Stay calm. Wait till it's dry.'

'It is a bit, a bit . . . short,' Bonnie managed.

'Yes, and it's very cool, or it will be when I've finished. This was a good decision, very much *of the moment*.'

Bonnie stared on, wondering if she herself was sufficiently *of the moment* to be able to carry it off.

Vincent spread a little mousse across his palms, worked it lightly into her hair and picked up the dryer. Switching it to the strongest blast of warm air, he attacked her scalp with his fingers.

'Scroggling,' he said loudly over the noise of the dryer, smiling at her in the mirror. 'That's what I call it. Some people call it finger drying. I think scroggling is a much nicer word, don't you?'

Bonnie nodded compliantly, unwilling to argue with him at such a crucial stage in the process of her dramatic transformation. Her spirits lifted a little as the short, flat, wet hair began to lift from her head.

'You've got great hair for this sort of style,' Vincent said. 'And your head's a good shape. You'll love it because it's so easy.'

Bonnie had lived with her greying parting for several weeks, torn between getting it redone and trying to let the grey grow through. Since she'd been back in Australia she'd been increasingly uncomfortable with the way she looked: hair, clothes, make-up, everything. The things that had worked in Switzerland seemed out of place here, unsuited to the life she was living. She needed a more casual style. And the hair, well, it just didn't seem to work anymore. That morning, knowing she had to meet Will's flight at twelve-thirty, she had called in desperation for an appointment and raced in hoping for a liveable-with solution to growing out the colour.

'There is only one solution, really,' Vincent had said. 'We just cut it, like, really short.' He picked up a strand of hair and slid his fingers down the shaft, stopping at the point where the grey began. 'Like to here.'

Bonnie gulped. 'That's awfully short.'

He shrugged. 'That's your only option – that or waiting until the regrowth is longer.' Bonnie's stomach lurched. 'A lot of women are having it really short these days,' Vincent said. 'I can show you pictures.' He turned away and brought out a hair magazine called *Short Cuts*. 'Look,' he said, flicking through the pages, 'cut well it can look great. See, here's Emma Thompson. Hers is shorter than yours will be, and she looks great, and see – it says here that Emma loves her new style, feels it's really liberating. Yours won't be anywhere near as short as that. Hers looks like a number two, and yours is thick so it'll have more volume.'

Bonnie took a deep breath, closed her eyes, exhaled and opened them again. 'Okay,' she said, sounding far more decisive than she felt. 'Let's do it.'

'I think you look fabulous,' Vincent had said forty-five minutes later as he removed the cape and brushed the hair from her neck. 'I give you forty-eight hours by which time you'll love it too,' and he put his hands reassuringly on her shoulders. 'If not, come back.'

It was, Bonnie thought, a rather pointless offer – after all, the hair was so short there was nothing Vincent could do about it now except sell her a wig, and Emma Thompson would have a lot to answer for. But as she stood up brushing down her sweater and straightening the waistband of her jeans, she caught a glimpse of herself from another angle, and thought that maybe, just maybe, she might look all right. Jeans, sweater, very short silver hair – it was so unlike her, but perhaps that was just what she needed.

The first of the passengers began to straggle out into the lounge and as Bonnie stood up she caught sight of him almost immediately. His height helped, and his relaxed, confident manner always seemed to make him stand out from a crowd. Will had a commanding presence just like his elder brother, but in Jeff it had seemed perfectly natural, because he had the whole successful businessman look: greying hair, three-piece suits, confident gestures, authority oozing from every pore. Will, on the other hand, looked younger than his forty-three years, and his light brown hair, almost collar length, fell across his forehead. He was wearing jeans, a black t-shirt and a leather jacket, and looked more like a film director than a stockbroker.

He saw Bonnie immediately and headed towards her, a big grin on his face. It was the first time she'd seen him since Zurich, when he had stayed on after the funeral to help her sort out Jeff's affairs. Bonnie felt the prick of grief-induced tears as Will put down his laptop bag and hugged her. To strangers the brothers had not looked a lot alike, but to anyone who knew them well the resemblance was strong, and more than skin deep. It hit her like a bolt of heat.

'You look fabulous, Bon,' he said, hugging her and then holding her at arm's length to look at her. 'I almost didn't recognise you. So cool! I *love* the hair!'

She smiled, relaxing quite suddenly. 'Really?'

'Yes, really, the hair, the clothes – the whole lot. You look younger, really cool and . . . you look like you're coping.'

Bonnie said, 'I'm coping. It's hard going but yes I'm coping. And you look great, Will, I'm so glad to see you.' She hugged him again. 'How long are you here for?'

'Just the two nights. I've got meetings all day tomorrow and then I'm off to Tokyo, and back to Hong Kong.'

Bonnie slipped her arm through his as they walked towards the baggage carousel. 'And how come you haven't got some gorgeous female in tow?'

He grinned. 'I have now,' he said, squeezing her arm against his side. 'My favourite sister-in-law.'

'Your *only* sister-in-law.'

'Don't quibble. Anyway, the last gorgeous female suddenly realised that I hadn't been lying when I'd warned her that I wasn't interested in settling down. It took her three months.'

'Smart woman.' Bonnie smiled again. 'Some of the others have taken longer to catch on.'

Will grabbed his suitcase from the carousel and swung it onto the floor. 'Jeff was the steady one in the family,' he said with a grin. 'It was up to me to be different, create a counterpoint. Here we are, there's just this one bag. Let's go.'

'How about I take you to lunch somewhere nice before we go

home,' Bonnie said. 'I've got a friend staying with me and I want to talk to you about something before we go back to the house.'

They sat at the same table she had booked for the first lunch with Fran and Sylvia. She liked the fact that even when the place was busy it was reasonably quiet. No distracting music, almost never any small children, an environment where noisy conversations were rare and when they did occur the carpets and soft furnishings soaked up the edge of the noise. Beyond the windows the river, steely grey, was ruffled by the wind, the sky overcast and threatening rain.

'So,' Will began, after they had both ordered, 'are you really coping okay?'

'Yes,' Bonnie said with a nod. 'I think I am now. The first weeks were a nightmare, but recently things have improved dramatically. I still miss him so much, Will, but I am starting to get my life together again.'

Will tasted the wine and nodded to the waiter to pour it. 'So what made the difference? Just time?'

'Partly. But I met up with a couple of old friends, my best friends from school, actually. We hadn't seen each other for nearly forty years, but it's changed everything.' She paused. 'That's what I want to talk to you about.'

'You want to trust me with your women friends?'

Bonnie laughed. 'No way! Look, this is all very vague but both these women are really terrific at what they do and I was feeling useless, not good at anything. Then a couple of weeks ago I realised . . . well, what I'm good at is what they both lack, business sense. I can really see their potential and I've got this germ of an idea that I'm playing with. I need to talk it through. I think it could really take off but . . .'

'But what?' Will asked, unfolding his serviette as the waiter began to unfold Bonnie's. She waved him away, taking it herself and spreading it across her lap.

'Jeff was always telling me I should have a business of my own; I never did, of course.'

'But you were invaluable in his.'

'So he always said. I know I helped him, but it was Jeff who did it. I was just a sounding board.'

Will picked up his knife and fork and paused, looking up at her. 'I think you're underestimating yourself,' he said. 'I don't think that's how Jeff saw it, and it's certainly not the way he talked about it. You're a very smart woman with terrific business and financial sense. Because you *didn't* take the final decisions doesn't mean you *couldn't* have done so. He always said that he would never have got his first two companies off the ground without you. In the end, when you wanted to wind things up you did take big decisions, decisions that would have had plenty of other people in a spin.'

'You helped me.'

'I was there. But you made the decisions on the shares, the property investments. You made sound decisions and you made them very quickly.'

'Did I? It was such an awful time it's all a bit of a blur.' She looked down and took a deep breath. 'Well, I'm thinking of starting a business now.'

'With friends?' he asked, a flicker of scepticism crossing his face. 'Always risky.'

'Maybe, but I think it's all in the way it's set up and that's what I need to talk through with you. I want you to tell me what you think and whether it could work.'

It was a disappointment to Irene that Marjorie had turned out to be a snorer. She lay in the darkness listening to the aggressive rise and fall of the snores that turned the stillness into something resembling a motor vehicle workshop. Marjorie at night, Hamish by day – what an exhausting holiday this was turning out to be.

'Shut up, Marjorie, you're snoring, turn over,' Irene hissed across the hotel bedroom, and Marjorie, with an affronted 'Hhhrrrump', turned on her side and promptly started snoring again, just as loudly but in a different tone. So much for all that rubbish about people only snoring when they lie on their backs, thought Irene, getting up and wandering to the window.

She drew back the sliding glass door and stepped out onto the balcony. The air was soft and still, filled with the scent of the pines and the hot residue of the day: sun lotion, unidentifiable but tempting foods, the briny smell of the sea and the dry and dusty heat itself. In front of her the sea stretched dark, fathomless, lit in the distance by the moon glinting off its surface. On the horizon the pinpoint lights of fishing boats barely moved on the still water.

Irene sat down on one of the banana lounges, musing whether it would be comfortable enough to sleep on. Unlikely, she thought, pondering the prospect of dragging her mattress out and putting it on the tiles. The idea appealed to her but she didn't quite have the energy. She didn't like this hotel as much as she'd liked the villa. There was something international and impersonal about it, but there was still a week of island travel ahead before they returned to the peace and comfort of the villa. Maybe when they got back there she would get a room to herself. There was plenty of space and she and Marjorie had only shared because that's what they'd agreed back in Australia. Sometime during the course of the next week she would suggest it, but carefully – Marjorie could be touchy at times.

And Hamish, what was she to do about him? When Marjorie had first suggested that Hamish was flirting, Irene realised that she was right. Since then Hamish seemed to have shifted into top gear. Somehow he always managed to commandeer a seat beside her at meals or in the bus, and he was always in close proximity to take her arm as they picked their way over the rough unmade paths to the beach, or into the next ancient ruin or gallery. He had taken to putting his hand over hers on the table when he wanted her attention, and to calling her 'my dear' in an old worldly sort of way that was quite nice, but also disconcerting. It seemed like an attempt on his part to change the nature of a friendship that went back decades to when she'd met Dennis.

Hamish and Dennis had been at school and university together, and each had been best man at the other's wedding. Hamish and

Gilda, Dennis and Irene had often been a foursome, until Gilda left Hamish for another woman, something he'd found very hard to come to terms with. A few years later he'd married a rather mousy woman called Celia, whom neither Irene nor Dennis could stand, and so they'd seen less of each other.

After Dennis's death, Irene had seen Hamish and Celia even more rarely and then, six years ago, when Celia died of some typically undefined, pale, wasting condition, Hamish had decided to take himself back to his Scottish roots for a few years. He had only returned to Australia in the last year, unable to tolerate the icy Highland winds and persistent rains that played havoc with his arthritis. Was it just the fact that they were on holiday, or was he seriously trying to change an old friendship into something else? She'd been alone for so long and liked it a lot – wouldn't a man be an intrusion, an unnecessary complication? Having Bonnie fussing around her had been difficult enough to cope with, but to have a man who, knowing the nature of men, would probably want *her* to fuss around *him* was something she really didn't need.

Some time after the loss of Dennis, Irene, then in her early sixties, had occasionally been on what could loosely be called dates, with men her own age. They had gone out for lunch or dinner, sometimes to the opera or a concert, and sometimes to formal functions that required a partner, but she had always ended up listening politely to tedious monologues that seemed to replace real conversation. Occasionally, she found herself sitting in a restaurant or café virtually comatose while a man droned on about the latest letter he'd written to the newspaper, or how he'd fix everything if he was in charge. So she started refusing the invitations without offering an excuse or reason, and the men accordingly drifted away, turning their attentions to less prickly women.

But Hamish was different. He certainly wasn't boring; he had cultivated the art of listening as well as talking, which made him positively unusual. Irene would be happy to have him as a friend, a companion, she thought, but anything else? What else was there at their age? Love? Sex? Surely not! She'd almost forgotten how to do it and the prospect of relearning all that stuff didn't seem very inviting – in fact, she thought it might be faintly ridiculous and embarrassing. She would have liked to talk to Bonnie about it but it would be difficult over the phone. On the other hand, of course, it wasn't night time in Melbourne; perhaps she could just mention it in passing.

Irene crept back into the bedroom and retrieved the mobile phone Bonnie had bought for her the week before she left. 'Much easier than messing about with hotel phones,' she had said, keying in the house phone number and handing it to her. 'All you have to do is press this button and you'll dial straight through to here.'

Marjorie had stopped snoring, and was so quiet that Irene wondered briefly if she had actually stopped breathing. But as she made her way cautiously back to the sliding door there was another blast like a motorbike revving up, and Irene fled to the balcony, closing the door behind her.

Bonnie, to her surprise, had some difficulty getting tickets to the Wine Club dinner where Fran was to speak. She'd assumed it would be a small affair and that she could just call nearer the time and book two tickets, but Will's visit knocked the subject out of her head and by the time he left, the dinner was just two days away.

'Members and guests only, I'm afraid,' the club secretary told her in a rather snotty voice. 'This is our peak event, three clubs are combining for the dinner, and I'm afraid it's not open to outsiders. We are mindful of security these days.'

Bonnie restrained herself from pointing out that she was a friend of the guest speaker and wasn't planning a terrorist attack. She had been away for a long time but she knew Melbourne well enough to understand the snobbery of some of its subcultures. She was sitting at the kitchen benchtop tapping the end of her pen against her teeth, trying to remember who she knew who might be a member, when the phone rang. Bonnie was surprised to hear her mother's voice and shocked to realise that it was over a week since they'd spoken.

'Anyway, dear,' Irene was saying as Bonnie tried to focus on

113

the conversation, 'it's beautiful out here on the balcony and I daresay I shall survive the snoring but I really rang to talk to you about Hamish.'

'Hamish? What's he been up to?' Bonnie asked distractedly. 'I thought he was in Scotland.'

'No, he came back to Melbourne a year or so ago. He's with us on the trip. The thing is, he's being rather strange.'

'What sort of strange?'

'Well . . . I don't know, really,' Irene said vaguely. 'Oh, this must sound so silly, but he seems to be – Marjorie says he's flirting with me.'

'How nice,' Bonnie said with a smile. 'Make the most of it.'

There was a pause before Irene said, 'It's just that – Bonnie, what do you think he wants?'

Bonnie's mind was a blank. Irene almost never asked her for advice and she certainly had nothing useful to say on this subject. 'Probably he's just enjoying your company,' she said with a slight shrug. 'You're not worried about it, are you? I mean, he's not making a nuisance of himself?'

'Oh no, not at all, it's just that . . .'

'What?'

'Oh dear, I don't know, this is silly of me, sorry to bother you with it. How's everything at home?'

'Fine,' Bonnie said, pleased to escape the topic of Hamish. 'Lots happening – lots to tell you when you get back. Will was here for a couple of nights. He sent his love. By the way, Mum, do you know anyone who's in any of the wine clubs?'

A couple of hours later, Bonnie had organised the tickets through an old colleague of her father's who was more than delighted to book for them, and would keep a couple of places at his table. She wrote the cheque for three hundred dollars, tucked it into an envelope and sat drumming her fingers on the benchtop in annoyance. People were coughing up one hundred and fifty dollars a head for dinner and wine and Fran, the star attraction, wasn't even being paid.

She sat for a while, making some notes about marketing Fran and her work, and it was almost an hour later when she got around to thinking about her brief conversation with Irene and wondered if she had been too distracted. The old anxiety returned with sudden force and she picked up the phone and dialled the mobile number, but she was greeted by her own voice on the message she had set up for Irene. Presumably Marjorie had stopped snoring and Irene had switched off the phone and gone back to bed. She'd call her in the morning. Meanwhile, she had quite a lot of work to do. It was years since she'd written a business plan, but talking to Will had helped. He was due back in Melbourne again in a couple of weeks and she had definite goals to meet before they discussed things again in greater detail.

Bonnie felt a surge of excitement at the prospect; an engine that had been idling within her had fired up again. The really hard part would be convincing the others. She would have to be very careful how she handled it. Will had been right, friendship and business could be a risky combination and the first risk lay in the way she put it to them. She would have to do a lot of work on that and make sure she got it absolutely right if she was not to risk losing the friendships that had become so vital to her.

Sandwiched between two club presidents on the top table, Fran stared enviously across to where Sylvia and Bonnie were deep in conversation with a small group at the far side of the room. This was the part of the evening she hated most. She could cope with interviews because they had an obvious direction and purpose, but making conversation with strangers over dinner was always a source of anxiety. Tonight the president on her right was a real estate agent who fancied himself as something of a gourmet cook and was keen to tell Fran about a recipe for a rabbit casserole he always used. The president on her left was a retired lawyer who had begun the evening by enquiring whether she had professional liability insurance. She hadn't, and by the time he had finished describing the hideous case of a food writer in the US who had been sued by someone who had followed her advice and subsequently poisoned himself, Fran was not only bored but suffering terminal anxiety. She picked at the grilled barramundi, which was not as fresh as the menu claimed, and prayed for the evening to be over.

Speaking engagements were a pain but the paper liked her to do them and there were always spin-offs, small commercial writing jobs that helped to pay the bills, and those jobs generally paid better than the newspapers and magazines. When it came to speaking, Fran knew she could deliver something entertaining and interesting as the diners, with several glasses of wine already under their belts, tucked into their dessert and coffee. But tonight she was nervous, and it wasn't just the insurance scare.

'I'm sure you'll be terrific,' Sylvia had said earlier as they waited for Bonnie to get back from parking the car. 'And you look wonderful.'

'Thanks to you,' Fran said. 'The only other time in my life that I went somewhere feeling confident about my clothes was the day I got married.'

Sylvia brushed a speck of dust from the shoulder of the velvet jacket and gave her a quick up and down glance. 'I admit it does look good,' she grinned. 'And I so enjoyed making it.'

Fran tucked her arm through Sylvia's. 'I'm feeling really nervous. Bonnie's wearing her business hat tonight. She's going to be sizing me up for marketability.'

'Exactly right,' Bonnie said, coming up behind them and taking them by surprise.' You're a mere product to me now, Fran, but a very well-dressed one, I must say.'

As the main course was cleared away, the presidents exchanged nods and Fran watched as a rich chocolate mousse swirled into tall glasses was delivered to the tables. The introduction was tedious and as she eventually rose to her feet to a round of applause, she was sure she had completely forgotten what she was going to say.

'Thank you so much for inviting me, I'm delighted to be here with you this evening,' she said, adjusting the microphone, taking her time to allow herself to calm down. The sea of faces looked up at her expectantly, half-smiles of anticipation, a few stares from eyes already glazed by a surfeit of fine wine. 'Tonight I want to talk to you about food and wine, not just the delights of both but what they mean – what we *make* them mean in our lives, our rituals, duties and celebrations. I want to talk about food and love and the messages we send each other as we prepare, present, eat and share food and pour the perfect wine to accompany it.' She paused, knowing now that she was okay, she could pace herself, play the audience. There was an almost imperceptible ripple around the room as the audience settled back to be entertained.

Bonnie breathed a sigh of satisfaction; she had sat through enough after-dinner speakers to recognise the magical combination of well-prepared content and stylish presentation. Fran had invited them on a journey and now she was carrying them along, not just with ideas and information but with literary and historical anecdotes and quotations, finely tuned jokes and references to popular culture, all perfectly suited to the occasion. She seemed to be gaining confidence each minute and she looked every inch the professional.

Bonnie sipped her wine and looked from Fran across to where Sylvia was leaning forward in rapt attention. Her idea would work, she was sure of that, it would work for the three of them. All she had to do now was finish the business plan, run it past Will and then convince them. A couple more weeks and it would be ready to go.

THIRTEEN

The morning after the Wine Club dinner, Sylvia woke at six feeling hopeless and vulnerable. Fran's talk had been a huge success; while her business management might be chaotic she was clearly talented and disciplined in every other aspect of her work. And now Bonnie too was focused on a business she was developing with Jeff's brother. To Sylvia it seemed that she alone had no talent or profession to turn to for focus or direction, no resources that would give her a grip on the future.

Her anger at Colin had largely dissipated, and she felt a detached fascination at the way they had both given up on the marriage so readily. The advice they might have dispensed to others in their situation – get counselling, take a break away together, or even a trial separation – hadn't entered into it and for that she was thankful. But what would she do now that she *was* free? She needed an income, a job and a place to live, and the challenge of finding them seemed insurmountable. This morning her anxiety about the future was crushing in its intensity. Who would employ someone with no formal qualifications, who had been out of the workforce for so long? Could she work in a shop, perhaps, or maybe a school?

She got up. It was pointless to lie in bed worrying – she'd been doing that half the night. She pulled on her tracksuit and walking shoes and, stopping only for a glass of water on her way through the kitchen, let herself out of the front door and set off along the wide, tree-lined streets in the early half-light.

Sylvia loved Gardenvale: the affluence, the beautiful old houses, the proximity of the beach, and most of all its familiarity from schooldays. She and Fran had both lived in Elsternwick and taken the train to school here, but Bonnie had lived close by and for years the three of them had roamed these streets and the nearby beach after school. Irene had always welcomed them and Sylvia relished not only the comfort and graciousness of the house, but also the precious memories. She was determined that she was never going back to Box Hill, which had become synonymous with the loneliness and sterility of her life with Colin, but Gardenvale was way beyond her financial means. Irene had insisted on the phone to Bonnie that Sylvia could stay on as long as she wished and had even suggested that she could move into the guest cottage, which hadn't been occupied for years. Apparently it only needed a few bits of furniture, an airing and perhaps a spring-clean, and she could live there fully self-contained.

'It's so good of her, but it doesn't really seem right,' Sylvia had said. 'I feel I'd be taking advantage of Irene.'

'It was her idea, Sylvia,' Bonnie said. 'You know I drove her up the wall when I first came back, but I think in a way it made her aware that having someone around isn't such a bad thing as you get older.'

'But you're here.'

'Yes, but my guess is she's not sure if I'll stay or if she wants me to.'

'What do *you* want to do?'

'Stay, I think, but I'll have to talk it through with her when she gets back, and when I'm clear about whether this business will work.'

Sylvia, like Fran, had an aversion to talk of business and finance, albeit for different reasons. It was an area of which she knew nothing and her ignorance made her fearful. The one thing she had never really understood about Bonnie was her ability to become involved in the mysterious world of finance, and a conversation about business plans would, she was sure, be beyond her.

'I'd certainly appreciate being able to stay on, either in the house or the cottage, until I get myself organised and find a job,' she said.

'Mum doesn't have a history of doing things she doesn't want to do,' Bonnie said. 'She wouldn't have suggested it if she wasn't happy about it. She likes you and Fran being around and she may be offering it as much for herself as for you.'

Sylvia walked on through the semi-dark streets turning down towards the beach, facing into the wind that was churning the water into choppy waves. A few early walkers and joggers were braving the chill, and by the time she had walked for twenty minutes the pearly glow of dawn was filtering through the trees. It was fully light by the time she reached the boatshed, and she stopped to read the real estate agent's board, and then wandered up along the boardwalk, leaning for a while on the rail, staring out to sea, remembering the times they had spent here, hoping to get noticed. Perhaps that had been the start of the waiting, trying to look right, to be right, to capture a flicker of attention, longing for a smile. She had been doing that throughout her marriage to Colin, waiting for warmth and affection, for passion; marooned in the suffocating shallows of duty and responsibility, in a companionship that had slowly deteriorated into habit and isolation.

'Get over it, Sylvia,' she told herself, 'you were your own worst enemy.' Straightening her shoulders she turned back towards the house. Colin had agreed to let her have the car as part of the settlement, and she would have some money, a reasonable amount once the investments were sorted out and divided. She was fortunate compared with many women in her situation. And there must be a job for her somewhere and once she had found it she would really be able to relish the start of a single life. The postie gave her a wave as he pulled away from the gate and she took the mail from the box and let herself in through the tall wrought-iron gate, her footsteps crunching over the gravel drive.

Bonnie was in the kitchen making tea. 'Impressive!'

'Couldn't sleep,' Sylvia said, dropping the mail on the benchtop. 'Did you know the kiosk is closed? The boatshed has a sold sign on it. I wonder what'll happen to it. It'll be a shame if it gets bulldozed.'

'I know,' Bonnie said, sifting through the mail. 'It was sold a couple of weeks ago. Great location.' She looked up. 'Remember after school, trying to talk to those guys by the boats? We thought they were so cool, and they're probably just boring old farts now. This one's for you.' She slid a bulky padded envelope across the counter.

The writing on the envelope was Colin's and Sylvia's stomach lurched with anxiety. There had been no real nastiness between them, but something in her kept expecting it to develop, kept anticipating a grenade to be tossed dramatically into the slow process of winding up their marriage. She slit open the bulky envelope and discovered two sets of car keys in bubblewrap, and a note wrapped around another envelope.

Dearest Sylvia

What can I say? Nothing makes this right, nothing can make up for the things I've done.

It sounds stupid to say I never meant to hurt you, but it's true. I know it all started to go wrong a long time ago and that we have passed the point of no return. I wish you happiness and peace of mind and hope that you can find it in your heart to forgive me.

I'm enclosing the car keys. I'm moving out on Friday so perhaps you could arrange to collect the car before then. Let me know when you're coming and I'll get out of the way.

The envelope contains a gift. I know you're concerned about money and this is not something you would buy for yourself at this time, but I hope you'll use it and that it will help with the new start.

With my love
Colin

Sylvia stared at the letter, moved by the simple emotion and aware of how difficult it would have been for him to write it.

'Are you okay?' Bonnie asked. She nodded, pushing the letter towards her.

Bonnie read the letter rapidly and looked up. 'What's in the envelope?'

Sylvia tore open the flap. 'It's a return air ticket to London,' she said, looking up at Bonnie in amazement, 'so . . . so I can go and see Kim.' She struggled to swallow a sob. 'For the last three years I've been begging him to go, but he kept saying we couldn't afford it.'

'That's wonderful. When's it for?'

'Three weeks time.' She stared at the ticket and then dropped her head into her hands. 'God, men! They're so weird, aren't they? Why does he wait until I've left him to start being thoughtful?'

'Not there, further back,' Lila called from the front path. 'I want them at the back, then in spring I can put purple pansies at the front.'

David, holding two pale mauve lantanas, took a step backwards. 'About here?'

'That'll be fine, dear,' Lila said. 'I'll leave you to it, then. I'm going in to put the kettle on – nearly bloodsucker time.'

'Bloodsucker?'

'Yes, young er . . . er . . . Judy, that's it, Judy's coming to take my blood. Always comes on the second and fourth Wednesdays, regular as clockwork.'

David glanced up at the sky as a couple of large raindrops landed on his head. He'd have to be quick to get the plants in before it began to pour. He started digging, working fast, and was just backfilling around the plants when down came the rain. Spade in hand, he bolted for Lila's back door. Kicking off his boots in the tiny laundry, he grabbed the hand towel from the side of the trough and wandered into the kitchen drying his hair.

'You only just made it,' said a young woman sitting at the table. 'Another couple of minutes and you'd have been drowned. I'm Jodie, by the way – we've met before.' She was setting out a series of tubes and a blood pressure monitor alongside a syringe in a sealed pack. David ran his hands through his wet hair and stared at her.

'Hi, I'm David. I'm not sure where . . . ?'

'I took your blood at the clinic the other day.'

David blushed. At the clinic and the hospital it was easy to pretend he was in a world unconnected to the rest of his life. He remembered her now, remembered the bright blue eyes and mouthwateringly clear skin, and his two worlds smashed together.

'Sorry, of course you did. Where's Gran?'

'Looking for something in her bedroom. She said to make the tea, so maybe you . . .'

'Yes,' David said. 'Sure, sure, how do you like it?'

'Milk, no sugar, please.'

He dropped tea bags into three mugs and got out the milk, feeling the back of his neck burning with embarrassment, cursing his scruffy wet clothes and hair, hating the fact that she knew him through his sickness.

'Ah, good,' Lila said, coming back into the kitchen clutching a handful of coathangers with purple and white knitted covers. 'You've made the tea.' She put the hangers down on the table in front of Jodie. 'There you are, dear, I know you liked the hangers I did for myself so I covered some for you.'

David put the cups on the table, trying not to stare at Jodie as she examined the hangers and thanked Lila with a hug. It was difficult because everything about her demanded his attention; the corn gold hair piled up on top of her head, the curves of her body accentuated by the clinic uniform. He swallowed hard, looking down into his cup, stirring his tea as she strapped the blood pressure cuff onto Lila's arm.

'Caro was in yesterday,' Jodie said. 'She seems to be doing well. Nervous, but everyone's like that with a first baby.'

Lila grinned. 'She'll be fine. She's a good girl, Caro – bit mouthy sometimes but she's got a good heart.'

'You know Caro?' David asked, leaning forward.

'We were at school together,' Jodie said. 'Same class. Caro and I were in year nine, far too lowly for you to notice. And now I seem to be making a habit of collecting your family's blood!' She slipped the stethoscope on and started pumping. 'Bet you don't remember me.'

David opened his mouth and shut it again, waiting until she took off the stethoscope.

'I don't think you looked like this back then,' he said, 'or I'd certainly have remembered.'

Jodie grinned and winked at Lila. 'He's got the right answers.'

'Oh yes,' said Lila, 'that's our David. He's a teacher, you know . . . very good, been in the desert somewhere, teaching the Arabs to speak English. Where was it, darling?'

'Qatar,' David said, fidgeting awkwardly. 'But Jodie doesn't want to know all that.'

'She might,' Lila flashed back. 'It's interesting working somewhere like that. He's not very well so he's working here now.'

'Gran!' David groaned and put his head in his hands.

'What? Nothing wrong with that. Jodie knows about these things, don't you, dear?' She leaned forward to Jodie. 'He's embarrassed, that's all. He was always a rather shy boy.'

Jodie grinned at David. 'Really? That's not how I remember him!'

David prayed for his grandmother to shut up but Lila rolled down her sleeve and stood up.

'I haven't finished with you yet, Mrs Whittaker,' Jodie said.

'I know, I know . . . got to do the bloodsucking but I want to get something to show you. A photograph, David's uni graduation. He looks so lovely in that black robe with the pale blue, just you wait there . . .'

'Oh, Gran, please no –' David began.

'Don't "Oh Gran" me,' Lila cut in. 'I'm proud of you, and you should be too.' And she disappeared out of the kitchen.

'Sorry,' David said with a shrug, trying not to look as mortified as he felt. 'She's a bit unmanageable these days. Sensitivity is not top of the list. I suppose you know about the purple passion.'

Jodie nodded. 'Oh yes, I've seen her once a month for the last couple of years so I've lived through quite a few stages of it. Don't be embarrassed, it's lovely that she's so proud of you. She talks about you all the time.'

'How tedious.'

'Not at all. You've acquired hero status.' She stood up to pour some boiled water from the kettle into a plastic medicine glass, and as she stretched forward over the sink he studied the tender flesh at the back of her knees.

'So, d'you live around here?' he asked, his throat uncomfortably dry.

'Collingwood,' Jodie said, sitting down at the table again. 'I share a house just off Hotham Street.'

David leaned forward, forgetting his discomfort. 'I just moved to Collingwood,' he said, 'round the corner from Gino's coffee shop.'

'Really? I haven't seen you; I go there most mornings for a coffee before work –'

'Here we are,' Lila interrupted, coming back into the kitchen with a photograph album open in her hand. 'I couldn't find the graduation one – shame, because he looks so handsome in that – but have a look at these. This is so sweet.' And she opened the pages to a large colour picture of a two-year-old David, stark naked in the paddling pool in the garden at Richmond.

Jodie raised her eyebrows and grinned at David. 'Hmm,' she said. 'I'd never have taken you for a nudist. I'll have to keep my eyes open around Collingwood in future.'

Irene lay in the dark gazing out of the bedroom window at the indigo sky scattered with stars, and wondered how she had got herself into this situation. Had she intended it or had it simply happened to her? The night was still and warm without a breath of a breeze, the only sound the occasional drone of the cicadas. She ran her hands cautiously down her body: soft, loose skin wrinkled at her touch and the brief burst of confidence she had felt half an hour earlier suddenly evaporated. She was an old woman with a worn and wrinkled old body – whatever did she think she was doing?

The bathroom door opened softly and Hamish hesitated in the doorway, outlined briefly against the light before he flicked the switch, plunging the room back into darkness. Irene took a deep breath, trying to calm the anxious throbbing in her head. He was wearing a pair of boxer shorts, and as he bent to sit on the edge of the bed she shifted to make room for him and he took her hand in both of his and held it.

'It's been a long time, Irene,' he said softly. 'I've probably lost the knack . . .'

'Me too,' she said. 'Maybe we're just too old for this. I feel quite ridiculous lying here.' She could sense his smile rather than see it.

'You're not ridiculous,' he said, tenderly stroking her hand. 'That's not a word that could ever be used about you. You're a wise and beautiful woman, Irene, always have been, always will be. And the theory is that we're never too old.'

He leaned forward and kissed her very lightly on the lips and Irene, the pressure of tears throbbing behind her eyes, reached up and touched his face.

'Come on then,' she whispered.

Hamish climbed into bed and lay on his side facing her, his head propped on his arm.

'Look,' he said, 'I know I started all this but I should warn you – I'm a bit lacking in the er . . . er . . . what I mean is that . . . I'm afraid erections are a thing of the past.'

'That's good,' she said with a smile. 'I couldn't be doing with all that grunting and heaving, anyway. I always thought that penetration was a bit overrated.'

'Really?' There was relief in his voice. 'Well, then, that's good, isn't it? Funny, really, this feels like . . . like the first time ever.'

'Yes,' she nodded. 'Hamish . . . ?'

'Yes?'

'I'm really nervous.'

'So am I,' he said, moving closer. 'Silly old things, aren't we?' He reached out to stroke her neck, and Irene sighed as the tenderness of his touch revived a part of her that had been long dormant.

She put her hand over his. 'Perhaps if you could just hold me,' she said, her voice tremulous in the darkness, and gently Hamish slipped one arm under her shoulders, wrapping the other over her, drawing her towards him.

'Beautiful,' he whispered, his cheek close to hers. 'How beautiful to hold you close like this.'

She sighed, relaxing against him as his hand stroked her back, realising that he too was trembling. 'I'd forgotten how it feels to be touched,' she said. 'I didn't think anything like this would ever happen again.' Anxiety about her age, her body and its limitations threatened to assail her but she pushed it away, grasping instead for the other, confident self within. Silently they clung together, remembering other nights, other lovers in other lives, savouring the memories of long forgotten pleasures, which slowly drew them into the present confident stirrings of desire.

Irene woke as the first light of dawn edged through the half-open shutters and a few birds began to scuffle in the bougainvillea. It was strange after all these years to wake beside someone and at first she lay perfectly still, as though any movement might change everything, make it evaporate like a dream. She listened to his breathing, turned gently onto her side to look at him. Hamish was sleeping soundly on his back, one arm thrown carelessly above his head, the sheet pushed down to his waist. It was the posture of a young man, a lover in a movie lying sated among crumpled sheets. He was in reasonable shape for a man of his age, but his skin had the thinning, crumpled softness of age, covering slackened muscles – comforting, she thought. She smiled, wondering how he would have looked in this pose as a young man. She'd known him for so many years and his face was entirely familiar, but his body, this physical closeness and vulnerability, was new territory.

Tentatively she reached out and laid her palm flat on the centre of his chest, feeling the warmth of his skin, the firm line of his sternum under her touch. Without opening his eyes Hamish put his hand over hers, holding it to him, and turned on his side away from her, drawing her arm around him. She closed her eyes, wondering briefly if she should send him back to his room. But surely they were beyond all that? Her pride rebelled at the thought of Hamish scurrying through darkened corridors to avoid discovery. They were among friends; it was a sad state of affairs if they couldn't do what they wanted without fear of disapproval. Irene rested her cheek against Hamish's shoulder.

'Thank God you don't snore,' she whispered against his skin.

'You do . . . a bit,' he said very softly, squeezing her hand, 'but I promise not to tell Marjorie.'

They must both have fallen asleep again, for brilliant sunlight was streaming through the window when they woke with a start to a sudden banging on the door. Irene's heart thumped in shock and Hamish sat bolt upright.

'Irene!' Marjorie called. 'Irene, wake up, it's half-past nine and we've got an emergency.'

She rattled the doorknob. 'Irene, for heaven's sake open the door. You're not dead, are you? Irene? We've lost Hamish! George said he never came back from his walk last night, his bed hasn't been slept in, and he hasn't shown up for breakfast. Irene . . . ?' There was a sudden pause and Irene and Hamish exchanged glances. Marjorie's voice dropped a few decibels. 'Oh my god! He's not – you're not . . . ?'

Hamish grinned and reached for Irene's hand. 'Yes, Marjorie,' he called, 'we are, but don't worry, Irene's quite safe and we'll meet you on the terrace in half an hour.'

'Oh my god,' Marjorie muttered, 'dear me.' She raised her voice. 'Okay, everyone, you can call off the search, Hamish is fine.' And they heard the steady thump of her footfalls as she walked away down the steps to the terrace.

'Whoops,' said Irene. 'I think we're in trouble.'

'Probably,' Hamish said. 'Disapproval? Embarrassment? What do you reckon?'

Irene shrugged. 'Probably both. Marjorie will interrogate me, but the others may behave as though nothing's happened.' She grinned suddenly. 'Shall I tell Marjorie that you're a great fuck?'

Hamish bellowed with laughter. 'Oh, please do, and make sure she tells George and Frank – in fact, tells everyone!' They leaned against each other shaking with laughter. 'Irene,' Hamish said eventually, turning towards her. 'This *is* very special. I care for you deeply and I'm too old for one-night stands.'

Irene smiled, looking down at their clasped hands, speckled with age. 'Me too. But, Hamish, I'm also too old to want to share my bed *every* night, or to want to change my life to accommodate someone else.'

'Understood entirely,' Hamish said. 'Not a domestic relation-ship . . . an affair?'

She laughed. 'At our age?'

'Why not? What else would you like to call it?'

She thought for a moment. 'Loving friendship,' she said slowly, and then, 'No! An affair – it sounds much more fun, positively raunchy, and after all, it's the last affair either of us will ever have.'

'Speak for yourself,' Hamish said. 'I'm only eighty-one!'

She punched him on the shoulder. 'I'll get Marjorie to counsel you if you're not careful.'

'Oh no, anything but that,' he said with a laugh. 'Speaking of which we should probably get up.' He raised her hand to his lips and kissed it. 'Come along, my darling, time to face the music.'

Caro sat at the kitchen table in her dressing gown staring at a glass of orange juice, wondering if she wanted to drink it.

'You could give up work now if you want,' Mike said. 'You feel so rotten and keep having to have days off – why not just give it away?'

'It might stuff up the maternity leave arrangement,' she said, lifting up one leg and resting it across his lap. Mike continued to eat his cornflakes with one hand while stroking her foot with the other.

'Talk to Des about it,' he suggested, 'you don't know till you ask. They all think a lot of you and they've said they want you back when the baby's born. He might re-jig it all for you.'

Caro pushed half a slice of dry toast around her plate. 'It's the nausea that's the worst thing,' she said. 'It makes me feel so weak and sort of light-headed. I thought you said it would be a text-book pregnancy.'

'Well, all the indications were that it would be,' Mike said, put-ting down his spoon and pushing his cereal bowl aside. 'You should be fine, but then all pregnancies are different, or so I'm told.'

'I wish you'd told *me*,' Caro said grumpily. 'I wouldn't have got pregnant if I'd known it was going to be like this. Look at my fingers – they're all swollen, and so are my ankles. You never told me about that.'

Mike stroked her hand and then studied her ankles. 'Mmm, you do look a bit puffy. Better keep an eye on that. Stay home, put your feet up and rest. Ring Des at the office and tell him you're not going in and ask him about leaving. And I wish you'd ring your mum. A girl needs her mother at a time like this.'

'Fuck off! You sound like an agony aunt. Is that what you tell your patients?'

Mike stood up and put Caro's foot gently back on the floor. 'Only if they're stubborn, temperamental pregnant women who need to talk to their mothers.' He picked up his cereal bowl and carried it to the sink, rinsing it under the tap. 'Seriously, babe, give Fran a ring. I don't know why you won't – she loves you to bits, and anyone can see she's dying to get involved.'

Caro pushed the toast away and sighed. 'I suppose,' she said, standing up.

Mike put his arms around her and hugged her. 'I love you to bits too, you know,' he said. 'Even though I almost can't get my arms round you.'

Caro grinned and looked down at the large bulge that had replaced her taut midriff.

'It'll be all right, won't it?'

'Course it will,' he said, kissing her. 'She'll be a beautiful, stubborn, crochety dame like her mother.'

'Or he'll be a great big boofy sex maniac like his father?'

'Yes, or that! Anyway, I've gotta go. The ER calls – oh, the glamour and romance of it all. See you later, babe. Ring Des.' And he was gone.

Caro wandered aimlessly around the kitchen and stood by the window staring out into the tiny paved courtyard, where a couple of honeyeaters fluttered competitively around the bottle-brush. Perhaps Mike was right, she should give up work. It was all getting a bit much, not at all as she'd expected. She wondered if she was not essentially a motherly sort of person, and felt, once again, a stab of the fear that had dogged her over the last few weeks, the fear that she would prove to be totally incapable of looking after a baby. So often she still felt like a child and had to remind herself that she was almost thirty.

She inhaled deeply, trying to breathe it away. What did you do with babies all day? Did they just lie around in between being fed? What would you do if they woke up at night? Fear of her own ignorance haunted her dreams as well as her days. Last night she had woken, sweating, from a dream in which a tiny wrinkled baby with unbearably knowing eyes and an expression of disgust had looked up at her from the pram. 'Really, Caro,' it said, 'you are so incompetent. I could die any minute and it would be your fault. Don't you know that babies don't eat steak?' The stupidity of it did not ease the effect. Two nights earlier she dreamed that she had completely forgotten about the baby, ignoring it for weeks, only to remember and discover it a starved, neglected corpse, swarming with maggots in an otherwise pristine crib.

Caro put her empty glass in the sink and sighed. She would do it: give up work, and talk to her mother. The trouble was that Fran was so good at everything, there was so much to live up to. Lots of Caro's friends and their mothers read Fran's columns and articles, followed her recipes and constantly commented on how lucky Caro was to be her daughter. She had long resented this irritating reflected glory that made her feel inadequate. For a long time she had felt that her only position of strength with her mother was grounded in her knowledge of Fran's insecurity about her weight and the way she looked. Slim, fit and cool Caro had, for years, been able to dispense fashion and grooming advice and roll her eyes in a superior, told-you-so sort of way as Fran crashed into and out of crash diets and punishing exercise regimes while her body remained unchanged. But now Caro's own body was out of control, her waistline had disappeared, she had become a blob; she craved pickles, rollmops and chocolate, and everything gave her indigestion. Aerobics classes were impossible, swimming made her skin itch, yoga bored her and nine months was proving to be longer than the whole of the rest of her life.

The honeyeaters flew off chattering at each other and Caro picked up the phone. She'd call Des, tell him that she couldn't come to work but that she would pop in around lunchtime because she needed to talk to him. By that time the nausea might have eased; she would tell him she wanted to stop work now. Then she'd call Fran, swallow her pride and own up to how truly awful she felt. It wouldn't be easy, but as David had pointed out recently, it would actually be an entirely grown-up thing to do. Holding Fran at arm's length was the behaviour of the sort of teenager who tacked pink ribbon across the carpet, not that of a responsible woman who was herself about to become a mother.

FOURTEEN

Fran stood outside the restaurant, stamping her feet against the cold and wondering if she should wait inside. She was early for the appointment but waiting added to her irritation. The last thing she needed was some tedious publisher wasting her time trying to schmooze her into writing glowing reviews of some wanky cookery books which were probably more style than substance. She was quite sure that was what this lunch was about, but he'd been so persistent that agreeing to it seemed the only way to get him off her back. He'd introduced himself as she was leaving the Wine Club dinner. Quite a distinguished looking older man, he'd congratulated her on the fascinating talk and given her his card.

'I really admire your work,' he'd said. 'I read your column online and I've seen some of your articles in *Gourmet Traveller* and the Qantas magazine.' Fran had smiled and thanked him, taken the card and prepared to make her way over to where Bonnie and Sylvia were waiting. 'I'd like to catch up with you sometime,' he persisted. 'Perhaps we could meet for lunch? I'm in publishing – Bannister Books, you might have heard of us. We're based in Sydney and we have a rather strong list of food, homes and gardens books. I'm Jack Bannister. Do *you* have a card? Maybe I could give you a call before I go back to Sydney?' Fran forgot about it until three days later when she found a message on her answering machine.

'Jack Bannister here, Fran, just hoping we can fix up that

meeting. I'm in Melbourne until Friday. Would you call me, please?' She decided to ignore it. He'd be gone in a couple of days, anyway. But on Friday morning there was another message saying he was just leaving and would be back the week after next. He hoped they could get together then.

'Just so I can give you some great publicity for your lousy books,' Fran yelled irritably at the answering machine before erasing the message. But when he called again ten days later, he caught her at home, and she'd agreed to lunch on the principle that for two hours and a good meal she could get rid of him. It was only now, as she waited outside the restaurant, that she realised she could have given him Bonnie's card and told him to contact her agent. She let out a short burst of laughter at the thought of ever being confident enough to say something like that, and pulled her scarf more tightly around her neck.

Fran was not at her best. Her anxiety levels were very high, she was sleeping badly and her eating was totally out of control.

'You really have to do something about your weight, Fran,' Glenys, her doctor, had told her the previous week. 'You're not getting any younger and your cortisol levels are very high.'

'What does that mean?' Fran had asked, rolling down her sleeve as Glenys folded up the blood pressure machine.

'Cortisol is the stress hormone. When you get stressed you create too much cortisol and that stimulates the release of insulin in your blood. So, your appetite increases, you crave carbohydrates, and you eat more of all the things that are bad for you.'

'That's me,' Fran said grimly. 'But food is my job, and stressed is a constant state. It's worse right now because I'm selling the house, Caro's pregnant and David, well, you know about David.'

'David's doing fine,' Glenys said. 'I've not seen Caro but pregnancy is a perfectly natural state for a woman, nothing to worry about. I know food is your job, but eating it doesn't have to be. Just try to calm down. Have you tried meditation? And remember to keep up the exercise.'

Fran flushed. She hadn't been near the gym for weeks. 'I'll try,' she'd said, and she really meant it, but when she got home she had this overpowering urge to whip up a batch of cheese and sun-dried tomato muffins, despite the fact that they were her favourites and there was no one else in the house, so she would inevitably eat several while they were still warm, and with lashings of butter. 'A last fling,' she promised herself. 'Tomorrow I'll really start a diet.'

Perhaps this Bannister person wasn't going to turn up, she thought now, glancing at her watch, but it was still five minutes before the time they'd fixed to meet. She snuggled further into her coat. It was a new coat and she loved it. Sylvia and Bonnie had forcibly removed her old leather one.

'It does nothing for you, Fran,' Sylvia had said.

'No,' said Bonnie 'leather is not the thing for you. It doesn't work for . . . well, for bigger people. Makes you look . . .'

'Bulky,' Sylvia had supplied.

'Yes, unnecessarily bulky. You need something softer, softer colour and fabric.' And they had marched her down to the outlets in Bridge Road and she'd ended up buying this coat in soft charcoal wool, light but very warm, plus a pair of chunky heeled leather boots and this gorgeous purple cashmere scarf.

'No,' she'd protested when Sylvia held up the scarf. 'It's lovely but it's purple.'

'Just because your mother has a purple fetish doesn't mean you can't wear it,' Sylvia said. 'Try it, the colour suits you.'

'It looks gorgeous,' Bonnie agreed. 'Just don't wear it when you go to see Lila or she'll pinch it.'

'I shouldn't be spending all this,' Fran said nervously, loving the scarf and the coat. She had already bought the boots.

Bonnie drew her into the fitting room and pulled the curtain. 'Look, this is a little bit of the money you'd saved for the tax. Use it, you'll feel better. You get so worried about your size and how you look, if you have a few good quality things that you know you look good in, you'll feel more confident. You have a financial plan now, we worked it all out. This is wise spending, Fran, you're not frittering it away.'

'Like I have in the past, you mean.'

'I didn't say that. How you spend your money is your business but you asked for my advice and I'm giving it to you. You need to look the part if we are going to start charging like a wounded bull for your services.'

Fran softened and grinned. 'I love you, Bonnie,' she said. 'For your subtlety!'

'Good,' said Bonnie. 'I love you too, for lots of things. Now shut up and buy the coat and scarf.'

'Fran,' Jack Bannister said, interrupting her reverie. 'I'm so sorry to have kept you waiting. I hope I'm not late.'

'No,' she said, trying to smile graciously. 'I was early – it's not even one yet.'

'I should have suggested we meet inside. You must be frozen.'

He steered her into the restaurant, where she relinquished her lovely coat and was glad that she had also succumbed to the black pants and the purple cashmere tunic that went with the scarf. Bonnie was right, a few well-chosen things made a big difference, and a large gin and tonic made an even bigger difference. Perhaps that was the answer to stress, she thought, more gin, and she began to unwind.

Jack Bannister looked older than she remembered, sixty perhaps. He had a rather nice, lived-in sort of face, thick grey hair and very bright blue eyes. He was also an entertaining companion, and before she knew it they had eaten their way through the entrée and the main course, and Fran, in a fit of conscience, was waving away the dessert menu.

'No?' said Jack. 'Perhaps just some coffee, then.' And the waiter disappeared to fetch it.

'Now, Fran,' he began, 'the reason I wanted to talk to you . . .'

Fran stiffened with resistance despite the gin and the wine. She had forgotten there was a price to pay for this delightful interlude. She straightened up and tried to look polite but firm and unapproachable.

'I'd been thinking for some time of contacting you and I was here in Melbourne and a friend invited me to the Wine Club dinner. You speak as well as you write and you have a great ability to draw together a range of ideas on a theme. I was wondering whether you might consider writing a book for us.'

Fran stared at him and then realised her mouth was open, so she shut it. 'Write a book?'

'Yes . . . along the lines of your talk the other night, but expanding on those ideas of food in relation to love, nurturing, lust, food porn, duty – all the rest of it. And, of course, including all those fascinating bits of history and the quotations you used, perhaps in sections with recipes in each one . . . is anything wrong, Fran?'

'You are asking me to write a book for you?'

'Yes.'

'Publishers don't just ask people to write books. Writers have to struggle and send manuscripts and get rejected, all that sort of stuff.'

'Well, yes, but it often happens the other way around. And, by the way, this is the point at which you're supposed to play hard to get.'

'You mean, like, I should say you'll have to talk to my agent?'

'That's a very good start. But you might want to tell me whether or not you're interested at all, because if you're not it will save us both a lot of time.'

'Interested? Of course I'm interested.'

'That's good, then –'

'I thought you were softening me up with lunch to get me to write about some of your cookery books.'

'Do I look like a sleaze?'

Fran blushed. 'Well, no, it's just that –' She jumped as her mobile rang loudly from her handbag. 'Sorry,' she said. 'So sorry, I should have switched it off.'

'Don't worry,' Jack said with a smile as the waiter refilled their coffee cups. 'Just take the call.'

'I'll take it and call them back,' she said. 'It's my son-in-law. Hi, Mike, can I call you –'

'Fran, Fran, listen, ' Mike interrupted and she listened, turning white as he spoke.

'Yes, oh god – yes, of course, I'll come immediately,' she said. 'I'm in the city, I'll get a cab.'

'What's happened?' Jack asked. 'You've gone very pale.'

'My daughter,' Fran said, getting to her feet. 'She's been in an accident. She's pregnant. I have to get to the hospital.'

'Of course,' he said, signalling to the waiter. 'Come on, get your coat, and I'll call a cab. Would you like me to come with you?'

She shook her head. 'No, no, I'll be fine. My son-in-law's there, he's a doctor. Thank you, Jack, and I really do want to do the book.'

'Don't worry about that now,' he said. 'Take care. I hope she's okay, and the baby too. I'll call you.'

FIFTEEN

The first time Will saw Sylvia she was standing by the window in Bonnie's kitchen drinking a cup of tea and wearing a paisley-patterned dressing gown in dark blue silk. Bonnie had mentioned that she had a friend staying, but they had gone straight to lunch from the airport and Sylvia was out when they got back to the house. As Will was out in the evening, their paths didn't cross until the following morning.

'You must be Will,' she said with a smile, and he felt something very strange happen to him: his heart seemed to speed up and he had trouble getting his breath. 'Would you like some tea, or maybe you'd prefer coffee?'

'Thanks,' he said, wondering if he looked as winded as he felt. 'Coffee would be great.' And he sat down on one of the stools at the benchtop while Sylvia refilled the kettle and got out the coffee plunger.

Will had not given a thought to what Bonnie's friend might be like. She was, after all, Bonnie's vintage, ten, maybe fifteen, years older than him, and he was not a man given to noticing older women. Not that he had anything against them. Will liked women of all ages but while he might flirt with older women who responded to a certain boyishness in him, he had never ever been attracted to one. He loved Bonnie like an older sister, and while he thought she looked good for her age, the idea that a contemporary of hers could interest him had never crossed his mind.

As he sat facing Sylvia across the benchtop Will wished he'd combed his hair, brushed his teeth, and hadn't come downstairs wearing just the pyjama trousers and t-shirt he'd slept in. He liked to be in a control of a situation, especially when it came to women, and he felt at a distinct disadvantage. He'd accepted Bonnie's invitation to stay at the house because it was the first time he'd seen her since they had been sorting out Jeff's estate together in Zurich, and he wanted to make it clear that he was there if she needed anything. Business required that he travel frequently from his home in Perth to Hong Kong, where he kept a flat, and he had just signed a deal with a company in Melbourne which meant that he'd be making frequent trips there over the coming months. He'd been wondering how he could organise it so that when he returned in three weeks' time he could decently stay in a hotel. Will was a hotel sort of person. There was a freedom and independence to hotels which he enjoyed, and you never knew when you would want five star accommodation on standby if you wanted to ask someone back to the room for a business meeting or something more intimate. But now, sitting across from Sylvia, Will was revising his future accommodation plans.

Cautiously he steered the conversation around to whether she might still be there next time he was in town. Having established that she almost certainly would be, he felt more confident, and then suggested that if she and Bonnie were free that evening he might take them both out for dinner.

'This must be a bit of a shock to your system, Will,' Bonnie had said as the three of them sat eating fish and chips in St Kilda. 'Fish and chips with the over fifties and probably home by ten.'

He grinned sheepishly. 'Youth and beauty have no age, Bonnie.'

'Shame on you!' she said. 'You're quoting Picasso, misquoting him, actually, and I don't think he was often seen eating fish and chips with older women.'

'It was you two who opted for the fish and chips,' Will said. 'I would have taken you anywhere you wanted. The world – or, at least, Melbourne – was your oyster tonight.'

'Thank you, Will, yes,' Sylvia said with a smile, 'it was, but this was what we both fancied, and I'm enjoying it very much.'

'Me too,' said Bonnie. 'I'm only teasing you. When we've finished, let's wander up Acland Street and go to that lovely coffee shop for coffee and Italian ice cream.'

That night Will had lain in bed feeling remarkably content. He'd had the best time he could remember for ages. He stared up into the darkness, thinking of Sylvia, seeing her smile at him across the table, remembering the way she used her hands as she talked, the slim line of her neck when she turned her head, and the way she tucked a soft strand of silver hair behind her ear. Only one thing bothered him; Sylvia, charming, intelligent and beautiful, seemed totally immune to him. Either she wasn't picking up his signals or she was choosing to ignore them.

Back home in Perth a few days later, he was unsettled, unable to concentrate on anything, and his ability to make sound and rapid trading decisions seemed to have deserted him. Swimming laps in the pool, staring out at the river from the window of his high-rise office or sitting in his apartment in the evenings half watching television, he couldn't get Sylvia out of his mind.

'Dinner Saturday evening,' his oldest friend Ryan said over the phone. 'Tania just got a promotion, so we're going to The Loosebox to celebrate. It's just won another Gold Plate Award.'

Will hesitated; he didn't feel like going out. 'Er . . . I'm not sure,' he began, thinking he'd rather lie on the couch listening to music, wondering if he could call Bonnie's place on the off chance that Sylvia might answer, and what he'd say if she did. 'I might have something else on.'

'What d'you mean "might have"?' Ryan countered. 'Either you have or you haven't. There'll be seven of us, but bring someone if you want. Tania'll be wrecked if you're not there, you guys go back a long way.'

Years earlier Will and Tania had had a fleeting relationship: friendly, light-hearted, great sex and lots of laughs. They had parted friends and when Ryan arrived in Perth to work as a consultant to the state government, Will had introduced them. The chemistry had been instant and Tania and Ryan had married six months later.

'Okay,' Will said, 'sure, of course, I'll, er . . . I'll cancel the other thing.' So he'd gone to dinner feeling strangely out of sorts among this group of close friends, three married (or almost married) couples and him. He studied the comfortable, tender, affectionate, teasing play between the partners and envied it; envied it for the familiarity, the permanence, the ease, and wanted it for himself. He felt a strange aching loneliness, a longing that went far beyond the sexual to something much deeper, something he hadn't felt for years.

'You're very quiet tonight, Will,' Tania had said, patting his thigh affectionately as the waiter poured the coffee. 'Positively broody. What's happened to you?'

'Feeling a bit odd,' he said, staring down into his cup. 'You know, all you guys fixed up, happy couples . . .'

'Never!' Tania said in amazement. 'Don't tell me you're getting settling-down twinges.'

'Maybe,' Will said. 'P'raps I'm having a midlife crisis, but don't let on to anyone else, it'll totally ruin my image!' He tried to laugh but it didn't quite work and Tania looked at him hard.

'Just a general idea or anyone in particular?' she asked.

'Oh . . .' He shrugged, looking away. 'Dunno, really; probably it's nothing,' and he mustered a smile. 'That's the thing with midlife crises, isn't it? You're never sure what it's about.' But in his heart, of course, he knew exactly what it was about.

Back in the seventies when he was doing his economics degree in Melbourne, Will had fallen instantly in love with a chunky, athletic physiotherapist called Glenda whom he'd met at a party. The minute he'd walked into the room he'd spotted her, dancing energetically. She had swinging red hair held back in an Alice band and was wearing a short glittery shift and flared pants. Everything about her seemed gleaming and mobile: her skin glowed, her hair shone, and the smile she flashed devoured him in an instant. They had gone home together that night and were joined at the hip for almost a year, until Glenda met a muscular vet and took off with him to Adelaide. For the first time in his life, Will was dumped by a woman and he was devastated. A month earlier they had discussed getting married, and Will had had their future mapped out. A character home in a leafy

Melbourne suburb, Glenda with her own practice and him, degree completed, taking over the Australian end of his brother's business.

At home, at school and at university, Will had always been a winner: good looking, intelligent and genuinely nice, he was a golden boy, captain of the rowing team, the hero in drama productions, and winner of medals for academic excellence. Losing at all was a new experience: losing Glenda was devastating. He was smart enough to know that a broken heart might be good for his soul in the long run but it wasn't an experience he planned to repeat.

'You must understand that I'm not a long-term investment,' he told the women he went out with. 'I'm not in the business of settling down.'

Some had believed him and enjoyed the fling. Others had ignored his warnings and, confident of their ability to change him, had secretly striven to be the perfect partner, believing they could lead him into a long-term commitment, and were shattered when Will declared it was time for him to move on. Right now Will was at a loss to understand how it had happened that he had this overwhelming yearning for a woman in her fifties who seemed immune to him.

By the time he got back to Melbourne three weeks later, Will was as nervous as a teenager on his first date. He'd told Bonnie not to bother meeting him at the airport, and as he paid the taxi driver and ran up the steps to the front door his heart was pounding against his ribs and a prickle of sweat was breaking out on the back of his neck. Sylvia opened the door wearing faded jeans and a white polo neck sweater, and eating a piece of carrot cake.

'Oh, Will!' she said, brushing a crumb from her lips, 'You're early, come on in. Bonnie's gone to the bank, but she'll be home soon.' She stepped back to let him in and Will abandoned the measured approach he had planned and decided on the spur of the moment to try some of his usual bravado.

'Sylvia! Great to see you. Do I get a welcome kiss?' he asked, with what women usually described as his winning smile.

Sylvia grinned. 'Of course! Welcome back.' She put her hands on his shoulders and kissed him lightly on the cheek. Will inhaled a delicate perfume, and tensed at the touch of her lips. 'Come on through to the kitchen,' she said. 'I've just made some coffee and this beautiful carrot cake, or do you need lunch? How was your flight?'

Will thought he had died and gone to heaven. Only a scenario in which Sylvia opened the door and flung her arms about him, kissed him passionately on the lips and then raced him off upstairs would have been better. That had been his fantasy on the plane, but it was a bit much to hope for in view of the nature and brevity of their acquaintance.

'Just coffee, please,' he said, 'and yes, some cake,' and he followed her into the kitchen and did a very daring thing. He stood beside her looking down at the warm, deliciously scented cake cooling on its rack, and as he did so he rested his hand gently on her shoulder and kept it there for as long as he dared. 'It looks delicious,' he said, lightly stroking her shoulder before dropping his hand and moving back to the other side of the bench, where he hitched himself onto a stool and sat, as he had sat that first morning, facing Sylvia as she passed him the plunger of coffee and cut some cake. 'You look terrific,' he said, feeling suddenly awkward and vulnerable again. 'Are things going well for you? Sorting things out with your ex?' He thought he sounded like a character in a daytime soap.

She nodded, putting the cake onto a plate, handing it to him and licking the crumbs from her fingers. 'Yes,' she said. 'Really well. I'm so excited, Will. Colin sent me a ticket to London, so I'm leaving in a few days to visit my daughter and grandchildren.'

Will choked unattractively on his cake, spluttering crumbs across the benchtop. Sylvia fetched him a glass of water and he drank it quickly. 'England? That's a surprise,' he managed. 'When do you leave, exactly?'

'Friday, for almost four weeks. I can hardly believe it. I haven't seen them for nearly four years.'

Will drank more water and tried to compose himself. 'That's terrific,' he said, trying to hide his disappointment. His plan had been to take things very gently, especially as he was going to be in

Melbourne for a few days. Bonnie, he knew, would not take kindly to his pursuit of her friend, so winning Sylvia over completely was essential before his sister-in-law became aware of what was happening. In his favour was the fact that Bonnie always teased him about his attraction to younger women, so he just hoped she wouldn't think for a moment that he could be interested in Sylvia. Will smiled and tucked into the cake, determined to make the most of this time alone with her, only to hear the sound of Bonnie's key in the front door.

Fran sat in an uncomfortably low vinyl armchair in the waiting area designated for people whose relatives were already being treated in casualty. Across from her an elderly couple sat silently, hand in hand, occasionally casting an anxious glance towards the doorway when a nurse or doctor flitted past. From time to time, as though in an attempt to reassure each other, they would smile and lift their joined hands slightly, squeezing them together in a gesture of solidarity. Were they there for an adult child, perhaps, or a grandchild? An ageing sibling? In the corner a pale teenage girl lay across two seats, her head in the lap of a boy who might have been a couple of years older. He rested his head against the wall, the peak of his baseball cap pushed forward to mask his eyes. Beyond them the open door showed the major emergency waiting room, packed with restless people waiting for action for themselves or others.

Fran yawned from weariness and lack of oxygen, staring at the television playing in a corner with the sound turned down. Her watch had stopped but clearly it was seven o'clock because the titles for *Frasier* appeared on the screen, and Niles and Daphne were stuffing a turkey in the kitchen while Frasier and Martin argued in front of the television. It was reassuring to see the familiar characters in situations that had played out time and again. Fran liked the acerbic wit and the Crane brothers' combination of pretentious snobbery and vulnerability. She could almost recreate the dialogue in her head. It was a relief from the mindless unfocused worry of the last few hours. She could barely believe it was after seven. She had arrived about two-thirty, and the intervening hours had been a mix of short bursts of activity and the tedium of waiting, all overhung with fear of the outcomes.

'It's okay,' Mike had said, greeting her at the entrance to emergency when she arrived. 'We don't think it's serious, but of course at this stage we can't be sure.' Taking her hand he had led her through to the curtained cubicle where Caro lay hitched to a machine that was monitoring her own and the baby's heartbeats. 'She was brought in by ambulance,' Mike explained. 'Apparently she drove across red traffic lights. The guy coming through on green swerved to avoid her but caught the wing and she spun round and ended up on the island of the intersection. Could have been a lot worse. She's not been making much sense since she got here. It's probably just concussion but they have to do some tests.'

'And the baby?' Fran asked, stroking Caro's hand.

Mike indicated the machines. 'Heartbeat's okay, which is good, but we have to check for abdominal damage, from the seatbelt and the steering wheel. Can't do anything at the moment until her blood pressure stabilises.'

Caro's eyelids, which had been half closed, flickered slightly and opened. 'Mum,' she said. 'I didn't mean to. I thought if I cut the steak up very small it would swallow it.'

Fran felt a chill of fear – Caro being unreasonable was familiar, but irrational was something entirely new.

'It's okay, Fran,' Mike said gently, putting his arm around Fran's shoulder and giving her a squeeze. 'It'll pass.' But looking at him for further signs of reassurance, Fran could see the anxiety written on his face, and the almost imperceptible tremble of his chin.

'Hey, babes,' he said, moving over to sit down on the edge of the bed. 'Look who's here. It's your mum. Can you open your eyes again and give us a smile?'

Caro opened her eyes and smiled a vague, empty-eyed smile in the direction of the curtain rail. 'Oh,' she said suddenly. 'Sorry, I don't know why I did that, the traffic lights, I wasn't sure what the colour was.'

Mike leaned down and kissed her gently. 'Don't worry, babe,

it's okay. Nothing to worry about. You just have a little rest,' he said, smoothing the sheet. As he stood up, Fran saw the glint of tears in his eyes, and went over to take his hand.

The hours had ticked by, each moment tense with anxiety, and over and over again Fran had wondered at how slowly everything seemed to happen when you were sure it all ought to be happening very quickly. Outside the window the afternoon light faded to dusk, and by the time David arrived in a gap between teaching classes, Caro's blood pressure had normalised and she was starting to make more sense. Fran had stayed with Caro while David took Mike, by now noticeably shaken and trembling, away for a cup of tea. When they returned, Mike took up the vigil and David steered Fran towards the café.

'So what do you think?' she asked him, stirring sugar into her tea.

David shrugged. 'How can you tell? The other doctor said he thought both she and the baby were okay but now they've stabilised her they can do the CT scan to check for head injuries.'

Fran sighed, slumping back in her chair. 'Poor Caro, she was doing so well, so strong and confident, and now this.'

'No, she wasn't,' David said. 'She's had all-day sickness, depression and she's scared shitless.'

Fran felt as though someone had kicked her in the ribs. 'But she told me –'

'Mum, I know what she told you, but she was lying, well – pretending.'

'But why? I could have helped her, I could have . . .'

'Search me! She just didn't want you to know. Both Mike and I told her to talk to you but she wouldn't. Mike says that the accident happened on her way to tell Des that she wanted to stop work because she felt so bad. Must have had all that on her mind, hence the red light. She's a pretty good driver, so it's really out of character.'

Fran shifted her position in the waiting-room chair and thought back over the conversation again. Caro had seemed invincible in her pregnancy, invincible and remote. Fran's attempts to indulge in the potential delights of prospective grandmothering – shopping trips for baby things, chats about pregnancy, labour, and the relative merits of flannel and disposable nappies – had been cut off at the pass. And because she'd grown accustomed to Caro's various taboos, Fran, while disappointed, had not been worried by it. But Caro had been crying out for help and she hadn't seen it. It never failed to amaze her that however hard she tried to get things right with her children, she so often ended up making the worst kind of misjudgments.

There was the hard line she'd taken with David while he still lived at home and she was sure he was smoking dope when he wasn't; and the soft line she'd taken when he left home and Tony was sure he was shooting heroin and he was. The time she'd argued vociferously with a mother and a teacher that there was no way her daughter would be shoplifting with the other woman's daughter, and then gone home to find lipsticks, bottles of nail polish and some hideous glittery beads in Caro's schoolbag. And in between these milestones of poor parenting, there had been all the smaller misdemeanours so common to mothers but perhaps especially to sole parents trying so hard to be good and bad cop at the same time.

'Fran?' Mike popped his head around the door and she jumped, struggling awkwardly to her feet from the low chair.

'What is it? What's happened?'

'It's okay. Come and see her. The CT scan's okay – it's just concussion, but she's improving,' he said, and she saw the relief on his face.

'So are they keeping her or can she go home?'

'No, no, she can't go home. There's no head injury but they're still concerned about the possibility of abdominal injuries. She's being sent to Royal Women's, where they can keep an eye on her and the baby. They'll probably keep her there for a couple of days.' He slipped his hand under her arm, guiding her along the passage, then stopping suddenly, he turned and put his arms around her. 'Oh, Fran, I was so scared. I know I ought to be used to this sort of thing but it's different when it's someone you love.'

She stood on tiptoe to hold him and could feel him fighting the sobs. 'It's okay, Mike,' she whispered against his hair. 'She's going to be okay, and it's fine for you to cry.'

He straightened up, rubbing his face and swallowing hard. 'Not here, it's not,' he said ruefully, running his hands through his hair. 'It's not that I'm being macho, but a bloke in a white coat and a stethoscope crying his eyes out is not a reassuring sight.'

He took a deep breath and gave her a weak smile. 'I'll save the tears for later. Talk to her, Fran, please, when she's better. I know she's a total pain in the butt sometimes but she does love you and she needs you right now.' And gently he pushed aside the curtains, and Caro looked up from her pillows.

'Hi, Mum,' she said. 'I really stuffed up this time, didn't I?' And she burst into tears.

SIXTEEN

Two o'clock in the morning and Bonnie still couldn't sleep. Sick of punching her pillows she gave in, put on the bedside light and got up. Pulling on her dressing gown she padded, shivering, down to the kitchen, switched on the kettle and leaned against the sink waiting for it to boil. The boatshed file lay on the table where she had left it after their meeting. She stared at it for a moment before turning back to make her tea.

Maybe she had been expecting too much too soon. Will had warned her to take it slowly, suggested that although *she* was rapt in the idea it might take the others a little longer.

'Just put it out there and stand back, Bonnie,' he'd said. 'You've been working up the business plan, doing the figures and the projections for four weeks, but it'll come straight out of left field to them. They don't even know you've bought the boatshed. You'll have to give them time.'

Of course it made sense, but even so she had hoped for more, visualised instant delight and commitment to the plan that had her bouncing around like Tigger, full of excitement and enthusiasm.

She had opened her curtains that morning to see that her prayers had been answered; early winter sunlight glinted off the rooftops, a gift after the freezing rain of the previous couple of days. It didn't matter how cold it was, she had just wanted sun; a long-vacated building in need of renovation was a much more attractive proposition with sun pouring through the windows than it was under a leaden sky. She had already had to postpone the meeting once because Fran was at the hospital with Caro, and in a couple of days Sylvia would leave for England. Bonnie was desperate to put the proposition to them both before then.

'You're being very mysterious, Bon,' Sylvia had said as they pulled up outside the boatshed. 'What are we doing here?'

'Returning to the scene of the crime,' Bonnie said with a smile, switching off the engine. She pointed to a small alcove at the side of the building. 'That's where you kissed Bill Munroe.'

'No!' Fran said in amazement, wrapping her scarf around her neck against the wind. 'You didn't really, did you, Syl? You always said he looked like a wombat.'

'He did,' Sylvia said, smiling. 'But I quite like wombats; at least, I did in those days.' They walked up the ramp, their feet clattering across the boards, their laughter swept up on the wind.

'I bet you three had all those boys on the run,' Will said, his gaze settling on Sylvia.

'No way,' Bonnie said, shaking her head. 'We were much too young, they didn't even notice us.'

'Bill whatever-his-name-was must have noticed,' Will said, unlocking the boatshed door.

'He didn't really count,' Sylvia said. 'He was the kid brother of the captain of the rowing team. Our aspirations were higher than poor old Bill.'

Sunlight poured through the salt-encrusted windows as Bonnie, breathless with anticipation, led them over to a large old trestle table and laid out the portfolios, unsure whether it was cold or nerves that was making her hands tremble.

'This is such a lovely old building,' Fran said, wandering over to a window. 'I've always liked it. Such a shame that someone doesn't do something with it.'

Bonnie looked up in delight. 'That's what I thought,' she said, 'And that's why we're here. Someone *is* going to do something with it. Me – or rather – I hope it will be *us*. I've bought it.'

Slowly, methodically, she laid out her plans: the renovations, the floor plan, the architect's impressions of exterior and interior as Will had suggested. 'Go for visual appeal,' he'd said. 'The last thing you want to do is to start off by boring them with figures and projections. Show them the plans, tell them what it can mean, Fran's profile, the associated products, the gallery, and so on – keep it simple.'

'Fran and Sylvia aren't stupid,' she'd said indignantly.

'I know they're not. If they were, you wouldn't be doing this and I wouldn't be encouraging you. But you're an accountant and a businesswoman, Bon. The detail in the figures, the costings, the trading projections are straightforward to you. You're familiar with the structure and language. They're not and it can be intimidating. Do the visual stuff and talk about how it can work for the three of you – jobs, income, working together and so on.'

Bonnie recognised the wisdom in what he was saying. Caught up in the planning and the excitement of it all, she'd lost sight of how removed they would feel. Her mishandling of the situation with Fran over the loan was a warning and she was desperate to get it right this time. She had thought long and hard about what it meant if financial security was just out of reach and there was no real prospect of narrowing the gap. She wanted this business, the Boatshed with a capital B, for herself, and for them too. She had fallen deeply in love with the concept for the restaurant and gallery. She looked from one to the other, trying to measure their reactions, guess what they were feeling. Surely they would see it as she did, a sound venture with great potential, solid returns and, best of all, the three of them working together.

'A restaurant!' Fran said in horror. 'I couldn't run a restaurant, Bon.'

'You wouldn't have to run it, Fran. The restaurant would be based on your menus and would make use of your reputation, but it would have a chef, manager and a full staff. I'd run the business. You would have an office here and continue what you're doing now, only a lot of the running around would be done by someone else. And I've allowed for a test kitchen, so you wouldn't have to do your recipe testing at home, and you can draw on the kitchen staff to help. Basically you'd be concentrating on what you are good at, writing and creating recipes, and actually being Fran Whittaker, prominent Melbourne food writer.

And there'd be a range of signature products carrying your name: pasta sauces, perhaps; dressings; chocolates, maybe.'

'Like Paul Newman?'

'I hope not,' Will said with a grin. 'Bonnie has a more exclusive range in mind.'

'And there would be other merchandise based on your name and the restaurant,' Bonnie said. 'Tea towels, aprons, perhaps some really nice kitchen utensils. And, Sylvia, this is where I saw you,' she said, indicating the area on the floor plan and putting it alongside the artist's impression. 'This area will be a gallery. I got the idea from seeing the beautiful silk and velvet cushions you made. I thought exclusive needlecraft and unusual jewellery. So – velvet and silk bags and scarves, cushions, throws, linens; I've found a silver artist and a woman who makes beautiful glass earrings – that sort of thing. We could also have some books, a range that fits with the ambiance. It would have tourism value as well as gift potential and it would be a terrific place for local people to display their work.'

She had hoped for a glint of excitement in their eyes but there was none. Confusion and anxiety, yes, but no excitement, and she felt her voice fading away in disappointment. She swallowed hard. 'And it's essentially a daytime concept,' she added. 'Breakfasts, lunches and afternoon teas, closing at six.'

Will got up and wandered through one of the doorways into the rabbit warren of rooms and passages at the back of the building, his footsteps echoing in the silence.

'But I wouldn't know where to begin,' Sylvia said. 'It's daunting. How would we get this place from being a wreck to the sort of place you want? And anyway, I've no idea how to run a gallery.'

Bonnie leaned forward, resting a hand on her arm. 'I know it looks huge but actually it's pretty straightforward. I'll be looking after the renovations, with an architect, a designer and the builder. Your first job would be tracking down suppliers, craftspeople with the sort of products we could sell. You and I can plan the interior of the gallery with a designer, and once it's up and running it would be your territory. I know how to manage this and so do you – you'll realise that as we go along. The three of us can

153

make this work.' She paused glancing across at Fran, who was standing with one knee resting on a chair, staring down at the drawings. 'It would be a job for you, Sylvia, working with things you know and enjoy.'

Sylvia stiffened. 'Bonnie, you've already provided me with a temporary home and even offered me the guest cottage; you don't need to find me a job as well. I *can* do *some* things for myself, I'm not a charity case.'

Bonnie flushed, struggling for words. 'It's not that,' she said. 'Believe me, it's not that all.'

'It is a bit full on,' Fran cut in. 'I mean, you've been so generous, helping me with the loan, being my agent and all that, but this . . . well, it's bigger than Ben Hur. I'm just a food writer, not an entrepreneur. I don't know if I can see myself in all this. Anyway, you didn't come back to Melbourne to rescue Sylvia and me from our work and financial worries.'

Bonnie, elbows on the table, chin resting on her hands, tried to hide the fact that she was trembling. 'Look,' she said, struggling to steady her voice, 'that's not how it is. You think I'm doing this to rescue you but it's really for me, it's what I want for myself. Jeff always wanted me to have a business of my own, but I never knew what I wanted. Now I do, I want it and I really need it. You're the inspiration, but I want it for myself. Jeff left me in an extraordinarily fortunate financial position, but it's not enough, I need something more. Before she went away, Mum told me to get a life. Well, I'm getting one. I'm going to restore this beautiful old building that's part of our childhood. Your talents inspired me, and I'd hoped we could do it together.'

She stood up, feeling extremely wobbly, and walked to the window, turning around to face them again. 'This is going to be my new life. The restaurant and the gallery will happen with or without you. This is a business proposition and I'm trying to recruit the best people. You also happen to be my best friends – the last thing I wanted was to offend you.' She shoved her hands into her pockets and walked out onto the deck, taking deep breaths to calm herself, drawing the sharp sea air down into her lungs, not knowing if she was hurt or angry or both.

Will was standing at the far end of the deck, his hair swept back from his face by the wind, his forearms resting on the rail. Bonnie felt a surge of affection for him. At least one other person was enthusiastic; he was an astute businessman, and he was satisfied it would work. Turning slightly to watch a seagull he saw her and straightened up, walking along to meet her.

'Hang in there, Bon,' he said, putting an arm around her shoulders. 'It looks a bit scary to them at the moment. Give them time.'

'How much time? Days? Weeks?'

'Weeks, probably.'

'They think I'm playing lady bountiful.'

He smiled. 'Dishing out jobs to the deserving poor? Perhaps that's to be expected. Look, you're a very rich woman, you can afford to do this, and you're a businesswoman. It can be an intimidating combination, and they probably haven't encountered that side of you before. Just give them the files you made up for them, let them go away and think about it. Meanwhile, you can get started on the renovations. Like you said, you're going ahead with it anyway.'

Bonnie turned out the kitchen light, made her way upstairs with her tea and climbed back into bed. There was nothing to do now but wait. She was exhausted by her own passion and the day's disappointment, and she sank back against the pillows, thinking gratefully of Will. He seemed different from the Will of old, the workaholic party animal; this week, he had even taken a day off work. They'd been eating breakfast in the kitchen when the radio news reported that snow had fallen overnight at Mount Macedon.

'Let's go and see it,' he'd said quite suddenly. 'We could just hop in the car, we'd be there in an hour and a half. I can cancel my meeting.'

Bonnie wasn't tempted. 'After more than twenty years in Switzerland I've seen my share of snow, thanks,' she'd said.

'Sylvia?' Will asked. 'What about you?'

'Well . . . yes, I'd love to,' she'd said. 'Last time there was snow there I tried to get Colin to go but he was too busy.'

By nine o'clock they were out of the door. Bonnie smiled to

herself, set her empty cup on the bedside table and slid down, pulling the quilt up to her chin. Perhaps Will was softening a little, changing, just like his brother had done at that age. She drew a spare pillow against her and curled herself around it, longing for the comforting and familiar warmth of Jeff's body, his steady, reassuring presence, the precious intimacy that was lost forever. From time to time she would convince herself that she was over it, but the enormity of her loss constantly returned to haunt her and his absence seemed sharpened by the fact that she was spending so much of her time with people who had never even known him. She talked to him still, often at night, and she felt him urging her to be brave and confident, but without him every step was a challenge. The Boatshed was a chance to build a new life, one Jeff would have been proud of, and she was determined not to lose sight of it, though after today's meeting she feared that in her passion for it she may have damaged something infinitely more precious.

SEVENTEEN

'I made you some of that special chocolate fudge,' Fran said, putting the package down on Caro's bedside table. 'Hope you can eat it.'

'Brilliant, thanks, Mum,' Caro said. She pulled off the plastic wrap and stuffed a piece of fudge into her mouth. 'I love this so much. One good thing about the accident is that the shock seems to have stopped all the nausea and vomiting.'

Fran took off her coat and sank down into the chair beside the bed, thinking carefully how to handle this. 'Sickness? I thought you'd escaped that,' she said. 'You said you were feeling fine.'

Caro flushed slightly and glanced away, helping herself to another piece of fudge. 'Yeah, well, I didn't want to worry you. Anyway, it's okay now. I can go home tomorrow.'

'So they're satisfied everything's all right with you and the baby?'

Caro, her mouth full of fudge, nodded and swallowed. 'I was really lucky.'

'And you're not worried about anything?'

'Uh-uh! Can't wait to get home.'

'And work?'

'I'm giving up. Des came to see me and I told him. I'll probably go raving mad with nothing to do but I s'pose it's for the best.'

Fran nodded, unsure how to pitch the conversation now. Both David and Mike had asked her to talk to Caro but what was she supposed to say? If Caro wanted to confide her fears about the pregnancy she had just had the ideal opportunity but clearly

157

she'd chosen not to take it. Fran knew her daughter well enough to predict that even subtle probing would simply bring down the shutters. All she could do was try to keep an eye on her once she was home; the window of vulnerability that had opened up when Caro had burst into tears a few days earlier was now firmly closed.

'So what do you think of the Boatshed thing?' Fran asked, nodding towards the portfolio that she'd left with Caro the previous day.

'This? It's cool, I reckon. Are you going to do it?'

Fran picked at a loose thread on the cuff of her jumper. 'I don't know. It all seems a bit much. I think I've got enough to cope with, juggling work, trying to sell the house and move . . .' In fact, she was feeling totally frazzled and Bonnie's proposal had come at the worst possible time. Sitting in the Boatshed a couple of days earlier she had resisted the urge to put her head down on the table and howl with exhaustion. She could see that her lack of enthusiasm had disappointed Bonnie but she wanted to shake her friend and ask her if she couldn't have waited a while before presenting her with the need to make yet another big decision.

'Yeah, I know,' Caro said, picking up the file and flicking through it. 'But the way this is set up you'd have an administrative safety net. Other people will do the shit stuff that you don't like. It'll leave you free to do the things you're good at. You used to say you were trapped because there was too much work but not enough income to take someone on to help you. This is a perfect solution. You get an agent and business manager and a share in the restaurant profits – she's even buying the use of your name. Terrific publicity, good returns. You'll be Melbourne's answer to Martha Stewart.'

'I hope not,' Fran said. 'She's just about to go to jail.'

Caro rolled her eyes in irritation. 'You know what I mean. Anyway, why ask me? You must know whether you want to do it or not.'

'I'm asking you because you're my daughter, and because you're the business manager of a small company and they think very highly of you, so you must have a feel for this sort of thing.'

'Maybe,' Caro shrugged. 'But in the end it's your decision whether you want to do it or not.'

'Do you think it's that simple?'

Caro sighed and ate another piece of fudge. 'You always have to make everything so complicated, Mum. Everything has to be analysed, dissected and discussed ad nauseum. No wonder you get tired. You wear yourself out thinking before you even get out of bed in the morning. Just do it or don't do it, for heaven's sake.'

The feeling of being crushed by Caro's disapproval settled on Fran with an awful familiarity, and she felt her defensiveness rise. Caro always managed to make her feel so incompetent. Breathing deeply she determined to stay calm and to try to get something good happening between them before she left the hospital.

Across the ward a heavily pregnant young woman tore the wrapping from a package and lifted out a tiny white hand-knitted matinee jacket. 'Oh! Mum, it's so cute. I didn't even know you could knit,' she said, leaning over to hug her mother. Fran shifted uncomfortably; somehow, unaccountably, she seemed to have missed the mark on motherhood. Now it looked as though she was heading to get it wrong as a grandmother too.

'Shall I come and pick you up tomorrow and take you home?' she offered.

Caro shook her head. 'Mike's not on duty till four o'clock so he'll come.'

'If you're not working we could go shopping later in the week. I saw some gorgeous baby things in Pumpkin Patch the other day.'

'S'pose,' Caro said, 'but I've probably got enough stuff already. We went out a couple of weeks ago and got clothes and nappies and stuff for the baby's room.'

Fran watched the pair across the ward examining the matinee jacket. She had no idea how to break through Caro's brittle exterior and no energy to attempt it. She was sick of trying to get it right and failing, sick of turning the other cheek, of trying to compensate for splitting up the family. She got up, reaching for her coat. It was time to go before she said something she'd regret. Caro picked up a copy of *Marie Claire* and began flicking through the pages.

'By the way, Mum,' she said, not looking up, 'I told Des I'd go back full time two months after the baby's born, but child care's so expensive I thought I'd find a place for three days a week and you'd have it the other two.'

Fran froze, her arm halfway into her coat sleeve. 'Just what do you want from me, Caro?' she asked, in a voice so unlike her own that Caro looked up from the magazine in surprise.

'Well, just two days a week, not every day.'

Fran stared at her daughter for a moment and then, swinging her bag over her shoulder, she walked to the end of the bed. 'You don't even know what I mean, do you? You don't want to share the least little thing about your pregnancy or the birth with me, why would I give up my precious time to help you?' she snapped. 'Frankly, Caro, you're a self-centred bitch, a complete pain in the arse and I don't know why I've put up with it for so long.' And she turned on her heel and marched out of the ward.

Irene thought the house felt different. On her return from previous holidays, Marjorie had always gone in the day before to air the bed, switch on the heating in winter and put basics in the fridge, but this time she returned to a house that breathed with life. She toured every room, stopping to sample the atmosphere, to ground herself in it again. Bonnie's presence was everywhere and although Sylvia had left for her holiday in England a few days earlier, her influence was obvious too, not simply in the room she had occupied, but in the vases of flowers and beautiful quilted silk and velvet cushions she had made for the lounge. And Will's laptop blinked away on the desk in what had once been Dennis's study. The house had a feel of the old days when they had been a family, Simon and Bonnie's friends coming and going, she and Dennis pursuing their shared and separate interests.

Sitting in her favourite chair, listening to a Schubert sonata and reading Bonnie's Boatshed proposal again, Irene realised the weariness of the jetlag was easing and she was beginning to feel more like her old self. The phone rang and she decided to let the machine answer, but hearing Hamish's voice she got up to intercept it.

'I've got the tickets,' he said. 'Is tomorrow still all right for you?'

'Fine,' she said. 'I'm feeling a lot better today. Emerging from the jetlag.'

'Good, me too. I could pick you up at two and we can do the exhibition and then have afternoon tea at the Windsor.'

'How elegant! It sounds positively pre-war.'

'That's me! My vintage,' Hamish said, and she could hear the smile in his voice. 'Have you told Bonnie yet?'

'Not yet, I haven't quite summoned up the courage. It seems odd just to sit her down and tell her outright. I'm sure she'll be fine but I have to find the best moment.'

'Hmm, I hope so,' he said. 'Not fair to keep her in the dark for too long. Anyway, I'll see you tomorrow at two.'

Irene went back to her chair and sat, the proposal on her knee, her head resting on the back of the chair, and closed her eyes. How significantly her life had changed in the last few months, with Bonnie coming home and now this. Since their first night together, Irene's feelings for Hamish had acquired more substantial form. Decades earlier her relationship with Dennis had begun with a hearty, energetic friendship forged in their mutual enjoyment of tennis, sailing and music. Their marriage had been lively and companionable. As Dennis neared retirement, Simon's tragic death at forty-two had bonded them in terrible grief; but a couple of years later his own death from a heart attack had changed both the present and her vision of the future. Now she found herself in a new phase, loved once again in an intimate, even romantic way. In Greece their friends had happily adjusted to the new situation as though it was the most natural thing in the world. Even the formidable Marjorie had pronounced her blessings.

Out in the drive a car door slammed and Irene jerked her head up, opening her eyes as she heard Bonnie's key in the front door. She glanced down at the proposal again. It was, she thought, a splendid plan. Both Dennis and Jeff would have been impressed by the scope and precision of Bonnie's planning.

'What do you think of it?' Bonnie asked from the hallway, where she stood clutching plastic bags of shopping with both hands, her coat thrown over her shoulders. 'I know you were too jetlagged to take it in yesterday.'

Irene got up, relieved her daughter of her coat and followed her through to the kitchen. 'I think you've done a wonderful job. I can see you making a huge success of this.'

Bonnie smiled and started to unpack the shopping. 'Thanks, Mum – you said I should get a life. I just wish Fran and Sylvia felt the same.'

'They'll be the losers if they don't,' Irene said, putting onions and lemons into a rack in the pantry. 'This would be excellent for Fran. It builds on everything she's done so far, gives her a context to work from.'

Bonnie crumpled the plastic bags. 'At the moment she doesn't see it that way. She – both of them are very uneasy about the whole idea. I think they're torn between being interested and feeling that I'm offering them charity.'

Irene shrugged. 'That's not how the proposal reads but their own sensitivities would affect their reading of it. Of course, you can make it work without them but it would have distinct advantages for all three of you if they were involved. What does Will think?'

'He thinks the plan is spot on, and he believes they'll come around, given time. You know, Mum, it never occurred to me that having money could actually cause problems with friends. I must be a bit thick.'

Irene filled the kettle and got out the teapot. 'Sylvia and Fran have both had to struggle financially. Money's a nightmare when you haven't got it and when you manage your way through crises there's some pride that you've coped. You need to remember that.'

'So I'm discovering, perhaps a little too late,' Bonnie said. 'Anyway, they've both promised to think about it. Fran's got a lot on her plate at present, and Sylvia promised to think about it while she's away. Meanwhile, there's plenty I can be getting on with. By the way, did you know the French Impressionists exhibition is on at the gallery? Sylvia and I went a couple of weeks ago but I'd happily go again if you want to see it.'

Irene poured the tea and handed Bonnie a cup. 'Thank you,

dear, but I've arranged to go tomorrow with Hamish, and afterwards we're having afternoon tea at the Windsor. I haven't done that for years.'

Bonnie smiled, sipping her tea. 'That sounds lovely. I hope it's okay with you, I told Will he could bring a business acquaintance back here tomorrow evening.'

'It's fine,' Irene said, her throat suddenly feeling a little dry. 'I won't be here, anyway; I'll have supper and stay the night with Hamish.'

'Oh, no need for that,' Bonnie said. 'If Hamish doesn't like driving in the dark, just ring me when you're ready to come home and I'll come and pick you up. I know you're not one for staying with other people.'

Irene took a deep breath. 'Actually, dear, I do want to stay with Hamish and I'll be doing so quite often from now on. And Hamish will stay here sometimes. We had a lovely time together in Greece. In fact, according to Marjorie, who is always very up to date with the vernacular, Hamish and I are now what is known as *an item*.'

Although she didn't actually *see* Bonnie drop her mug, she heard the smash as it hit the tiled floor.

EIGHTEEN

London was drenched in August sunshine. It glanced off the angles of recently cleaned buildings, and lit the darkest corners of narrow streets. Even the normally murky waters of the Thames appeared fresh and sparkling. From the front seat on the open-top bus, Sylvia gazed out over a very different city than the one she remembered. Both her previous visits had been in the dank, freezing darkness of February.

'Look over there, Grandma,' eight-year-old Charlotte cried, scrambling up in her seat. 'That's the Tower of London where they cut people's heads off.'

'Used to, darling,' Kim said as Sylvia grabbed her granddaughter by the back of her denim jacket. 'Please don't lean over the rail like that, you might fall. They don't cut people's heads off anymore.'

'They drown them in boiling oil,' James said ghoulishly. Two years younger than his sister, he was a serious little boy whose slight squint was being corrected by glasses which, he told Sylvia, were just like Harry Potter's.

'Gruesome, aren't they?' Kim said. 'I didn't realise kids were quite so bloodthirsty.'

'You used to like the most revolting stories,' Sylvia said. 'I remember one about an ugly dwarf being cut in half by a wizard and the two halves being thrown from the castle ramparts and turning into dragons as they hit the ground.'

'Did I?' Kim said in amazement. 'I can't remember that at all.

Do you want to get out at the Tower or shall we stay on the bus? There seem to be queues everywhere.'

'Stay on, I think,' Sylvia said. 'It's so lovely up here, being able to see everything and not be caught up in the crowds.' The crush of people in London had come as a surprise to her. The streets were packed with tourists, and she had felt quite claustrophobic as they'd emerged from the underground at Oxford Circus and been swept along by the crowd pouring out onto the street.

Sylvia had been in England a week and was slowly adjusting to the smallness of everything, particularly Kim and Brendan's house. She had almost forgotten how cramped she had felt on the last visit, although by English standards it was a comfortable middle-class family home, one that they could never have afforded had Brendan not inherited it on the death of an aunt a year after he and Kim were married. Standing in its own quarter acre of garden in the Surrey commuter belt only twenty minutes by train from central London, it was now worth a small fortune in Australian dollars.

Kim had met Brendan at a party in St Kilda ten years earlier. He had been backpacking around Australia, but the travel came to an abrupt halt when they met and he stayed on in Melbourne until his visa expired. Six months later Kim went to join him in England and together they slipped out of London for the weekend and were married in a registry office in York. Charlotte was born eighteen months later, and Sylvia and Colin had paid their first visit. They were there again for James's second birthday. Now the babies were children and as she clung to Charlotte, who still insisted on leaning as far as possible over the rail, Sylvia felt a pang of regret for the time she had missed with them.

The bus continued on the last section of its route, back past the Houses of Parliament and Horse Guards Parade, depositing them finally at Victoria Station. There they bought the children milkshakes and caught the train back to Croydon, where Kim had left the car.

'Tea for you two and early bed,' Kim said as they made their way back into the house. 'It's nearly six o'clock and we've been out for hours.'

165

'I'm not in the least little bit tired at all,' said Charlotte deci-sively, putting her pink plastic shoulder bag on the hall table. 'I'm going to stay up for ages and teach Grandma how to play the witchy game.'

Sylvia put her hand on her heart. 'Well, you may not be tired, Charlie, but I'm exhausted. Why don't you and James go and see what's on television, I'll help Mummy with the tea and then you can have fun in the bath and I'll read you both a story. You can teach me the witchy game tomorrow.' Charlotte and James wandered off to switch on the television and Sylvia watched them fling themselves onto the sofa. 'Wherever do they get their energy?' she sighed, washing her hands in the sink.

'God knows, but they'll be out like lights quite soon, so we'll feed them quickly and get them off to bed, then we can have a quiet evening. Bren's got a meeting tonight so he'll eat in town. Shall we have a sandwich now with the kids?'

Sylvia nodded. 'Good idea. Shall I make that while you do theirs?'

They worked companionably side by side in the kitchen. During the long periods of separation Sylvia felt out of touch with her daughter's adult life, often thinking of her still in terms of the teenager who had lived at home. Watching her now she could see the competent woman her daughter had become and she wished, albeit fleetingly, that Colin was there to share this pleasure in a way that only parents could.

'You haven't said much about Dad,' Kim said later, handing her a glass of wine and settling down in a large armchair in the living room. The children were fed, bathed and in bed and the long summer evening was fading to darkness.

'I thought I said enough the night I arrived,' Sylvia said.

'Yes, but since then hardly anything at all.'

Sylvia shrugged. 'What more *can* I say? You know it all. I'm sad and shaken, but also relieved. I was furious with him at first, now I'm thankful that everything came to a head.'

'So there really is no chance of you going back to him?'

Sylvia looked at her in amazement. 'For heaven's sake, Kim. Your father has left the ministry, lost his faith and is living with

166

his girlfriend in a townhouse in Williamstown. No – I am not going back to him. I don't want it and neither does he.'

'Sorry, sorry, Mum . . . I just wanted to make sure. I mean, maybe you might have felt you wanted to try and make a go of it again.'

Sylvia realised what was happening. 'Kim, darling, I can see where you're coming from. But this is very different from what happened with you and Brendan. Your father and I . . . well, it was over long before the other woman came along. We both hung in there making each other quietly and inexorably miserable. It really is over. Some time in the future we'll probably be friends again, but the dust will take a while to settle.'

Kim nodded, sipping her wine, looking out across the garden to the dovecote, where two pairs of fantailed pigeons were settling in for the night. 'Dad said he might come over at Christmas.'

'Really?'

'He wants to bring her, this Jennifer person, bring her here, but I said no. I know she's living with him but I don't think that means I have to have her here in the house.'

Sylvia shrugged. 'That's your decision.'

'But it affects you.'

'Maybe, but it doesn't horrify me. When a bit more time has passed you may feel you want to meet her and let her meet the children.'

'Perhaps,' Kim said, 'but not yet. Anyway, it may not last. Perhaps she's just some sort of replacement for God and eventually he won't need her anymore.'

'You sound very bitter,' Sylvia said, curling her legs underneath her on the couch.

'I am bitter. All my life God came first with Dad. He was never involved with me. There were so many things we didn't do, so many times when he was too busy. You can't argue or be jealous when it's God who's getting all the attention. Complaining about it seems shallow and selfish.'

'That's rather how I felt,' Sylvia said.

'Yes . . . so now he dumps God and gets himself a girlfriend who's not much older than me.'

Sylvia saw the first tear slide down Kim's cheek and she went over to her, perching on the arm of her chair and putting an arm around her shoulders. 'It must feel awful, Kim. I'm so sorry we've hurt you so much. But your father and I are just very ordinary people who made a mess of things, and in the end we have to sort it out in our own way. And there is one other thing to remember: through all those years your father's faith was rock solid. He really did believe in his vocation and that his duty to God must come before everything else.'

Kim nodded, drying her eyes on a tissue. 'I know all that, but it's sort of scary when your parents split up. You're being very nice about him.'

Sylvia shook her head. 'I wasn't at first, I assure you. But what's the point in bitterness? The only person it hurts is me. I have to recognise my own part in it, my collusion, resenting it for years but doing nothing while I felt I was dying inside. It's not as though Colin is a bad person.'

They sat in silence for a moment while outside the doves cooed and shuffled and the evening star emerged from behind a wisp of cloud.

'The thing is,' Kim went on, 'the thing I . . . Bren and I wanted to ask you is if there's no chance of you getting back together, would you think of coming here?'

'Here? To England? To live, do you mean?'

Kim nodded, and Sylvia got up from the arm of the chair and wandered over to the window. 'You could get a place near here. We'd love it, and so would the kids.'

'But what would I do, how would I live?'

'You could get a little flat or something, maybe share a house with another woman,' Kim said.

'I doubt I could afford it. Australian dollars are worth nothing here. Back home I'll probably be able to get a job, but here . . . anyway, people can't just come and live in England, there'd be all the immigration problems.'

Kim seemed brighter now. 'Bren thinks not,' she said. 'After all, you were born here, and even though you were two when Gran and Grandad moved to Australia, you still have the right to live here. Anyway, that's what he thought – we could find out for sure.'

Sylvia settled back on the couch staring at her daughter in amazement. 'I've never even thought of it. Of course, it would be lovely to be close to you and Brendan and the children but –'

'Exactly,' Kim cut in. 'You could rent somewhere nearby and we'd see you often. In fact, what I had in mind was . . . Mum, I'd *really* like to get a job and it would be brilliant if you could look after the kids, you know, meet them from school, be here for them in the holidays, all that stuff. You'd love it, and so would they, and it would be the perfect for solution for Bren and me. Please say you'll do it, or at least think about it.'

Sylvia stared at her empty glass, unable to think straight. 'I don't know,' she said. 'I don't know. I'd have to have a job, so how could I do that and look after the children? And it's a big thing, moving to a new country, my whole life . . .'

'But your life is sort of gone now, isn't it?' Kim said eagerly. 'I mean, it's all a mess. This would be lovely for you, a new start.'

Sylvia was totally confused. On the one hand, the prospect of spending time with Kim and the children, watching them grow, being an active part of their lives, was hugely attractive; on the other, there was a distinct uneasiness that she couldn't really pin down. 'I'll have to think about it,' she said cautiously. 'Of course, it's lovely of you to suggest it, but I will have to think about it.'

'Yes,' Kim said, clapping her hands. 'Do, and I'm sure the more you think about it you'll see it's the perfect solution. Have another glass of wine to help you think.' And she refilled her mother's glass as Sylvia sat there shaken, anxious, and totally incapable of thinking rationally about anything at all.

Late the following Saturday, Sylvia had the house to herself. Kim, Brendan and the children had gone to a friend's for a barbecue, but she had cried off on the grounds of tiredness. She wanted time to herself. She wasn't used to the full-on presence of the children nor, in fact, to being with an adult who talked quite as much, and as intensely, as Kim. Surrounded by people and noise from dawn to dusk she tired quickly and couldn't think straight,

and she was feeling oppressed by Kim's constant, hopeful anticipation of a decision every time she opened her mouth.

For a while she rested, enjoying the silence, and then she
remembered the small church she'd noticed on the way to the
local shops. Fetching a jumper from her room she set off up the hill.
The church stood on a corner and from the lych-gate there was
a view across the rooftops and some small areas of wooded park-
land to where the setting sun and the distant lights of the city
washed the darkening sky with a pink-gold glow. She could hear
the far-off sound of a train, and the muffled cries of children playing outside in the mild evening air. Could she live in this place?
England in summer had surprised her with its beauty, but the
memory of dark, bleak winters remained and it was more, much
more than that.

Drawing her jumper around her shoulders, Sylvia stepped
into the dim interior of the church, lit only by the fading light
through the stained-glass windows. Everything she knew was at
home – friends, acquaintances, a whole way of life. And despite
the dramatic change in her circumstances, it was still a way of life
that she knew. Starting again in Melbourne seemed hard enough
– how would she manage in a strange country? What sort of life
would she have here? Meeting the children from school, being
here for them in holiday times, part of her longed for that sort of
involvement. But how could she earn a living and do that, and
what about the rest of her life? What about those times when she
wasn't needed, the times that would increase in frequency and
duration as the children got older?

The previous day they had walked to the park to let Charlie
and James play on the swings. Turning out of the street where
Kim and Brendan lived into a less affluent one of older, three-
storey houses built in the thirties, Kim had touched her arm.
'Look, Mum,' she said. 'A lot of these big old houses have been
made into flats and they're really nice. Art deco, some of them.'

As Sylvia paused to look, an elderly woman opened the front
door of one and bent to pick up a bottle of milk from the step. She
straightened up and as she looked ahead to where they were
standing, Sylvia could see that she was sixty perhaps, certainly no

more. But there was something old and lost about her, something very different from the way Sylvia saw herself.

'That woman's not much older than me,' she whispered, catching a glimpse of a possible future, and feeling uneasy about it. 'She looks so . . . old.'

'They make really nice flats,' Kim said. 'High ceilings with cornices, and bay windows. They'd be big enough for you to have the children to stay overnight.'

'It would be very different,' Sylvia said, watching the woman turn back into the house. 'A very different sort of life.'

Kim took her arm. 'I know, Mum, but that's what you want, isn't it? Something different. Wouldn't you love seeing Charlie and James almost every day?'

Would she? The whole idea had disturbed her in a quite profound way that she couldn't yet put into words.

Sylvia stared at the altar and above it the magnificent jewel colours of the leadlight depicting the Light of the World. 'What do *you* think?' she asked, staring into the eyes of the Christ figure. 'You got me into it all in the first place. I know I've neglected you, but surely you have some answers for me.'

The glass eyes stared down unmoving, and Sylvia sat on in the church until the evening chill sent a shiver through her and it was almost too dark to see. Then she got up and walked back down the hill to the house.

'You didn't need to wait up for us,' Kim whispered as they came into the hall. James was draped, fast asleep, across Brendan's shoulder. Charlotte, drowsy and irritable, trailed behind her mother.

'I wasn't waiting up,' Sylvia said. 'I've been doing some thinking.'

Charlotte reached her arms up to Sylvia and she picked her up.

'Grandma, take me to bed,' Charlotte said, and Sylvia staggered slightly with the weight of her.

'You're too big for me to carry upstairs, darling,' Sylvia said. 'I'll come with you but you have to walk.' Charlotte began to cry, rubbing her fists into her eyes, and Brendan, who had already deposited James fully clothed on his bed, came down again and took her from Sylvia.

'Come on, sourpuss,' he said, and carted her off upstairs.

'So,' Kim asked eagerly, 'you had some time to think. Have you made up your mind yet?'

'Don't keep hassling me, Kim,' Sylvia said, suddenly annoyed at the pressure. 'It's wearing me out. What you're asking – it's a big thing, a huge decision for me. I can't make up my mind in a few days with you breathing down my neck like this.'

Kim turned to go into the kitchen. 'I thought you'd like the idea,' she said. 'Jump at it, actually. We're your family, and now Dad's gone off with someone else, and your life is such a mess . . . besides, we need you. I can't go back to work unless I have someone to take care of the children.'

'Hang on,' Sylvia said, following her daughter into the kitchen. 'Don't keep saying that. My life *isn't* a mess. I've been living your father's life ever since we were married and now I've got the freedom to live my own.' And as she said it she knew what had been troubling her. 'If I come here I'll have the pleasure of being with you and the children, seeing them grow up, all that, but I'll be living *your* life, building my days around *your* needs, just as I did with Dad. It's lovely that you want me here, Kim, I'm grateful for that, but for the first time since I got married I can now choose what I want to do and where I want to live.'

'I know all that,' Kim said. 'That's what I mean – you can pick England and us. And you go on and on about living in the church houses but they were always okay. You had it pretty cushy, really, you didn't have to go out to work.'

Sylvia was angry now. 'It didn't always feel that way. I gave up my career to marry Dad, so I could work and keep him till he got his PhD. By the time you came along I had a really interesting job, and naturally I gave that up. I was glad to be able to be at home with you when you were little, but your father's life in the church made huge demands on my time and energy. And for the last fifteen years at least, I would have much preferred to go back to work. I no longer have to live Colin's life, and I'm not sure that hooking myself into yours is the best choice I could make for myself right now.'

Kim's face clouded and her bottom lip trembled as she turned to face her mother.

'I can't believe how selfish you're being,' she said. 'I thought you'd *want* to help. You keep saying how much you've missed seeing your grandchildren; now you've got the chance to see them every day and you don't want to. That's typical of your generation, isn't it? The stupid, selfish baby boomers, all the time me, me, me, what do *I* want, what's best for *me*. Never mind about what's best for anyone else. Well, don't let me interfere with your nice new life, I'm only your daughter, after all.' And, pushing past her mother, she strode out of the kitchen and up the stairs and Sylvia heard the bedroom door slam shut.

NINETEEN

'I thought I might find you here,' Jodie said, and David's head shot up from the front page of the paper. She was standing beside him holding a takeaway coffee. 'Mind if I join you?'

'Please do,' he said, tossing aside the paper and moving the other chair so she could sit down. He'd gone to the coffee shop almost every morning of the three weeks since he'd met her, hoping she'd turn up. Just that morning he'd decided that this would be his last attempt. Obviously she wished she hadn't told him where she went for coffee and was going somewhere else to avoid running into him.

'I've been away,' she said with a smile, lifting the plastic lid off her coffee and borrowing his spoon to scoop the foam. 'Got sent to do emergency cover at the clinic in Gisborne. My sister lives there so I stayed with her – better than driving backwards and forwards every day.'

David laughed. 'I thought you were avoiding me,' he said.

'Well – that too,' she said with a laugh. 'Won't do my reputation much good to be seen with a nudist.'

'I've given it up,' he said. 'Cross my heart.' Her eyes flashed with light as she laughed and he looked into them just that little bit too long and suddenly they were marooned in silence.

'So,' he said, embarrassed now at his own awkwardness, 'you're back.'

Jodie nodded. 'Yes. How's Caro?'

He gave a grim smile. 'Full-scale family drama. She had a car

174

accident – she and the baby are okay but she was in hospital for a few days, during which time she and Mum had a bit of a blue and now they're barely speaking to each other.'

Jodie pulled a face. 'Whose fault?'

'Fifty-fifty, I think. No, that's wrong – probably eighty-twenty. Caro can be such a pain, especially where Mum's concerned.'

'And your gran?'

'Making something called a Tiffany lampshade; purple, of course.' He was dying inside. He'd always found it easy, talking to girls, asking them out. But since the shock of his diagnosis, embarrassment about his illness seemed to have extinguished the spark of flirtation. What right did he have to get involved with anyone? He was a hopeless liability with nothing to offer. He stared down into his empty cup feeling like a clumsy teenager, totally lost for words. In a few minutes she would be gone, and if he didn't stop behaving like a complete wanker she wouldn't bother with him again. Somehow, though, the words wouldn't come.

Jodie downed the remains of her coffee and stood up. 'Gotta get on,' she said, picking up her bag. 'I'm a bit late already. Do you want to get something to eat tonight? That Thai place round the corner is nice.'

David's breath was trapped in his chest. 'Yes,' he said. 'Yes, I'd like that. Shall I . . . shall I pick you up?'

She pulled a pen from her bag and scribbled an address on the top margin of his paper.

'Why don't you wander round about half-past six and we can walk down there,' she said with a smile. 'See you later, then.'

'Yeah,' he said. 'Sure, see you later.' And he picked up the paper and stuffed it inside his coat as he watched her cross the street to her car. 'Half-past six,' he said softly to himself. 'Half-past six, I'll be there, you bet your life I'll be there.'

And he was, just as he was the next time, when she suggested a pizza, and the time she asked him to go the cinema, and so on . . . until the day he went to answer the doorbell and discovered his grandmother standing on the doorstep.

*

Lila didn't know what was wrong with them all – Fran and Caro not speaking, Fran deciding to move, and now David, whom she'd set up with the nice little bloodsucker, was about to let her slip through his fingers. Jodie, or was it Judy? Anyway, she'd told Lila that they'd already been on several dates, but only because she'd asked him.

'He seems keen enough when we're out together, Mrs Whittaker,' she said as she plunged the needle into Lila's arm, 'but he never asks me out. I always have to do it. I really like David, we have a good time together, we go for a meal, or to the movies, and once we went up to the Victoria Markets, but he'll never come back to my place and he won't ask me back to his. I don't know what I'm doing wrong.'

'It's nothing about you, my love,' Lila told her, pressing the tiny pad of cotton wool onto the puncture mark the needle had left. 'It's him being silly. You leave David to me.'

'Oh! Well, no, I don't want you to say anything to him,' Jodie said, flushing at the prospect. 'I'm just confiding in you.'

Lila knew everyone thought she was losing it, and she knew she was forgetful about names and dates, but when it came to all the important things she was still as sharp as a tack. She had always prided herself on speaking her mind, but recently she'd found herself holding back a bit, didn't want to seem an interfering old bat. Now here they were, falling apart. It was time, she thought, to sort them out. In some families the older woman was the matriarch, the children and grandchildren took notice, deferred to her, but in this family nobody gave a stuff what she thought. A lifetime of experience was going to waste.

A year or so ago Lila had had a fall, cracked her elbow and broken her ankle, and they had taken a while to heal. The shock had knocked her sideways and she'd lost a bit of confidence, come to rely on Fran or Caro, and more recently David, if she wanted to go out. The retirement village had a free bus service to the shops and she managed that all right, but she just hadn't got back into the swing of going anywhere else without someone to take her. But now she'd been asked out for coffee. It was a sign, she thought, a sign that she should step back into life again, and the family would be the first step.

Lila straightened her shoulders and looked at herself in the mirror. A couple of weeks earlier she'd bought a very nice pale mauve coat in the recycling shop. It went very well with the purple scarf Fran had been wearing last time she was there. Fran had let Lila try it on and she'd forgotten to give it back. Still, Fran wouldn't mind her wearing it – after all, purple was *her* colour. She thought she looked rather nice, certainly suitably dressed to go out for coffee with Irene and Hamish.

After her holiday Irene had called in as promised to admire Lila's purple décor, and to show her the photographs of Greece, and she'd brought her new gentleman friend. Now, this morning, they had called to say they were going to be right near her, on the way to visit a friend in Fitzroy, and they wondered if she'd like to go out for a coffee. Lila had thought Hamish was a very nice man and she was surprised to hear that Bonnie was being so silly about it. She'd always seemed such a sensible girl. In fact, what Lila remembered very clearly from the days when their daughters were at school together was that despite their money both mother and daughter were straightforward, friendly people, with no pretensions. That, she'd always told Fran, was a sign of good breeding, something that no amount of money could buy.

'So has Bonnie got over it yet?' Lila asked Irene as they sat in the café while Hamish queued at the counter to order the coffee.

Irene shook her head. 'No, she's very disapproving still,' she said, 'but I'm determined not to give in.'

'Good, you've got to stand your ground,' Lila said. 'Does she want you to give him up or what?'

'I don't think she knows what she wants really, she just knows it makes her uncomfortable.'

Hamish returned to the table carrying a plate with three tiny Portuguese custard tarts.

'To tempt you ladies,' he said, putting down the plate. 'Coffee's on its way. What are you plotting?'

'Just talking about Bonnie,' Irene said. 'Her disapproval.'

'Aha!' Hamish said with a smile. 'Strange creatures, one's children. As teenagers they're repelled by the realisation that their parents have a sex life, and that never really changes.' He reached over and took Irene's hand. 'It's all right if I take Irene out, wine and dine her, Lila, even go on holiday and fall in love with her, as long as I don't share her bed.'

Lila laughed loudly, and picked up one of the little tarts. She was enjoying herself enormously. 'Oh yes,' she said, 'our children! Because they were teenagers in the sixties they think they invented sex. I blame Woodend.'

'Woodend?' Irene queried.

'I think you mean Woodstock,' Hamish ventured.

'Yes, that's it, Woodstock, all that singing about sex, and doing it in public. Why not just get on with it quietly and enjoy it, I say. No need to share it with the rest of the world. Now tell me, Hamish, what do you think about all this Viagra business?'

Hamish, startled, glanced at Irene, who was grinning widely. 'Well, Lila,' he said, 'I really couldn't say. Never felt the need for it myself.'

'Isn't that good, then,' Lila said, thoroughly satisfied with his answer. 'Now, I wonder if you'd mind dropping me off in Collingwood when we leave here. I want to pop in and see David.'

David stared at the vision in purple that greeted him as he opened the door.

'Gran, what a surprise. Are you on your own? How did you get here?'

'Got a lift with friends,' Lila said. 'Besides, there're trams and buses, you know, I'm not helpless. Aren't you going to ask me in?'

He stepped back and she marched into the huge room and over to the tall windows that looked down onto the street below. 'This is very nice, very modern.'

'Yep, it is. Would you like some tea?'

'Just had coffee and cake, thanks,' she said. 'And I'm not here to mess about, David, I've come to sort you out.'

'Really? I can hardly wait.'

'Don't you be a smartarse with me,' she said, and David flinched at a word he would not have used in her presence. She perched on the edge of a scarlet cube-style sofa that Matt had helped him choose, her feet barely touching the floor. She looked strangely misplaced, like a small doll that had been put on the wrong shelf in the toy shop.

'This whole family's in a mess and it's time I did something about it and you're first,' Lila said.

David pulled a face. 'Sounds like I'm in trouble.'

'If you are it's of your own making. Now, what are you up to with Judy?'

'Jodie.'

'Don't change the subject.'

'I'm not, and I'm not up to anything.'

'Exactly! Not up to enough, if you ask me,' Lila said. 'No good to keep going out with her if it's not going to go any further than that. She's a lovely girl, you just don't know when you're well off.'

'It's not as easy as that,' David said, fidgeting with embarrassment. 'Jodie's fantastic, but it's complicated – you wouldn't understand.'

'Oh, I understand all right,' Lila said, 'But hepatitis isn't the worst thing in the world, you know. A lot of people have HIV as well – be thankful that hasn't happened to you. You have to take care of yourself, don't get too tired, don't drink, and be careful of your diet, and practise safe sex.'

David looked at her, surprise outweighing annoyance and embarrassment. Just like Matt, she sounded as though she had memorised the support group leaflet. 'How do you know all this?'

'I read it. Went down to the library and looked it up. It wasn't easy because they hadn't got it in large print, but the librarian helped me. You can live a normal life, you know, you just need to look after yourself and use condoms. No children, though – you can't have children.'

David, elbows on his knees, hid his face in his hands. He had never expected to have a conversation like this with his mother, let alone his grandmother, and he wondered what she'd come out with next.

'Don't get all uptight about it,' Lila said, leaning forward. 'In my day we weren't supposed to talk about these things. But now sex is everywhere, people are doing it and talking about it and filming it everywhere, it's even on the ABC, but talk about important things with your own family – oh no, that's not on. Doesn't make sense to me.' She struggled to her feet and walked back to the window. 'Come over here,' she ordered, pointing out into the street. 'Look at this.'

David joined her at the window, looking down to where a couple of teenage girls in revealing halter tops, low-cut jeans and bare midriffs were joking with some boys on the opposite side of the street. 'Look at them,' she said. 'Midwinter and they're half naked. Nothing left to the imagination, let it all hang out. I don't get it. What's it all for if people still can't talk frankly when it's important? All that free love, the pill, getting rid of taboos, but you can't talk to Judy and you think I shouldn't even know about it.'

'It's not really as simple as that, Gran,' David began.

'It's only as complicated as you make it.' Her eyes had an unusual watery brightness about them. He slipped his arm through hers and led her back to the couch.

'Come and sit down,' he said. 'No need to get upset.'

'Well, I am,' she said, rummaging in her bag for a handkerchief. 'I don't like this business with Fran and Caro, and I don't like you being unhappy. You've got to have courage, David. I know you're thinking I'm a stupid old woman who's losing her marbles –'

'No,' he protested.

'Yes you do, you all do. Maybe I'm a bit forgetful, and maybe I do like a bit of tinned ham and go on about the old days, I don't mind you all having a laugh about that. But I still know what's what, and what I know is this, that's a lovely girl you've got there, and she's not stupid, you know. Give her a bit of respect, for goodness sake, talk to her about it. Let her talk to you. Be brave, take a risk, sort it out. Otherwise you're going to be a lonely old man before you're forty.'

Lila blew her nose loudly, and then took off her glasses and wiped them with a tissue. 'That's what I came to say. And don't tell her I told you, otherwise she'll be really upset with me. Now you can make me that cup of tea and then you can drive me over to Caro's place. I need to set her straight, and then your mother. I really don't know what this family's coming to.'

Fran dropped the Boatshed proposal on the table and sank down onto the wooden bench. 'Lord give me strength. Thanks for meeting me, Bonnie. You are the only fixed point of sanity in my crazy world.'

Bonnie, who had been waiting anxiously for her to arrive, and was unsure how having had time to peruse the proposal would have affected her, raised her eyebrows in surprise, but decided not to push her luck. 'Tell me about it over lunch. The minestrone here is always good.'

'That'll do me,' Fran sighed, unbuttoning her coat, 'With heaps of parmesan and some Italian bread.'

'I see you got your scarf back.'

'I did. Almost had to rip it off Mum's neck. She thinks she has first rights on anything purple. She turned up on my doorstep wearing it a couple of days ago.'

'A visit?' Bonnie said. 'I thought she only went out with you or the kids.'

'So did I, but she decided that we all needed a good shake-up, beginning with David. Not sure what that was about – she said it was confidential. But then she got him to drive her to Caro and then to me, because she wanted to fix things up between us.'

'Two minestrones, bread and couple of glasses of the house red,' Bonnie told the waiter. 'Do they need fixing up?'

'Yes,' said Fran, 'but that's another story, and it'll take more than the purple people-eater to fix that. Mothers! Honestly, they can really be a pain in the bum.'

Bonnie nodded. 'Must be something in the air. Mine's been really weird since her holiday. She seems to be going through some sort of teenage phase again.'

'Oh well,' Fran said, 'I guess we've got this to look forward to in twenty-five years' time. Promise you'll tell me if I get like that?' She put her hand on the Boatshed file. 'This is great, Bon, I want to be in it, and I'm sorry for being so negative. It came at a bad time, too much happening, and I was scared of the whole thing. But I've had time to think about it and – well, it's great.'

'Really?' Bonnie was cautious – the leap from antipathy to enthusiasm was a big one and it had come more quickly than she had expected after that first meeting. 'Have you talked to anyone else about it?'

Fran nodded. 'Caro first, before we fell out. David. And Tom, who's the business and finance editor at the paper.'

'That sounds good. You must have some questions.'

'Yes, but they'll wait. The main thing is I want you to know that I'm in, and that I'm really grateful for the chance –'

'Don't, Fran.' Bonnie held up her hand. 'This is business, not charity.'

'I know, but it's an opportunity that I wouldn't otherwise have had, and that, and your faith in me, means a lot. It's changing the way I feel. And there's something else. Two things, actually.'

They sat back as the waiter arrived with two huge bowls of soup and their wine.

'Cheers,' said Bonnie, raising her glass. 'To the Boatshed. So, tell me the rest of it.'

'I've had an offer for the house. I've got it here with me. I thought you might have a look at it and tell me what you think. And I should have told you this before, but what with Caro's accident it slipped my mind. Remember that publisher we met at the dinner, the one I grumbled about because I thought he wanted me to review his books? I had lunch with him the day of Caro's accident. It turns out he actually wants me to write a book. He called me again this morning, and I gave him your number.' She grinned and took another sip of her wine. 'I told him to contact my agent!'

TWENTY

Will could hardly believe his luck. Here he was waiting at Hong Kong airport for Sylvia to arrive on the Cathay Pacific flight from London, and then come back with him to his apartment, and he had Bonnie to thank for it. Not even in his wildest dreams could he have imagined this perfect situation falling into his lap, especially after he'd discovered that Sylvia was going away just a few days after he had arrived in Melbourne. He had been cursing fate and rummaging around for what to do next, when God obliged by sending snow to Mount Macedon.

When he'd suggested driving up to see it he'd thought that for sure there would be three of them, but Bonnie, bless her, had opted out, and he and Sylvia had spent a delightful day, walking, having coffee and then lunch, and browsing through a couple of excellent second-hand bookshops. She still seemed to be ignoring his signals but Will was sure he must be making progress. And then, the very next day, two days before Sylvia was due to leave, it happened.

'I think I might make a little change on my return flight,' she'd said at breakfast. 'That is, unless they're going to charge me a huge amount for it.'

'Think you'll stay a bit longer?' Bonnie had asked from behind the newspaper.

'No, it's not that, but I have this half-day wait in Hong Kong on the way back, and I've always wanted to go there. I thought I might stay a day or two, do a bit of sightseeing before I come home.'

183

Will, who was pretending to be buried in the *Australian Financial Review*, refrained from leaping up and punching the air. Instead he waited to see what would happen next and it just got better and better.

'Good idea,' Bonnie said. 'I love Hong Kong, so does Will – in fact, maybe you could stay at his place there. Will, what do you think?'

Will kept on looking at the paper, feigning intense concentration. 'Will, wake up! Sylvia's thinking of stopping off in Hong Kong on the way back. I said maybe she could stay at your place.'

Will looked up, affecting the uninterested manner he sometimes used in meetings. 'By all means,' he said, forcing his eyes back down to the paper. 'You're welcome to use it any time, Sylvia. Just let me know when and I'll call the concierge and tell her to get it ready for you.' Turning his attention back to the paper he was amazed that, despite his excitement, he was able to play it so cool.

Eventually the two women agreed that Hong Kong would be worth three nights, especially as Sylvia wouldn't have to pay for a hotel.

'All right, Will?' Bonnie asked. She called out the dates and Will slowly folded the paper, went over to his briefcase, which was lying on a nearby chair, took out his Palm Pilot and pretended to consult his diary.

'Yes, that's fine,' he said. 'There's a chance that I'll be there myself then, but there are two bedrooms and you won't be in my way at all.'

'Splendid,' said Bonnie. 'And maybe you can show Sylvia around a bit if you've got time.'

'Oh, I don't want to be a nuisance,' Sylvia said. 'I'm sure I can find my own way around.'

'I'm sure you can,' Will said. 'Just the same, it'll be a pleasure – I can certainly fit in a brief stint as tour guide.'

Sylvia fetched her tickets and reached for the telephone. 'I'd better call Cathay,' she said. 'I hope I can switch to a later date. Do you think they'll charge extra? I travel so rarely, I'm not used to this sort of thing.'

'It depends on the basis of the fare that Colin booked for you,' Will said. 'Look, would you like me to do that for you? I have to call them about my own bookings.'

Like a lamb to the slaughter, Sylvia handed over her tickets with a grateful smile. 'Would you really, Will? That's kind of you. But if they want a big fee for changing it . . .'

'I won't commit you to anything without telling you,' he said. 'I'll do it today.' He slipped the ticket into the inside pocket of his jacket, and stacked his plate and coffee cup in the dishwasher.

'Gotta get off now,' he said, glancing at his watch and realising he really was cutting it fine for his nine o'clock meeting. 'See you both later.'

He let himself out of the house, and only when he was safely ensconced in the hire car and had turned the corner out of Bonnie's drive did he let out the yee-ha that was bursting to escape. Then he switched the radio on to Triple J and began singing along very loudly with Bono in the wrong key.

It had cost Will a stupid amount to change Sylvia's flight, not that he cared about that, he'd told her it had been simple with no charge. And he'd rapidly rearranged his schedule to accommodate Sylvia's visit to Hong Kong.

A few weary looking passengers began to emerge from customs, gazing around hopefully for friends and relatives, manoeuvring trolleys laden with luggage. Will shifted impatiently from one foot to the other. He was wearing an open-necked blue shirt and his favourite beige suit that was made from a mightily expensive linen and silk blend. He hoped he looked relaxed but also as though he was busy and had just come from some mid-level meeting, rather than having spent a long time wandering back and forth between the bedroom and bathroom thinking about what to wear and how he wanted her to see him.

The trickle of passengers seemed extraordinarily slow and with every moment Will grew more and more tense. Finally the doors opened again and there, behind a huge man in an anorak and baseball cap, he saw her. She was wearing a navy blue cotton shirt and stonewashed jeans, and she had a pale blue jumper draped over her shoulders, the sleeves tied in a loose knot below the open neck of her shirt. Will breathed a huge sigh of relief and his stomach lurched in excitement. She didn't see him at first, but then, she wasn't expecting him, so it was only as she passed through the guard rail out into the main concourse and he stepped up to her that she saw him and broke into a smile.

'Will, how lovely!' she cried, leaning forward to kiss him on both cheeks. 'How kind of you. I didn't expect you to meet me. I was going to brave my first Hong Kong taxi.'

Will took hold of the trolley and steered it through the crowd. 'We can do that together,' he said. 'I always think it's nicer to be met when you're in a strange place. How was your flight?'

'Oh, long and exhausting. I was in the window seat and that huge man in the baseball cap was next to me. He sort of overflowed, and when he fell asleep he expanded even further.'

A taxi stopped in front of them and the driver sprung the boot and jumped out to load the luggage.

Will handed Sylvia into the back seat, slipped in after her and gave the address to the driver.

'Fasten seatbelts,' he said with a smile. 'There's nothing quite like Hong Kong taxis, and Hong Kong traffic – you take your life in your hands.' And, true to form, the driver slammed his foot on the accelerator and they shot forward.

Sylvia emerged from the shower feeling as though she had been reborn. The journey had left her tired and irritable and as they were coming in to land she had wished fervently that, much as she hated the confines of the plane, she could just stay put, fly on and get back home to a normal life. When she caught sight of Will in the arrivals hall she'd had mixed feelings. There was the initial relief of seeing a friendly face in a strange place, but she'd hoped for solitude. Will, however, was surprisingly sensitive; once they were inside the tiny flat in Kowloon he made her some tea, showed her the essentials and then announced that he had things to do and he'd be back around six. Perhaps she'd like to have a rest and a shower, and then, if she didn't have other plans, he'd love to take her out for dinner.

Enormously relieved, Sylvia opened her bag, hung a few things in the wardrobe and flung herself on the bed. She had more than three hours to herself and, while she was tossing up the relative merits of having a shower first, she fell fast asleep and woke just before six to darkness and confusion about where she was. She sat up rubbing her eyes, feeling dirty and wretched. Her mouth was dry, her eyes scratchy and she shivered in the sudden chill of waking. Stripping off her clothes she staggered blindly under the shower, waiting for the hot water to wash away the remnants of the flight and the memory of the awkward, painful parting from Kim and the children. Slowly her mood began to lift and by the time she stepped out and started to dry her hair, she was revived and ready for the evening. She could hear Will, singing in his own shower.

'So, tell me about your holiday,' Will said as they sat in the softly lit restaurant overlooking the harbour. 'Did you have a good time with your daughter?'

She had hoped he wouldn't ask but now the question came as a relief and she knew she needed to talk about it. 'Yes and no,' she began. 'It was wonderful to see them all. The children have grown so much you can actually have conversations with them and they're so sweet and funny. So that was lovely, and England in summer was beautiful, so different from my other visits, but . . .'

'But?' Will prompted, signalling the waiter to pour the wine.

'But two small children all day every day can be exhausting, and then there were some other complications . . .' This would be so tedious to a young single man who would probably prefer to be having dinner with a girlfriend or business associate. 'Oh, never mind,' she said, 'I won't bore you with all that.'

'Tell me,' he said. 'I'd like to hear it and you look as though you need to talk about it.'

'Well, yes,' she agreed, 'I do . . .'

*

'And so, you see, it became an incredibly hot potato,' she said with a sigh, having related Kim's suggestion and her own very mixed feelings. 'It seemed to overhang everything we did together from then on. But, Will, I couldn't decide, not just like that, not with Kim standing over me for an answer. And then Bonnie called a couple of times to see if I'd decided about the Boatshed. It was all just too hard. What do you think?'

The waiter removed the remains of the light, fragrant soup, and placed clean plates and cutlery in front of them. Will twisted the stem of his wineglass.

'It doesn't matter what I think.'

'But how does it sound to an outsider? Am I being unreasonable and indecisive?'

He emptied his glass and reached out for the bottle, pouring some first into Sylvia's glass.

'Not in the least. In fact, you *are* being decisive – you're deciding not to make any hasty decisions. That's a decision in itself. A sound one. If you *really* want to know what I think, it's that you should just take your time. You've spent your life doing what other people expected of you; don't let anyone hassle you now.'

'But Kim needs an answer and so does Bonnie.'

'Sorry if I sound harsh about this,' Will said, his tone brisker now. 'I don't know your daughter, but as well as wanting you there because you're her mother and she loves you, she's got her own agenda. If she wasn't anxious to go back to work she'd be giving you time to make up your mind. As for Bonnie, it's much the same – you've got the skills she needs, and she wants to work with you because of your friendship. But you don't have to let their priorities dominate. They'll both survive without you if that's what you decide, and both of them will, in the long run, accept your decision.'

Sylvia nodded. 'You're right, I suppose, but I feel I owe Bonnie something because she's been so good to me.'

Will shook his head. 'Bonnie wouldn't see it that way, I'm sure. But she does need to get on with the business. Can I stick my neck out and offer a bit more overbearing male advice?'

'Please do.'

'Moving to England is the big question – you must take your time – but you don't have to see the Boatshed as a decision for the rest of your life. You need a job and Bonnie can give you one. Work for her, set up the gallery, enjoy that while you make up your mind.'

As they left the restaurant and joined the busy crowds of evening shoppers and sightseers, Sylvia felt as though she was in a luxurious space-time capsule isolated from her anxieties about the future.

'Thanks, Will,' she said as they strolled towards the harbour. 'The conversation, the meal, everything . . . you probably don't realise what a help it's been – just what I needed.'

Spontaneously she took his arm, then felt him press it to his side. He placed his other hand over hers and they walked on in silence to the harbour wall. The water was a gently swaying mass of lights and beyond them the dark silhouette of Hong Kong Island, speckled with more lights, was outlined against the night sky.

'Would you like to go across to the island tomorrow?' Will asked. 'Lots to see and the views from the Peak are magnificent.'

She nodded. 'I thought I'd get the ferry.'

'Would you like a tour guide?' he asked.

'Well . . .' she faltered. 'I don't want to take up your time, you've got business here . . .'

He turned to face her, taking her hand in both of his. 'Nothing that won't wait,' he said. 'There's nothing I'd rather do than introduce you to Hong Kong.'

It was after ten the following evening when, sated with the sights and sounds of Hong Kong – the streets hung with Chinese banners, dazzling shop windows, the colours and spicy scents of the markets, and the breathtaking views from the Peak – they stepped off the ferry from the island and made their way back to the apartment. Sylvia slipped off her shoes and padded to the French windows, sliding them open and stepping out onto the balcony, hypnotised once again by the lights of the city and harbour. She loved the humidity that turned tiredness into exquisite languor and she stood on her toes, stretching her arms above her head, enjoying the awareness of her own body in the night air.

She didn't hear Will behind her but when he slipped his arms around her waist it felt totally natural to lean back into him, and gently he bent his head to rest his cheek on her hair before letting his lips brush the length of her neck. She stretched again, responding to his touch, relishing the feel of his hands on her body, his mouth against her skin. It was so long since she had felt desire she had forgotten its power, and now her body surged with life and she turned in his arms and reached up to touch his face.

'I've dreamed of this,' he whispered. 'From the moment I first saw you in the kitchen I've wanted you.' And in that split second of anticipation before he kissed her, Sylvia wondered what she was doing. She pulled back slightly but, sensing her hesitation, Will drew her closer, his mouth closing on hers.

She was nervous at first – Colin had been her only lover and always a somewhat distracted one. Even in their first months of marriage he was cautious and polite, gentle but uninspired, and she had followed his lead. As Will drew her into the bedroom she feared her own awkwardness and inexperience, but his touch seemed to ignite her passion so that she was yearning to abandon herself to him in a way she had never imagined. As the night wore on and merged into morning and they finally fell into exhausted sleep, Sylvia discovered that she could be wild and uninhibited, that she could take the initiative as well as simply responding. The old Sylvia had been blown away and in her place was a woman confidently rejoicing in her sexuality.

Two days later, on the morning of her fifty-sixth birthday and the day she was due to fly back to Melbourne, Sylvia woke, for the first time ever, to breakfast in bed.

'Not really! Not ever before?' Will asked in amazement, slipping back into bed beside her. 'Not even on your birthday or Mother's Day?'

'Especially not Mother's Day,' Sylvia said, looking down at the tray covered with a white serviette, the toast cut in triangles.

'Mother's Day is a big day for the church but it doesn't leave much time for church wives, or, at least, it didn't in our house. But I did get breakfast in bed in hospital when Kim was born.'

Will pulled the bedclothes up to his waist, shaking his head. 'What a strange life,' he said, turning to her to take her hand. 'I don't want to go home.'

She smiled. 'Me neither – this feels totally decadent. Perfectly in line with your reputation.'

'Bonnie warned you, then?'

'Warned me? No – I doubt it crossed her mind that I would be in a position to *need* a warning.'

'So d'you think I'm an opportunist?'

'Possibly.' She reached out to stroke his shoulder, sliding her hand down over his chest. 'But weren't we both making the most of the opportunity? Here we are in the same place at the same time. It's not as though you lured me here!'

'I meant what I said that first night,' he said, trapping her hand and holding it. 'I wanted you right from the start. I schemed and dreamed and tried to look and sound really cool, but for the past few weeks I've been burning up inside.'

Sylvia tilted her head to rest it on his shoulder. 'Dear Will,' she said. 'You made me feel young again, made me feel very special.'

'You *are* special,' he said. 'Stay here with me, Sylvia. Let's change the flights and stay a bit longer.'

She shivered slightly and turned to look at him, drawing the sheet over her, conscious suddenly of her older body against his smooth flesh. His touch, the scent of his body, his sexual energy thrilled her, but his intensity also threatened to overwhelm her.

'I need to go back, Will, make the next step of this journey.'

Will sighed. 'This time tomorrow you'll be in Melbourne and I'll be in Perth, thousands of kilometres between us. Is that what you want?'

She shook her head. 'Of course not.'

He slid down in the bed, drawing her with him. 'I don't want to let go of you,' he said softly.

'I thought that letting go was your thing.'

'It has been, but not now.'

'Ah, Will,' she said, sliding closer, curving her leg across his. 'I don't have any illusions. This has been a wonderful adventure, you've transformed me. But you'll soon file this in your black book and move on, and that's as it should be.'

'You have no idea, Sylvia,' he said, his voice husky with emotion. 'You simply have no idea.'

TWENTY-ONE

Bonnie stared into the mirror and peered closely at her face, inspecting what looked like enlarged pores on her nose and broken veins across her cheekbones. Just before Jeff died she had been thinking about cosmetic surgery: Botox for her forehead, an eye lift, perhaps, her lips, and maybe doing something with the telltale pad of flesh under her chin that screamed middle age. But since then she hadn't given it much thought, it hadn't seemed to matter so much back here in Melbourne, at least not until now. Not until her mother started behaving like a teenager.

Bonnie put a hand on either side of her face and gently drew the skin tight towards her hairline. She looked ridiculous, but if she slacked the tension a little she looked good, and she held it for a moment, contemplating a younger look. Who would she be doing it for? Herself?

Jeff had always been against it. 'You're beautiful as you are, Bon,' he'd said whenever she mentioned it. 'Why do you want to change? Growing older is okay. I'd rather have you than some bland looking thirty-year-old. Your face tells a story, our story, and I love it.' But without Jeff around, there was no one to share the story written in her face.

She released the mask she'd created and looked at herself again. The haircut had been a sound decision, and overall she looked pretty good. Perhaps she just shouldn't look at herself so closely with her glasses on. She took them off and straightened up – a little bit of distance was a big improvement. Anyway, no one cared what she looked like; she could go out looking like the Witch of Endor and no one would take any notice.

It didn't seem so long ago that heads turned whenever she walked down the street. Europeans weren't so hung up on youth as Australians; in Switzerland she had constantly felt noticed and admired as a woman, whereas here she might just as well have been invisible. But it was ironic how visible she suddenly became when someone, a man, realised that she had money. The architect, the builder, the designer, the project manager – all of them had treated her in a bored, dismissive manner until it became clear that she was not only talking big money, she actually had it. Then they started to take her seriously. She didn't doubt that if she had been twenty years younger, or male, the original response would have been very different. There was considerable satisfaction in the knowledge that she could tell them all to get stuffed and she'd find someone else, but it had shown her that to be an older woman and not have the power of money behind you would make life a very different prospect.

Bonnie had encouraged Fran to respond to the offer for her house with a counter offer, driving the price up by another five thousand dollars, and she had gone with her to the real estate agent's office. Watching Fran's anxiety as they waited for the agent to call the potential buyer, she was reminded again of how comfortably insulated she had always been from the sort of financial concerns that had dominated her friends' lives. To Fran, the five thousand additional dollars represented a great deal more than just a well-done deal.

Bonnie turned out the bathroom light, went downstairs to the kitchen and stared at the fridge, wondering what she would eat. It was strange being alone in the house. Sylvia was away, Will had left for Hong Kong and now, this evening, for the third time in a fortnight, Irene was out and presumably not coming home. Bonnie, thankful that at least she hadn't yet been faced with Hamish in his pyjamas, realised that her own behaviour was probably holding this reality at bay. She had been so shocked when Irene told her that she and Hamish were 'an item' that she had actually dropped her cup and it had smashed on the kitchen tiles. The job of cleaning up the broken china and the tea had given her a few moments' breathing space but when it was done she and Irene had stood there looking at each other and Bonnie had been totally lost for words.

'You look rather shocked, dear,' Irene had said, returning to the task of unpacking the shopping.

'I am,' she managed to say, wondering if it was really just shock that she felt. 'You mean . . . you mean, you and Hamish are . . .'

'Having a relationship,' Irene supplied, not looking up. 'Yes.'

'Are you sure?' Bonnie said, realising before the words were out of her mouth that it was a perfectly ridiculous question. 'I mean,' she said, blushing, 'well . . . a relationship.'

Irene put a packet of flour into the pantry and turned to face her daughter. 'Look, Bonnie, we both know what a relationship involves, or do you want me to spell it out? Hamish and I are old friends, and while we were in Greece we spent a lot of time together. I called to talk to you about it one night but it was awkward, you were busy. Anyway, our friendship has developed into something deeper, more intimate. We're both very happy about it, and so are our friends.' She paused, taking in Bonnie's face and her body language. 'I hoped you'd be happy too. I've been on my own for a long time and I never expected to love someone or be loved again.'

Bonnie's shock and embarrassment outweighed sensitivity. 'But you're eighty, Mum!' she said. 'People don't have . . . aff . . . relationships, at eighty.'

'Of course they do, Bonnie, don't be so naïve. People have affairs when they're even older than us, even when they're in hostels and nursing homes. It's just that everyone pretends it doesn't happen. People don't stop being sexual once they draw the pension, Bonnie.'

Bonnie held up her hand. 'Don't! Please don't! You're my mother, for goodness sake.'

'Yes,' Irene said, clearly both irritated and hurt, 'and you're old enough to know better than to behave like this.' With that she marched out of the kitchen leaving Bonnie alone, confused, and surrounded by unpacked shopping.

Since then the atmosphere had been arctic, but Bonnie couldn't overcome her embarrassment and distaste. Why couldn't they just be friends? Surely they were both old enough to know better than to disrupt everyone's lives by behaving like teenagers. She had been too embarrassed even to tell Fran about it, and she just hoped it would all be over soon, certainly before Sylvia got back, and then no one else need ever know.

There was a plastic container of soup in the fridge and Bonnie took it out, put some in a bowl, popped it into the microwave and ate it sitting alone in the kitchen. She tried not to think about the fact that it was eight o'clock on Saturday night and here she was alone in the silent house. Sylvia's presence had saved her from the emptiness she had felt when her mother first went away, and somehow she hadn't expected to feel like this again. Now that she had the Boatshed her days were busy and satisfying, but suddenly her aloneness struck her with greater force than before. Fran had her mother and her children, Sylvia had Kim and her grandchildren and now, even her own mother had someone special. Bonnie couldn't actually bring herself to say, or even think, the word 'lover'. It wasn't that she had anything against Hamish personally, it just seemed so undignified and confronting.

It was cold downstairs and Bonnie washed her soup bowl and decided that the cosiest place would be bed. She took a hot shower and climbed into bed at quarter to nine, surrounded by pillows, and flicked through the television channels to find something to watch. Harrison Ford and Julie Andrews seemed to be caught up in a European hotel avoiding some spies and she settled back to watch. It was in one of the commercial breaks that she heard the front door open. She flicked the mute switch and heard voices, her mother's and Hamish's deeper one. Bonnie sank back onto her pillows, staring at the soundless pictures. Was Hamish going to stay the night? Would she have to face him in the morning?

Harrison and Julie climbed into bed together and Bonnie was consumed by a flush of heat as she pictured Irene and Hamish doing the same at the other end of the house. The thought that they might be having sex under the same roof while she lay alone in bed watching a movie had a horrible fascination. She flicked off the mute and the sound came up. Trying to force the images out of her mind she watched the remainder of the movie without really seeing it, until finally she turned off the lights and lay down in the darkness, wondering where they were and what they were doing, and what *she* would do when she saw Hamish in the morning.

Jacka Boulevard was busy with traffic and pedestrians. Despite the cold wind, the arrival of spring seemed to have brought everyone out of their houses. Fran turned away from the water-front and slowly made her way in the stream of traffic across Acland Street back towards St Kilda Road. She had driven past the house countless times but this was the fourth time she had arranged to go inside, and this time was different. This time she almost owned it – the contract was signed, the deposit paid and in three weeks' time she could move in.

She parked on the opposite side of the street, got out of the car and stood looking at it, imagining herself inside her new home, her own things around her, familiar furniture filling the rooms, her books on shelves, pictures and photographs on the walls. Each time she saw it she was more convinced that she had made the right decision. She took a set of kitchen steps out of the boot, locked the car, crossed the road, and went in through the wrought-iron gate and up the three steps to the front door. She wanted to do some measuring, work out what would fit where and what would simply have to go. In her pocket she had a list of things to check, a measuring tape and a copy of the floor plan.

It was a small Federation terrace, one of six, renovated in trad-itional style, but with all the convenience of a new townhouse. The walls of the original entrance hall had been removed so that the front door opened into a light living room, with a broad shal-low arch to the kitchen. Beyond that, the old sleepout had been converted to a breakfast room with glass doors opening to a small courtyard enclosed by walls of recycled brick. Upstairs there were two bedrooms and a bathroom fully tiled in black and white. If she had to design a place for herself, Fran thought, it would have looked like this. Not for the first time, she sighed with pleasure at the sunlit spaces, the pale polished timber floors and the freshness of the new interior within the original shell.

She glanced at her watch. David had promised to come and help her but there was plenty to be getting on with until he arrived. Carefully she checked the measurements of the fridge alcove. Her commercial fridge was to go to the Boatshed, as was the huge freezer. How nice it would be to have a normal domestic kitchen, to keep her work away from her home. Sylvia was due back the following day and Fran wanted to get her ideas about curtains and colour schemes as soon as possible. She measured the width of the lounge windows and set up the ladder to measure the height of the glass doors at the rear.

'Come on in, it's open,' she called when she heard a tap at the front door. 'You're just in time to help me with this. I need you to read the height measurement.' And she twisted slightly on the ladder and saw not David, but Caro, an awkward, rotund figure shifting her weight from one foot to the other in the middle of the empty room.

'Hi,' Caro said. 'I came to see the house and . . . well . . . you.'

Fran stepped down and stared at her daughter. It was more than four weeks since she had seen her at the hospital and Caro seemed to have got much bigger very quickly. 'Hi,' she said. 'You'd better sit down,' and she carried the steps through so that Caro could sit on them.

Mother and daughter looked at each other across a silence charged with unspoken accusations and misunderstandings.

'How are you?' Fran asked, breaking it.

Caro nodded. 'Okay, I suppose, I don't know, really. I don't know how it ought to feel.'

'No one does,' Fran said quickly. 'Best not to worry, just take it one day at a time.' She knew she must sound pathetic but she was operating in a purely mechanical way, unable to summon any feelings, as though a surfeit of them had made her shut down.

There was silence again. Caro rubbed the toe of her shoe against the edge of the steps. Fran, wary and wondering why she had come, leaned against the kitchen bench and folded her arms.

'So, what do you think of it?' she said eventually.

'Lovely, really lovely,' Caro said, looking around. 'Two bedrooms upstairs?'

Fran nodded. 'You must be pleased,' Caro said.

Looking beyond Caro, out through the front window onto the street, Fran could see David sitting in his car reading the paper. Obviously this was a put-up job, an ambush. 'Why did you come, Caro?' she asked. 'Was it the visit from Gran?'

Caro looked away, brushing her eyes with the back of her hand. 'Partly . . . we did have a talk.'

'I bet you did,' Fran said dryly, surprised at her own cynicism. 'And she told you to come and see me and apologise.'

Caro nodded. 'She explained a lot of things, and she told me what she thought about the way I've been. Not just now, for a long time.'

Fran waited, trying to quell the resentment that was rearing its head. What was she supposed to do, open her arms to Caro only to get knocked back yet again? It had happened one time too many. 'I'm sure you had your reasons,' she said, hearing the flat, uncompromising tone of her own voice. 'But thanks for coming. I wanted you to see the house.'

A few weeks earlier Fran would have grasped this moment irrespective of the emotional cost, but that day in the hospital she had crushed the inner victim that had for so long dominated her relationship with her daughter. She loved Caro as much as ever, but they had to move on to something new and different, and she knew it would take more than this tense encounter to get them there. Caro's eyes were bright with tears. Fran handed her a packet of tissues from her bag and slipped an arm around her shoulders.

'David's out there in the car,' she said. 'Why don't you go and tell him to come in. I can finish these measurements and then we can go down to Acland Street and get some lunch. You shouldn't be standing about here like this.'

*

Lila was quite pleased with herself. Her crusade to sort out her family had been at least partially successful. She was pretty confident that she had straightened David out and brought Caro back into line – only Fran had remained recalcitrant and told her to mind her own business. But Fran had always been stubborn and Lila had to admit that she'd put up with a lot from Caro over the years. Even so, she remained concerned about the two of them. Caro needed her mother right now and Fran would always regret it if she let her pride get in the way of sharing this time with her.

Lila realised she might have to put a bit more work into resolving that particular crisis; meanwhile, she had other things on her mind. Taking the initiative had done her good, brought back the confidence she'd lost. She was only eighty, or maybe a bit more, not that it really mattered. She had plenty of energy but she couldn't walk as far as she used to, and that interfered with her independence. There were a few people in the retirement village who used four-wheeled motor scooters to get around, and one even had a sun canopy. Now that, she thought, might be just what she needed to help her get out and about a bit more.

'I want to buy one of those scooter things, Ray,' she said, sitting down on the chair in the village manager's office. 'Something like Mr Pirelli has up in Eden Close.'

Ray Barton got up from the desk and took a box file down from the shelf. 'Easy-peasey, Mrs Whittaker,' he said, shuffling through some brochures. 'Lots to choose from. Have a look at some of these. I can even get the salespeople to bring a couple over for you to try out.'

Lila liked Ray, but she did wonder why he insisted on always wearing a safari suit. She didn't really follow men's fashion but even she knew that safari suits had been out for years. She'd often thought of mentioning it to him but had never found quite the right moment. She also detested it when he said things like 'easy-peasey' or 'okey-dokey', which she was sure he only said to the residents – he'd hardly be talking like that to his mates at the golf club where he played a round every Wednesday and Sunday. But he was a good-hearted man and he ran the place efficiently, so she hadn't said anything.

'They run on rechargeable batteries,' Ray explained, spreading the brochures out on the desk. 'Most of them do about thirty kilometres per charge. They start at just under three thousand dollars, but we can get a better price for you if you buy it through the village. This is the one Mr Pirelli's got.' He pointed to a smart looking scooter with gleaming silver paintwork and a black trim. 'Very reliable and absolutely stable, easy to get on and off.'

Lila looked at the pictures with a rising sense of excitement. She'd been worried about the price, but they weren't as expensive as she'd expected. It would be an investment, a small price to pay for independence. She'd spent a bit in the last couple of years what with changing her colour scheme, but she could still afford this.

'Will I need a licence for it?'

Ray shook his head. 'No, but of course it's pavements and footpaths only. No tearing up and down the freeway.'

Lila turned over another page and saw a slightly sleeker design, this time finished in canary yellow, with a shiny black basket on the front.

'That's nice,' she said. 'Pity it's not purple.'

'It comes in a range of colours, I think,' Ray said, picking up the brochure. 'Yes, look here. Available in a range of colours: cobalt blue, emerald, ebony, crimson and purple. Just your colour, Mrs Whittaker. Want me to arrange an inspection?'

Lila walked back up to her unit holding the papers. Ray had photocopied the brochure for her, and given her an article from *Choice* magazine comparing the merits of various brands. He'd even got on to the sales rep while she was there and arranged for a couple of models to be brought over for her to try out later in the week.

'I'd like you to come along too, Ray,' she'd said. 'You're experienced in this sort of thing.'

'My pleasure,' he replied. 'And you don't have to make a decision on the spot. Try them out and then you'll probably want to talk to your daughter about it, get her to come and have a look. The rep can always come back.'

'Absolutely not,' Lila said, feeling pretty sure that Fran would not approve of the idea. 'Fran's got enough on her plate at present. I trust your advice, and I'm going to have a chat with Mr Pirelli.' But as she put her key in the front door, Lila knew for sure that very soon she would be cruising around Hawthorn and Abbotsford under her own steam, and she thought she'd go for yellow. She could see herself in her purple pants and jacket astride the yellow scooter – she'd always had a flair for colour combinations.

David had not recovered from Lila's visit. His grandmother's desire for his happiness had touched him deeply, there was something strong and proud about her determination to sort them all out, but her method had embarrassed him. Worst of all was the thought of Lila and Jodie discussing him over the blood samples. If there was anything designed to make him panic and back off even further it was that. The morning following Lila's visit he didn't walk down to the coffee shop, and he didn't go the next day, or the day after that. And when he got off the tram in the evenings after teaching late classes, he walked a longer route home to avoid passing Jodie's house. But all the time he was desperately trying to avoid her, he desperately wanted to see her.

About four days later he hurried from the shower to hear her leaving a message on the answering machine and stood there naked, dripping onto the polished boards, listening to her telling him she'd missed seeing him around, and wondered if he was okay and did he want to go to a party on Saturday.

'You're a total dickhead, Davo, you know that, don't you?' Matt said at half-time as they sat with a pizza miserably watching Geelong make mincemeat of Essendon in the semi-final. 'You are going to fuck this right up if you don't sort yourself out, mate.'

David reached out for another slice of pizza and drew back again as his liver flagged a warning. 'I know,' he said, 'but I don't know what to say to her.'

'Just have it out,' Matt said, getting up to fetch a second Coke from the fridge. 'You can't go on like this. Your gran's right. Look, what's the worst that can happen? You talk to her and she tells you to fuck off. At least then you'll know where you are. Better than being stuck here in no-man's land. If you're not careful she'll tell you to fuck off anyway, for being a dickhead. What have you got to lose?'

What he did have to lose, of course, was hope. A mindless sort of hope that somehow he'd wake up one morning and it would all be all right without him having had to do anything about it. It wasn't much of a consolation but it did form the basis of most of his daydreams at present. It was only when reality got in the way that he was reminded that he was simply being childish.

Finally, on the Monday morning after Jodie's unreturned phone call, he summoned up the courage to walk down to the coffee shop, playing mind games with himself all the way. If she was there it was a sign that he should bite the bullet, ask her out and then have 'the conversation', which had by now assumed ridiculous proportions in his imagination. If she wasn't there it would be a sign that it wasn't meant to be.

Turning the corner to the coffee shop, his heart was thumping as though he'd done a couple of circuits of the park at a fast run. He was half a block away from the café when he saw the glass door swing open and Jodie walk out, coffee in hand. He jogged a few steps to catch up with her but stopped in his tracks as a man followed her out and over to her car. He watched as they both got in, talking, sipping coffee from identical cardboard beakers. He was too late, there was someone else. David wasn't a natural pessimist but he couldn't avoid the feeling that this was the way his life would be from now on.

TWENTY-TWO

'Now, Fran, I really want you to try and play it cool,' Bonnie said. 'Don't be too enthusiastic, we want to strike a good deal. Bannister Books want you and it's up to them to come to the table with a good offer.'

'But I want to do it anyway,' Fran said. 'Even if they weren't paying me anything I'd want to do it. It's what I've always wanted. This must sound ridiculous coming from me but the money almost doesn't matter.'

Bonnie shook her head as she clicked the remote control to lock the car. 'I know that, but it's the principle. We have to get it right. The concept has to be what you want and they've got to demonstrate a commitment by paying for it. We need to make sure they'll market and promote it effectively. And you have to have a say about the photographs and the cover, all that. They know the deal, they're not expecting to get you for nothing, not even for peanuts, so wind your neck in and try not to look as though you just won Lotto.'

'I may have stuffed up the negotiating position already, actually,' Fran admitted. 'I almost kissed Jack Bannister the first time he mentioned it. In fact, I was so ecstatic that if it hadn't been for having to race off to the hospital I'd have had sex with him on the restaurant table if he'd asked. But then, he probably wouldn't have asked anyway.'

'Don't be so negative,' Bonnie said, taking her arm. 'He should be so lucky, to get you to write a book let alone have sex with him anywhere. Self-esteem, Fran, come along now. What's he like, anyway?'

'Not bad looking, very nice, sense of humour. You'll like him.'

'Not till I see the colour of his contract,' Bonnie said, decisively straightening her shoulders as they walked through the Sofitel Centre. 'He's bringing someone called Len with him. He's the food books publisher, the person who'll work with you on the book.'

Fran was more than a little impressed to find herself on the way to a meeting with a publisher, accompanied by her agent. She took a deep breath as they knocked at the door, and then another even deeper one when she saw the size of Jack's hotel suite and the stunning views from the windows. Bonnie squeezed her elbow painfully hard just as she was about to launch into a flood of nervous appreciation.

'It's lovely to see you again, Fran,' Jack said, leading the way through to an alcove off the main area where a meeting table was set up. 'I hope your daughter's doing well. This is my sister Len – Lenore. She's in charge of our food books. Please make yourselves comfortable. Would you like coffee or a drink?'

The sight of Lenore Bannister pushed all Fran's worst inadequacy buttons. She was probably around sixty, and from the top of her wildly curly mop of grey hair to the toes of her elegant black boots, she oozed power and energy.

'I've read many of your columns, Fran,' she said, 'and the transcript of your speech. I'm really looking forward to working with you.'

She wore a long-sleeved black t-shirt and a long black skirt, and around her neck was a heavy silver chain with a large turquoise pendant almost the exact same colour as her extraordinary eyes. Beneath the close-fitting top the powerful muscles across her shoulders and upper arms were obvious and her large, strong gestures reminded Fran of some exotic bird. This was a woman who worked out. There wasn't an ounce of fat on her, and while her face carried signs of age, her complexion glowed with health. Fran, who had reluctantly gone back to the gym to pursue her painful relationship with the cross-trainer the previous week, felt a surge of self-pity combined with hostility.

It was a bad start, and she sat down at the table, hoping to disguise her bulk. Bonnie had nothing to worry about, she thought: she would be keeping very quiet during this meeting.

Jack had ordered coffee and it was delivered along with a selection of pastries that almost had Fran drooling, but with admirable restraint she waved the plate away. There was no way she would be caught eating such sinful food in front of Lenore, who probably lived on miso, carrots and tofu. But to her amazement, Lenore tucked into the éclairs, strawberry tartlets, and *mille-feuilles* with enthusiasm. It was immediately clear who would be doing the deal. Food and wine was Lenore's area and while Jack was the managing director, she too had a seat on the board as well as being the publisher of gourmet titles. But while Lenore was clearly out to strike the best possible deal, so was Bonnie, and Fran watched in awe as her friend dealt with Lenore's offer, playing through the deal until she got exactly what they had agreed to try for.

'Impressive, aren't they?' Jack whispered to her as he refilled her coffee cup. 'Lenore always leaves me for dead when it comes to doing deals.'

'I don't believe you,' Fran said. 'You're a team, you do the softening up and then in comes Lenore with both barrels blazing.'

He laughed. 'Well, Bonnie has a few barrels blazing herself,' he said. 'And that Boatshed project is a stunner. I'd like to see our books in the gallery there.'

It took about forty-five minutes to nut out the basics of the contract and Fran, delighted by the results, began to relax at the prospect of leaving.

'Can we have some more coffee, Jack,' Lenore said. 'And some sandwiches and bottles of water. I need to talk to Fran about the concept.' Fran stiffened as Lenore turned her turquoise gaze on her. 'We need to firm this up now, Fran, so you can start working on it as soon as possible.'

Fran was transfixed by Lenore's mesmerising eyes. She opened her mouth and shut it again.

'Contact lenses,' Lenore said. 'Just got them last week. What d'you reckon?'

'Amazing,' Fran said, relaxing a little. 'Stunning but also a bit scary.'

'Very scary to do deals with,' Bonnie said. 'I think I'll have to get some.'

'You don't need them,' Lenore countered. 'You've got great eyes. They turn to steel – I was terrified.'

They laughed and Fran thought she would probably survive the next stage of the meeting. But she had no idea what was ahead. It was another hour before they left, an hour in which Lenore challenged everything Fran said. An hour in which she had to argue to defend everything she wanted in the book, and in which Lenore made counter proposals which Fran was driven to argue against. When they finally sat back after reaching an agreement with all Fran's original ideas intact, she was totally exhausted and extremely irritable.

'Wonderful! ' Lenore said. 'It's a winner, Fran, great concept. I know we can do well with this. It's hard to find new angles for food – there's so much competition – but yours is a winner.'

Fran's jaw dropped. 'But you've been arguing with me about everything,' she said.

'Devil's advocate! I need to know you're clear about it all and that you'll organise the material, come up with the new recipes, use the historical, literary and sociological material effectively. We have to work together on this, Fran. I needed to be infected with your passion, and now I am. So, what about the title? Did you have one in mind?'

Fran hesitated, struggling with uncertainty about how they'd react. 'All the years I was thinking about the book, long before it became a reality, I did have a title in mind,' she said, glancing around the table. 'But now I think it's not really suitable.'

'So what was it?' Lenore asked, leaning forward, chin on her hands.

'Well . . . because it's obviously about food, and it links attitudes about food to love and sex and eroticism, and then there's the part about how those things really transcend levels of wealth or poverty, I'd thought of calling it *Food, Sex and Money*.'

Jack flinched and Lenore drew her breath in sharply through

her teeth. '*Food, Sex and Money*. I love it. What do you think, Jack?' she asked. 'Does it do it for you?'

Jack paused, frowning slightly. 'It does and it doesn't. I mean, I think it's valid as a title but I'd be concerned about perceptions. It might not set the right tone. This is a prestige publication . . . I'm not sure. People might be drawn to it for the wrong reasons.'

'What do you mean "the wrong reasons"?' Lenore asked.

Jack shook his head, trying to find the right words. 'I suppose I mean that they might be buying it either because of the possibly sleazy connotations around sex and money, or, indeed, *not* buying it for the same reasons.'

'I think they'd buy it in droves with a title like that,' Lenore said.

'I think Jack's right,' Bonnie said. 'It's risky.'

'Risky or risqué?' Lenore said with a laugh. 'Come on, guys, it's a great title.'

'I think they're right, Lenore,' Fran said. 'Although it's been in my head for so long, I'm not really comfortable with it now. Maybe we could have food and love in the title, instead of food and sex.'

Lenore raised her eyebrows. 'Not suggesting that they mean the same thing, I hope,' she said, looking hard at Fran, who blushed.

'No, but love is in the book – you know, the preparation of food is often about love, and . . . it's often about duty, so –'

'Food, love and duty!' Lenore cut in. 'I like that. Not as much as the other one but it works. Jack? Bonnie?'

Yes,' said Jack. 'Connotations of history and tradition, good – I like that.'

'Me too,' Bonnie said. 'It's much better.'

Fran took a deep breath, 'Okay, then?'

'Done,' Lenore said. 'I still prefer the first one, but I bow to your collective sensitivities. *Food, Love and Duty*, it is.'

'Thanks, Bon, you were brilliant,' Fran said, leaning wearily against the side of the lift. 'I've no idea how you managed it. That woman is a nightmare, and I have to work with her.'

Bonnie smiled. 'She was a tough one, but I liked her, liked them both. I think it'll be okay, Fran. You do your bit, she'll do hers. And as long as you deliver she'll stay off your back.' She swapped her briefcase to her other hand. 'While you were busy with Lenore, Jack and I were discussing the Boatshed. I'm going to take them down there tomorrow. Want to come?'

'I think I'll take a raincheck,' Fran said with a grin. 'Sylvia's going to come and see the house and then take me shopping for curtain fabric. I don't think I can face another marathon with Lenore quite so soon.' They walked together out of the lift and into the bright cold of the spring afternoon.

'Do you think Sylvia seems different?' Bonnie said as they reached the car.

Fran shrugged. 'Not really. She's probably just adjusting to being back. I thought she looked very well when we met her at the airport. More relaxed, I suppose.'

'Mmm . . . you're probably right. Maybe it's just my imagination but she looks like the cat that got the cream.'

'After all those years with the Incredible Sulk, if anyone deserves the cream it's Sylvia,' Fran said. 'Maybe she met some rich and handsome Englishman who swept her off her feet. Has she made up her mind about the Boatshed?'

'I don't know,' Bonnie said. 'I didn't like to ask her last night but I'll talk to her this evening. By the way, after you'd gone last night I did notice she'd bought a mobile phone, quite a flash one, and someone called her on it. She and Mum and I were in the living room and when it rang, Sylvia went out of the room to take the call.'

'There you are then,' Fran said triumphantly. 'I bet you anything you like she's met someone.'

'Not so soon after Colin, surely?' Bonnie said.

'It's not soon, really,' Fran said. 'Sylvia and Colin were over a long time ago. It was just that the separation was a long time coming.'

'Maybe,' Bonnie said. 'Well, good luck to her. I hope he's young and cute.'

*

Irene was determined not to let Bonnie's attitude deter her from enjoying herself with Hamish. She felt it was really too silly for words, as well as being quite hurtful and insulting. The only concession she had been prepared to make to Bonnie's sensitivities was that she had agreed with Hamish that he would not spend a night at the house just yet. She resented it somewhat – after all, it was her home and she felt she should be free to do as she wanted in it. If this had happened a year ago it wouldn't have been an issue. Irene was sure that had Bonnie been safely in Zurich with Jeff she would have been delighted to know that her mother had someone special in her life.

In her efforts to be fair, Irene had thought very seriously about how she would feel if Bonnie brought a man back to the house, and she realised that it would take some getting used to, but it certainly wasn't something she'd disapprove of. How would she feel if she bumped into Bonnie's lover in the mornings? Uncomfortable at first, she thought, but she'd accommodate it, and that's what Bonnie would have to do. Just the same, she'd decided to hold off for a while to give her daughter time to adjust, and because she really didn't want Hamish to find himself in an uncomfortable situation. A few nights earlier, Bonnie must have heard them come home after they had been to a concert. Hamish had left about eleven o'clock, but the next morning it was clear from Bonnie's stilted manner, and the way she kept glancing around surreptitiously as though expecting Hamish to materialise beside her, that she assumed he had stayed the night.

'Tell her to mind her own business,' Marjorie had said. 'It's your house. If she doesn't like it she can stay somewhere else.'

'She's my daughter and I love her, and it is her home too,' Irene said. 'You're not a mother, Marjorie. Despite all your training you don't understand what a minefield that relationship can be.'

'No, thank God,' Marjorie said. 'Far too complicated. All the same, Irene, Bonnie mustn't be allowed to spoil this for you and Hamish. You have every right to do what you want. Bonnie should be happy for you, all your friends are, even an old harridan like me.'

'I think she will be eventually,' Irene said. 'I suppose it's a surprise for her, and in a way I think it's making her feel the loss of Jeff all over again. I don't want to hurt her feelings, but at the same time I am getting a bit fed up with all this.'

'She might just be jealous, I suppose,' Marjorie said, 'although being jealous of your eighty-year-old mother is a rather extreme reaction for a mature woman.'

Irene conceded that there might be an element of jealousy along with loneliness for Jeff in Bonnie's reaction, but she thought it was more subtle and complex than that. 'It's not the idea of me having a man friend she objects to,' she said, 'it's the fact that we sleep together. She's shocked, and I think it's more than just the shock everyone feels when they have to acknowledge that their parents have a sex life. The real problem for her is that Hamish and I are old and old people having sex is somehow indecent or obscene. We're supposed to be past it.'

'Human beings are never past it,' snorted Marjorie.

'Obviously! But you know what it's like – younger women think we're old crones, that we used to be women but aren't anymore.'

'Bonnie's no spring chicken herself,' Marjorie said. 'I wonder what age she thinks is the dividing line.'

Irene shrugged. 'Goodness knows. Anyway, Sylvia's back now. A third person in the house makes it a little easier.'

Sylvia's return had certainly made a difference. The careful dances that Irene and Bonnie had been performing around each other were less apparent, the awkward silences were diluted somewhat and Sylvia's was a calming presence. Irene hoped she would stay, take the guest cottage and settle down. Now that Bonnie had the business, Irene had plenty of time to herself and Bonnie's friendship with Sylvia and Fran was an added pleasure for her too. All she wanted now was to sort out the present tension. She needed equality in the relationship with Hamish and while she could only stay at his place it was too one-sided. He might start to think about her moving in and that was definitely not on the cards. Love and companionship were enriching her independent life, but cohabitation was the fast route to domestic disharmony.

Irene ran her fingers over a beautiful length of pale green silk that Sylvia had brought her from Hong Kong. 'I know you love this colour,' she'd said, 'so I thought I could make it up for you – a dressing gown, or even a jacket. I could line it with the same colour or perhaps cream, if you like.'

Irene slipped off her jumper, stepped out of her skirt and stood in front of the bedroom mirror in her slip. She thought her skin looked like that crumpled fabric that was so popular at the moment. You wouldn't get old women wearing it, that's for sure: there'd be a puzzle to work out where the fabric ended and the skin began. She picked up the green silk and draped it around herself. It fell in sensuous silky folds over her body and she smiled at herself in the mirror. She was a different woman from the one who had set off to Greece, more like the old Irene who for so long had been aware of herself as a joyfully sexual being.

Dropping the silk she stared again at her body, the body of an old woman and entirely lacking sex appeal, but a body that once again was providing her with sensual and sexual pleasure. She understood that Hamish loved her for herself but she couldn't really understand why he loved her body and at first she had been alert for the slightest sign of disappointment, but his appreciation was evident. He loved her and wanted her, just as she loved and wanted him. He had told her that he too feared her response to his body, while she had been delighted by it. She had thought that sex and sensuality, tenderness and love were over, only to discover those precious gifts were hers once again. And, despite what Bonnie might want, Irene was determined to enjoy them to the full.

TWENTY-THREE

Sylvia was back in Australia only twenty-four hours before the cocoon of pleasure and self-indulgence established in Hong Kong melted away, and she found the new woman was still faced with the old dilemmas. In Will's apartment she had felt like a goddess, but she had also faced the reality of her age. The full-length mirror had revealed a much less than perfect body, a complexion showing the ravages of time, a woman looking good, very good, but also, very obviously, in her late fifties.

Will was an adventurer, she too had been having an adventure, and she was determined to exit with the magic intact. She would not hang on until he was ready, as he inevitably would be, to discard her. And so, despite his pleading with her to stay on, she stood her ground and insisted on travelling home as planned. Will began to talk about his next visit to Melbourne, and about keeping in touch – he would call her daily, he said, he would need to hear her voice because without her he would be bereft.

'And I bought you this,' he said, on that last morning, handing her a small silver mobile phone, with a pack of phone cards. 'I don't want to call you on Bonnie's number, that would be very awkward.' Sylvia had never owned a mobile before, although Colin had one, and Bonnie and Fran used theirs all the time. 'I'll call often,' he said, 'and text you too.' And then he had shown her how to use SMS, and she smiled and stroked his hair and teased him about his intensity when he explained pre-emptive text and how to change symbols and insert numbers.

Against her better judgment, Will had persuaded her that it was best to say nothing to Bonnie at this stage. 'Hearing about you and me is probably the last thing she needs right now,' he said, explaining that he had spoken to her on the phone a few days earlier and she seemed upset, maybe jealous, about Irene's new friendship with Hamish.

And although Sylvia thought Bonnie's reaction was probably based on something more complex than jealousy, she agreed to keep the secret for a while. It couldn't hurt, she thought, for once they left Hong Kong this relationship would have a very short life. Back home in Perth, Will would soon find another, younger object of his affections. The mobile phone connection would be short and sweet, shorter perhaps than the life of one phone card. And so when Fran and Bonnie met her at the airport, Sylvia told them at length about England, about Kim and Brendan and the grandchildren, and only briefly about her time sightseeing in Hong Kong.

'And Will looked after you well?' Bonnie asked.

'Wonderfully well,' Sylvia said. 'He was a delightful host and tour guide.'

'He's a lovely man,' Bonnie said. 'And he's been so good to me since Jeff died. Mum's fond of him too. She's back home now, of course, and looking forward to seeing you.'

The following evening, after Bonnie had given her a blow by blow account of the contract meeting with the Bannisters, Sylvia opened up the subject of the Boatshed, telling her first about Kim and about her own dilemma over the future. Bonnie looked stricken.

'But you wouldn't, would you?' she asked. 'Your life is here. Everything, everyone that matters to you is here . . .'

'Well, not exactly, Bon. Obviously Kim, Brendan, Charlotte and James aren't here, and that's what this is all about.'

'Oh yes, of course, but all the same . . .' Bonnie blushed at her own insensitivity. 'Would you really want to live in England? What sort of life would you have there?'

'That's what I'm trying to work out,' Sylvia said. 'It's a big decision and I don't want to make it in a hurry, which, of course, brings me to the Boatshed.'

214

'You don't want to do it, do you?'

'It's really a matter of whether you're able to meet me halfway,' Sylvia said. 'It's not the same for me as for Fran. She has her profile to invest and that's something you can actually build the business around. Obviously Fran has to be in for the long term if she is going to be in at all. It's different for me. I think I could get the gallery going, and I'd love to work with you, but at this stage I can't make a long-term commitment. If you're happy with that, I promise I'll work my bum off getting the gallery up and running and, if I do decide to go to England, I won't leave until it's going well and we can find someone to take it over.'

Bonnie shot out of her chair and flung her arms around her. 'Yes,' she cried, 'yes yes, of course. I understand, and it's fine. Not as perfect as having you sign away the rest of your life, but terrific just the same. You're on, Sylvia. I'll put you on the payroll from next week, on the terms we discussed before. And I warn you I shall be utterly ruthless in manipulating you into staying.' She bounded out to the kitchen and returned almost immediately with a bottle of champagne and three glasses. 'Let's celebrate,' she said. 'Mum? Mum, where are you? Come and have a glass of champagne to celebrate Sylvia working at the Boatshed.'

Irene wandered through from the study and briefly it seemed that the tension between mother and daughter was forgotten as they drank the toast.

'I'm so glad, Sylvia,' Irene said as Bonnie went to phone Fran and give her the good news. 'I was only next door and I couldn't help overhearing. It sounds like a wise decision, but don't let Bonnie bully you. In the long run you may decide that being with your family is what you want.'

'I think I've given up being bullied,' Sylvia said, 'but I know what you mean. I certainly felt bullied by Kim, and Bonnie's very good at getting her own way.'

Irene nodded. 'Exactly. Mothers and daughters, we all think we know what's best for each other. But Bonnie can't get her own way about everything, and she's going to find that out sooner than she expects.'

*

The birthday party was Caro's idea, born as she sat in the kitchen crossing days off the calendar and wishing she had stayed on at work. Not that she had the energy for it, but she was bored shitless with nothing to do and as soon as she started something, anything, she just wanted to lie down. Four weeks to go, twenty-eight days, possibly more, of rolling around like a beached whale, eating like a horse and having to ask Mike to paint her toenails. Her concentration was shot to pieces, she could barely get through half a page of Marian Keyes's latest book that normally she'd be sitting up half the night to finish, *and* she seemed to spend most of her life peeing.

Caro sighed, ran her finger along the calendar counting the days, and stopped at the date of her mother's birthday. Only two weeks away. She circled it – better not forget it, not when she so desperately needed to find some way of mending her fences. So much for her grandmother's advice. It was going to take more than rolling up unexpectedly and trying to apologise to put things right.

It was later, when she was lying on the bed flipping through the pages of a *Mother and Baby* magazine, that she had the party idea. There was an adorable picture of a baby in a tiny striped t-shirt and paper hat sitting alongside a birthday cake with one candle on it. 'Celebrate that special day' the caption said. It was an advertisement for disposable nappies but it got her thinking. As far as Caro could remember, Fran had never had a party, not any real sort of celebration on her birthday. She flushed with guilt at the realisation that year after year Fran had organised parties for her and David, even up to twenty-firsts, and then her wedding. This had to be the way to show her that she really did want to put things right. The trouble was that Caro had no idea what Fran would like. Of course she'd want the family and these new–old women friends, but what else?

She got out a pencil and paper intending to plan it but half an hour later all she had was the date at the top. She needed help. David would be at work, Mike was on the evening shift, and anyway, what would they know? What she really needed were these women, Bonnie and Sylvia. Caro sat at the table doodling, wondering how to find them without tipping Fran off, and then she remembered that Lila was friendly with the mother of one of them who'd just come back from Greece. With a sense of triumph she dialled her grandmother's number.

'Well, of course I'll give you Irene's number, dear,' Lila said, and Caro could hear her rustling through paper at the other end of the line. 'But why do you want to talk to her?'

'Erm . . . I just wanted to ask something about Greece,' Caro lied. If she let Lila in on the idea at this stage, Fran and everyone else would soon know about it.

'Oh yes, Irene had a lovely holiday. She'd probably show you her photographs if you want,' Lila said. 'Here it is. By the way, Caro, I'm getting a scooter,' Lila said, lowering her voice as if wary of eavesdroppers. 'What do you think of that?'

'Really, Gran?' Caro said distractedly, imagining the shiny bright aluminium job that the twelve year old next door was constantly racing up and down the street. 'Do you think it would be safe for you, pushing yourself along on one leg like that? Suppose you had another fall?'

'Oh, not *that* sort of scooter! A proper scooter, a grown-up scooter.'

Caro rolled her eyes, imagining Lila on a Vespa. She'd never get a licence, so no worries there – anyway, she'd probably forget about it in a couple of days. 'Oh, a proper scooter, silly old me,' she said.

'That's what your mother says to me, Caro. She says it when she actually means "you silly old thing", so please don't talk to me like that.'

'Sorry, Gran,' she said. 'Can I get the number from you now?'

Lila read the number to her and then read it again in case she hadn't got it down the first time. 'And you don't need to mention the other business to your mother,' she said.

'Other business?'

'The scooter, of course. Whatever is the matter with your memory, Caro? It's worse than mine.'

*

'What a lovely idea,' Bonnie said when Caro called. 'Sylvia and I were thinking of doing something but this is a much better idea. What can we do to help?'

'Tell me what she'd like . . .' Caro paused. 'I know I ought to know that myself but I don't,' and, to her horror, she burst into tears.

'Why don't Sylvia and I pop over?' Bonnie suggested. 'I'm sure we can sort something out. Sylvia's here. We could come now, if you like. We've both been dying to meet you, Caro, and we won't breathe a word to Fran.'

'I'm not sure Fran will be too happy about this,' Sylvia said as they made their way through the rain and the rush-hour traffic to North Melbourne. 'She'll think we're interfering. She and Caro are going through a difficult time. She mightn't appreciate us taking Caro over like this, rescuing her.'

'We're not rescuing her,' Bonnie said, switching lanes rather erratically, 'or taking over. We're helping Caro to organise a surprise birthday party for Fran. It's just that she sounded very upset, and Fran is not in a frame of mind to do peace deals at the moment.'

'And you think the party might help?'

'It's a start. It's a genuine effort by Caro to bridge this awful gap. I think it's worth a try.'

A phone rang and Bonnie reached automatically for the button on her mobile in its cradle on the dashboard. 'Oh, it's not mine,' she said, and Sylvia reached into her pocket.

'Hi,' she said. 'Can I call you back?' There was a pause and Bonnie strained to hear the voice at the other end, without success. 'A couple of hours, maybe? Okay, talk to you later.' She ended the call, switched off the phone and slipped it back into her pocket.

'I noticed you'd got a mobile,' Bonnie said. 'I don't know how I'd manage without mine. Did you get it in Hong Kong?'

'Yes,' Sylvia said, thankful that Bonnie couldn't see her blush. 'It's one of those that you buy cards for. I've put the number up on your phone list in the kitchen.'

'Oh good. I love those earrings too, freshwater pearls are my favourite.'

Sylvia touched the earrings that were Will's birthday present to her, and which she had barely taken off since she got home. They had cost a bomb – Bonnie would know that and was probably wondering why she had spent so much money at a time like this.

'I loved them too,' she said. 'Loved them so much I just couldn't resist them.'

'We have to treat ourselves sometimes, Sylvia,' Bonnie said, 'especially when there's no one special around to do it for us.'

Sylvia felt as though a neon sign above her head was flashing 'Liar, liar – pants on fire' in big red letters. Lying was not something she was good at, and although she acknowledged that for a large part of her married life she had been living a lie, lying to Bonnie now seemed a worse offence. 'I think we must be nearly there,' she said, changing the subject. 'Yes – that's it, next turning on the left, and from the directions you wrote down it should be the third on the right with a white gate.'

What Caro couldn't understand was how it was so easy to talk to these women. From the minute they arrived at the door and hugged her she burst into tears again and began to pour out everything: how she hated being pregnant, how scared she was, all her guilt and confusion about her mother. Until then she'd felt a faint sort of hostility towards them, perhaps even a jealousy that Fran seemed to enjoy them so much, and to be closer to them than to her. In fact, she realised that while things had been difficult between her and Fran for years, they had definitely deteriorated since the reunion with Bonnie and Sylvia had taken place around the same time she had found she was pregnant. Caro felt a deep hot flush of shock at the thought that she had resented her mother's friends returning just when she was expecting to be the centre of attention. She was thankful that she had called them – it felt as though they were on her side.

'But, Caro, there aren't any sides,' Sylvia said. 'It's just that all relationships are really hard work and the longer you hide from the problems the more difficult they are to deal with. Take it from me, I've spent an awfully long time hiding from problems.'

They must have been there for over an hour before they actually got around to talking about the party, to helping her draw up the guest list, decide on the food, the music, the birthday cake, and how to keep Lila from spilling the beans. It was ten o'clock when they got up to leave and Caro, exhausted by the relief of unburdening herself, fell quickly into bed and fast asleep.

'Well, we're in it up to our ears now,' Sylvia said as they drove home. 'Let's hope the party does the trick. If it doesn't, Fran will just see us as interfering and duplicitous.'

Bonnie nodded. 'I see what you mean. We can only do our best. Don't you think she'd understand that our intentions were good?'

'I hope so,' Sylvia said, unnerved by the fact that not only was she caught up in the lies surrounding her relationship with Will, but now she was also entangled in this precarious situation between Fran and Caro. 'I certainly hope so, or we're going to be in deep shit.'

Lila had spent a long time considering the various merits of canary yellow versus purple. Once she had had a ride on the demonstration scooter she was convinced that it was just what she needed; only the serious matter of colour remained. Eventually, she had opted for the yellow.

'That's a surprise, Mrs Whittaker,' Ray Barton had said. 'I thought you were the all-purple lady for sure.'

'Can't be too predictable, Ray,' Lila said, stroking the shiny black control levers affectionately. 'I've always liked a bit of contrast and yellow is the colour of new life.' She was disgusted that she had to wait two weeks for delivery but she crossed the days off on the calendar and thought of the satisfaction she would get from not relying on other people.

One day she took the bus up to the shops and in Dymocks she bought herself a street finder. There was a storage space under the scooter seat where she would be able to keep it. Meanwhile, she sat at her kitchen table plotting routes from Hawthorn where she lived, to Fran's new house in St Kilda, David's in Collingwood,

Caro's place in North Melbourne, and Irene's in Gardenvale. Some of the trips looked as though they might take a while, but she was in no hurry, and her time was her own. At her age, Lila thought, it was important to enjoy the journey as much as the destination.

The scooter was delivered quite late in the day. 'It's a good idea to keep your first trips really short, Mrs Whittaker,' said the nice young man who delivered it. And he went on to demonstrate the controls.

When he had gone, Lila settled herself in the leather seat and took a gentle turn around the village. The next day was Saturday and she was getting her hair cut and set in the morning ready for Fran's party in the evening, so she would ride into the outside world and down to the salon. When Caro had phoned her, swearing her to secrecy and promising that Mike would collect her, Lila had thought she might volunteer to get there under her own steam, but she had thought better of it. It would be night time and she might want to have a drink or two at the party; she shouldn't drink and drive.

Despite the threat of a storm later in the day the morning was glorious, small white clouds scudding across the sky, and as she cruised out through the village gates Lila felt a huge surge of delight in her own freedom. It was years since she'd driven a car and she'd never enjoyed it much but this was exhilarating, and she increased her speed down the quiet, tree-lined pavement. Ahead of her two boys were messing about on skateboards and Lila tooted her horn. They turned and stared at her, pausing at first as she bore down on them, and finally jumping out of the way.

'Go, Granny, go!' one of them called, and Lila tooted again, waved and sped on.

She was at the top speed now, testing it, tingling with delight at the freedom and the sensation of the breeze rushing through her hair – she'd have to take it slower on the way back if she wanted to preserve her shampoo and set. It reminded her of a song, something about being thirty-seven and realising that she'd never ride through Paris in a sports car with the wind in her hair.

Lila tried to sing it but couldn't quite remember the words. When she reached the hairdresser's, she dismounted, locked the scooter and gave it one final loving look before she went in to the salon. The song kept on buzzing through her head while the young apprentice washed her hair, and she was humming it when Sandy the stylist arrived to start her cut.

'D'you remember this song, Sandy?' Lila asked, singing the Paris in a sports car bit.

'"The Ballad of Lucy Jordan",' Sandy said, drying off her hair and running the comb through it. 'Fancy you knowing that, Mrs Whittaker.'

'That's right,' Lila said, 'Marianne whatsername . . .'

'Faithfull,' Sandy supplied. 'It's such a sad song, about that woman's life.'

'I never thought so myself,' Lila said. 'Life's what you make it, Sandy, thirty-seven or eighty, just what you make it.'

Lila had been a good bit older than thirty-seven when she first heard 'The Ballad of Lucy Jordan'; in fact, she'd been nearly sixty, and she'd realised many years earlier she wouldn't be going anywhere with the wind in her hair. She had married Mal Whittaker in a rush in nineteen-forty, when she was twenty years old and pregnant, but the baby was stillborn, and Fran didn't arrive until eight years later. After the war, Mal had been full of plans. He was an ideas man, or so he said, couldn't be tied down, so he ended up as a salesman, travelling around with a case of samples – cheap perfumes, face and hand creams, and home perm kits. He was away most of the week, returning home on Fridays to do his paperwork and spend most of the weekend at the pub, and at the footy in winter and the cricket in summer.

'Business, Lila love,' he always said. 'Got to keep up with what's going on.'

'I know just what's going on,' Lila had told him. 'A lot of drinking and a good bit of betting. Business, my foot; you're a big waste of space, Mal Whittaker. Who knows what you get up to when you're away? At least you could stay home at the weekends. What about little Fran? She waits around for you all week and then all you can do is go down the pub.' But it made no difference and when it finally became clear that he had done a moonlight flit to North Queensland with a woman half his age, Lila breathed a sigh of relief.

During the war she'd worked in a factory, but by this stage it was 1959 and she was nearly forty and she wanted something better. She'd always been good with figures, and meticulous in the way she managed things, and she got a job in the post office. The following year, when Fran got the scholarship to the convent, Lila had been over the moon, although she knew there would be extra expenses – uniforms, books and outings, and other bits and pieces – but there was no way that she would have Fran going without anything that the fee-paying girls had. When Fran first brought Sylvia home, Lila was relieved to find that she was another scholarship girl, but she worried when they got involved with Bonnie.

'Just be careful,' she'd told Fran. 'They're a different sort of people to us. Don't go getting any ideas, she might be just . . .' But she wasn't quite sure what she was trying to say. 'Well, she might just drop you,' she finished. And Fran, who at twelve was already familiar with the process of dropping and being dropped, just shrugged and, as time passed, Lila's fears about the rich girl slowly faded away. The hard work had paid off: Fran had a good education, good friends, and prospects, the sort of prospects Lila had never had.

It was Fran who had been playing 'Lucy Jordan', while she contemplated ending her marriage.

'Don't you ever play anything else?' Lila had asked one day when she turned up to sit with Caro while Fran went out with a friend.

'Hardly ever,' Fran replied. 'Not at the moment. I seem to need to keep playing this one.'

'She'll have me singing it next,' Lila grumbled as she dished out beans on toast for Caro and David.

And sure enough it had seeped into her consciousness and haunted her for weeks. Lila liked the earthy rasp of Marianne Faithfull's voice but she thought that Lucy Jordan was a bit of a wuss; you took your life in your own hands and made it into something. That was what she'd done, and eventually Fran had done it too. Lila was proud of her daughter. She kept scrapbooks of all her columns, and the magazine articles, and filed her recipes in a set of dated folders. But more than anything she was proud of the person Fran had become.

For the seventh time in half an hour, Will dialled Sylvia's mobile and was diverted to message bank. In frustration he threw the mobile onto the couch and slumped down after it. Friday afternoon – he had a briefcase full of work, half a dozen telephone calls that needed returning, and he hadn't even bothered to look at the previous day's close on the Dow or the NASDAQ. The truth was, since he'd got back from Hong Kong he hadn't been able to concentrate on anything. He'd start reading a contract or going through correspondence, and his thoughts would just drift off to Sylvia, and then he couldn't get his concentration back. He would fall into bed exhausted, longing for the sleep that continued to evade him, reliving the nights in Hong Kong, driven mad with desire and haunted by loneliness. When he did fall asleep he would wake with a start a few hours later to the miserable emptiness of his own bed, aching to feel her there beside him. Sometimes he was convinced he could still capture the scent of her body on his skin, but as swiftly as it came it would evaporate and he would go to the wardrobe and pull out the jacket he had worn with her and bury his face in it, hoping to find it once again.

He had tried to get on top of his feelings with exercise, with long, punishing runs through Kings Park at dawn, swimming laps or relentlessly pumping iron in the gym. But each time he returned to the emptiness of his apartment, it seemed barren and lifeless because not only was Sylvia not there, she had never even seen it.

'Just come over here for a few days,' he had begged her that morning. 'I can show you Perth, we can have more time together.'

But she had made a commitment to Bonnie and she wouldn't budge. 'I'll see you soon anyway,' she said. 'You'll be over here early next month.'

'Too long,' he replied, knowing he sounded childish and petulant. 'It's almost four weeks since Hong Kong. I may have to jump off the Narrows Bridge – that's where desperate Perth lovers go to top themselves.'

'Dear Will,' she had said, and he could hear the smile in her voice. 'I do remember that you told me you're an excellent swimmer.'

'For all you know it could be a railway bridge,' he said sulkily.

'It's a bridge over the Swan River,' she said firmly, but with a note of tender indulgence. 'I've been reading the lovely book on Perth you sent me.'

She was humouring him and the worst thing for Will was that while she was clearly looking forward to seeing him again, she wasn't driven crazy with longing as he was. She called him regularly, but he called her obsessively; she told him she missed him but he told her he longed for her. She told him about her visits to studios and warehouses searching out stock for the Boatshed gallery, about Bonnie's efficient management of the project, about their sorties among the ladders and cables and plaster dust as they inspected the renovations, and about the plans for Fran's surprise party. He told her about his failure to work, his attempts to distract himself, and how he had dreamed that she came to him in the night.

'I could come over there for the weekend and come to the party,' he had said plaintively the previous day.

'Don't you think that would look rather strange?' Sylvia said. 'After all, you're the one who said Bonnie shouldn't know just yet.'

And so he was left with nowhere to go, faced at all turns with her relentlessly gentle firmness and good sense.

He picked up the phone and dialled again, flicking it aside as he heard it divert. Why did this have to be so hard? For the first time in his life Will didn't know where he stood. Not since Glenda had he felt anything more than a mix of affection and lust for any woman, and never had one taken over his head, his heart and his erotic imagination in the way that Sylvia had. Will knew he was in love and he longed to plunge headlong into it, to do all the crazy, irrational, glorious things that lovers do; the things that they had done in Hong Kong. But first of all he had to tell Sylvia how he felt, and what held him back was the terrifying feeling that while he was in it up to the neck and sinking, she had simply dipped her toe into the shallows.

The mobile rang and he pounced on it.

'So sorry, Will,' she said in the voice that melted his insides. 'I did get your messages but Bonnie and I have been delivering stuff to Caro for Fran's party.'

He lay down on the couch, soothed momentarily by the fact that she was there on the line talking to him, connected directly to him by some miracle of science that held him jerking and twisting like a fish on a line. He closed his eyes and saw her on the balcony in Hong Kong, standing on tiptoes stretching her arms above her head as he walked up to her and took her in his arms. He felt the warm weight of her body leaning into his.

'You know I love you, don't you?' he said, and his voice sounded unreal, wobbly, totally unlike himself. He hadn't meant to say it, not now, not like this. There was silence at the end of the line and then he heard her take a breath and he could see her face beside him, close enough to touch, close enough to feel her breath on his cheek.

'I know you *think* you do,' she said softly, and he was angry suddenly, sitting bolt upright on the couch, his body tense with emotion.

'Don't patronise me, Sylvia,' he said. 'Don't do the wise, enigmatic older woman thing. I can't bear it. I love you, no thinking about it, no deluding myself, I'm in love with you . . . and I'm falling apart.'

TWENTY-FOUR

Fran stepped into the long velvet skirt Sylvia had made for her and was surprised to find that it was a little looser than the night she had worn it to the Wine Club dinner. In fact, it was so much looser that she really ought to move the button, but being short of time she opted for a safety pin, and put on the cream silk shirt, wondering briefly if she was overdressed for wherever it was they were going. David had told her to dress up because he was taking her, Caro and Mike out for dinner to celebrate her birthday. It was a gesture designed, she was sure, to help heal the rift between her and Caro. She would actually have preferred to have a quiet dinner with them at home in the new house, especially as she had worn herself out unpacking boxes. But now that the time had arrived she found she was looking forward to it, and when she saw David's car draw up outside she switched off the lights, grabbed her umbrella and ran down the path.

It was an appalling night, the strong wind driving the rain in almost horizontal torrents, and she slipped thankfully into the front seat. They set off, crawling along streets where water pooled and gushed in the gutters, the wipers working overtime, the gale force wind pummelling the car.

'Why are we here?' Fran asked as David turned into Caro and Mike's street and drew up outside their house.

'I said we'd pick them up.'

'Can't they get there under their own steam?'

'They could, but I'm the designated driver, so they can get stuck into the champagne with you.'

Fran leaned back in her seat, thinking that it wasn't a good idea for Caro to be drinking at all, especially if she was still throwing up. But she decided that it might be best to keep her nose out of it and try to enjoy herself. 'Just hoot,' she suggested as David opened the car door. 'They can run out.'

'Caro wants to show us something,' he said. 'Come on, it won't take a minute.'

Fran struggled out of the car, which was low and awkward for someone her size. She felt it was irritatingly typical of Caro to make everything more complicated, and putting up her umbrella she took a stride across a huge puddle and hurried up the path. The front door was ajar and she pushed it open and walked into the dark hall.

'Caro, Mike!' she called. 'We're here!' There was no answer. A slice of light showed under the door to the living room.

'Best go on down,' said David, and with her irritation growing, Fran strode on down the passage and opened the door to face a room decked with streamers and heart-shaped balloons, 'Happy Birthday' banners, and the smiling faces of her family and friends, who immediately burst into song.

'Happy birthday, Mum,' David said, pressing his hand in the small of her back, pushing her gently forward, and Caro, looking as though she might drop the baby at any minute, took her hand and drew her gently into the room.

Fran's heart plummeted as she struggled to cope with the shock. She had always hated surprises. It went back to childhood, to the day her father had promised her a surprise on her eighth birthday. She had convinced herself it was going to be a visit to the zoo and afternoon tea with pink-iced buns, fruit cocktail in jelly, and strawberry milkshakes. But when the day arrived Mal had taken her and Lila down to the footy club, installed them in the family lounge and produced lemonade and a small birthday cake with seven candles. His mates had trooped through from the bar, sung 'Happy Birthday' and disappeared again, taking Mal with them. Fran had stared miserably at the candles that proved her father didn't know how old she was, and then burst into tears.

For more than an hour she and Lila had sat alone in the silent lounge waiting for his return, waiting for even a glimpse of his face around the door. Finally, Lila told Fran to put on her coat, and led her out of the club to the tram, with the promise that she would take her to the zoo the following day. Hours later, Fran had woken to the sound of her father staggering drunkenly into the house, demanding to know why they'd left. Since then she had maintained a strong, sometimes perverse need to know just what was being planned, when and by whom. It had been the start of a lifelong mistrust of surprises, and her unwillingness to trust others to do anything for her. Faced now with this extraordinary demonstration of affection, Fran swallowed the shock that threatened to choke her, and gripped Caro's hand. There was no mistaking the nervous brightness of her daughter's eyes, nor the anxiety with which she searched her face for approval.

'I wanted to surprise you, to make it really special,' Caro said, cautiously, as though sensing Fran's ambivalence. 'I hope . . . I hope it's okay.'

Crushing the strange mix of hostility and panic that she felt, Fran smiled. 'It's lovely, Caro, really lovely, thank you so much,' she said.

'Happy birthday, Fran,' Mike said, kissing her and handing her a glass of champagne. 'And many happy returns. Next birthday you'll be a grandmother.'

Sylvia, who had registered the flash of mixed emotions that crossed Fran's face as she opened the door, was wary. She knew that Fran's reaction to Caro's efforts in planning the party, and her own and Bonnie's involvement, could go in one of two very different ways. Bonnie had been cavalier about the whole thing, confident that the genuineness of Caro's purpose justified the secrecy; but Sylvia, highly sensitised to the subtleties of offence, defence, confusion of intent and misinterpretation in her own presently awkward relationship with Kim, had been on tenterhooks for the past ten days.

'See,' Bonnie whispered, 'I told you it'd be okay.'

'It's not,' she whispered back, watching Fran take in the presence of everyone in the room. 'Not yet, she's still being polite. We're not out of the woods yet.' Even so, she began to relax as Mike put on some music and the level of noise in the room rose to a lively buzz, drowning any traces of awkwardness.

But Sylvia had more on her mind than Fran's reaction to the party. In the four weeks since she'd got back from Hong Kong, her relationship with Will had taken an entirely unexpected turn. She had been sure that the insistent telephone calls would soon stop. But it seemed that he had abandoned all routine and was instead working at odd, disorganised hours, dropping out of his social life, and focusing all his attention on her. Even from the other side of the country his neediness was smothering her. She had taken to leaving the mobile switched off for quite long periods to give herself a break from the constant calls, and because she was sure that their frequency would alert Bonnie to the fact that something strange was going on.

On more than one occasion Sylvia had been tempted to confide in both Bonnie and Fran, but it was clear that Bonnie was, for some as yet unexplained reason, distressed about Irene's friendship with Hamish, and Fran was not only exhausted but anxious and concerned about Caro. And so, uneasily, she had kept her own counsel, hoping that time and distance would eventually do its work. But Will's blunt declaration of love had made her realise that she was enmeshed in something much more complicated than she had realised.

'You look anxious, Syl,' Fran said, coming over to hug her.

'Just hoping you're happy about this,' she said. 'Happy birthday, Fran. You look gorgeous – and thinner.'

Fran displayed the safety pin. 'I think I've lost a bit. Look at this! Bonnie might be right about low carbs being the answer.'

Sylvia hugged her again. 'Well done! I hope this'll fit,' she said, handing her a package wrapped in silver tissue. 'I made it but I may need to take it in a bit now.'

Fran made her way around the room. 'What is Lenore Bannister doing at my birthday party?' she hissed into Bonnie's ear as she hugged her.

'It's difficult,' Bonnie said awkwardly, turning Fran away slightly so that they couldn't be overheard. 'I stuffed up. The day I took her and Jack to the Boatshed she mentioned she was going to be in Melbourne again, and we arranged to meet and have dinner this evening. Thing was, I forgot to put it in my diary. So when she rang this afternoon I bluffed and suggested she come along. Do you mind very much?'

'I'm just getting used to the idea of the party,' Fran said. 'Lenore is a minor hurdle.'

'And I'm afraid Hamish is here too,' Bonnie said. 'Mum insisted on bringing him, although I told her she shouldn't.'

'Why ever not?' Fran asked. 'He's a lovely man, and he and Irene get on so well. She was telling me that they've known each other for years.'

'Don't!' Bonnie said, holding her hand up, palm outwards. 'I don't want to discuss it.'

Fran shrugged and moved on to hug a couple of former neighbours, and Bonnie glanced across the room to where Irene and Hamish were deep in conversation with David. At least they looked okay together. Perhaps this was just a phase they were going through, grasping at youth and the idea of a holiday romance. Surely Irene should be getting over it by now?

Lila had found a soul mate. She had spotted her the minute she walked in the door, a strong, energetic looking woman with curly grey hair, dressed entirely in purple with a turquoise pendant on a silver chain around her neck.

'Hello, I'm Lila, Fran's mother,' Lila had said, thrusting out her hand, and the woman had taken Lila's hand in both of hers and fixed her very bright turquoise eyes on her.

'I can see that you are,' she said. 'I'm Lenore, I'm going to be working with Fran on her book. You and I are a matching pair – you love purple too?'

And Lila had led Lenore over to the window seat and told her how she had coloured her life purple.

'I know that poem,' Lenore said. 'And, Lila, do you know about the red hat society? Well, you know the poem talks about wearing purple with a red hat –'

231

'And the hat clashes with the purple,' Lila cut in.

'Right! Well all around the world there are red hat groups, women who wear purple with red hats, to beat that feeling of invisibility and the idea that older women are irrelevant.'

'You mean there are other women?' Lila asked. 'Other . . . purple women?'

'Thousands,' Lenore said with a grin. 'There are lots in England and the US, I think there are a couple of groups in Sydney, and maybe one here in Victoria. I could find out for you.'

Lila clasped her hand. 'Yes, yes please, I haven't got a red hat yet, but I've been thinking about it, a big one, with a wide brim and some lovely tulle or chiffon wrapped around it. Only between you and me, Lenore, I thought everyone would just laugh at me. They already think I'm a bit of a joke.'

'Take no notice of them,' Lenore said, patting Lila's arm. 'This is the time of your life to make a statement, Lila. There's a novel written about it too, I'll mail you a copy.'

'I wish you'd come and see my place, Lenore,' Lila said. 'What are you doing tomorrow?'

'I have to meet an author and a photographer in the morning,' Lenore said, 'but I'm free after that and I don't go back to Sydney until Tuesday morning.'

'Splendid! Here, I'll write down my address for you.' She leaned forward and lowered her voice conspiratorially. 'I may not have a red hat, but I do have something else. It's a secret, I haven't told anyone yet, but I've just bought a scooter, so I can get around a bit on my own. If you pop over tomorrow afternoon I'll show it to you.'

'A scooter? Good for you, Lila,' Lenore said. 'Purple, I hope?'

'Canary yellow,' Lila said with pride. 'Lovely combination, don't you think?'

'Stunning,' Lenore said. 'And a red hat will top it off. Maybe I can have a ride on the scooter . . . ?'

David strolled outside onto the deck to get some air. Three hours in and the party was in full swing. He had done his turn on the dance floor with his grandmother, his mother and sister; he'd even managed a very sharp samba with Bonnie and a rather surprising jive with Sylvia. He closed the sliding door behind him, breathing in the fresh cold air. It was good to be outside. Sometimes the effect of light and noise combined with the slightest hint of tobacco smoke would make him nauseous. Leaning against the wall out of the path of the wind, he watched as it ripped through the tree tops and the light from the windows transformed the driving rain into sheets of silver. It was the worst night he could remember for a long time, but at least everyone, and particularly Fran, seemed to be having a good time. What would it be like to have Jodie there with him, in the heart of his family, dancing with him, holding his hand? Pushing away the images he cursed himself for the stupidity of the past that had so dramatically affected his life, and for his more recent failure to grasp the opportunity that had been offered.

The door slid open and Mike staggered out, burping loudly, and lurched towards him. He'd been playing rugby that afternoon and had sunk a good few beers in the bar before collecting Lila, and had made it home half an hour before the party. Now he was quite drunk, bumping into furniture, hugging people at the least invitation, and constantly telling anyone who would listen that he was about to become a father.

'Hey, Davo,' he said, thumping him on the shoulder. 'Great party, mate! Need you to do drinks and stuff, I wanna dance.'

David steered him back into the house, pointed him in the direction of Caro, opened some more wine, topped up glasses and checked the oven. The food looked done and he took out the quiches and the tray of filo pastry parcels filled with spinach and ricotta, and lined them up on the benchtop.

'I'll help you,' Fran said, appearing beside him.

'You will not,' he said. 'You're the guest of honour. You just get out of the kitchen and enjoy yourself. You *are* enjoying it, aren't you? I wasn't sure at first.'

She hugged him as he put down the tray of food. 'Very much,' she said. 'It was a bit of a shock, that's all. Now I've got over that it's wonderful, the first time I've ever had a party for me.'

'Then off you go,' he said. And she drifted away and was collared by Hamish, who swept her onto the floor with a flourish.

Caro danced slowly, her arms around Mike's neck. It was after ten and apart from champagne for the toasts she had drunk only water and eaten nothing at all. She had felt strange all day, queasy, light headed and on and off she'd been getting quite painful squeezing sensations.

'Braxton-Hicks contractions,' Mike had said when he got back from rugby. 'Tightening-up practice for the real thing.'

'I know what Braxton-Hicks feel like,' Caro had said irritably, 'I've been having them for weeks. Everything tightens and squeezes and you feel as though your eyes are going to pop out. These are different, more intense – painful, actually.'

Mike leaned over and patted her enormous belly. 'Not long now, babe. Have a rest, put your feet up for five minutes before they get here.'

Across the room on the window seat, Caro could see Fran deep in conversation with Lenore; she looked as though she was enjoying herself. Maybe now was the time to give her the other present, the present that was either going to be absolutely perfect or totally misunderstood. Caro took a deep breath; if she was going to do it she might as well do it now.

'Hang on, Mikey,' she said, pushing him gently away. 'Gotta do something urgent.' And she went up the four steps from the living room through the passage to the bedroom and returned almost immediately with a small package wrapped in pink tissue. She crouched down on her haunches beside Fran.

'Sit here, Caro,' Lenore Bannister said, making space for her on the seat.

Caro shook her head. 'No thanks, I'm fine. Been practising this position at antenatal classes.' She held out the package to Fran. 'This is for you, Mum.'

Fran looked at her in surprise. 'But you already gave me a present,' she said, 'these gorgeous earrings.' And she put her hand up to touch her silver and amber birthday present.

'It's a different sort of present,' Caro said, nervous now as Fran tore open the tissue paper and looked in confusion at the grubby, discoloured contents.

'Whatever is it?' she asked, touching the frayed fabric that had stiffened with age and wear.

Caro waited, desperate for her mother to recognise it. Fran put the tissue aside, staring at the gift in confusion as it started to unravel.

'It's the ribbon,' Fran gasped, looking up at Caro. 'The barrier ribbon from your old bedroom.'

Caro nodded. 'I don't need it anymore.'

Fran shook her head and swallowed hard, turning the ribbon over in her hands, watching as it dropped into a scruffy coil. 'This is the very best birthday present ever.'

Caro nodded, speechless with emotion and flooded with relief that she had got it right. She braced herself to stand, putting her hand on Fran's knee, but as she pushed down she felt a warm gush of liquid between her legs, followed swiftly by a sudden intense contraction that made her cry out with pain.

'Oh my god,' she said, abandoning her attempt to stand and lowering herself carefully to the floor. 'I think my waters have broken, Mum, help! Where's Mike?'

Someone turned off the music and David, who had been watching from the kitchen, ran through to the bathroom, where Mike had headed a few moments earlier. Caro let out a bellow of pain and thrust herself back against the window seat as she tried to breathe. Fran slipped onto the floor beside her and took her hand.

'Hang on, darl,' she said, 'Mike'll be here in a minute.'

Caro was incoherent with the pain.

'Caro, you might be more comfortable on your hands and knees,' Lenore suggested, kneeling beside her. 'It'll take the pressure off your back.' Caro nodded, grim-faced, and with Fran and Lenore's help twisted around onto her knees.

'Is this the first pain?' Fran asked as Caro began to relax.

'I've had pains on and off all day, but nothing like this.'

Fran and Lenore looked at each other. 'She's in labour, isn't she?'

235

Lenore nodded. 'And if she's been getting mild contractions all day –'

'She could be well on the way,' Fran cut in.

When she thought about it later, Fran realised she had never seen a room clear so quickly. One minute everyone was laughing, talking, drinking and dancing, and the next minute the crowd seemed to evaporate. People slipped away to the bedroom and returned clutching their coats and bags, called out their good-nights from the doorway and disappeared into the storm, anxious to escape the drama that was about to unfold. Only Bonnie and Sylvia, Irene and Hamish, Lila and Lenore remained.

'Where's Mike?' Fran asked, looking around desperately for someone who knew what to do.

'Mike's passed out on the bathroom floor,' Hamish announced from the top of steps by the passage. 'He seems to have had rather too much to drink. David's trying to bring him round, but I wouldn't hold your breath.'

'Christ!' Caro hissed between her teeth. 'Isn't that bloody typical? And my midwife's in Noosa till Wednesday.'

'Perhaps we'd best just put you in the car and get you to hospital,' Fran suggested. 'I'll come with you and David can drive.'

'Those contractions are coming pretty close together,' Lenore said. 'Can you start timing them, Sylvia? Fran, I don't think this girl's going anywhere in a car. She needs an ambulance, but they'll have to hurry up.'

'Right,' Caro murmured, breathing easier now. 'Yes, an ambulance please, and quick.'

'I'll do it,' Fran said, struggling to her feet. Sylvia and Lila dragged some cushions off the chairs and Lenore pushed them under Caro's knees and hands as she let out another roar of pain.

'One and a half minutes,' Sylvia said, and the women looked at each other in dismay.

'There's a long delay with the ambulance,' Fran called from the kitchen. 'Lots of accidents because of the storm. I've told them it's an emergency but they're asking if anyone here has ever deliv-ered a baby.'

'I have,' Irene said.

'Oh don't be silly, Mum,' Bonnie snapped. 'She said *delivered* a baby, not had one.'

'I know that, Bonnie,' Irene said, giving her a steely look.

'So have I,' Lila said.

Fran was holding the phone away from her ear. 'You mean –' she began.

'Yes, dear,' Irene said. 'Lila and I can probably cope if necessary,' and she took the phone from her. 'I'll have a word with the ambulance people. Can you get me a pen and something to write on?'

'Mike's come round but he's very drunk and throwing up,' Bonnie said, returning from the bathroom. David and Hamish are pouring cold water on him.'

'The ambulance will be at least forty-five minutes,' Irene said, hanging up the phone, 'and I don't think Caro's going to last that long.'

Lila got to her feet. 'Come on then, Irene, you and I better scrub up.'

'Shit,' Caro said, 'I don't believe this is happening. Gran, are you sure you know what to do?'

Lila got down on her hands and knees again and put her hand on Caro's cheek. 'Course I do, darling. Irene and I are old hands at this.'

Caro let out a sigh that ended as a groan. 'I suppose it's better than a drunk and unconscious doctor. Use our bathroom, there's lots of clean towels in the linen press. And shouldn't someone boil some water?'

'Absolutely,' Irene said. 'Fran, come over here and sit with Caro. Bonnie, don't just stand around there, start boiling, the kettle, large saucepans, anything you can find, and rustle up some coffee for Mike. Sylvia and Lenore, I want you to find every pillow and cushion you can get your hands on, stack them around Caro, cover them with sheets and towels, try to make a comfortable space for her.'

'D'you think they know what they're doing?' Bonnie hissed at Sylvia.

'Well, I think they know more than we do, and they're the best we've got in the circumstances,' Sylvia replied. 'Come on, Lenore, let's get those big cushions off the settee in the other room.'

'How long since you did this, Lila?' Irene asked as they stood side by side washing their hands and arms in the ensuite bathroom.

'Donkey's years,' Lila said. 'Just after the war. What about you?'

'Nineteen fifty-five, my neighbour went into labour in her kitchen,' Irene said, drying her hands. 'But I think we'd best not mention how long it's been. How confident are you?'

Lila turned off the tap and took the towel, looking at Irene in the mirror. 'Not at all, but she's my granddaughter, Mike's useless, and you and I are all that's left.'

'Exactly, and however nervous we *feel* we need to *look* confident. Now, do you think we should keep her off her back and on her hands and knees if that's comfortable for her?'

Caro rocked back and forth, trying to relax between contractions. With any luck, she thought, Mike would be there in a minute. She allowed her weight to sink against the pile of cushions, and when the pain gripped her again she yelled out at the agonising pressure bearing down on her.

'Push,' she yelled. 'I have to push!'

'No, Caro – no, not yet,' Irene cried as she and Lila struggled down onto the floor. 'Don't push yet, pant.'

Caro panted, remembering the classes and how it had all seemed so easy then. As the pain eased she lurched sideways again, bracing herself for the next onslaught.

'I think she's nearly there, Irene,' Lila said, twisting around awkwardly to get a pillow under her own knees. 'But she mustn't push just yet.'

Irene crawled across the sheets and cushions to look Caro in the eye.

'Okay now, Caro, it's going to be fine. Lila and I can look after you, but you must listen to us. Remember your breathing and don't push until we tell you. Someone get a clean flannel and wipe Caro's face.'

'Are you sure it's okay?' Fran asked, gripping her mother's arm.

'There isn't any choice, Fran,' Lenore cut in. 'Caro's probably been in labour all day and now this baby's not waiting for Mike or an ambulance.'

'Fran! Pull yourself together and breathe through it with her,' Lila ordered. 'She mustn't push until we tell her.'

Caro let out a low groan that built to a roar as her body threatened to split open.

'It's crowning,' Irene cried. 'Pant, Caro, pant, it's too soon to push yet. Just pant. You're nearly there.'

'Thank god it's the right way round,' Lila said. 'That was definitely the head.'

The dark bulge slipped back and Caro breathed more easily again, waiting for the next contraction.

'I think it sometimes helps to count, Caro,' Irene said, and Fran, wiping the sweat from Caro's face, began to count aloud and Caro followed her.

Mike appeared at the top of the steps, staggering between David and Hamish, his head and shirt soaking wet.

'S'okay, babe,' he managed. 'I'm here, I'm here.'

'No way,' Caro panted. 'You're still pissed – stay right out of the way.'

'Okay, Caro,' Irene said, her hand gripping Caro's ankle. 'Now listen, take it gently. We mustn't let it come too fast.'

'Right,' Mike called from across the room, 'not too fast.'

'Shut up,' Caro growled, steeling herself for the next contraction. Fran rolled the flannel and held it out to her.

'Bite on this if you need to.'

Caro felt a tiny lull in the pain and then it ripped through her again and she roared, a great crescendo of sound that seemed torn from unknown recesses of her body. The breathing lessons forgotten now, she groaned and ground her teeth on the flannel as she fought the overwhelming urge to push.

'Next time, I think,' Irene called. 'Next time, Caro, you can push.'

Caro's head rolled back and she threw out the flannel and grasped Fran's arm, her nails biting into the soft flesh. 'Oh my god,' she cried, 'I have to push . . .'

'Yes, darling, push now,' Lila yelled. 'Go on, Caro, push now.'

And thrusting down on her lungs, her face clenched and purple, her legs and arms trembling, Caro pushed and pushed and pushed again, until, just as she thought she must burst or die, her muscles contracted a final agonising time and something warm and wet thrust itself out between her legs.

'Good girl,' Lila cried. 'We've got the head.' And Irene gently eased the cord over the baby's head to free it. 'Pant now, then next time, darling, push long and slow for the shoulders.'

'Strong and steady,' Irene agreed.

Caro pushed, growling deep in her chest with the effort, the promise of relief hovering close as the slippery body was freed in a final triumphant whoosh of moist warmth, and she heard a splutter and a cry, and the gasp as the other women caught their breath.

'It's a girl!' Lila cried, cradling the baby. 'A beautiful little girl.'

'Well done, Caro,' Irene said, sinking off her knees to sit on a pillow. 'Well done, dear, splendid.'

Irene and Fran helped Caro to lean back against the cushions as Lila cleaned the mucus from the baby's nose and mouth and laid her on Caro's chest.

'She's so beautiful,' Caro breathed. 'Oh Mum, isn't she beautiful!'

Fran took a warm towel from Bonnie and wrapped it gently around her granddaughter, leaning forward at the same time to kiss Caro's cheek.

'She's gorgeous, darling, just gorgeous, and you were perfectly wonderful.'

The tiny red face crumpled and the baby let out another cry, a robust one this time, squeezing her eyes shut against the light.

'She looks a bit cross,' Caro said.

'Not surprised,' Lila said, touching the wrinkled forehead with her finger. 'Bit of a shock arriving so fast in the middle of a party.' And Sylvia helped her up off her knees and onto the window seat.

'Is it all right – being so quick?' Caro asked, suddenly anxious.

Mike, who had sobered up rapidly at the sight of his daughter being born on the other side of the room, searched his medical bag for sterile scissors, and sank down beside Caro, kissing her gently, stroking the baby's head.

'Of course it is,' he said, 'it's brilliant. So sorry, babe, useless bastard. I love you,' and he bent forward, kissing her first and then the baby. 'She's almost as beautiful as you. Can I sort out the cord and the placenta?'

Caro grinned at him. 'Boofhead,' she said. 'Thank god for Gran and Irene.' She held the baby closer, shivering with shock and exhaustion.

Fran, tears running down her cheeks, moved the edge of the towel to look again at the baby's face.

'Your granddaughter,' Caro said with a smile. 'Rebekah Frances – she shares a name and a birthday with her grandmother.'

TWENTY-FIVE

'There you are, you see,' Bonnie said as she drove up to the house. 'Hamish is here. One o'clock in the morning – he must be staying the night.' Irene and Hamish had left the party shortly after Rebekah's birth, and it was almost three hours later when Bonnie and Sylvia had finished clearing away, washing up and restoring Caro and Mike's house to order.

'Mmm, so I see,' Sylvia said, longing for her bed.

'I suppose I'll have to have it out with her, although I don't really know what I'm supposed to do.'

'Do? Why do you have to do anything?'

Bonnie switched off the engine and leaned back with a sigh of irritation. 'I can't just ignore it . . . it's . . . it's all wrong. I mean, Mum's over eighty and Hamish is even older. It's embarrassing, I have to put a stop to it.'

Sylvia woke up a bit and stared at her. 'Sorry, not with you – what's embarrassing?'

'This thing with the two of them. I mean, it's nice that they're friends, but the rest of it . . . it's so embarrassing.' She twitched her shoulders.

'Embarrassing for whom?'

'Everyone . . .'

'It's not embarrassing for them, obviously,' Sylvia said. 'And it doesn't embarrass me or Fran. If you mean *you're* embarrassed by it, I'm not sure why – you like Hamish. Is it just that they're sleeping together?'

242

Bonnie leaned her head back on the neck rest and closed her eyes, thankful for the darkness. 'Well, of course,' she said. 'How would you feel if it was your mother?'

'She's dead,' Sylvia said thoughtfully, 'but I think I'd feel happy for her, if she had a friend who became her lover. I think it would be lovely for her, and it wouldn't be any business of mine.'

Bonnie's head snapped up. 'But they're old, they should be over all that.'

Sylvia laughed out loud. 'Oh Bonnie, really! Are *you* past it?'

'No,' Bonnie replied, affronted, 'of course not, I'm just recovering from Jeff, but I'm twenty-five years younger than them.'

Sylvia smiled at her through the darkness. 'And at what age do you think you'll cross the line into too old?'

Bonnie hesitated. 'Well . . . I don't really know . . . but certainly before I'm eighty.'

Sylvia opened the door and got out of the car. The wild weather of a few hours earlier had subsided to stillness, leaving the air heavy with moisture, the garden a wreck of flattened plants, scattered twigs and branches ripped from the trees by the wind. 'Don't be so ridiculous,' she said, irritated now. 'People go on being sexual until they die. It's just that, like you, no one wants to acknowledge it.' She slipped her key in the front door and walked into the dimly lit hall.

'But she's my *mother*, for god's sake,' Bonnie whispered, following her in and closing the front door.

Sylvia grabbed her by the wrist, drew her through into the kitchen and shut the door. 'Okay, she's your mother, but she's much more too. She's a woman with a mind and life of her own, Bonnie. She just delivered a baby – you didn't think she was too old to do that.'

'I did really –' Bonnie began but Sylvia cut her off.

'If this was someone else's mother you'd admire her. It's like you not wanting her to go to Greece. That wasn't about *her*, it was about *you*. *You* needing her to be your crutch, your standby now that's Jeff's gone. Don't you see how selfish you're being? This is not about Irene at all, it's about *you*.' She wanted to shake Bonnie for her blindness, her inability to see what she was doing.

'Until you get out of this, Bon, you aren't going to be able to move on,' she said sharply. 'Boatshed or not, you're still trapped in your own neediness. I know it's all been terribly hard for you but you can't do this to Irene. You can't keep trying to control her life because of your own neediness. We're single women, Bonnie, you and I and Fran, we're alone and we have to make ourselves be enough. Fran's done it for years. She doesn't co-opt her mother's life or her kids' lives. You and I have to learn to be like that, because until we do we're going to be stuck in the past.'

Bonnie stared at her, white with shock at this sudden onslaught from one who was generally so restrained. She started to speak and then stopped, realising she had no idea what she wanted to say.

Sylvia put an arm around her shoulders. 'Look after yourself, Bon, and let Irene look after *herself*. She's been doing it extraordinarily well for years.' She was unnerved by Bonnie's silence. 'Come on, I'll make us a cup of tea,' she said, steering her towards a stool.

'But, but they're sleeping together, having sex . . .' Bonnie said.

'Probably, and why shouldn't they? Anyway, it's none of your business,' Sylvia said firmly, filling the kettle. 'Don't interfere. Irene didn't interfere all those years ago when you were bonking the banker.'

Bonnie gasped and her hand flew to her mouth. 'You know about that?'

Sylvia turned to her, smiling. 'Of course, we both knew, Fran and I, and Irene.'

'But how?'

'That woman you shared with, Stephanie?'

'Stella.'

'Yes, Stella, she called both of us because she was worried about you, thought you might get into some sort of trouble. She wanted us to do something about it. We told her you were an intelligent adult and knew what you were doing. So she rang Irene and then Irene rang us so we told her the same thing. She said that was what she thought too and she'd leave well alone.'

Bonnie's face had gone from white to crimson and now she

buried it in her hands. 'Oh my god. You mean she knew . . . Mum knew about it?'

Sylvia nodded, pushing a mug of tea across the benchtop towards her. She had softened now, her anger suddenly evaporated, replaced by affection. 'Oh yes, we all knew.'

'Weren't you shocked?'

Sylvia shrugged. 'No, actually, Fran and I were quite impressed at the time. I've often thought of it since then, how spunky and single-minded you were, while I was so ready to give up everything and do what Colin wanted. I didn't even finish my degree, and there you were, a real woman of the sixties.'

Bonnie sat, silent for a moment, staring into her tea. 'Mum – she would have been shocked . . . horrified.'

Sylvia paused for a moment. 'She was certainly concerned, don't know about shocked.'

'How will I face her in the morning?' Bonnie said, looking like a twelve year old caught smoking.

'Easily,' Sylvia laughed. 'Nothing's changed for her; she's probably forgotten all about it.'

Bonnie shook her head. 'I thought I'd been doing so well,' she said. 'The Boatshed and everything, I thought I'd let go . . . now . . . well, now I don't know what to do.'

'Concentrate on yourself, Bon,' Sylvia said gently. 'Stop looking for answers in other people. Our lives, yours and mine, have changed so much this year. We're on the road to sixty, we have to find the future within ourselves.'

Bonnie nodded cautiously. 'I suppose you're right. I feel safe while you and Mum and Fran are around, while I'm part of everything you're doing. Being without that seems really scary.'

'I know,' Sylvia said. 'Really I do, but we have to crack this, both of us, if we don't want to turn out to be tedious clinging old women, and a burden to the people we love.'

'Yes,' Bonnie said. 'Yes, I see what you mean.'

There was a silence in the kitchen and Sylvia could see that Bonnie was still uneasy. 'Just imagine it was Lila who had a lover,' she said. 'Wouldn't you be saying good for her?'

'I suppose I would.' Bonnie paused and sipped her tea. 'I feel so embarrassed by it, though.'

'Look, that's just teenage stuff, discovering that your parents and the Queen actually have sex – not together of course,' Sylvia laughed. 'But we're not teenagers, and Irene and Hamish have every right to this happiness.'

Bonnie rubbed her hands over her face. 'You're right,' she said finally, 'it is about me. For years I knew I was the most important person in Jeff's life. Now I don't come first with anyone and that's what's so hard to get used to.'

Sylvia nodded. 'Me too, although I realised over a period of time that I could never come first with Colin. But at the same time I was in a relationship in which I was *supposed* to come first, one that I had the right to call on and demand priority if I needed it. Just knowing that provides a sense of safety. But it's a new life for both of us now.'

Bonnie looked up from her cup. 'What about Hamish? What shall I say if I come down here in the morning and he's in the kitchen in his pyjamas?'

'How about "Good morning, Hamish",' Sylvia said with a smile, getting up to rinse her mug. 'And then "Would you like tea or coffee?". That sounds like a reasonable start.'

David sat in the flickering half-dark not watching an old black and white movie on the television, struggling with a mass of conflicting emotions. It had begun with his aloneness at the party, an emptiness and a regret that had bugged him all evening. Now the birth of Rebekah Frances had upset him in ways so profound that he could hardly bear to think about it, and he had turned it into anger against Mike, an anger that he could barely contain as he helped Bonnie and Sylvia to clear up, called a cab for Lenore, and then drove Lila home. Mike's failure to be there in a state to deliver the baby, to be with Caro, to share fully in that unique experience, had David, usually the mildest of men, seized with the urge to punch him full in the face and pummel him to the ground.

'Congratulations, mate,' he'd said eventually, slapping his brother-in-law on the back, but inside he was seething. Later, when he went out on the deck to get some air, Hamish joined him.

'Well, we finally got him vertical,' Hamish said with a laugh. 'He's never going to be allowed to forget this.'

'No, and he shouldn't,' David said, hearing the anger in his own voice. 'He behaved like the worst sort of macho prick.'

'No point getting upset about it,' Hamish had said. 'In the end it was his loss – he won't forget that in a hurry.'

But David couldn't shake off the fact that Mike had stuffed up the opportunity to be a part of something precious, something that he himself could never have. He managed to appear cool, cuddle his niece, hug Caro and Fran and her friends and cling briefly, albeit almost desperately, to Lila and Irene. He was awestruck by the way they had taken charge, deployed the other women and managed Caro. Some ancient female wisdom had been at work and David's respect stood alongside his resentment and jealousy.

Staring unseeingly as Gary Cooper rode across the desert on a dapple-grey horse, David wondered if staying home in Melbourne had been the right decision. He had been travelling for years, six months here, a year there, easily finding work wherever he went, first in Asia then Europe and finally in the Middle East. He enjoyed teaching, meeting the students, making friends among the eclectic crowd of people who lived similarly peripatetic lives, using their work as a way to see the world. It seemed fine to be alone discovering new places, but being alone at home felt different; like failure somehow, as though giving up travel should be about settling down and building something new. But here he was, doing in Melbourne just what he had done in Chiang Mai, Prague, Budapest, Florence, Bahrain and finally Qatar. Only now it was different because in those places it was adventurous, and here it seemed . . . just lonely and rather tedious, as though he was waiting for something that wasn't going to happen.

David got up and wandered to the window, looking down into the darkened street and then up and beyond the rooftops to the city buildings and the eerie charcoal sky blushing with the first

247

iridescence of dawn. If he leaned to one side slightly he could see the rooftops of the houses in Jodie's street. He thought about Caro's baby, the tiny wrinkled creature that had burst so dramatically into the world; the furrowed little brow under the wispy hair, the bright blue eyes and those minute hands, fingers spread wide, grasping at life. He'd never seen such a tiny baby before, never a life so new and raw, glistening with its mother's moisture, staking its claim on the world. The thought of not being able to have children hadn't bothered him before, but now he knew it was the killer factor. Most women, he was sure, would want children. It could never have worked with Jodie. She was younger than him – in a few years' time she would have felt the ticking of the biological clock and that would have been the end of it.

So Caro and Mike were parents now, and soon it would be Matt. His partner was pregnant too and they were getting married at Christmas. Couples, babies, families – they were all around him and he was teetering on the edge of the large and meaningful relationships of life unable to step into them. He flicked off the television and crawled back under the doona yawning, shivering with exhaustion and emotion. He had the lease on this place for six months, perhaps he should stay on until Matt's wedding and then let it go, take off again. Maybe Morocco this time, or Turkey perhaps, anywhere that would lift him out of this abyss of inaction, this sense that the most important things in life were lost to him.

A birth changed things, Fran thought as she backed slowly out of the narrow driveway. No one there was untouched, she had seen it in their faces. Being there had brought them together, bonded them in a very special way.

She turned out of the street and headed for Hawthorn. The day had that sparkling sunlit stillness that so often follows a wild and stormy night. It reflected her mood. While the others had been clearing up after the party and the birth, she and Mike had helped Caro into bed. Fran had prepared Rebekah's crib, and then washed her, sponging the strong little arms, the hands that punched at the air, the legs that kicked against the towel. She fumbled with

248

the nappy, the tiny vest and stretch suit, as though she had never done it before, relishing the privilege of being the first person to dress her granddaughter. She had stayed the night and when Mike dropped her home at midday, Fran wandered around her new house imagining Rebekah crawling across the floor, sitting in a highchair in the kitchen, taking her first staggering steps through the lounge. This was a birthday she would always remember; her first party and the birth of her granddaughter, surrounded by people she loved.

It was three o'clock when she reached Hawthorn and she stopped to buy a large bouquet of daffodils and purple iris for Lila. She was planning to surprise her by taking her out for tea and then to see Caro and the baby, and she drove slowly, enjoying an unaccustomed sense of contentment. It was only as she turned into the retirement village and onto Lila's street that her heart leapt and her body jerked to attention in the driving seat. There, in the turning circle at the top of Malthouse Close, was Lila, all in purple, cruising the empty street on a gleaming yellow contraption. And standing watching – Lenore, in black with a purple leather jacket, her silver hair gleaming in the sunlight.

'Fran, Fran!' Lila cried in delight, rocketing down the street towards her. 'What a lovely surprise. I thought you'd be too tired to come over today. You're just in time to see my scooter. Come along, park the car and get out. You can have a ride if you like.' And she swung back up the hill to the house. Fran swallowed hard and tried to contain her shock at the sight of Lila on a scooter, and her resentment at finding Lenore there.

'Lila invited me to see her scooter,' Lenore said, greeting her cautiously as she got out of the car.

Fran smiled distractedly and walked around the scooter pretending to inspect it, but really playing for time, searching herself for a genuine reaction.

'Who's is it, Mum?' she asked. 'It looks like Mr Pirelli's, only a different colour.'

Lila gave her a huge grin. 'It's *my* scooter,' she said proudly. 'I got it on Friday and rode it to the hairdresser's yesterday. I was going to tell you last night, but then the baby decided to arrive.'

'Yours? You mean you've hired it?'

'Bought it, it's all my own, all paid for. Come on, Fran, sit on it, try it out.'

'Bought it? You can't have done . . . what . . . on your own?'

'Ray helped me,' Lila said, adjusting the seat slightly. 'I didn't want to bother you. You were so busy with the business and everything. Now, just sit on here and then this is the accelerator, and the brake is over here. Don't go too fast, it takes a while to get used to the controls.'

'You mean you've been out on the road on it?'

'Course I have,' Lila said. 'Well, not on the road, I'm only allowed on the pavement. It's a glorious feeling.'

'I wish you'd talked to me about it,' Fran said.

'I'm perfectly capable of managing. You didn't ask me when you bought a new house.'

Fran gulped. 'No, but . . .' She stopped herself and changed tack in an effort to hide her feelings. 'Can you afford it? It must have cost a bomb.'

Lila straightened up and looked her in the eye. 'I can also manage my money, thank you, Fran. Now stop being so grumpy and have a ride.'

Fran looked suspiciously at the scooter, and put a tentative foot on the platform. 'Are you sure it's safe for you?'

'Course it is. Safe as houses, completely stable,' Lila said. 'And it makes me independent. You can't argue with that now, can you?'

Fran hesitated. 'I might be too heavy for it,' she said.

'Rubbish,' Lenore cut in. 'There's plenty of people much bigger than you who ride these things. Go on Fran, give it a go, it's really lovely.'

Fran settled herself in the seat, examined the controls, and then set off cautiously down the sloping street in the grip of two overwhelming emotions – panic at the prospect of her mother careering around the streets on a motorised vehicle, and resentment that not only had Lila taken this step without consulting her, but Lenore had been there first. She gritted her teeth, braked and turned the scooter in a circle. It certainly handled nicely. She took her time circling before going back, trying to get a grip on herself to avoid sounding ungracious.

'Well, it certainly handles very well,' she said, hearing how grudging she sounded. 'It'll be great for you to get out and about again. But you will be careful, won't you?'

Lila waved away the warning and climbed triumphantly back onto the scooter. 'You must think I'm losing it, Fran. Of course I'm careful,' she said, and Fran saw the wink she directed at Lenore, and the way Lenore attempted to ignore it so as not to be drawn further into the tension.

Lila started the scooter and headed for the backyard. 'Come on, you two, we'll have a cup of tea before Lenore has to go,' she said, negotiating the narrow gateway with some skill. 'Close the gate behind you.'

Fran made the tea and nursed her bruised feelings with as good a grace as she could muster while Lenore was given a guided tour of the house.

'You are so lucky, both of you,' Lenore said, having done an admirable job of greeting each aspect of Lila's purple décor with appropriate levels of appreciation. 'But you deserve it, what a beautiful family.' She put her hand on Fran's arm. 'Thank you, Fran, it was a privilege to share your birthday party, and as for the rest of it . . . what can I say? Unforgettable.' She finished her tea and stood up. 'Lila, I must get a move on. I have to meet someone at five.'

'I was going to take Mum to see Caro and the baby. Could we drop you off somewhere?' Fran offered in an attempt to compensate for her earlier chilliness.

Lenore shook her head. 'I'll be fine. I came by tram and I've got a return ticket.'

'Take her to the tram stop, Fran, while I clear up here,' Lila said, hugging Lenore. 'You'll find out about those red hat clubs for me?'

'I will,' Lenore said. 'And I'll get the book for you too. Meanwhile, you need to find yourself a red hat – something with lots of chiffon, totally unsuitable for a great grandmother.'

'You're not happy about the scooter, are you?' Lenore said to Fran once they were in the car.

Fran sighed. 'Not really. I can see what it means in terms of her independence, but I wonder if she's safe on it.'

Lenore shrugged. 'Fran, at eighty-four with a dodgy ankle, she's probably as safe on it as she is on her feet.'

'She could have an accident, roll it over, hit something.'

'And she could just as easily trip over in the kitchen and crack her head, or fall down the steps of the bus. But because this is new and motorised, it seems more dangerous.'

'I suppose so,' Fran said. 'She's so thrilled with it, with the prospect of being independent. I don't want to spoil it for her.'

Lenore nodded. 'The senescent illusion of freedom,' she said. 'The last gift of time. It all seems more precious the older one gets.'

'I don't think I've reached that stage yet.'

'No, you wouldn't. It's sixty when it happens, or at least it was for me, the sudden realisation that one is an older person, that time is limited. Occasionally you think you glimpse the end, and you know it could happen any day.'

'It could always happen any day,' Fran said. 'An accident, sudden illness, a heart attack.'

'Of course,' Lenore replied, 'but after sixty it all becomes just that little bit more real.'

'How old are you, Lenore?'

'Sixty-two next week,' Lenore said. 'I'm a Libran, like you.' she paused. 'Fran, I think I've upset you.'

Fran parked the car in the forecourt of a disused building across the street from the tram stop. 'It's complicated,' she said. 'I don't know how to explain it.'

'Let me guess,' said Lenore. 'I muscle in on your party, and on the birth of your granddaughter, and then when you come to see your mother the next day I'm there and I've already seen and test-driven the scooter. A series of intrusions, and while I never intended to hurt you I can see that I have. Is that right?'

Fran nodded. 'It must seem really petty,' she said.

'No. I must seem pretty insensitive. And I'm sorry. I was having such a good time, but I should have been more thoughtful, especially about coming here today.'

Now that her feelings were named and out in the open, Fran felt stupid and childish. 'It's been a bit of a difficult time,' she said. 'I think I was overreacting. I'm sorry too.'

'And there's more, isn't there?' Lenore said. 'You're really worried about the scooter.'

'Yes I am,' Fran said. 'She's very forgetful. She may get lost, not be able to find her way home. But the other thing . . .' She paused, remembering she was talking to Lenore but also needing to say it. 'I don't know how to put it, really, but this purple business, I've found it a bit hard to cope with. It seems so eccentric, and now the yellow scooter . . . I suppose I don't want people to laugh at her. This must sound ridiculous, but it's like when I was a teenager and I used to worry about what she wore at school concerts. I suppose we all worried that our mothers would embarrass us, and our friends would laugh. It's like that.'

'But who would laugh?' Lenore asked. 'Not your friends, or the people in the village who know her and like her, not people whose opinions really matter. If I saw Lila coming along the street, I'd think she must be a great character. I'd admire her, and, in fact, that's just what I do feel anyway.'

'You think I'm being stupid.'

Lenore undid her seatbelt and put her hand on Fran's arm. 'Not in the least. I think you're having a perfectly normal reaction. Whoever we grow up to be, Fran, we are always our mothers' daughters.' She picked up her bag and got out of the car. 'This was all very special, something I won't ever forget, and I hope I haven't spoiled it for you.'

Fran took a deep breath and got out of the car. She wasn't sure whether she wanted to laugh or cry. 'You haven't spoiled anything, Lenore. Really. I'm sorry for being a pain in the bum.'

Lenore smiled. 'I'll see you soon, then,' she said. 'Will you be able to make time to work on the book?'

'I'll do my best. A lot of it is written in bits and pieces. I just need to make it come together.'

'You'll do it,' she said, walking around to Fran's side. 'And if you don't, I'll be after you with my big stick.' She hesitated slightly, and then leaned forward and kissed Fran on the cheek.

'Thanks for the lift,' and she darted between the cars to the other side of the road just as the tram rattled to a halt.

Fran stood watching as it jolted forward and resumed its journey, and Lenore waved to her from a rear window. She felt uneasy now about her ungenerous attitude. Lenore was a strange and disturbing presence, both attractive and intimidating, and Fran was left wishing that she could have the last two hours back again to do it all differently.

TWENTY-SIX

The builders had moved out of the Boatshed the previous week, taking with them heaps of rubble, lengths of surplus wood and boxes of tools. Now the decorators were putting the last touches to the paintwork. By the end of next week, the kitchen fitting would be complete. Bonnie checked the schedule on her clipboard; she had booked the floor finishers and the cleaners for the week after that. Time to advertise for staff, a chef first, then a manager for the restaurant, and she needed to make a final decision about the furnishings, and for that she needed Sylvia and Fran: Sylvia for her strong visual sense, and Fran because, as the restaurant would trade on her name, she had to feel comfortable with it.

The interior walls had been sanded and repainted gleaming white, reminiscent of the hull of a boat, and the new hardwood floorboards would be stained to a warm cedar tone and then varnished. Bonnie wanted white wooden tables and chairs in bright primary colours – scarlet, royal blue, emerald, purple, yellow and orange. Sylvia had agreed that the bold colours would work, but Fran was more cautious.

'We can drop purple, if you like,' Bonnie had suggested with a smile. 'If it's making you nervous.'

'On that basis you'd also have to drop yellow too,' Fran replied. 'But it's not that, it just feels like too much mixed-up colour.'

So Bonnie had the designer draw up an interior with simple

white painted tables, each surrounded by chairs in a single different colour. The effect was remarkable and she could hardly wait to get Fran's reaction.

She wandered through into the gallery where the paintwork was now complete, and stood studying the drawing of the shop fittings she and Sylvia had chosen, visualising the rich colours and textures of the fabrics, and the glint of silver, bronze and bead jewellery displayed in the glass cabinets. By the time Will arrived at the end of the following week, she thought, he would see a major transformation.

She wandered outside to get away from the smell of paint while she waited for the signwriter to turn up. A couple of plastic crates were stacked on the boardwalk right where the few scruffy kiosk tables used to be and she perched there, in the same place she had sat brooding on the day her mother left for Greece, the day that she and Fran had rescued Sylvia from the vicarage. Sylvia's late-night lecture had shaken her, confronting her with her own selfish neediness, and then that question about what age would be 'too old'. But toughest of all was what Sylvia had said about them all being alone; that in the end each had to be enough for herself. Bonnie had gone to bed that night battling fear and confusion, and frequently breaking out in hot flushes of shame about her behaviour towards her mother and Hamish.

But it was the vision of herself and her future that was so confronting. 'I never think of myself as single,' she'd said while Sylvia made the tea. 'Jeff and I were married for more than thirty years. Even though he's gone I still feel married to him.'

'I know,' Sylvia said. 'And I do know how hard it is for you, but yes, he's gone. You're on your own now, Bon, and you do have to get to grips with that.'

Bonnie realised that in many ways she was still behaving as though Jeff was alive, and would eventually return and take over the reins.

'So what do you think about the kitchen design?' she'd ask him at night, or 'D'you think I've gone over the top on the projected turnover?' She felt his advice and acted on it and she sensed his approval around her like a safety blanket. But Sylvia had forced reality on her – Jeff wasn't coming back, and her mother's life was her own. She would need more than the Boatshed to sustain her through the vast expanse of the future, but in the meantime it would serve to distract her from the other emotional maelstrom that had threatened to engulf her since the birth of Fran's granddaughter.

The morning after Rebekah's birth, Bonnie had staggered downstairs in her dressing gown to find Hamish in the kitchen drinking coffee and reading the paper.

'Good morning, Bonnie,' he'd said, getting up. 'Can I get you a cup of coffee?'

Weary and bewildered, Bonnie felt the dialogue was the wrong way round. Surely she was supposed to do the asking? It was supposed to be her move, her olive branch, but he had beaten her to it.

'Thanks, Hamish,' she said, getting a glass of purified water from the cooler, 'that would be nice.' She drank the water and sat down at the benchtop observing him as he discarded the contents of the plunger, rinsed it and put in fresh coffee.

'I've been up for a while,' he said. 'This lot is a bit stewed, I'll make a fresh pot.'

He was not, thankfully, in his pyjamas, but wearing an immaculate pair of chinos and a light blue shirt. Bonnie's first and uncharitable thought was that obviously the sleepover had been planned, as he wasn't wearing the same clothes he'd had on at the party. But she realised she was thinking like a mother with a troublesome teenage daughter.

'Quite a night, last night,' Hamish said. 'A once in a lifetime experience for me.'

'Me too,' Bonnie said, feeling as though she had lost some battle, one that hadn't really been worth winning anyway.

'Wasn't your mother splendid? She and Lila – such remarkable women.'

The slight Scottish accent that he had never quite lost, although he had come to Australia as a teenager, sounded pleasant, melodious. In fact, he was quite a nice looking man for his age.

'Don't you think so, Bonnie?' Hamish prompted.

'I thought they were amazing,' she said, sipping her coffee. 'None of the rest of us knew what to do.'

She watched him get out Irene's favourite cup and saucer, fill it almost to the top with coffee and add a dash of cream, just as she liked it. He looked relaxed, pleasantly domestic; there was something reassuringly solid about him. Hamish had been involved with her parents for as long as Bonnie could remember; a childhood memory of her running towards him and being caught and swung around in the air, squealing with delight, came with a burst of nostalgia, a taste of childhood joy she had forgotten, and she remembered too her teenage appreciation that he always took her seriously. And yet she had not taken him seriously, had seen him merely as an interference; he was so familiar and yet entirely new.

'I'd better take this up to the boss,' Hamish said, slipping a couple of digestive biscuits onto the saucer. 'She likes her coffee really hot.'

Bonnie reached out and put her hand on his arm. 'Hamish . . .' He paused, looking down at her in surprise. 'Hamish . . . I'm sorry . . . really. I don't know what got into me.'

He put down the cup and took her hand. 'No need to apologise, Bonnie.' He lifted her hand to his lips and kissed her fingers lightly. 'I've known you since you were as small as Rebekah Frances, and this is a bit of a shift for all of us, but you're a wise and generous woman, just like your mother.' And he patted her on the shoulder, picked up the cup and was gone.

Facing her mother loomed as a rather more awkward hurdle in Bonnie's guilty imagination. It was hard to rid herself of the feeling that Irene was suddenly going to confront her with a reprimand about the banker and the share portfolio; the fact that Irene had probably forgotten all about it years ago didn't seem to make it any less of a threat. Eventually, around midday, Irene had come into the study where Bonnie was working to give her the Sunday paper.

'I've finished with this, Bonnie,' she said, dropping the paper onto the desk.

Bonnie, who hadn't heard her come in, jumped nervously to her feet, and took off her glasses.

'Thanks . . . er . . . thanks, Mum.' Every line that she had rehearsed now seemed fatuous, pretentious or both. 'Mum, I . . .' She looked down at her feet. 'I've been really stupid and selfish.' She paused, hoping her mother would rescue her but Irene, standing straight-faced in the doorway, was clearly waiting for more.

'About Hamish,' Bonnie began again. 'I'm sorry, really sorry. I always think I know best but I was wrong.'

'Thank you, Bonnie, I'm glad you've come to terms with it.'

'Yes . . . and I was so proud last night, you and Lila were wonderful, and I'm . . . well, I'm ashamed of myself.'

Irene walked back into the room. 'Don't be, there's no need. Sometimes being close to someone makes it hard for us to see each other clearly.' She paused and fleetingly Bonnie was convinced she was going to mention the banker. 'I was worried about you last night,' Irene said. 'The baby . . . I thought . . . I saw your face and wondered whether . . .'

Bonnie's heart began to race and she raised her hand. 'It's okay, Mum, I'm okay. I wouldn't have chosen to be there but it happened, and I'm fine, happy for Caro and Mike, and of course for Fran and Lila.'

Irene said nothing at first, just looked her straight in the eye and eventually Bonnie had to look away. 'Well,' Irene said, 'if you're sure . . . as long as you're really okay.' And she patted Bonnie gently on the arm and left the room, closing the door behind her.

Bonnie sank into her chair gasping for air. With her elbows on the desk she buried her head in her hands, taking deep breaths to calm herself. A fine film of sweat broke out on her skin and her head was spinning. She thought she had carried it off well last night, concentrating on doing practical things, then on her annoyance with Hamish and finally, when she was alone, forcing the feelings down by focusing instead on what Sylvia had said to her. But of course her mother knew, would understand how it felt; indeed, she too would be caught in her own grief as she helped deliver Lila's great granddaughter. And in that moment Bonnie knew that by referring to it Irene had forced their shared grief to a place where it could not be ignored for long.

The signwriter's white flatbed van drew up in the street outside and Bonnie got to her feet, straightened her shoulders and walked out to meet him. Keep busy, that was the thing, keep busy and distracted for long enough and the pain might go away, she might be able to smother it again. What she must not do was to think about the baby and the fact that one day, probably quite soon, Fran would have Rebekah with her and she, Bonnie, would be expected to admire her, touch her, hold her – because she was afraid that when that day came, the decades old bandaids would no longer be strong enough to contain the wound.

TWENTY-SEVEN

Sylvia was counting her money, not in piles of coins, but carefully working out her capital, how much interest she would get on the investments that had been her share of the settlement, and how much she would have left from her pay from the Boatshed after tax was deducted. What she had said to Bonnie had also worked as a reminder to her that she was now really all she'd got. But she was also well aware that her situation was somewhat different to Bonnie's and it wasn't just a difference in financial status.

Comparatively early in her marriage, Sylvia had recognised that she would have to take responsibility for her own emotional and spiritual needs and had developed her ways of coping with the painful discovery that loneliness within a relationship is more acute than being alone. Already Colin's presence in her life was shadowy, different entirely from Jeff's constant presence in Bonnie's consciousness. He was in every respect Bonnie's point of reference; for Sylvia, on the other hand, the issue was one of direction tied to a restless sense of something she hadn't yet been able to grasp.

She was very close to deciding against England, but at the same time the prospect of running the gallery felt like a compromise. Just as moving to England would be hooking her in to Kim's dreams and aspirations, so the gallery locked her into Bonnie's. In Hong Kong she had discovered the passionate, assertive, sexual woman she could be and it was thrilling, but it was just a stage in the unfolding challenge – and she would not compromise this journey for Kim, for Bonnie and the Boatshed, or even for Will.

'I've always had this idea,' Irene said as they discussed the use of the garden cottage, 'that single women should reorganise their living arrangements as they get older. We don't need all these separate households when we all have different things we can offer each other.'

'I thought you liked your solitude,' Sylvia had said.

'I do. I like to know I have spaces where I won't be disturbed. But the older I get, the more I see the value in having people close to me as well. The thing is, Sylvia, some of us are lucky enough to have money or property or both, others are less well off financially but can contribute in other ways – energy, companionship, a safety net as one ages. I have more than I'll ever need, and I really hope you'll stay. It's as much for my own sake as for yours.'

The cottage was the size of a one-bedroom apartment, simple, comfortable and sufficiently detached from the house to give her the feeling of being in a place of her own.

'We'll get the flying domestics in next week,' Irene said, pulling the dustcovers off the sofa. 'Open up those windows, Sylvia; let's get some sun and fresh air going through.'

The furniture she had put in storage when Colin vacated the house could stay put for a while, but there were lamps, ornaments and pictures, cushions, and other bits and pieces which would give the cottage a familiar and personal touch.

'For as long as you want it, dear,' Irene said. 'And I personally hope it will be a long time.'

'Couldn't you go somewhere else?' Will asked when she told him. 'Somewhere you and I could be together?'

'I need somewhere that suits *me*,' she said. 'Besides, why would I get somewhere for you and me? You're only here occasionally.'

'I could be there more often,' he suggested, but Sylvia decided not to respond.

'Come in, Sylvia, come in,' Veronica Waters said, drawing her into the living room. 'It's lovely to see you, I was so glad when you phoned.'

The room was bright and warm with afternoon sunshine, and Sylvia remembered that the last time she was here, she had thought it clearly reflected its owner, a woman who was entirely at ease with herself and what she wanted. It was essentially well organised but also confidently scattered with books, newspapers and other bits and pieces – there was no plan here to impress a visitor, or to impose a particular décor. The contents were entirely compatible with Veronica's personality.

'This is such a lovely place,' Sylvia said.

Veronica moved some books from a chair so that they could both sit down. 'Thank you,' she said. 'I like it. I'm not the tidiest of people but then it doesn't really matter when one only has one-self to worry about. How are you, Sylvia? I've thought of you so often but didn't like to call. I thought you might be wanting to forget about Box Hill, create a little distance.'

'I did at first,' Sylvia admitted, 'but time's moved on now and I certainly didn't want to lose touch with you.'

'Well, I'm delighted,' Veronica said. 'Of course, we have a new minister now, you know, and a new minister's wife.' She pulled a long face. 'It takes a bit of getting used to when one is so involved and someone very different takes over. They're from England, and rather stodgy, I'm afraid. He's amazingly patriarchal and she's very much the bossy vicar's wife. Still, I think they have good hearts. I guess we'll get used to them eventually.'

It was strange to be back in the heart of what had been Colin's territory and yet be separate from the responsibilities and expectations of that life. Sylvia relaxed into her chair and while Veronica produced tea and a delicious banana cake, she told her about her trip to England, and her work in preparing the gallery.

'So, a time for big decisions,' Veronica said, setting the tea on a small side table. 'Practical decisions. Have you had a chance to work out what you really want?'

Sylvia shook her head. 'No, there seems to be something hovering just over my shoulder but I haven't yet worked out what it is. So many years of doing what other people wanted – now I'm not clear about what it is that I want.'

'I suspect that your daughter isn't making things any easier,'

Veronica said. 'Young people do tend to see things in black and white, and there's nothing like a beloved child wanting something from you to get the maternal guilt going.'

Sylvia nodded vigorously as she stirred her tea. 'Tell me about it! The guilt and anxiety are crippling. I feel that if I decide against it I'll be a bad mother, and a worse grandmother, that it *ought* to be the thing I want most. But you know, Veronica, even if they were here in Australia I'm not sure that I'd want to lock myself so fully into Kim and Brendan's lives, but there aren't many people I'd admit that to.'

Veronica went to the dresser and picked up a framed photograph of a smiling couple flanked by two rangy teenage boys and a rather younger girl. 'My daughter Heather, her husband Brian and my grandchildren,' she said. 'This was taken about ten years ago. The boys are in their twenties now, and Linda's nineteen this year. They live in the Northern Territory, a remote cattle station. Brian's a cattle farmer, and Heather's one of those people who does everything, makes butter, rides with the stockmen, she even educated the children through the School of the Air.

'Twenty years ago they begged me to move there with them to look after the babies. Financially, it would have been very practical for me, and of course I would have had a very special relationship with them all, but I couldn't do it, Sylvia. I'm a city person, I like to be near cinemas and libraries, good cafés and bookshops, go to concerts and be involved with the church and my work for the Red Cross. Some women would have jumped at it and I admire them for that, but it would have been death for me.

'I see them now, once or twice a year, and we all get on well, but I don't think Heather has ever really forgiven me for not going. But I would have been no good to her or the children because I would have been resenting the fact that I had sacrificed what I wanted for them. I made an uncomfortable and unpopular decision and it took a while for the dust to settle, but at least I was true to myself.'

Sylvia sat for a moment, staring down at the photograph and then gazing thoughtfully out of the window. 'Did you have something you very clearly wanted to do?' she asked. 'A sense of purpose, a direction?'

'Not really. And I think that made it harder for Heather to accept. I wasn't saying no thanks, I've got a relationship I don't want to leave, or a job I want to stick with. I was just saying no thanks, it doesn't suit me because I want to do a whole range of other interesting things which I can only do here. After all, it's assumed that we mothers and grandmothers want to take on this sort of care and involvement, but not all of us do. Anyway, it should be more straightforward for you, you *have* got a job, but the most important thing, surely, is your creativity – you never had time to develop that with the church always around your neck. Now you have, and it's tapping you on the shoulder.'

Sylvia stared at her, feeling as though a very large penny had dropped inside her. 'My creativity . . .'

'Yes,' Veronica said, pouring her another cup of tea. 'Your beautiful designs, the children's costumes you made, the clothes you created for yourself.' She paused. 'I remember you showing me a wonderful selection of designs for lingerie based on the fashions of the thirties . . . surely you haven't forgotten?'

The stillness in the room was broken only by the entrance of Veronica's tabby cat pushing his way in through the cat flap and looking imperiously around for a place to settle.

'Won't you be developing all that through your gallery?' Veronica asked, looking up to see Sylvia still staring at her in surprise. 'You're not just thinking of buying and selling other people's work, surely? You have a real gift, Sylvia, now is the time of your life you can really explore it.'

Caro stretched out on the lounge with Rebekah, replete from a recent feed, sleeping on her chest. She picked up one tiny hand, examining the rosy fingers that curled strongly around her own even in sleep, and nuzzled the sweet-smelling warmth of her daughter's head. This, she decided, must be the reward for a ghastly pregnancy and a sudden shock birth, this extraordinary connection to another being who seemed to know her so intimately without the need for words.

'She's three weeks old today, you know,' she said to David, who was sitting across the room from her. 'Three weeks, imagine that.'

'You look positively angelic,' he said with a half-smile. 'Is this really the same tortured delinquent of six months ago?'

She stuck her tongue out at him, and stared down again at the baby. 'Be nice to me, I'm a mother, I deserve respect.'

David rolled his eyes and groaned. 'Oh please! Do me a favour and promise you won't say that to Mum.'

Caro laughed. 'All right, all right, I know, discretion is not my strong point but I'm not that stupid even if I am demented from loss of sleep.'

'How will you cope when you go back to work?' David asked.

'Ugh! Don't remind me,' Caro said with a groan. 'I said two months – that's only another five weeks. I can't bear the thought of it.'

'Don't tell me you want to be a full-time mum?'

'What's wrong with that?' Caro said defensively.

'Nothing at all, it just doesn't sound much like you.'

'I'm not really like me anymore, that's the problem.' Caro sat up, cradling Rebekah in one arm while she folded her own legs underneath her to sit cross-legged. 'Like, I don't want to go back to work. I guess I will want to work eventually, but not as soon as I thought, and not full time. And definitely not at Desmond Records. Going back there seems like a death sentence.'

'I thought you loved it there,' David said.

'I did, but now, well, it doesn't seem so great. I mean, they're nice guys but they're such dags, they're like a load of fifty-year-old teenagers. That's probably why I liked it but it feels different now.'

David shrugged. 'Doesn't suit the new holistic earth mother? So, will you look for something new?'

'I suppose so,' Caro said, 'but not till after Christmas at the earliest. I just don't think I can cope with work and motherhood quite so quickly. Anyway, I can't bear the thought of putting her in child care just yet.' She got up and carried Rebekah over to David.

'You have her for a bit.' She walked over to the window, stretched her arms above her head and then dropped over from the waist to touch her toes. 'I still have a roll of fat around my middle,' she said, pinching it as she stood up straight. 'By the way, d'you think Mum's lost weight?'

David shrugged and stroked Rebekah's head with his finger. 'Dunno, hadn't noticed.'

'I think she has. She told me she was doing some low-carb diet from the *Women's Weekly*. She's certainly looking better.' She bent again, hanging lower this time until she could get her palms flat on the floor. 'Jodie came over the other day, she was asking about you. Said she hadn't seen you in the coffee shop for ages.'

'I stopped going there,' David said, not looking up. 'I go to the one down the other end.'

Rebekah, eyes still closed, opened her mouth in a huge yawn and stretched her tiny arms.

'You are *such* a dickhead, David,' Caro said, straightening up. 'Don't you like her or what?'

'Jodie? Sure, I like her a lot, a helluva lot, but I stuffed it up. Couldn't get my head around talking to her about . . . you know. By the time I got up courage she was on with some other guy.'

'She *is not!*' Caro said as vehemently as if she herself had been accused of infidelity.

'She is,' David said. 'I saw her with him, saw them a few times, although I don't think she saw me. First time was only a few days after she called to ask me to a party. He's a tall guy, wears an old brown leather flying jacket with a fleecy collar, looks vaguely familiar. They get their coffee together in the mornings.'

Caro looked at him, hands on her hips, head on one side. 'Duh! That's her brother, stupid. He was at school with us, name's Owen. We were in year nine, Owen was in year ten and you were in year twelve. Don't you remember? He's just moved back here from Brisbane. One of Jodie's housemates moved out and he moved in. Honestly, David, you can really be a thicko sometimes.'

She walked over and reclaimed Rebekah. 'Come back to Mummy, darling, dopey Uncle David can't be trusted to look after himself, let alone beautiful girls!'

'What do you *mean*, the trade fair?' Fran said, staring at Bonnie in horror. 'I can't go to Sydney, Bon, we have to interview chefs and then I'll have to work with him or her on testing the menus. There's the signature products, we've got find a floor manager, there's far too much to do.'

'It's only for three days and it's a great promotion opportunity,' Bonnie said, perching on the edge of Fran's new desk. 'It'll be seething with useful people from the tourism and hospitality business and publishers who do gourmet type books and, most importantly, the media. Food editors from magazines, restaurant review writers.'

'Look, Bonnie, I know what it is,' Fran said. 'I went once a few years ago and it's quite nice, but there's too much to do here. There's no way you're taking on a chef without me vetting him or her.'

'I wouldn't dream of it,' Bonnie said. 'We can do that before you go. Lenore has got you the spot as guest speaker at the dinner. You can do your stuff and they'll mock up coloured samples of the cover of your book, posters, all that . . .'

'But I haven't finished it yet,' Fran protested. 'Nowhere near.'

'It doesn't matter,' Bonnie said. 'Advance publicity. It'll get your name out and around the traps, in somewhere other than Melbourne. We can rush through some of the Boatshed publicity for you to take with you, and we'll overstamp it with the opening date. We can't afford to miss this, Fran. We need you to go.'

'Bloody Lenore,' Fran grunted, sifting through the label designs for the Boatshed products.

'Oh yes, and she says you can stay at her place in Surry Hills,' Bonnie continued. 'She's got plenty of space and it'll be really convenient.'

'Oh no! Don't do this to me, Bon, not three days and nights of Lenore.'

'Well, there's always the gorgeous Jack as compensation,'

Bonnie said with a grin. 'Now that you've signed the contract it's okay to have sex with him on the table!'

'Fall asleep underneath it is more like it, the way I feel,' Fran wailed. 'I can't believe you're making me do this, Bonnie.'

'I'm marketing you and the Boatshed, Fran,' Bonnie said with a smile and a wave. 'All in the cause of business and profits. Anyway, you'll probably enjoy it once you stop whingeing.'

Fran stared out of the window trying not to think about the trade fair. She was just getting on top of things and now this. She looked around her at the room that was slowly taking shape as her office, just like Bonnie's room next door. Both had desks, shelves and telephone, but as yet no chairs. Fran's, though, had a light box for transparencies, a luxury she had never had before, and both had wall-mounted whiteboards.

Even through her dismay, Fran's pleasure wasn't diminished for long. Her delight in her granddaughter and the sudden release of years of tension between her and Caro had her waking each morning with enthusiasm for the day rather than the anxiety that had been a constant presence for longer than she could remember. Being out of debt and knowing exactly what income she could expect had increased her confidence. For once her financial situation was under control, and even her eating habits seemed to be changing. As she assumed her role in the decision-making about the Boatshed, Fran felt she was sprouting new muscles that she would soon start to flex.

'Okay, okay, of course I'll go. Anything you say, Madame Lash.'

Bonnie laughed and struck a whip-wielding pose. 'By the way, that long narrow room at the back, up that little flight of steps? Sylvia's asked if she can use it.'

'Whatever for?' Fran asked. 'It's not good for stock, she'd have to keep carrying stuff up and down the staircase.'

'It's not for stock,' Bonnie said. 'A studio of some sort, she said she'd tell me more later, but if we weren't using it she'd like to.'

Fran shrugged. 'Fine by me. It's very narrow but the light and the view are lovely, almost like the bridge of a ship. Impractical for us, though. Where *is* Sylvia, anyway, getting more stuff for the gallery?'

'Suppose so,' Bonnie said. 'It's a bit different now she's in the cottage. I don't see her come and go. I really miss her being in the house, but I'm trying not to interfere. She was out until very late last night – I heard her drive in after midnight. Maybe she did find herself a toy boy in Hong Kong. I'm dying to ask her. On the other hand, I could ask Will, he arrived the night before last and he's coming over to look at the Boatshed this afternoon. Maybe he knows what Sylvia got up to in Hong Kong.' She turned back to look at Fran. 'How much weight have you actually lost?'

'Five kilos,' Fran said, 'and not a cross-trainer in sight.'

TWENTY-EIGHT

Outside the window of the fourth-floor boardroom on Southbank the sky was a leaden grey. Rain fell as relentlessly this afternoon as it had since daybreak and the room was filled with a dull steely light that seemed to be fading by the moment. At the other end of the boardroom table the recently appointed executive director, who was clearly uncomfortable at this first board meeting, fidgeted and cleared his throat. His lack of confidence irritated Will, nudged him with concern that they may have made a poor decision in appointing him, reminded him that this was the sort of business set-up that he had vowed always to avoid but had drifted into at the start of the year with Jeff's encouragement, just before he died.

Halfway down the table on his right-hand side, the company solicitor, who had been summoned to attend the meeting to report on the contract negotiations with the Japanese joint venture partners, graced him with a stunning smile and a look that conveyed a great deal more than professional interest. It was the sort of overtly adventurous look from an attractive, confident woman that had always had the power to turn him on. Will had never responded to girlish women who looked up from under their lashes like Princess Diana, as though they were ready to wilt in his arms. It was power and confidence that got his juices flowing, the challenge from someone who could match him, a woman who was ready to play hard. But he let this one go through to the keeper and turned his attention to the papers in front of him, and the tedious monotone of a fellow director explaining his concerns about the environmental impact of the resort development.

The solicitor tossed her head, flicking the fall of blonde hair back from her face, her eyes resting on him in a beam of heat, and he was visited by an unpleasant flashback of how he would so recently have responded. The pattern was familiar: match the gaze, hold it, let her see him appraising her, break the gaze briefly and then lock it in again while planning a strategic move for when the meeting broke up. Now he met her eyes with deliberate coldness, in a look that signalled a dislike aimed really at himself, and he saw her hesitate before switching off the beam and turning her attention to the environmental impact statement under discussion. He was not used to not getting what he wanted. Powerless was a new feeling, and frustration made it worse.

'Just come for dinner and stay with us your first night,' Bonnie had said on the phone before he left Perth. 'Come and be family before you go off to be a tycoon in the city. It's weeks since you were here.'

His original plan had involved going straight from the airport to the serviced apartment and meeting Sylvia there. For weeks he had comforted himself by imagining passionate nights and busy days punctuated by intimate breakfasts, cosy lunches, and long romantic evenings. Despite his unease about the depth of Sylvia's feelings, he had managed to convince himself that once they were together again, everything would be as it had been in Hong Kong. This would be, and he pardoned himself for the pun, the bedding down of their relationship. From here they could plan the future.

'Why don't we just tell Bonnie?' Sylvia had said on the phone when he told her he felt bound to accept Bonnie's invitation for the night of his arrival. 'I'm not comfortable about this at all and the longer we hide it the harder it will be to tell her.'

'No,' he'd insisted. 'Absolutely not, not yet. I want to see how she is and we need to pick the right time. Please, Sylvia, don't say anything just yet. Promise me.' And he heard in her voice how much it cost her to make the promise.

There was, of course, no reason not to tell Bonnie, no reason except Will's own fear that her reaction might influence Sylvia in a negative way. Ever since his declaration of love over the telephone he thought he had sensed her drawing back, wary of his intensity. There had been women in the past who would have melted to hear those words from him, but despite everything that Will knew about women, he was not prepared for someone like Sylvia, a woman whose identity was grounded not in a knowledge of sexual attractiveness or her ability to deal at his level in his world, but in an innate and mature female wisdom, a singular spiritual and emotional strength that meant she would not play games of submission and dependence, or compete with him at his own game. He had tried to match her by pulling back a little too, behaving more like the old Will, the one with whom she had been happy to throw snowballs and browse bookshops, to trust as a tour guide on the giddying funicular to the Peak, and as a mature and confident lover in the bedroom of his Hong Kong apartment. The Will he had been before the parting at the airport had sent him into a miserable spiral of lovesick longing.

Arriving at Irene's house from the airport in the early evening he had expected Sylvia to be there. She had, after all, said she would see him at dinner. But there was no sign of her and it was not until he had dumped his bag in the spare room, washed and wandered down to join Bonnie, Irene and Hamish for a drink, that he felt able to enquire, as casually as possible, how and where she was.

'She'll be over for dinner,' Bonnie said, handing him a glass of wine. 'She's moved into the cottage now, and she had something she needed to finish tonight.'

Will nodded and sipped his drink, attempting to look calm while waiting for the sound of the kitchen door. He passed the next hour in nervous anticipation masked by attempts at relaxed conversation. It was while Bonnie was checking the status of the meal that he heard the door open and voices in the kitchen.

'Will,' Sylvia said, crossing the room to him. 'How lovely to see you.'

And the brief pressure of her body against him in the hug, the scent of her hair and the brush of her cheek against his, were like an injection of some powerful calm-inducing drug. He felt safe again, just as he had as a child when his mother came to collect him from the hated boarding school and take him home for the holidays. He was flooded with warmth and with the confidence that nothing bad could happen while she was around. He made a mental note never to mention that because it was the sort of immature, needy, unsexy thing that she would hate.

It was hard for Will to get through the evening without giving in to his desire for physical contact, and when Sylvia returned to the cottage and the others retired to their rooms for the night, the feeling of her being so near but so far away was torture and he called her on the mobile.

'I could slip out of the back door,' he whispered into the phone. 'No one would hear me. I could be there in your bed in less than a minute.'

'No, Will,' she said firmly. 'You're the one who wants to keep this a secret. What if Bonnie or Irene spots you skulking around the garden in your jocks?'

'I'll get dressed —'

'No! We'll be together tomorrow. When Bonnie finds out, I want it to be because we told her, and I want that to be soon. Darling Will, it was lovely to see you tonight, and I was dying to pounce on you too, but you set it up like this and now we just have to wait.'

He eventually fell asleep cursing himself for bad management, for his failure to think ahead and lie to Bonnie about the day and time of his arrival, which would have allowed them a night or two together while Bonnie thought he was still in Perth.

The following morning he had appointments back to back and they finally met at his apartment early in the afternoon. Within minutes he was wondering what he had been worried about. The torture of the intervening weeks was washed away and it was Hong Kong all over again. They made love, ordered takeaway, made love again, watched a movie on the house system and made love again. It was only at midnight that Sylvia, who had fallen asleep, woke suddenly, kissed him and got out of bed to go home.

'No!' Will protested, sitting up and grasping her hand as she stood beside the bed. 'Stay, you have to stay the night.'

'And what if Bonnie notices that my car isn't there, or pops across to speak to me early in the morning?' She zipped up her skirt and went to the mirror to brush her hair, looking at his reflected face. 'We have to be sensible, Will, either that or let's get it out in the open.' She walked back to the bed and leaned down to kiss him. 'Don't look so grumpy. I'll meet you for lunch and see you tomorrow evening. Remember, Hamish is taking us all out for dinner.'

'Yes, and I'll have to share you again, and you'll go home with them,' he complained.

'You sound like a sulky schoolboy,' she said, laughing and roughing up his hair. 'You need a good spanking by the headmaster.'

'No, the headmistress,' he said, tugging her back onto the bed on top of him. 'Please stay.'

She kissed him again, wrapping her arms around his neck. 'No, much as I'd love to. I don't want to be asked questions by Bonnie or Irene and have to lie.'

The talk around the boardroom table had stopped and everyone was looking at him expectantly. Will shuffled his papers together.

'I think we all need time to think this over,' he said. 'Let's sleep on it and we'll meet here tomorrow at ten and make a decision.'

Back at the apartment he flung his briefcase on the bed and stretched out on the sofa, mulling over the idea that had come to him during the meeting. He had organised it so badly, just assuming that Sylvia would be there with him, constantly available, fitting in with his plans. Next time he would organise it better, plan it with her in advance. Meanwhile, perhaps he could persuade her to engage in a little more subterfuge. He loosened his tie, kicked off his shoes and dialled her number.

'I've had an idea,' he said when she answered. 'I'm supposed to go back to Perth on Friday, but suppose I don't, suppose I rebook it for Sunday night but pretend I'm still going home. We could go off somewhere to the country for the weekend.'

There was silence on the other end. 'I don't know,' she said eventually. 'What would I tell Bonnie and Irene?'

'Couldn't you invent a friend somewhere that you're going to visit?'

He could tell she didn't like it, the deception, lying to Bonnie again, but he could also tell that she wanted to go. 'Please,' he wheedled. 'Let me ravish you in the glorious Victorian countryside. We can go for walks, eat delicious food, taste wine, we'll have plenty of time and no one looking over our shoulders. After that it's only just over three weeks until I come back for the Boatshed opening, and we'll tell Bonnie then.'

'Promise?'

'I promise,' he said, and he believed it. He believed that away from Melbourne he could break down her resistance and get some commitment for the future, something that would withstand Bonnie's possible disapproval.

'All right,' she said. 'All right, it would be lovely, I'll come. But I'll also hold you to that promise. When you come back for the opening, we tell Bonnie.'

'I've booked it,' he whispered to her that evening. 'The best suite in the best hotel in Queenscliff. Friday to Sunday.'

'I can hardly wait,' she said, smiling at him, and the warm pressure of her leg against his under the table convinced him that she meant it.

TWENTY-NINE

'It's all right, Fran,' Sean said, folding his arms and leaning back against the kitchen wall. 'You can safely go away, I shan't do anything terrible to the kitchen while you're not here, and when you get back we can test cook the whole menu.' A dark haired, dark eyed thirty-five year old from Galway with a melodious Irish accent, he had been the first applicant for the chef's position, the first interviewee, and was head and shoulders above all the others in experience. He was also looking for a day job. Graeme, his partner, was breakfast chef at a central city hotel, so the breakfast and lunch schedule was perfect for him. Now Fran stood in the centre of the restaurant looking around with satisfaction, her suitcase alongside her.

'It's not that I don't trust you, Sean,' she said. 'I just don't want to leave the excitement.'

'Sure'n there'll still be enough excitement when you get back,' he said. 'Now look at herself there waiting for you, you'd better get going.'

She gave him a wave and looked around her as she walked to the door. 'You were right, Bonnie, those white tables and coloured chairs are great,' she said.

'I knew it'd be okay,' Bonnie said. 'The day Mum and Hamish brought Lila in to have a look around I showed her the artist's impression. Lila said the colour scheme was perfect!'

Fran laughed. 'Good thing you didn't tell me that at the time – it would have frightened the life out of me. Just over two weeks, Bon, and we'll be open. I can hardly believe it.

'You won't take on any waitstaff while I'm away, will you?'

Bonnie shook her head. 'No, Fran, I promise, now come along or you'll miss your flight.'

'Fran,' a voice whispered above her. 'Fran, it's me, Lenore. It's five o'clock and I'm going power walking. Just thought I'd check if you wanted to come.'

Fran rolled over, forcing her eyes open to the unmistakable light of dawn. She had arrived at Lenore's home, tucked in a narrow lane near Oxford Street, the previous evening, in time for dinner with Lenore and Jack and some of their acquaintances who were in Sydney for the trade fair. It had been a pleasant evening with good food and delightful company.

'Oh good,' Lenore said, 'you *are* awake, I wasn't sure.' She was wearing a black tracksuit and purple sneakers and was bouncing easily from one foot to the other as though warming up. 'I always go at this time. Forgot to ask you last night, and then I thought that if you got up while I was out you might be worried. It's a glorious morning.' She pulled the curtains back a little further, letting in more of the early light. 'Do come, it's such a great start to the day.'

Fran couldn't imagine anything she would like less than power walking at five in the morning, except, of course, for a run. 'I doubt I could keep up with you, Lenore,' she said, hoping this would be sufficient discouragement. 'I wouldn't want to slow you down.'

'No worries,' Lenore said. 'I can steam on ahead if I want and then wheel back to meet you.'

Fran dragged herself up into a sitting position and yawned again.

'Great! I'm so glad,' Lenore said, taking her semi-vertical position as acquiescence. 'I'll wait downstairs. I'll have a nice glass of hot water with lemon ready for you.'

Fran weighed up the prospect of another couple of hours in bed against an ungracious response to her hostess and slowly hung her legs over the side of the bed.

'I can't believe I'm doing this,' she told herself, thinking of the glee with which Caro would devour the story when she told her about her first morning in Sydney.

Lenore handed her the threatened glass of hot water and returned to the doorjamb against which she had been flexing her calf muscles.

'Good to warm up a bit, especially if you're not used to it,' she said, beckoning Fran to join her.

Fran drank the water feeling incredibly virtuous and thinking longingly of her first cup of coffee of the day, which was always her first choice on waking. Warily she stretched her arms up and bent over at the waist, as she had seen Caro do, and hung there for a moment before copying Lenore's stretches.

'Good,' Lenore said. 'We can get going now.' And she led the way out of the front door, along the lane and out towards Oxford Street where a waiter in a long white apron was hosing down the pavement in front of an Italian cafe, and a greengrocer was rolling up the shutter door of his shop.

Fran swung her arms and breathed deeply. There was something rather nice about the gentle pace of dawn in the heart of a city – now she was up and out, the prospect of exercise didn't seem quite so horrific. Lenore bounced along beside her in companionable silence as they made their way down the slope towards Hyde Park.

'I might just power on a bit now,' Lenore said, pulling her baseball cap further down over her eyes as they hit the entrance to the park. 'You take your time and I'll meet you back here in about half an hour.' And off she strode, her body a power pack of energy, her arms swinging back and forth.

Fran walked on past the war memorial and the Pool of Reflection gleaming like glass in the sunlight. Ahead of her through the broad, tree-lined path, sunlight filtered through the branches of the trees, patterning the deep shade, and a couple of old men who had obviously been sleeping rough rolled up their blankets and struggled to their feet. Lenore was striding on, widening the distance between them, and Fran, keeping to a comfortable pace, thought of mornings at home, falling out of bed at the last possible moment, a mug of strong coffee drunk while defrosting a couple of homemade muffins or croissants. Then a second coffee while she piled on butter, jam or honey, one ear on the radio, an eye on the newspaper, and her hand tapping nervously on the pad while she listed things she needed to do. The edginess of that time defined the day, but on this glorious, still Sydney morning, it all seemed such an unnecessary waste of energy.

'I'll do it again tomorrow,' Fran told Lenore as they sat at the table in the back garden drinking lemon and ginger tea and eating poached pears with Greek yoghurt. 'Don't go without me – I feel perfectly splendid.'

'It's a date,' Lenore said with a smile. 'It's such a good way to start the day, and you look great, you've lost weight.' She paused, looking at Fran. 'You have such a great complexion, Fran, and the most wonderful eyes. You're a really beautiful woman.'

When David walked into the coffee shop he felt as though everyone knew why he was there. He ordered his long black at the counter and sat at a table with the newspaper. The first time he'd seen Jodie here she had taken him by surprise, but that wasn't going to happen this time. He had tried out various scripts for what he'd say but none of them sounded convincingly natural, so now he planned to trust to luck. As the minutes ticked away, though, his head began to throb with the tension. When he saw her open the glass door, he got up from the table and intercepted her on her way to the counter.

'Hi ,' he said. 'Can I get your coffee for you?'

She paused. 'Okay,' she nodded. 'Cappuccino, please.'

'Are you on your own?' She nodded again, and as she made her way to the table, David waited impatiently for the coffee, resenting the seconds that were giving her time to make up her mind to tell him to piss off. Finally he set the cup down in front of her, realising too late that she usually got a takeaway.

'Sorry,' he said, 'I forgot. Will I get them to put it in a beaker for you?'

'It's fine,' Jodie said, picking up her spoon to skim off the foam.

They sat in uneasy silence while David tried to calm himself. 'I met your niece the other week,' Jodie said. 'She's beautiful and Caro really seems to have taken to motherhood.'

David nodded. 'Yes, yes, she does . . .' He tried to force out more words but they stuck in his throat and there was another longer, even more awkward silence.

'You didn't return my call,' she said eventually. 'If you didn't want to come to the party, you only had to say so.'

David flushed deeply, heat flooding his body and leaving its traces in an embarrassing glow on his face and neck. 'It wasn't the party,' he said. 'It's more complicated than that.'

Jodie raised her eyebrows and sipped her coffee.

'I'm thinking of going away,' he said. It wasn't at all what he had wanted to say and it felt really stupid now. Maybe she thought he wanted to say goodbye.

'Soon?' she asked.

'Early in the new year. Turkey, maybe.'

'Why?'

He shrugged, flushing again. 'Feeling a bit unsettled here, I suppose.'

Jodie gave him a long look and then looked back into her coffee. 'And going away will solve that?'

David thought he might be going to throw up; his tongue seemed stuck to the top of his mouth and he couldn't remember ever feeling so useless and incompetent. 'I don't know,' he managed to say, putting his hands palms down on the table. 'I could possibly be running away, in which case it would only make things worse.'

Jodie set down her cup rather suddenly and rather hard, and shocked him by putting her hands on top of his. 'I realise this is hard for you, David,' she said, 'but could we cut the crap and get on with it? If you want to apologise for running out on me and want to ask me out, could you just please do it, because then I can say yes please and it will all be much easier.'

'Well,' he said, sitting up straighter, exhaling deeply as though something had attacked his lungs with a pump. 'Yes, in that case, yes, I'm really sorry, I behaved like an idiot and I want you to go out with me.'

'Good,' she said. 'That's saved us at least an hour. Tonight okay?'

He nodded, exhausted by the sudden release of tension. 'Yes, brilliant but, Jodie, before . . . well . . . I need to explain about my health and . . .'

The hands that were resting on top of his grasped them suddenly, turning them slightly to get a firm hold. 'David, I'm a nurse, I know all about it. I know what it means, what you can and can't do. I probably know as much about it as you do.' She glanced down at her watch. 'Whoops, gotta get to work. Pick me up at my place at six-thirty, okay? Unless, of course, you're planning to leave for Turkey before then.'

THIRTY

'Come inside, tell me what you think,' Sylvia said, opening the door and ushering Irene in. 'It's an odd sort of room, I can't imagine what it could have been used for. Anyway, I'm calling it the design studio because it sounds professional and that might help me convince myself.'

Irene stepped inside, looking around. It was a narrow room that ran the length of the rear wall of the Boatshed, and it had the same white-painted walls and timber floor as the rest of the building; the line of windows looked out over the open water. Two cutting tables stood in the middle and at one end there was a drawing board with a stool and at the other, Sylvia's electronic sewing machine and a couple of dressmaker's dummies. Adjustable shelves had been fitted along one wall and some were already stacked with fabric. Nearby stood a long, shoulder-height rail designed to hang clothes.

'It does look very professional already,' Irene said. 'I don't know what you need for something like this but to me it looks perfect.'

Sylvia pulled out a chair for her. 'I think so too. The light in here is wonderful, and it has a very nice peaceful feel. It's far enough away from the restaurant and kitchen to be very quiet.'

'Is this all the fabric you brought with you when you left Colin?'

'Yes. It's good to be able to unpack it. I've been buying odd lengths and trimming for years, just stuff that I liked, ends of rolls, things I saw in sales. Now I can spread them out, have a good look at what I've got and use them to make up some of my designs.'

Irene smiled, turning away from the sheaf of designs spread out on the drawing board. 'These are beautiful, Sylvia,' she said, 'and this studio should help to build on them. What do Bonnie and Fran think?'

'They haven't seen it yet,' Sylvia said. 'They've both been so busy, I don't think they've even noticed me coming and going up here. Besides I'd really like to get everything sorted out before they see it.' She felt like a child with a new playroom.

'And tell me,' Irene said, getting up and walking over to the window, 'what's happening with you and Will?'

Sylvia's heart missed a beat and she felt a deep flush spread up from her neck. 'What do you mean?' she asked, her voice sounding high and unnatural. But Irene said nothing, just raised her eyebrows and continued looking at her. Sylvia sighed. 'How did you know? We thought we'd been so careful.'

Irene laughed. 'Well, you probably have, but it was Will. The night he arrived he was like a cat on hot coals until you turned up, and then he spent the evening looking as though he'd won the lottery. Hamish noticed it too. It was the same the next evening when we all went out. We couldn't understand why you seemed to want to keep it secret.'

'It was Will's idea,' Sylvia said, relieved to be able to talk about it. 'He felt we shouldn't tell Bonnie yet. When I got back from Hong Kong she was already upset about you and Hamish, and he thought it would make her feel more lonely. But the longer it goes on the worse I feel about keeping the secret. I've made him promise that we'll tell her when he comes back for the Boatshed opening. You know, Irene, I actually think he's afraid she'll disapprove as well as be hurt . . .' She paused. 'Do *you* disapprove? After all, he's a lot younger than me.'

'Of course I don't disapprove,' Irene said. 'I'm happy for you, but I do wish you'd told Bonnie. It doesn't matter if she disapproves, but I mind that she could get hurt because she feels deceived.'

'That's just what I said, but Will's adamant and I've promised I won't tell her without him here.'

'Are you in love with him, Sylvia?' Irene asked.

Sylvia hitched herself up to sit on the end of the table. She had asked herself this question so often. 'No,' she said, decisively. 'I'm very fond of him and being with him has been wonderful, incredibly liberating for me. But no, I'm not in love with him.'

'And he *is* in love with you?'

Sylvia nodded. 'So he says, and he thinks he can make me be in love with him if he digs in. He's a man who's used to getting his own way through sheer force of will and he can't quite understand why that isn't working this time.'

The Queenscliff weekend had been a disastrous step and Sylvia regretted that she had ever agreed to it. She had hoped she could make Will understand and accept the nature of her feelings and her reservations, but she had returned exhausted, knowing that despite her honesty he had gone home to Perth convincing himself that the time together had sealed their relationship.

'I believe you do love me,' he'd said when she explained the complexity of her feelings. 'It's just that it's difficult for you, still being married to Colin, but once the divorce is dealt with you'll feel differently.' As he picked up his briefcase on cue for the call for business-class passengers to board the flight, she made her case one more time, reminding him of his own history of brief and affectionate relationships with women with whom he had not been in love.

'But this is not the same,' he said.

'But I'm telling you that's just how this is for me,' she insisted.

'This is the real thing,' he said. 'I know it. This weekend was magic and I know it can be like this for us always. You feel that too, I know you do, you just have to believe in it. Your new life – this is it.'

She had watched him go with a mix of affection and frustration, and since then it was the latter that had haunted her. As she went back over their conversations his refusal to hear what she was saying, and his ability to counter everything with his own rationalisations, now seemed more extreme than they had at the time.

Irene leaned back against the window, shaking her head. 'I think there may be something else at work here,' she said.

'What do you mean?'

'I don't know Will all that well, but he's very like his brother. Jeff was a great strategist, it was part of his success. Will has it too. His love for you may be making him deaf to what you're telling him, but he may feel that if Bonnie does disapprove, then that will influence you.'

'I see,' Sylvia said, thoughtfully. 'And do you think she *will* disapprove?'

'Who knows! It never occurred to me that she would react as she did to my relationship with Hamish. But it made me realise that in the past Bonnie's sense of security has come from an idea of ownership and it may well be that she's transferred that to you, Sylvia, and possibly even to Will. Your daughter's on the other side of the world and Will is very much alone, his parents and his brother are dead. Bonnie has become involved with both your lives – who knows what's going on in her head and how she'll react when she finds out about this?'

Sylvia rested her forehead against the cool glass of the window, gazing out over the ruffled grey sea. Since Irene had left she had replayed the conversation over and over again in her mind. She shuffled together the papers on the drawing board, and stood silent in the dusky light before wandering downstairs and through the empty building.

'I've done it again,' she had said to Irene. 'All those years of volunteering for martyrdom, and I've done it again.'

'What do you mean?' Irene asked.

'Right from the start I let Colin dictate what we should do. I gave way to his needs and his opinions and ended up resenting it. Now I've done just the same thing with Will. I thought I'd moved on, broken the hold of the past, but I've just done the same thing all over again.'

'Possibly,' Irene said.

'Definitely,' Sylvia insisted. 'Different person, different sort of relationship, but when it comes down to me, to who I am in the relationship, I haven't changed at all.'

'You're talking about the habit of a lifetime, Sylvia,' Irene said. 'You can't expect to change overnight, so don't be too hard on yourself.'

'But it's a shock, you see. I thought I was different – it felt so different, so liberating, to be with someone like Will. He's a person who takes what he wants where it suits him, he does what he wants and I thought I was learning to be that way.'

Irene smiled. 'Don't get me wrong, dear, I'm very fond of Will, but he's not much of a role model.'

'No, no, but there's a single-mindedness about him; he puts himself at the centre of things. I wanted to stop being on the fringe, an appendage in someone else's life, and be at the heart of my own.' She stopped and got up, wandering over to the window. 'Do you know, Irene, in a way I almost felt superior to Bonnie because I was moving forward and she was still hanging on to the idea of Jeff's presence, trapped in the past. But all the time I've been just as stuck as she is.'

'This stuff is so hard, isn't it?' Irene said. 'But it seems to me that it is in fact the combination of your strength and your generous nature that lands you in these situations. Certain very needy people unconsciously detect it and are drawn to you like heat-seeking missiles. You sound as though you feel you're a pushover but I think it's a great deal more complicated than that . . .'

A surprisingly brisk wind was blowing from the sea as Sylvia locked the Boatshed doors. On impulse she turned away from the road home and walked up to the church. A few low lights were burning and Sylvia slipped gratefully into a pew. The organist was practising parts of a familiar Haydn mass and she sat back, closing her eyes and abandoning herself to the peace of the church and the beauty of the music. The regular spiritual practice that had been so closely tied to her life with Colin had, at first, seemed to sit uneasily with her changed circumstances. It was strange to be among people who no longer practised their faith, or no longer held it, but she was grateful that her friends had not adopted fashionable cynicism.

'It seems like a sign of sophistication these days,' she'd said to Fran one night, 'that even people who respect Aboriginal spirituality and Islam have so little respect for Christianity. It's okay to believe these days, as long as it's not in a Christian god.'

'I know,' Fran had said, turning to her quickly. 'It's really weird, such a contradiction. I gave it away years ago, but I've often wondered how people arrive at that position. It's an odd take on political correctness.'

Some long lost sense of peace seemed to be returning as Sylvia sat in the church. Her faith had kept her sane through the barren years of her marriage, now perhaps it was time to reclaim it as her courage for the future. In so many ways she could say she had lived a good life, but her willingness to do what others wanted and act against her own better judgment was the fault line that always undermined her integrity. Despite her changed circumstances she again felt at the mercy of wills stronger than her own; but were they really stronger? Perhaps they were just more needy, more demanding, preying perhaps, as Irene had suggested, on her own greater strength and goodwill? The challenge, she knew, was to dispense with compliance and compromise and establish her authenticity.

An hour later, Sylvia let herself in to the cottage, switched on the lights and drew the curtains against the darkness of the garden. It was time to stop the equivocation. She must call Kim and let her know that she could not go to England. Then, as soon as Will returned she would end the relationship, and together they would tell Bonnie. Perhaps telling her it was over might in some way assuage the hurt of their former deception.

'It's very nice of you to pick me up and take me there, Caro,' Lila called from the bedroom. 'It's a bit far for the scooter and I don't want to lose my hat on the way.'

'It's fine, Gran,' Caro said. 'I wanted to bring Rebekah over to see you, anyway.'

Lila came back into the living room wearing her best purple dress. 'Just one more little cuddle before we go,' she said, reaching out to take the baby, holding her up to her shoulder, swaying and patting her gently. 'Are you managing all right, dear? Getting some sleep?'

Caro nodded. 'Yes, she's pretty good, really, although getting up twice at night is a bit wearing.' She thought Lila's face looked strange, a little lopsided. 'Are you okay, Gran?'

'Fit as a fiddle,' Lila said, looking down at Rebekah. 'She's such a little beauty, aren't you, darling? Just like you were, Caro, and just like your mum.' She handed her back. 'Better go and put my hat on or I'll be late.'

'What is this thing you're going to, anyhow?' Caro asked, tucking the baby back into her capsule.

'Afternoon tea,' Lila called from the bedroom. 'It's the red hat club, I'm sure I told you, the ladies who wear purple with red hats. I spoke to the organiser on the phone and she said I should just come along today. What do you think of my hat, dear?'

Caro looked up from fastening the strap on the capsule and blinked in surprise at the wide-brimmed hat that seemed to overwhelm Lila's small frame.

'It's beautiful, Gran,' she said. 'It's very large and such a lot of chiffon.'

'Yes, you see you can tie the chiffon under your chin so it's like a bonnet if it's windy,' Lila said, demonstrating. 'Or just ruche it up around the crown for a more formal effect. I think that's what I'll do today, and then pin on this lovely silk rose.' She took the hat off, swirled the chiffon around the crown and pinned the silk flower carefully to hold it in place against the shiny red straw beneath. 'I had to look around a bit to get something suitable,' she said.

'I'm sure you did,' said Caro, still uncertain about the hat. She had never seen Lila wear one before, although there was a photograph of her in a small pillbox with a veil at Fran and Tony's wedding. 'It's a real Melbourne Cup sort of hat – you could win a prize with that. Has Mum seen it yet?'

Lila shook her head. 'Not yet. She said she'd come over when she gets back the day after tomorrow.'

'She'll be impressed,' Caro said, thinking that Fran would be impressed in a rather different way from how Lila imagined.

'I think I'll wear it to the Boatshed opening,' Lila said, adjusting the hat in front of the mirror. 'I want Irene to see it. I tried to get her to come with me this afternoon but she says it's not really her sort of thing.'

'Know who else you'll see at the Boatshed opening?' Caro said with a grin, picking up Rebekah in her capsule.

'Hamish?'

'No . . . well, yes, of course he'll be there, but I meant Jodie.'

'Jodie?'

'Yes. Come on, Gran, you know, Jodie, who takes your blood. She's coming with David? He finally sorted himself out and talked to her. They've been going out together again.'

Lila straightened her shoulders and looked at her hat in the mirror. 'Can't say I can recall her. But it's good if he's happy. Is she a nice girl?'

Caro's throat went dry and her face felt uncomfortably hot. 'Yes . . . she's lovely . . .' She faltered, trying to carry on as normal. 'I'm really pleased for him. He needed something good to happen. He seems to have lost all his confidence since he got sick.'

'Sick?' Lila said, swinging around to face her. 'What's the matter with him?'

Caro felt as though she was in a play for which she had been given the wrong script. She bent down again to tuck one of Rebekah's hands under the cotton blanket.

'You know, Gran,' she said, not looking up in her embarrassment. 'The Hepatitis C – that's why he came back to Australia.'

Lila stared at her in amazement. 'What do you mean?' she asked. 'No one told me David was sick.'

Caro's heart started to beat faster and her legs felt weak. There was something profoundly unnerving about this sudden and shocking loss of memory. 'Yes, we did, Gran,' she said, trying to sound calm. 'When he first came home. And that's why he stopped seeing Jodie. Remember – you went to the library to find out all about it, and then you went to his place in Collingwood –'

'Oh, rubbish, Caro,' Lila interrupted. 'You don't know what you're talking about. David lives in Richmond with your mother. Well, I'm sorry he's not well, probably this virus that's going around. There's a lot of it about but if his girlfriend is a doctor, she'll look after him. You know, Caro, there were hardly any lady doctors when I was younger – shame, really. Come along now, dear, let's get going, I don't want to be late.' And she set off down the front steps to Caro's car, leaving her granddaughter to lock the door behind them.

'And after that it's all a bit of a muddle, really,' Caro told Fran on the phone early that evening. 'I drove her to the hotel and dropped her off, and she seemed okay. I went back at five to pick her up and she'd had a lovely time. But she seemed surprised to see me, as though she wasn't expecting me. It was spooky, Mum. Different from before, and she was quite aggressive about it too, not like her at all.'

Fran felt as though a lump of lead had landed in her stomach. 'And you're sure she was okay when you dropped her at home?'

'Yes, fine. I checked the Webster pack, and she'd taken her pills this morning, and I got her to take the evening ones before I left.'

'Good,' Fran said. 'Good. And she really seemed okay?'

'Absolutely,' Caro said. 'She was just the same as ever, but I reminded her again about David and she just told me I was being silly. It's like that whole little block of information has disappeared. Before, you'd remind her of something and she'd remember and correct herself, she *knew* she'd forgotten or got it wrong, but this was different.'

'Okay, I'll go over there as soon as I get back.'

'And, you know, she doesn't look too good, more vague some-how, and her face, well . . . it seemed a bit lopsided. I didn't notice that at first and then I couldn't really see properly under that great big hat and I didn't want to make an issue of it.'

Fran felt physically sick. 'Should we call the doctor, do you think?'

'I don't think she'd be too happy about it,' Caro said. 'She might know her face is different but I don't think she's really aware that anything else has changed, so she wouldn't understand why.

Leave it for tonight and I'll pop over tomorrow. Just to make sure she's okay.'

Fran switched off her mobile cold with fear. She had been bracing herself for just this moment, the defining moment when benign memory loss morphed into something more sinister, but it was still shattering. She sat for a moment, the phone clasped in her hand, her insides churning with anxiety. Maybe it was just a one-off thing and tomorrow Lila would be back to normal, but in her heart she knew that this was no glitch. It foreshadowed decline, the progress and shape of which were totally unpredictable.

'Ready when you are, Fran,' Lenore called up the stairs. 'We should really get going. Okay for the guest speaker to be fashionably late, but not very late.'

'Just give me a couple of minutes,' Fran said. 'Something I forgot to ask Caro,' and she hit redial.

'Me again,' she said. 'I got so caught up with Mum's memory stuff I forgot to ask – this Jodie who takes her blood, how long has she been going out with David?'

'Another wonderful speech last night, Fran,' Jack Bannister said as they sat in slow traffic on the Harbour Bridge the following morning.

'I couldn't let you think I only had one speech up my sleeve,' she said with a laugh.

'I didn't,' Jack said. 'And it was great publicity for the book and for the Boatshed, all those fliers we produced have gone. I must talk to Bonnie when we come down to Melbourne for the opening. I've a got a few ideas for some spin-offs and I'd be interested in investing in the company.'

Fran looked out of the window to the Opera House, its landmark sails outlined in stark white against the grey sky that threatened rain. 'It's certainly Bonnie you need to talk to about that,' she said. 'She's the business brain and her money's behind it. It's entirely thanks to her that all this is happening.'

If Fran needed any sort of reminder of the value of being part of Bonnie's business, it was this visit to Sydney. Five years earlier at this very same trade fair she had been a struggling freelancer with a small local profile and a few good contacts. This year she was a speaker at a key function, and her face and name were plastered over posters and fliers alongside the blurb about the forthcoming book, and some clever shots of the Boatshed, taken weeks earlier from angles that avoided the incomplete renovations. And now they were on their way to Bannister Books' office to meet with the food stylist who would work on the book.

Fran hated styling and was thankful that they had engaged one of the best in the business. While she loved cooking and developing new recipes, the painstaking, detailed job of styling the food so that it worked for the camera was another thing altogether. Undercooking things to keep their colour, moving tiny bits of garnish with dental tweezers, drizzling a miniscule drop of oil in the right place, or lining up the grill lines on a chicken breast time and time again were things she could well do without. The relief of handing over the parts of her work she really didn't enjoy was just one of the many perks of the new situation.

She looked across at Jack. 'I'm sure Bonnie'll be happy to talk to you. She's very excited about it all. Jeff, her husband, was a merchant banker, with all sorts of business interests but this is the first time Bonnie's ever had a business of her own.'

'You shouldn't underestimate your contribution,' Jack said, negotiating a lane change and breaking out of the snarl-up in the traffic. 'Your profile in Melbourne has given Bonnie a head start; it would have been much harder for her without your name and reputation attached to it.'

She nodded. 'I know that, but I also know that this has made my life a lot easier. Freelancing has its advantages but it's a struggle. I'd got to a point where there were opportunities for heaps more work but I couldn't fit in any more myself, and I couldn't afford to take on anyone to help me. And I know business is not rocket science but it might as well be for all I know about managing that side of things.'

'My son's a bit like that,' Jack said. 'I was hoping he'd take over Bannister Books but landscape gardening is his passion. So god knows what will happen to the business when Lenore and I fall off our perches.'

'Lenore doesn't have children, then?' Fran asked.

'She does, but they're in America,' Jack said, slipping into a parking space outside Bannister Books' office. 'And they don't speak to her. She hasn't seen them since they were four, not since the marriage broke up.'

Fran undid her seatbelt and twisted round to look at him. 'That must be terrible for her.'

'It was pretty bad for a very long time,' Jack said. 'But I think she's learned to live with it. Their father's American, and he whisked them back to his family in Texas straight after the divorce.'

'But couldn't Lenore have got custody?'

Jack switched off the engine and turned to look at her. 'It was all very messy,' he said. 'Lenore was only eighteen when they got married and twenty when the twins, two little girls, arrived. It was a bit of a shock but they were so gorgeous, they made us think Dick couldn't be quite as awful as he seemed.'

'What sort of awful?'

'A Texan version of the original Australian redneck,' Jack said with a grin. 'Ignorant, narrow minded, a real arrogant, loud-mouthed bastard. Our parents couldn't stand him, none of us could, and we couldn't understand what Lenore saw in him, and by that time nor did she. Anyway, to cut a long story short, Lenore fell in love with someone else, left Dick and took the children with her. He grabbed them back, went to court and got custody.'

'But that's appalling,' Fran said. 'I thought women always got custody back then.'

'They did,' Jack nodded, 'unless they could be proved to be an unfit mother.'

'Unfit?'

'Lenore left Dick for another woman. It was the early sixties. Dick's mother flew over here, and went to court with him and promised to raise the girls in a god-fearing home. Lenore's never even seen them since, despite trips to Texas to try. The family won't have a bar of her. God knows what they told the girls but when they were old enough to decide for themselves, they didn't *want* to see their mother.'

He glanced at his watch and took the keys out of the ignition. 'It's a hideous story and I've only given you the bare bones of it. She'll tell you more about it one day, I'm sure. Anyway, time's getting on, the food stylist will be here any minute. I want to make sure you're happy with her.'

THIRTY-ONE

On a glorious sunny afternoon, two weeks to the day before he was due to fly to Melbourne for the Boatshed opening, Will drove from his office in West Perth to the jeweller in Claremont recommended by Tania and Ryan.

'So what do you want a jeweller for?' Tania had asked the night before.

They had met at the opening of an exhibition at a local gallery and after an hour of canapés and a very dry champagne, the three of them had wandered into South Perth for dinner.

'To buy jewellery,' Will said with an enigmatic smile as the waiter arrived with the pasta.

'You can't do better than this guy in Claremont,' Ryan said. 'That's where I bought Tania's engagement ring.'

'And this bracelet,' Tania said, stretching out her hand so that Will could inspect both. 'And we bought beautiful pendants there for the bridesmaids too.'

'Good,' Will said. 'Thanks.' And he tucked the piece of paper with the name and address into his top pocket.

'But what sort of jewellery?' Tania persisted. 'Who for?'

Will took a sip of his wine and contemplated being mysterious and remote, but he was really dying to talk about it. So far he hadn't told anyone about Sylvia, not even during the lonely weeks after Hong Kong, or since his return from Melbourne. Now the prospect of sharing his happiness with his best friends was too tempting to resist – besides, they'd know soon, anyway. He was sure he could convince Sylvia to spend Christmas with him in Perth and he was already planning a dinner party to introduce her to his friends. As soon as he started to tell them, he knew it was the right thing.

'Well, I'm delighted, mate,' Ryan said. 'About bloody time you took things seriously.'

'But she's still married, you said?' Tania asked.

'Yes,' Will said, 'but the marriage is definitely over. Just a matter of dealing with the divorce.'

'Married long?' Ryan asked, reaching for the wine bottle to top up their glasses.

'Thirty-three years,' Will said.

'Christ!' said Ryan, incurring a look of disgust from an elderly woman at the next table. 'How old is she?'

'Fifty-six,' Will said, holding up his hand to forestall any comments. 'I know, I know, not my usual sort of woman at all, but she's wonderful, mate, honestly.' He reached for his wallet and drew out a photograph of Sylvia taken on the balcony in Hong Kong. 'See what I mean.'

Tania and Ryan inspected the photograph in awkward silence. 'She's certainly a beautiful woman,' Tania said cautiously, 'but . . . that's a big difference in age, Will, she's nearly fourteen years older than you.'

Will smiled and took back the photograph, giving it another loving glance before returning it to his wallet. 'It doesn't matter,' he said. 'Age is immaterial. I'm in love with Sylvia, and I don't even think about age. All my life I've been chasing the wrong sort of women and I didn't even know it.' He paused. 'Come on, guys, don't be so sexist. If the ages were reversed you'd be cheering me on.'

Tania cleared her throat and fiddled with the stem of her glass. 'Yes,' she said, 'yes, of course, and we do want you to be happy, Will.'

Ryan took a very large gulp of his wine. 'So, what are your plans, then?' he asked.

'Well,' said Will, sublimely unaware of their concern, 'first I want to get her over here for Christmas, so she can meet everyone and I can show her Perth. Then we can decide where we want to be. I think Sylvia will love it here.'

Tania and Ryan exchanged glances as Will stowed his wallet back in his pocket.

'Let's drink to it,' he said, picking up his glass.

'Oh, yeah . . . sure,' Ryan said, nudging his wife. 'Come on, Tania, here's to Will and er . . . and Sylvia. Cheers, mate, all the best.'

Tania sipped her wine and put down her glass. 'So, what are you going to buy?' she asked. 'If she's still married, you can't get engaged.'

'Why not?' Will asked, smiling broadly. 'Who says we can't?'

'You're going to buy a ring?'

'Sure am.'

'Have you asked her yet, Will?'

'No. I'll do it when I'm in Melbourne in a couple of weeks.'

'Might be better to wait with the ring, you know,' Ryan said.

'Yes,' Tania cut in. 'You could buy her a bracelet or earrings.'

Will shook his head. 'No. The ring is right, I know it. This has never happened to me before. I have to do it properly.'

'You were engaged to Glenda,' Ryan reminded him.

'Another life,' Will said. 'Another life. Sylvia is something else, she's the love of my life, and I'm going to make everything perfect for her in every possible way.'

Will locked the car, crossed the street and inspected the display in the jeweller's window. He didn't really have much idea what he wanted, but he knew that he would recognise the right ring when he saw it. And ten minutes later he did see it: a wide, irregularly shaped, rose gold band with three large but not ostentatious square cut diamonds set at an angle. The moment the jeweller laid it on the black velvet cloth he knew it was made for Sylvia. The man looked at him with caution as he told him the price but Will didn't even blink.

'One condition,' he said producing a piece of paper on which he had secretly traced the inside of one of her rings while she was in the shower. 'It has to be made to this size, and I need it by next Friday.'

'No problem, sir,' the jeweller said, jotting the details in his book. 'It'll be ready for you on time. I'm sure the lady will be delighted, it's a very rare piece.'

'Surprised and delighted.' Will said, handing over his platinum credit card.

On her first day back in Melbourne, Fran drove to Hawthorn to see Lila. There was an unfamiliar white Barina in the driveway, and she pulled in behind it and walked round the back of the house, past the yellow scooter gleaming in the sunlight, tapped on the back door, pushed it open and called out to her mother.

'In the living room,' Lila replied, and Fran walked through to the front of the house where Lila was sitting at the table with a young woman who was drawing blood from her strapped arm.

'Come in, come in,' Lila said. 'I can't get up until the nurse has finished with me.'

Fran paused in the doorway, shocked by her mother's crooked smile. The left side of her face had dropped, there was a puffy bag of flesh below the eye, the cheek was sagging, the side of her mouth drawn down.

'Hello, Mum,' she said, trying to hide her shock. 'How are you? Caro tells me you went off to tea with the red hat women.'

'Did I? Oh yes, that's right, Caro took me there the other day. We had a lovely afternoon.'

Fran's anxiety lifted a little. If Lila could remember the outing, there couldn't be much wrong with her memory. Maybe Caro had simply misunderstood her. The nurse withdrew the needle, dropped the phial of blood into a plastic container, and put a small pad of cotton wool and a plaster over the tiny red mark on Lila's arm.

'There you are, Mrs Whittaker,' she said, standing up. 'Don't get up, please, I still have to take your blood pressure.' She turned to Fran. 'I'm sorry,' she said, 'couldn't stop in the middle of that. I'm Jodie. I've been taking your mother's blood for some time now.'

Fran was hurt that it had been left to Caro to tell her about David and Jodie, but mothers, she reasoned, were unlikely to be the first people that sons confided in about a new relationship.

'Caro told me,' she said, holding out her hand.

'I'm sorry, that should have been David,' Jodie said, blushing. 'He's been putting a lot of energy into trying not to worry anyone. Anyway, I'm really pleased to meet you at last.'

'Me too,' Fran said. 'I know Mum thinks the world of you.'

'Um, yes . . . that's awkward right now . . .' Jodie began.

'What are you two mumbling about over there?' Lila asked, standing up and rolling down her sleeve.

Jodie turned to her, 'Blood pressure, Mrs Whittaker, we'll do that now, shall we?' And quickly she put a hand on Lila's arm to press her back into the chair.

'All right, all right,' Lila said. She turned to Fran with a smile. 'She's bossy, this one, isn't she? What did you say your name was again, dear?'

'Jodie, Mrs Whittaker, you remember. I come every month. I'm a friend of Caro and David.'

Lila shrugged. 'No, I don't think so, dear. David's away, you know, somewhere in the desert.'

Shock hit Fran like a bullet in the chest, and she steadied herself against the doorjamb before walking over to the table to sit beside her mother, as Jodie strapped the cuff on Lila's arm.

Lila looked around her, smiling.

'Did you have a good time, Fran?'

'I did, and I stayed with Lenore. She sent you her love.'

'Who?'

'Lenore, you remember her, she told you about the red hat ladies.'

Lila shrugged. 'No, no. I read about them in the poem, Fran, the one you gave me. And somebody sent me a book about it. I've invited some of them to the Boatshed, for the opening.'

'That's fine,' Jodie said, unstrapping the cuff. 'All done, Mrs Whittaker, thank you.'

'Good-o,' Lila said, getting up. 'I'll put the kettle on. You'll stay for a cup of tea, won't you, dear?' And she went off into the kitchen.

'What's happened?' Fran asked.

Jodie lifted her shoulders and sighed. 'Not sure, really; it's not for me to make a diagnosis.'

'But you know her well, and you must have noticed her face. You're a nurse, don't you have any idea?'

Jodie glanced towards the kitchen. 'I think you need to see a doctor, a geriatrician, and do it soon. I do see a lot of elderly people and my guess, and it *is* only a guess, is that she's started having TIAs – transient ischaemic attacks. They're tiny strokes that wipe out little bits of what makes a person who they are.'

Fran looked at her in horror. 'But if she'd had a stroke we'd know, surely . . . ?'

Jodie shook her head. 'TIAs are so minute that the person doesn't even know they're happening. She won't have felt anything, she won't even know that anything's changed.' She looked at Fran, who had gone white. 'Are you okay, Fran?'

Fran nodded weakly. 'Yes, it's the shock, I don't know what to do . . . Would those TIA things account for her face as well?'

'Almost certainly, although there's also a thing called Bell's palsy that can have that effect, but I think if she *is* having TIAs then they're responsible for her face too.'

'Milk and sugar, dear?' Lila asked, popping her head around the door and looking at Jodie. 'Jennifer, did you say?'

'Jodie, and milk, no sugar, thanks,' Jodie replied before turning back to Fran. 'She's completely forgotten that she knows me, and she thinks David's still away. She's probably lost other things as well but they haven't shown up yet.'

'But just now she remembered the red hats, and about the Boatshed opening – going from the past to the future quite easily,' Fran said, shaking her head in confusion. 'It doesn't make sense.'

'No,' Jodie said, 'and it won't from now on. Imagine tiny cigarette burns that each eliminate something, some part of her or her memory.' She closed the blood pressure machine and packed it away. 'Look, I'm talking way beyond my competence. You need to get her to see someone, Fran, and you need to do it soon.'

A week later, Jodie's diagnosis was confirmed. The geriatrician was a pleasant, softly spoken man and Lila took an obvious liking

301

to him, but as he went through her medical history the gaps in Lila's memory became increasingly apparent. She couldn't remember how many pregnancies she'd had, or the fact that she was diabetic.

'And your date of birth, Mrs Whittaker?' Dr Parkes asked, and Lila looked at Fran in confusion.

'Well,' she said, 'I think it's just slipped my mind. You know, don't you, Fran?' And she looked so confident when he asked if she knew who was prime minister. 'Bob Hawke,' she announced triumphantly. 'Yes, Bob Hawke; well, that's who I voted for.'

The doctor tried again. 'So who's the prime minister *now*?'

Lila looked around in confusion. 'Hawke,' she said again, with a shrug. 'He's the prime minister now. I met him once, you know, at a morning tea. A very good-looking man. Lovely silver hair.'

There was silence and Fran, trembling inside at the awfulness of it all, had to turn away.

'She's certainly had some TIAs,' Dr Owen said to Fran while his nurse helped Lila to dress after the CAT scan and the physical examination. 'And she has Alzheimer's disease. What the TIAs do is accelerate its effects, so you may see quite rapid deterioration from now on. I'll get someone from the Seniors Health Assessment Team to see her. You may need to start thinking in terms of residential care.'

THIRTY-TWO

The Boatshed was due to open on the first Friday in December, with a special invitation-only brunch for the media, some tourism and food people, as well as family and friends. By seven-thirty that morning the newly employed sous-chef hadn't turned up and wasn't answering his mobile phone. Sean, who had recently acquired the title of King of Cool, totally lost it, had a fit in the kitchen and phoned his partner, Graeme, who fortunately was having a day off. Within half an hour, Graeme was there in his chef's whites and Sean was back to cool again.

'Don't worry about him,' Graeme told a frantic Bonnie. 'He always has a drama at the start, that's his process; he'll be steady as a rock from now on.'

'But we still need a sous-chef,' Bonnie wailed. 'Suppose he doesn't turn up at all? What about the weekend? We're open now!'

Graeme patted her shoulder and handed her a large mug of coffee. 'Sous-chefs are ten a penny,' he said. 'I'm off for the next three days and I'll help out, but Sean and I can find you one by tomorrow, probably.'

Bonnie gulped her coffee and sank down onto a chair. 'My fault,' she said. 'All my fault. I picked him over the guy Sean wanted. He said this one was dodgy right from the start.'

'She's right,' Sean called from the kitchen. 'He had very funny eyes, that boy, and I'm not having him anywhere near my kitchen after this.'

'There you are, you see,' Graeme said. 'Drink your coffee and

303

don't worry, we'll take care of it. You'll have a new sous-chef by tomorrow or Sunday at the latest. I'll stake my virginity on it.'

In the gallery, Sylvia was showing Caro the till and stock book. The new part-time assistant couldn't start until the following week and Caro had volunteered to fill the gap. Fran stood at the entrance to the kitchen wondering if she should offer to help or stay out of the way.

'Don't breathe down their necks, Fran,' Lenore whispered. 'You're the ideas and the inspiration, you have to leave the rest to them.' And she took her arm and led her away from the danger zone.

'Ten o'clock,' Bonnie said. 'Time to open the doors. Here we go, guys, we're open.'

It seemed that one moment they were drinking a quiet glass of nerve-calming champagne and the next the invited guests were arriving and Bonnie began the ritual of meeting and greeting, answering questions, discussing the menu, encouraging people to try the first range of signature products and to check out the gallery. She wondered if Jeff was watching, and thought he would be proud of her. She had hoped Will would confirm that but, while obviously pleased with the end result, he seemed to have something else on his mind.

'Missed you dreadfully,' Will whispered to Sylvia as she gift-wrapped a beaded handbag. 'I nearly raced across the garden last night and hammered your door down.'

He had arrived the previous evening, and this time he had been happy to accept Bonnie's invitation to stay at the house, confident that within a couple of nights at most he would be moving his suitcase to Sylvia's bedroom in the cottage. The opening would be over by early afternoon and he had plans for the rest of the day. A late afternoon drive down to his favourite spot on the coast. He patted his jacket, reassuring himself that the small leather box was still safe in his inside pocket. Sylvia flushed, looking up at the customer, who had turned away to admire some earrings.

'Just be careful, and don't do anything silly,' she told him sharply. 'I'm worried about Bonnie, and I need to talk to you, seriously, later, when this is all over.'

304

'My thoughts exactly,' he said, ducking out of the way of a couple who were inspecting the bookshelves. 'This afternoon can't come soon enough for me.' And he stroked her hand and slipped away as he saw Bonnie coming through from the restaurant. He was impressed by the way it had all come together, but he was absorbed in the prospect of the life that was soon to be his, the life that would begin in earnest at the end of this day, when he could have Sylvia to himself.

David pulled up as close as possible to the entrance and leapt out of the driving seat to open the car doors. He had been dispatched to collect Lila and her red hat friends. It was not a job he relished; he hadn't seen his grandmother since the sudden deterioration in her memory and he feared that she might not recognise him. As he turned into the bottom of Malthouse Close he saw them, Lila and three other women, all in purple with big red hats, waiting for him on the front path.

'Here he is, that's my grandson,' Lila cried, holding out her arms to him. 'Hello, darling, I'm so glad to see you. Such a long time you've been away. Did you have a good flight? I was worried about you, terrible things happening over there.' And one by one she introduced him to her friends, telling them he'd just come back from Iraq. Despite the warnings from both Fran and Jodie, it came as a shock.

'Don't argue with her,' Jodie had told him that morning. 'You'll hate it, but it really is best to go along with what she says. That's her reality now, and you'll just make it harder if you try to correct her.'

David helped the three women into the back of the car and handed Lila into the front, hugging her again as he did so. Her lopsided face and incongruent memories made her seem like a stranger, and he felt sad and bewildered without the grandmother whom he had known all his life.

Lila, however, was having a wonderful day. Several times she mixed up the names of the red hat women, but they ignored it and piled cheerfully out of the car and up the steps to the boardwalk, anxious to meet Fran and tell her how closely they followed her column and used her recipes.

'I can't believe it,' David said, standing under the trees by the car, watching them surge into the building. 'Such a short time, her face, it's so . . . so shocking. And she doesn't even know you, she just walked right past you.'

Jodie, whom he had dropped off before going to collect the women, slipped her arm around his waist. 'Try to remember that your gran is quite happy. She most probably doesn't realise that she's changed. Even if she does it's clearly not bothering her. It's you and your mum and Caro who have all the adjustments to make.'

David put an arm around her shoulders. 'You'll think me an awful wuss but when I saw her this morning I just wanted to cry.'

Jodie moved closer, rubbing her cheek against his. 'It's awful to watch someone you love slowly disintegrate, and it's worst of all for Fran. She'll need your help with this, David.'

'I know,' he said. 'I do love you, Jo, I'm sorry I was such a stupid wanker all those weeks. You're the best thing that's ever happened to me.'

'And you to me,' she said. 'It wasn't really complicated at all, was it? Just a question of knowing what we both want.'

He drew her back behind a tree, into the cool shade where the sun dappled patterns on the grass. 'It's the children bit that still worries me, though,' he whispered against her hair.

'There are other things in life, David,' she said. 'Not everyone has to have children to feel fulfilled. Anyway, we're getting too intense, let's go and rescue your mum. She's being swamped by red hats.'

'Magnificent, Bonnie!' Jack Bannister said, leaning back against the deck rail and watching a group at a nearby table tucking into eggs Benedict.

'You've done an extraordinary job. This place will soon be the talk of the town.' He raised his glass and she chinked hers against it.

'I admit to being absolutely thrilled,' she said. 'Modesty is not my thing this morning but I'm trying not to look smug. These guys obviously like it but the real test is when we open to the public.'

'The public will love it too,' he said. 'Let's talk later, I've got some other ideas that might interest you.'

She smiled. 'I've got the bit between my teeth now, Jack,' she said with a grin. 'Flushed with my own success, I'm probably going to turn into Melbourne's answer to Donald Trump.'

Jack spluttered into his glass. 'That's a really scary thought,' he said with a laugh. 'But I doubt it, you're much more attractive and have better hair.'

'How's it going, Fran?' Lenore asked, handing her a glass of water.

'Terrifying,' Fran admitted, drinking it gratefully. 'How did you know I needed this?'

'Champagne before midday, very bad for you,' Lenore said. 'We'll all be staggering around with headaches this afternoon if we don't drink plenty of water.'

'D'you think it's okay?'

'Okay? It's a roaring success. Bonnie's done a terrific job, you all have. But look, I just had a chat with Lila. I don't think she knew me, and her poor face . . . it's serious, isn't it?'

Fran stared at the empty glass and nodded. 'Yes, and the weird thing is that she doesn't seem to realise it. Moving her into care is going to be terrible but I don't think she can stay where she is for long.'

'The worst thing I ever had to do was put my father into residential care,' Lenore said. 'In a way it was worse than parting with my kids, because they were taken away I had no option, but with Dad I actually had to do the deed. He didn't understand what was happening or why and he never forgave me. If there's anything I can do . . . I've only known her a few weeks but I've grown very fond of her, and of you. I'd like to help.'

Mike drew up in a corner of the car park and unpacked Rebekah from her capsule. She opened her eyes and stared at him, her face breaking into a big smile.

'Who's Daddy's gorgeous girl, then?' he said, locking the car and hitching her into the pouch against his chest. 'Look at all those ladies in the big red hats, Bek. That's your great gran over there, and your gran, and there's Mummy – look, she's running to meet us.'

Caro was indeed running towards them off the boardwalk steps and down the path.

'Thank goodness you're here,' she said, taking Rebekah from him. 'Can you get your bag and hurry, there's a guy collapsed in the restaurant.' She shouldered her way back into the building ahead of him, through the groups of chatting guests who had spread across the deck and the boardwalk onto the grass. Inside the restaurant an elderly man was slumped across one of the tables, surrounded by a cluster of anxious onlookers.

'Apparently he was panting and then his eyes rolled back and he just seemed to pass out,' Caro said. 'Can you move back, please, the doctor's here now.'

She turned to Bonnie, who was standing nervously beside her, and thrust Rebekah into her arms. 'Can you take her, please, Bonnie,' she said, 'I might need to help Mike,' and Bonnie, whose worst fear when she saw the slumped figure was food poisoning, had no alternative but to take Rebekah and clutch her awkwardly against her chest, her face white with shock.

Mike tilted the man's head to one side, put his fingers to his neck, checked his pulse, and then pushed him backwards so that he could prise open his eyelids. 'Looks like dehydration,' he said, drawing a syringe out of his case. 'Can someone bring some water, please, and can you all stand back a bit.'

The man's eyelids flickered and opened cautiously and Bonnie sighed with relief. She looked down in dismay at Rebekah, who smiled at her and reached up a tiny hand to grab her face.

'Phew,' Will whispered, 'let's hope Mike's right. I was thinking –'

'Food poisoning,' Bonnie cut in. 'Yes, me too. Here, have you met Rebekah? Fran's granddaughter? Look after her, will you, there's stuff I have to do.' And she thrust Rebekah into his arms and hurried away to the kitchen, hoping neither Fran nor Caro had seen how desperately she hadn't wanted to hold the baby.

'It's a lovely club, Irene,' Lila said. 'Lovely women, most of them younger than me, but very nice and friendly.'

'That's good,' Irene said. 'They certainly look a very jolly group and the hats are gorgeous. And how are you, Lila?'

Lila looked around to make sure Fran wasn't within hearing distance. 'Not all that good, really. It's a funny thing but I could swear something's happened to my face. It's all down on one side, but no one seems to have noticed it. Even the doctor Fran took me to last week – he asked all sorts of questions but didn't say anything about it. Look at it, Irene, what do you think? It looks funny, doesn't it?'

'It does look a little different, Lila,' Irene said cautiously. 'A little bit one-sided. These odd things happen to us as we get older, don't they? Best not to worry about it. Do you *feel* okay?'

Lila glanced over her shoulder again. 'Not the best. I've done a couple of odd things this week. Found myself walking round the garden in my nightdress in the middle of the night. Now, that's a silly thing to do, isn't it? I don't want Fran to know, though; don't want to worry her. Might be all the excitement, you know – David's just come home, and then there's my scooter,' She paused and put her hand on Irene's arm.

'Who's that woman over there in black, the one with the very bright blue eyes? She says she knows me and had a ride on my scooter.'

Irene tucked a hand under Lila's arm and steered her into the shade. 'It's Lenore, Lila, you remember her. She was there the night we delivered Rebekah. She told you about the red hat club.'

'Really?' Lila said, staring across at Lenore. 'Well, she said something like that, but I didn't know whether to believe her. You can't be too careful these days, you know, people will tell you anything. I don't know what to believe. And where did we deliver Rebekah to?'

Hamish had found them a quiet table on the shady part of the deck, and Irene dropped thankfully into a chair and watched him passing an extra chair to a group at another table. He was wearing her favourite blue shirt with a silver grey cashmere sweater thrown over his shoulders. She was struck by how distinguished he looked, and wondered how she could have known him almost all her adult life without noticing things about him that she now found so attractive.

'I didn't want to ever have a relationship again,' she said as he sat down, and he looked up at her with a smile.

'Me neither,' he said. 'It took me years to get over Gilda, and I think I married Celia because I was lonely and we didn't get along too badly. When she died I was never going to get involved again.' He took her hand. 'I'm awfully glad I did.'

Irene smiled, feeling the prick of tears in her eyes. 'Me too. I was just talking to Lila . . .' she paused. 'Suppose that happens to one of us?'

'Why don't we worry about that if and when the time comes?' Hamish said. 'After all, it might *never* happen.'

'It's so sudden and so dramatic,' Irene said. 'I feel desperate about it for her and . . . this is so selfish – for myself and you too. I thought I'd live in my own home until I died. Now I look at Lila and . . .'

'Ssh, Irene,' Hamish said, stroking her hand. 'At this time of life, we just have to take one day at a time and live it to the full. The fear's always there, just don't let it get to you. There's two of us now.'

It was well after six by the time Will managed to prise Sylvia away from the others. He'd planned a long and lazy drive to somewhere romantic where they could watch the sun go down, but time was not on his side, so he opted for the terrace of a small and quiet Federation hotel a little way down the coast, where he remembered a magnificent view and an air of restrained elegance. Leaving the city he put his foot down with a sense of joyful anticipation and a noticeable sigh of relief as he shook off the irritation and impatience that had filled his day.

'Not yet, Will,' Sylvia had said early in the afternoon, when the crowd had drifted away and they had closed the doors of the Boatshed. 'I need to check the sales register, and the till, and anyway, this is a special day for us – we're all going back to Bonnie's.'

Will had made some small effort to feign an interest in the post mortem. A large, noisy and elated group had gathered at the house and persisted in reliving the event minute by minute; the overall success, the minor disasters, the lessons learned. Will thought he'd die of boredom if he heard the story of the missing sous-chef or the food poisoning scare one more time. Despite his genuine interest in the Boatshed he found this all too tiresome for words, and in his desire to be with Sylvia he was like a restless teenager longing to get away from a crowd of boring adults.

'At last,' he said, smiling across at Sylvia as she leaned back in the passenger seat. 'I thought I was never going to get you alone.'

'Yes,' she said. 'Well, now that we *are* alone, where are we going? Not too far, Will, I'm really tired. Let's just go somewhere quiet where we can talk. I'm going to flake out quite early tonight.'

Will, imagining them flaking out together in Sylvia's bed, relished the moment and tuned the radio to something soothing on Classic FM.

The light was fading as they settled at a candlelit table on the terrace with a frosty bottle of rosé. It was surprisingly quiet and for a while they had the terrace to themselves. Will raised his glass and the pink wine flashed crimson in the candlelight. He felt an almost unbelievable joy – he had waited so long for this moment that he wondered if he'd be able to speak. He wanted to capture it and hold it forever, a memory they would share through the coming years.

'Will,' Sylvia said, sipping her wine and putting her glass back on the table. 'There's something I have to say to you –'

He set his glass on the table and smiled at her, putting his finger to her lips to silence her. 'Me first, please,' he said softly. 'You'll understand why in a moment.'

He thought she looked irritated but he pressed on, taking her hand in his and kissing it. 'Ever since we met, Sylvia, I haven't been able to get you out of my mind.'

'Will,' she persisted, 'this is not the –'

'Please let me finish,' he insisted. 'I know you think I'm some sort of playboy and that this was just an adventure on my part, but I love you, Sylvia.'

311

He reached into his inside pocket, drew out the ring box and opened it, and the diamonds flashed satisfyingly. 'Sylvia, I know you feel the same. Marry me, please say you'll marry me.'

He took the ring from the box and reached for her hand but she withdrew it suddenly and when he raised his eyes to hers he saw, not the rapture he had expected, but an expression of pure shock.

THIRTY-THREE

Fran always found it difficult to squeeze herself into Caro's Beetle, but she had deliberately left her car at home that morning, knowing she'd be drinking. Mike had gone to work at four that afternoon and Rebekah, who was now fast asleep in her capsule in the back seat, had spent the afternoon and evening being handed around between Irene, Lenore, Hamish, Sean and Graeme, managing to get them all to fall in love with her.

'Isn't she just as good as gold?' Fran said, twisting awkwardly around to look at her granddaughter. 'She never cried the whole day.'

Caro eyed her daughter in the rear-view mirror and started the engine. 'No, she's saving it for tonight.'

Fran straightened up and buckled her seatbelt as Caro pulled out of the drive onto the street. 'Is she still waking twice a night?'

'No, we're down to once now, thank god, but she messes about with it and takes ages to settle again after that. When d'you think she'll start sleeping through?'

'It's hard to remember,' Fran said. 'David was going through the night by three months but you took much longer. You woke up every night long after I'd dropped the two o'clock feed. I just gave you boiled water and then you'd go back to sleep again – sometimes!'

'So this is karma, I suppose,' Caro said. 'Ah well, I guess I should be thankful she usually sleeps well in the middle of the day. By the way, did you think Bonnie seemed a bit odd this evening?'

Fran shook her head. 'No, I don't think so. Although now you come to mention it, I don't remember seeing her hold Rebekah. I expect she's just tired. We all are, it's been an exhausting few weeks. She probably just wasn't in the mood.'

'Maybe,' Caro said. 'Anyway, did I tell you I've told Des to advertise my job? I'm not going back.'

Fran smiled. 'I never knew how you coped with all those wrinkly rockers in the record company, anyway,' she said. 'You'll find something else when you're ready. And thanks for helping out today.'

'It was great,' Caro said. 'I loved it, and I really like Sylvia. And I've been dying to ask you this all day. What's going on with her and Bonnie's brother-in-law?'

'Bonnie's brother-in-law? Oh, Will . . . nothing, I don't think, why?'

Caro shrugged and turned off Barkly Street into the end of Fran's street. 'Heavens, Mum, don't say you haven't noticed. He was hanging around her all day, like a faithful Labrador. In fact, she got a bit pissed off with him at one point and told him to stop mooning round the gallery and go and mix with the guests. Then they took off from Bonnie's together in the car about six. I saw them when I came out to the car to get a new pack of nappies.'

Fran's hand flew to her face. 'No! Are you sure? Bonnie said she thought Sylvia had gone back to the cottage because she was exhausted.'

Caro shook her head. 'No way, and his car wasn't there when we left, and it's after ten now.' She glanced across at Fran and grinned. 'Secret love affair, d'you think? He's a lot younger than Sylvia, isn't he? Why are you looking so shocked?'

'Oh . . . well . . . I don't know, really. Yes, he's younger than her, not that that matters. Actually, when Sylvia came back from Hong Kong, Bonnie and I thought she might have met someone there, but now that you've said this, I . . . Sylvia stayed at Will's place in Hong Kong. Maybe she . . . maybe they . . .'

Caro laughed out loud and slapped her hand on the steering wheel. 'Yes, maybe they did! Good for her. He's pretty cute, really, and probably very rich – good old Sylvia.'

'Oh dear,' Fran said. 'Oh, shit . . .'

'What's the matter? Heavens, Mum, you're not going to disapprove, are you?'

Fran shook her head. 'No,' she said. 'No, not at all, it's just Bonnie . . . if Bonnie finds out, she's not going to like this one little bit.'

Bonnie carried the remaining glasses out into the kitchen and stacked them in the dishwasher. Irene and Hamish had gone to bed some time ago, but Fran, Caro, the Bannisters and Sean and Graeme had stayed on until the exhaustion of the day finally sent them in search of their beds. Sylvia, Bonnie guessed, must have fallen asleep in the cottage hours ago. Will, on the other hand, had disappeared early in the evening and not come back. Bonnie was disappointed and just a little hurt, but she wasn't going to let his desertion spoil her satisfaction.

'I really want us to get together and talk about some other possibilities,' Jack Bannister reminded her. 'I know you're in for a hectic few weeks but it would be good to talk sometime soon.'

'Love to,' she'd said. 'I've got the bit between my teeth now, although I have to tell you I don't know anything about books.'

He smiled. 'You didn't know anything about running a restaurant and a gallery until you bought the Boatshed,' he said. 'Anyway, it's not books, or at least not *solely* books. Lenore's the book person now, I want to branch out a bit . . . so let's talk another time, but soon.'

She liked Jack, who was similar in many ways to Jeff: solid, reliable and he treated her with the same courtesy and attention she'd grown accustomed to in Europe. Bonnie realised she had sorely missed that sort of interaction with men since she came home.

She left the back door on the latch for Will and made her way upstairs, stopping on the half-landing to look out into the moonlit garden. There was a low light on in Sylvia's window; she must have fallen asleep. Bonnie felt a tiny flicker of guilt. A week or so earlier she had been looking for Sylvia and had gone into the studio room. The designs on the table and the made-up garments on the rack had surprised her with their individuality and style. She had known Sylvia was good, but not quite that good; perhaps this was something she'd like to develop. As she stood looking at the drawing board, Bonnie glimpsed another prospect for expansion and felt a surge of excitement at the idea. But they'd been so busy she hadn't even mentioned it to Sylvia. Now that the opening was behind them she could start to focus on other things. In the morning, she'd talk to her about it, find out what plans she had for her designs.

Bonnie kicked off her shoes and let her clothes fall on the floor. Tonight she was too tired to go through all her usual hanging and tidying, too tired even to take off her make-up and clean her teeth. She climbed into bed, anticipating that special last moment before sleep when she always told Jeff about her day. But now she was just one satisfied sigh away from sleep and was gone the moment her head touched the pillow.

'For goodness sake, Irene, calm down and come to bed,' Hamish said. 'There's absolutely nothing you can do.'

'I know, I know,' Irene said, wringing her hands, 'but I wish there was. Something awful's going to happen, I know it is.'

Hamish got out of bed and went over to the window where she was peering through the curtains to see if Will's car was back. 'Don't be so dramatic,' he said, closing the curtain and putting his arm around her shoulders. 'What's the problem? Will and Sylvia took off together, then you saw him bring her back and he drove off again on his own. He's probably gone somewhere for a quiet drink.'

'But it was the *way* they came back,' Irene said, twitching the curtain open again. 'He drove in and Sylvia got out of the car almost before he stopped and ran into the cottage. Then Will got out and hammered on the door but she didn't let him in. That's when he got back in the car and drove off. That was a couple of hours ago – it's after midnight now.'

Hamish sighed and led her back to sit on the foot of the bed.

'I know, my dear, you've told me all that. So, they went off for a meal or a drink or something, had a bit of a tiff and she's sulking in her place, and he's gone off to sulk somewhere else. It's their business, Irene, nothing you can do.'

Irene knew that Hamish was being perfectly logical but she couldn't get rid of the feeling that the whole thing spelled trouble. She was worried about Sylvia and Will, but she was also worried that whatever had happened between them tonight was going to bounce back on Bonnie.

'I was thinking I might put on my dressing gown and pop across to see if Sylvia's all right,' she said.

'No,' Hamish said in an authoritative voice she'd never heard him use before. 'It's after midnight, Sylvia's probably fast asleep by now. If she wants to talk to you she'll do so in the morning. But my bet is that by the time we wake up, Will'll be back here, sleeping off a hangover, and it'll all be forgotten. Things always look better in the morning. Come on, why don't I read to you? A few pages of Tim Winton'll take your mind off it.'

Sylvia put down the phone and sat for a moment in the dark, her skin prickling with shock and panic. The call had woken her with a start from a heavy, restless sleep peppered with fragments of incomprehensible, troubling dreams and she had sat bolt upright in bed, heart pounding, fumbling around in the dark to find the mobile. The green figures on the digital clock said it was three-thirty. Snapping on the bedside light she got out of bed, dragged on a sweater and a pair of jeans, brushed her hair, splashed some water on her face and grabbed her bag and car keys.

At the doorway she paused briefly, wondering if she was doing the right thing. Would it be better to go alone? But it was only a fleeting moment of indecision, keeping the secret from Bonnie had been bad enough; she couldn't compound it further by excluding her from this. Besides, she needed someone with her, this was something she couldn't face alone.

She closed the door of the cottage and ran through the shadowy garden to the back door of the house. Fortunately, it was on the latch – presumably Bonnie had left it that way for Will – and she crept through the darkened kitchen to the hall, ran up the stairs two at a time and tapped lightly on Bonnie's bedroom door.

'Bonnie, Bonnie,' she whispered. Getting no answer, she opened the door. 'Bonnie, are you awake? It's me, Sylvia.'

Bonnie's head popped up from under the quilt. 'What? Who's that?'

'It's okay,' Sylvia said, going over to the bed. 'It's me.' She put her hand on Bonnie's arm and sat down on the edge of the bed.

Bonnie struggled up from under the covers and switched on the bedside light, blinking and putting her hand up to shade her eyes. 'Sylvia? What is it? Are you okay?'

'I'm fine,' Sylvia said, taking a deep breath. 'It's Will, he's in the Alfred Hospital. I'm not exactly sure what happened but he fell into the river and is quite badly injured.'

'Fell into the river? Oh my god, how? Was he drunk or something?'

'I think he probably was but I don't have any more details. I said we'd be there straight away.'

Bonnie struggled out of bed and headed for the bathroom. 'I'm probably over the limit still,' she said. 'Can you drive?'

Sylvia pulled out onto the road into town, shivering with the chill of night-time waking and with dread of what the next few hours might bring.

'I can't understand it,' Bonnie said. 'Will's usually pretty careful what he drinks. Mind you, we all started drinking early in the day. But where did he get to this evening? And how did he manage to fall in the river?'

'I think they said he fell off the Princes Bridge,' Sylvia said, shooting through traffic lights on orange.

'Fell off the Princes Bridge! You can't just fall off that bridge,' Bonnie said in amazement. 'I mean, it's got great thick concrete balustrades, you'd have to climb up on them to fall off. Oh, for goodness sake, he couldn't have been so drunk that he'd climb up there, could he? Men, honestly, don't they ever grow up? Who was he with, for heaven's sake?'

'I think he was on his own.'

'Will, drunk, on his own, climbing over the Princes Bridge – it doesn't make sense.' Bonnie let the car window down a little to get some air. 'So what else did they say?'

Sylvia swallowed hard and tried to concentrate on the road. 'Just that he was unconscious and they weren't sure how serious the injuries were. I was so shaken by the call that I didn't ask any of the right questions.'

'Yes, yes, of course, sorry,' Bonnie said. She sat quietly for a moment. 'Hang on, why did they call you? How did they get your number?'

Sylvia hesitated. It was the moment she'd been dreading, and there was no escape.

'Will had a card in his wallet with his blood group and on it he'd listed me as his next of kin.'

'Next of kin! You? He hasn't got a next of kin, not since Jeff died. I'm probably his closest relative, so why did he . . .' She paused, and it seemed to Sylvia that she could actually hear the connections happening in Bonnie's head. With her eyes still on the road, she saw in her peripheral vision that Bonnie was turning to face her, very slowly and deliberately. 'Okay, Sylvia,' she said, and her voice was low now, her tone measured. 'Do you want to tell me why Will had you listed as his next of kin?'

THIRTY-FOUR

'I don't *know* what happened, Fran,' Sean said, cracking eggs into a mixing bowl. 'All I know is that Bonnie rang and said she wouldn't be in until later. She and Sylvia are at the hospital because that weirdo brother-in-law had an accident. She tried to phone you but your mobile was switched off.'

'Shit!' Fran said. 'I forgot.' She pulled the phone from her bag, switched it on and picked up the message from Bonnie, but it told her nothing more. Her head reeled in panic. Six-thirty on the first day of trading and they were due to open at seven.

'Don't worry, darl,' Sean said. 'We're all cool, Graeme's here, the sous-chef starts tomorrow and Graeme'll stay on for a bit if we need him.'

'We'll owe you two a fortune,' Fran said gratefully.

'Naturally,' he said with a grin, and batted the kitchen hand on the shoulder with an egg whisk. 'Coriander – get me a big bunch, kiddo. I assume you know what it looks like. Chop it really fine.'

Out in the restaurant, Tan was checking the table settings and calling instructions to the waitstaff.

'It's okay, Fran,' she said. 'It's a shame Bonnie miss the first morning, but we got good staff, we be fine.'

Fran decided to believe her and went up the stairs to her office, wondering what could have happened. Since her conversation with Caro, all Fran's instincts told her that Sylvia and Will were having an affair and trouble was not far ahead. She sat down at her desk and dialled Caro's number.

'Sorry to call you so early,' she said. 'Any chance of you rolling up this morning to keep an eye on the gallery?' Even in her present anxious state, Fran relished the ease with which she was able to ask the favour, and Caro's willing response. She paused, wondering whether to call Bonnie or Sylvia, or just get on with the job of opening the Boatshed, and decided finally that it was probably best to leave them to it. She'd wait until the first customers were happily tucking in to their breakfasts before she called, then she could at least reassure them that everything here was under control.

She sat in the silence, getting a grip on the fact that it was opening day and she was here alone. But of course it wasn't like before, there was a whole infrastructure in place, and while her presence was useful and desirable, it wasn't essential. What would Bonnie expect her to do? Just be there, talk to people and keep an eye on things. She must control her urge to get into the kitchen and try to take over there, stay calm and remember she was running a business.

Fran walked through into the small washroom between the offices and stared at her face in the mirror. She thought she looked confident and professional. Her nervousness didn't seem to show and she wondered how much creative energy she had wasted in the past worrying about her weight and appearance. What might she have achieved if she had been able to ignore the relentless cultural pressure to look different?

'Go on then,' she said to her reflection, 'this restaurant is trading on your reputation, Fran Whittaker, and you're in charge.' She paused and fiddled with a stray strand of hair. 'And you don't look half bad either,' she said, and she made her way down to the restaurant, where Tan was giving the waitstaff a final briefing.

'Okay, guys?' Fran asked sticking her head into the kitchen, and Sean gave her a thumbs up.

Outside the restaurant doors, a few people were chatting on the grassy slope, a car drew up and a couple got out and headed for the steps, as two more cars pulled into the car park, and three Lycra-clad cyclists chained their bikes to the rail at the edge of the boardwalk. Fran checked her watch; it was a couple of minutes to seven.

'You guys ready too, Tan?'

'We been ready ages,' Tan said with a smile, and the others nodded.

'Okay,' she said, 'here we go.' Reaching up she unbolted the glass doors and stepped outside to fix them back. 'Good morning,' she said. 'Welcome to the Boatshed.'

And the first customers made their way into the restaurant.

Sylvia sat on a vinyl-covered hospital bench, eyes closed, head resting against the wall. It was seven o'clock in the morning and the twelve hours since Will had sprung his proposal on her seemed like an escalating nightmare. Against the harsh soundtrack of hospital activity – the rattle of trolleys, ringing phones and the cacophony of voices – she went over events again in her mind.

She had been determined that as soon as they had time alone she would tell Will that it was all over, and was careful not to do anything that he might take as encouragement. But Will had focused his attention on her in a way that rapidly became overbearing. He seemed to have no interest in anything or anyone else, and while Bonnie was clearly looking to him for reassurance and support, he had detached himself completely from that role.

'For goodness sake, Will,' Sylvia had said to him shortly after the guests started to arrive, 'get out there and help Bonnie. She's counting on you being there for her – your approval means Jeff's approval.'

'Huh?' he'd said, looking as though he had no idea what she was talking about. 'What d'you mean?'

Sylvia sighed, leading him away from the counter where Caro was helping a local journalist choose between two different pairs of turquoise earrings.

'Look, this place is Bonnie's way of doing what Jeff would have wanted her to do. Getting a life of her own, being strong, moving on. She wants to know he'd be proud of her. You're his brother and as far as the Boatshed's concerned, you're a de facto Jeff – she needs you to be there for her.'

Will looked confused. 'What am I supposed to do? Channel him?' he'd asked irritably, attempting to stroke the side of Sylvia's hand without anyone seeing.

Sylvia rolled her eyes and snatched her hand away in annoyance. 'Just *be there* for her, Will, show her you're behind her in this. Let her know what a terrific job she's done.'

'Okay,' he'd said, shrugging his shoulders. 'If you say so. What time d'you think we can get away?'

'God knows. Late afternoon, early evening probably. Now please, just go and back Bonnie up.'

He'd strolled off into the restaurant, and Sylvia caught a glimpse of him with Bonnie and then, a few minutes later, talking with Jack Bannister, but he was soon back in the gallery, leaning against a display case, chatting idly as he watched her. And from then on he had been a constant oppressive presence in the gallery, making her awkwardly conscious of her every move.

'Who *is* that?' Caro had asked at one point, and when Sylvia explained she let out a low whistle. 'Chick magnet!' she said, and nudged Sylvia. 'He can't take his eyes off you, Sylvia.'

'Rubbish,' Sylvia had said, blushing deeply. 'You're imagining things, Caro,' and she had hurried out to the storeroom to fetch some more gift wrapping.

When the guests had left and the staff debrief was done, they had gone back to the house and dissected the whole thing, celebrating the success of the launch, the excellent staff, and Bonnie's brilliant organisation and planning. Sylvia's irritation grew as Will mooched around casting impatient glances at her. In the end it was Hamish who had marshalled them in a toast to Bonnie's vision and management, to Fran's work that had given the restaurant such a solid trading base, and her own efforts in organising and stocking the gallery. But Sylvia felt it should have come from Will, and from the moment they left the house her anger at him, and at herself for allowing the relationship to get to this point, simply increased.

On the hotel terrace she could barely wait for the waiter to pour the wine so that she could say what she had to say. But as she started to speak, Will had stopped her, putting a finger to her lips to silence her in a gesture she found shockingly patronising. She could only imagine the shock that he must have seen on her face when he asked her to marry him.

'No, Will!' she'd said, drawing her hand away in dismay and folding her arms. 'I'm sorry, but no. I don't know what you're thinking of. Anyway, I'm still married.' Tactically it was a disastrous thing to say, for he read her reply to mean that it was only her current status that stood in the way of his dreams.

'But you won't be for much longer,' he said. 'Of course we can't get married now, but we can be engaged, we can be entirely open about this. I know you want to tell Bonnie. She'll be happy for us, I know she will.'

Sylvia's head spun. 'Will, you don't understand. I don't *want* to marry you, not now, not ever.' She pushed away the hand that was once again reaching to take hers. 'Look, we've had a wonderful time together, it was a gift, and of course I do care for you –'

'There you are, then,' he said, smiling, 'I knew it –'

'No! Listen to me, please,' she said. 'I care for you, Will, but I'm not in love with you. I won't be engaged to you and I won't marry you. Please try to understand.' She saw the pain and confusion on his face and hated herself for hurting him. 'Look, Will, this is beautiful, really, that you should ask me but . . . but that's not how it is for me. I'm sorry, really, but I don't have those feelings for you. Since that weekend in Queenscliff I knew I had to end it. I felt you didn't understand what I was saying to you.'

'You said you loved me,' he said in a small voice edged with anger. 'I asked you.'

'I said I cared for you and loved you as a dear friend. I said it several times and each time you refused to hear that qualification. I told you then, and I'm telling you again, Will, I'm *not* in love with you, I don't want to marry you. I'm sorry but we have to finish this now.' He stared at her, saying nothing, just shaking his head. 'I intended to tell you this evening, anyway,' she continued, 'as soon as we had time alone. I never dreamed . . . never dreamed that . . . Will, I'll always treasure it, but it's over now, it has to be, and we have to tell Bonnie. I don't want her finding out sometime later, down the track.'

'Fuck Bonnie!' Will said, the pain on his face turning to anger. 'This is nothing to do with her. This is about us, Sylvia, you and me.'

Sylvia reached out and put her hand over his. 'No, Will, there isn't an us, not anymore.'

He snatched his hand away, sending his glass crashing onto the brick paving. 'What do you mean, not anymore? I love you, Sylvia, we're right together . . . Hong Kong, Queenscliff, it can be like that all the time . . .'

'It can't, Will, that's what I'm telling you. It's over for me.'

'Over for you? What about me? What's supposed to happen to me?' He was on his feet now, staring down at her.

A waiter with a dustpan and a damp cloth materialised to sweep up the broken glass and wipe the spilled wine from the table.

'Should I bring you another bottle of wine, sir?' he asked.

'No,' Will said, waving him away. 'Go, just go away.'

Sylvia caught the waiter's eye. 'Could you bring some water, please?' she asked, and the young man nodded and disappeared back into the bar.

Will leaned over her, his hands on the arms of her chair, peering close into her face. There was something threatening about his manner and Sylvia drew back.

'Stop it,' she said angrily. 'Stop it, Will, you don't intimidate me.'

'Hah!' he cried, straightening up again. 'No, I can see that. It doesn't even touch you, does it, the way I feel? What sort of woman are you, Sylvia?'

She was extremely angry now and she stood up, pushing past him to move out of reach. 'I'm a very ordinary sort of woman really, Will,' she said. 'I've been married for over thirty years, and as you yourself pointed out I've spent far too much of my life doing what my husband and other people wanted me to do. You told me to do what I wanted, don't let anyone hassle me, do something for myself. That was good advice and I took it. I did what I wanted to do; I had an affair with you. It was thrilling, exciting, wonderful in every way, and yes, I *did* think it was an adventure. The same sort of adventure you've been having with women all your life. I thought it was the same for both of us. But you changed the rules. I didn't ask you to fall in love with me, but I accept that I should have made it clear to you by ending it when you told me that day on the phone. I'm sorry if you think I misled you, Will. But it really is over.'

A group of four people strolled out of the bar and settled at a table in a nearby corner. Sylvia walked over to the low wall, leaning against a planter filled with pink and white geraniums. He came up behind her and gripped her arm; he was pleading now, the anger subsiding as suddenly as it had flared.

'I'm sorry,' he said, 'I'm sorry, Syl, I shouldn't have shouted. But this is wrong, it's so wrong . . . I love you, don't you see?'

'Take me home, Will, please,' she said quietly. 'Take me home now, or if you prefer it I'll call a cab.'

But it was another hour before she managed to get him to leave, and in the meantime he drank three double whiskies and his mood changed from pleading to anger and back to pleading again.

'I think you'd better let me drive,' she said as she finally coaxed him out into the car park.

'I'm fine,' he said, the anger returning.

'You've been drinking all day,' she said, 'and you haven't had anything to eat for hours.' She reached out to take the keys of the rental car from him, but he twisted away from her.

'Shut up and get in the car,' he said.

Sylvia hesitated, and then, against her better judgment, slid into the front seat beside him. Will switched on the engine, reversed out of the car park and swung into the road,

'You don't have any lights on,' she told him and she saw his knuckles tighten on the steering wheel before he flicked the switch. He took off at a ridiculous speed until she cautioned him to slow down and he responded by swinging into the fore-court of a disused building and stopping completely. And the second round of the battle began, flaring and subsiding time and time again until Sylvia finally persuaded him to take her home and they made the last stage of the journey in painful silence.

'Now we can talk.' Will said, swinging the car into the driveway with a shower of gravel that she was sure would have everyone looking out of the window.

'No,' she said immediately. 'No, not tonight, I can't take any more of this. Tomorrow if you want, but it won't make any difference, Will, it's over.' And she opened the door and got out as he stopped the car, and ran up the steps, let herself into the cottage and slammed the door behind her. She leaned back against it in relief, until he hammered on it and she moved further away and into the lounge wondering whether, if she refused to let him in, he would barge into Irene's living room and make a scene. But then the banging stopped and she heard the car door slam and the wheels spun once again across the gravel. Sneaking a look through the gap in the curtains she saw the tail lights at the gate and he roared out again into the street.

An ambulance, its siren still blaring, drew up at the hospital entrance and Sylvia straightened up, opening her eyes as an orderly and a couple of nurses raced to meet it with a trolley. Getting to her feet she wandered over to the drinks machine to get herself a bottle of water. It had been fairly quiet when she and Bonnie had arrived three hours earlier; they must have hit a lull in the emergency department. Linked only by their anxiety about what they might find, they had walked briskly from the car park in frosty silence. Bonnie's hurt and resentment had emanated from her in waves as Sylvia explained the situation.

'And you let him drive in that state?' she'd said as they reached the reception desk. And Sylvia opened her mouth and shut it again, realising that to say that Will was an adult and responsible for his own behaviour would only make things worse.

Will, his face ashen, was breathing through an oxygen mask, and there was a deep cut on his forehead which had been cleaned but not yet stitched. His neck was in a brace, and what looked like small sandbags were packed down each side of him to keep him lying straight.

'We're worried about neck or spinal damage,' the doctor told them. 'We need to keep him immobilised until we can stabilise him and then get him up to x-ray.'

'I couldn't really see what he was doing,' said the young police officer who had dived into the river to haul him out. He was a red haired man in his early twenties, sitting wrapped in a blanket drinking a cup of tea, waiting for his colleague to return to the hospital with some dry clothes. 'We saw him up there on the wall on the side of the bridge, he seemed to be clambering around a bit, then he sort of tipped forward and fell in the water. Good thing we were down near the water or it would've been too late.'

Facing Bonnie across the bed, Sylvia was overwhelmed by exhaustion and sadness. Tears ran uncontrollably down her cheeks and she sank into a chair.

'He tried to kill himself, Sylvia,' Bonnie whispered when the doctor left the cubicle for a moment. 'He tried to kill himself.'

Sylvia shook her head. 'No,' she managed to say, grabbing a handful of tissues from a box near the bed. 'No. Not Will, I don't believe he'd do that.'

'Huh!' said Bonnie, stroking Will's arm. 'You didn't think he'd fall in love and look how wrong you were about that.'

Sylvia unscrewed the bottle of water and wandered to the doorway to get some fresh air. The ambulance was pulling away and the fierce burst of activity had subsided. She stood outside taking deep breaths. If she had acted sooner, if she and Will had come clean before this had happened, they would have shared the burden of Bonnie's hurt. But now everything was changed. Sylvia tossed the empty water bottle in the bin and turned back into the hospital. At the far end of the corridor she saw the orderly wheeling Will on the trolley with Bonnie by his side, on their way back from the x-ray department.

'No spinal damage,' Bonnie told her curtly. 'His blood pressure's up, internal bruising and they think his head's okay, but he's not in the clear yet.'

A nurse pulled back the curtains to the cubicle, and she and the orderly transferred Will back to the bed. His eyes flickered open

328

and settled on Sylvia, and for a second he seemed to lift his hand towards her and then, almost as quickly, he dropped it and turned his head away.

'Will,' she said. 'Will, it's okay, we're here with you, Bonnie and I.' She took his hand in hers. 'Will, can you hear me?'

Across the bed, Bonnie seemed to draw herself up. 'Leave him alone, Sylvia,' she hissed. 'Don't you think you've done enough damage? Leave him alone.'

THIRTY-FIVE

'I think you're being unnecessarily hard on yourself, Sylvia,' Fran said. 'On reflection, yes, it would have been better if Bonnie had known about you and Will right from the start, but I don't think you had any responsibility to tell her. It really wasn't anyone else's business.'

'But in the interests of friendship, and in view of Bonnie's generosity to me –' Sylvia began.

'I know all that,' Fran interrupted. 'But at the same time, you weren't sure where all this was going. You thought you were having a bit of a fling, and Will wanted you not to say anything. I understand that Bonnie might feel hurt, but frankly I think she's way over the top.'

It was the Monday morning after the opening and they were sitting at an outside table eating Sean's baked eggs with tomatoes and basil. The first weekend of trading had been comfortably busy and free of problems, and managing it without Bonnie had made Fran feel more confident. Since the morning of Will's accident, Bonnie had made only two fleeting visits to the Boatshed, spending the rest of the time at the hospital, waiting for Will to regain consciousness. Sylvia, distressed by Bonnie's hostility, had abandoned the vigil, calling in at the hospital two or three times a day but continuing to run the gallery with Caro's help.

'So what do *you* think he was doing up on the bridge?' Fran asked, savouring the scent of her freshly baked roll as she broke it in half. 'Was he suicidal when he left you?'

Sylvia shook her head. 'No, he was angry and upset and he'd drunk far too much. But it was the anger that was predominant, that's why I wouldn't let him into the cottage, I simply couldn't cope with it.' She paused, putting down her fork. 'I don't think Will is the sort of person who'd try to kill himself. I *did* see another side of him that night, though, I saw that he was the sort of man who could get drunk and get into a fight, do stupid, irrational, possibly violent things, but suicide? No, not Will. That's not what Bonnie thinks, though.'

'Bonnie's not very rational at the moment,' Fran said. 'She's leapt to this conclusion on circumstantial evidence, and I think this is as much about her losing Jeff as it is about Will and you. Just hang on, Sylvia, it can only get better.'

'I certainly hope so. Being ostracised is very difficult. I feel like some sort of pariah and I don't know whether I should be at the hospital or not. Bonnie just seems to have taken Will over completely.'

'What does Irene think?' Fran asked, seeing Hamish's car draw into the Boatshed car park.

'Much the same as you,' Sylvia said, 'although of course she's very concerned about Bonnie.'

Fran watched as Irene and Hamish got out of the car and walked towards the restaurant. Their shared ease and affection were obvious and she was shocked that she felt a stab of envy.

'Come and join us,' she called, making space for them at the table.

'We fancied a really good breakfast,' Hamish said with a smile.

'The baked eggs are spectacular,' Sylvia said. 'Sean has excelled himself.'

'Sounds good to me,' Irene said. 'How are you this morning, dear? Any news from the hospital?'

Sylvia shook her head. 'I called in earlier but there was no change. And it's too difficult for me to be there with Bonnie feeling as she does.'

Irene nodded. 'I know. We'll call in ourselves later. Try not to let it get to you, Sylvia. The main thing is that Will comes through all right. Bonnie will sort herself out eventually.'

The door of the gallery swung open and Caro clattered noisily down the boardwalk, half running, holding Sylvia's mobile phone in her hand.

'Sylvia,' she called. 'Sylvia . . . you left your phone on the counter, I answered it. It's Bonnie. Will's conscious, he's asking for you, you need to go to the hospital.'

David pushed the buggy along the coastal path enjoying the breeze on his face and the sound of the circling gulls overhead. He'd been sick since the night of the opening but, feeling better this afternoon, he'd offered to mind Rebekah while Caro covered for Sylvia at the gallery. He wondered what it would feel like to be pushing a buggy with his own child in it, having not just the pleasure but also the responsibility of fatherhood. There was a wooden bench ahead and he picked up his pace and made for it, sitting down and turning the buggy to face him as Rebekah blinked up at him.

'Hi, Bek,' he said softly, moving the edge of her jacket away from her face. 'Want to come out for a bit? Sit on my knee?' She smiled as though she understood him, and he unstrapped her, lifted her out and cuddled her close to his chest, rocking her gently back and forth.

He and Jodie had planned for her to move into his apartment the morning after the Boatshed opening and he'd been counting the days, but then he'd ruined it by being sick. He'd risked a glass of champagne at the opening, and then a second, and by the end of the day that, combined with too much food, had knocked him sideways. On Saturday morning, all he could do was stagger sweating between the bathroom and bedroom and watch the ceiling circle dizzyingly above his head.

'Matt's going to come and get your gear,' he'd told Jodie on the phone. 'Unless you want to hang on until I get over this.'

'No, I'm dying to move in,' she said. 'Can't wait. Owen's here, he'll help.'

So David had lain there propped up with pillows while her boxes, plants and few bits of furniture were carried up the stairs and distributed through the apartment.

'I feel like a complete waste of space,' he'd complained at one point.

'You are,' Matt said with a grin, dumping Jodie's suitcase in the bedroom. 'Can't think why this gorgeous woman is even bothering with you.'

The movement around him, the coming and going, had made him dizzy and he was thankful when Matt and Owen left and he and Jodie were alone at last. 'Sorry, Jo,' he said sheepishly, gripping her hand when she came to sit on the side of the bed. 'Now you can really see what a loser you've taken on.'

'Stop it,' she'd said, pulling her hand away and standing up. 'You have to stop this, David.'

'Stop what? I can't stop the illness, you know that, you said you understood . . .'

'I do. What I mean is that you have to stop behaving as though you're a leper.'

'A leper?'

'Yes. You've still got the idea that your illness makes you a liability.' She stopped for a moment and walked over to the window, and then turned back to him again. 'It's like you think the Hep C is all you're about now, that it defines you, controls you. Well, it doesn't, or at least it doesn't have to.' She walked back to the bed and climbed onto it, sitting beside him, with her legs stretched out in front of her. 'It's horrible that you have this disease but it doesn't have to dominate our lives. I know you'll be sick like this sometimes, but you seem to think that the disease is all that people see when they look at you. You're more than your condition, Dave; at least, you are if you'll let yourself be.'

A seagull swooped down onto the seat beside him and, steadying Rebekah with one hand, David pulled out a packet of Tic Tacs, flipped it open and spilled some onto the seat for the gull. Rebekah turned to look at David and he hugged her closer.

'Big bird, Bek,' he said, 'a big bird,' and he watched as the gull circled and swooped back for another mint. In that moment, clutching the baby to him and watching as a few more gulls lined up on the seat, David knew that this strangely wonderful feeling was called contentment, something he had never known before.

He held Rebekah up above him and she gurgled joyfully, dribbling on his hair. 'You dag, Bek,' he laughed, lowering her into the buggy, and together they made their way back along the path to the Boatshed.

Bonnie was exhausted with waiting; waiting for Will to open his eyes, to speak, to show any sign, however small, that he was going to be all right. Even when she wasn't at the hospital she was waiting. On her brief visits to the Boatshed she was waiting for people to stop updating her on the first few days of trading, so that she could get away. And when, at night, she finally gave in to exhaustion and returned home to sleep, her dreams seemed to be full of waiting for a variety of strange things to be finished so that she could wake up.

'I'm back, Will,' she said each time she returned to the chair by his bed. 'It's Bonnie, I'm here, can you hear me? Squeeze my hand if you can hear me, Will.' And occasionally she would think she had felt a change of pressure against her hand, but it was so minute that she couldn't be sure. From time to time he would stir, and his eyes flickered open and closed again and he would mumble something incomprehensible, but there was no real improvement.

'We'll be able to tell more when he regains consciousness,' the doctor had explained. 'But apart from the extensive bruising, broken collarbone, cracked ribs and that head wound, I can't find much else wrong. But when he does come round, he's going to be very sore for a good few weeks.'

Bonnie stroked Will's hand. 'It's okay, Will,' she said. 'I'll take you home as soon as I can, there's a room ready for you. I'll look after you, nothing to worry about; you just concentrate on getting better.' But apart from the odd flicker of his eyelids, or a slight shift of position, there was no change.

As she sat by the bed unable to read, unable to concentrate on the television flickering softly overhead, Bonnie thought he looked more and more like Jeff. There had always been a fraternal likeness, but as the hours passed, the resemblance seemed to grow until sometimes it was as though they were the same person. A couple of times she even found herself calling him Jeff, and she laughed awkwardly and corrected herself, thankful there was no one else around to hear her. So it seemed a cruel stroke of fate that on the Monday morning when Will did finally open his eyes and start to make sense, Bonnie was three floors down in the café, getting herself a cup of coffee and a croissant. Making her way back up to the ward, clutching the cardboard beaker and the bag with the croissant, she pushed open the door of Will's room and found a nurse she hadn't seen before, taking his blood pressure and talking to him.

'Oh good,' the nurse said, straightening up and smiling at her. 'He's back with us at last, aren't you, Mr Logan? I've sent for the doctor. I guess you must be Sylvia – he's been asking for you.'

She undid the blood pressure cuff and smoothed down Will's sleeve. 'Keep talking to him, please. The doctor will be here in a minute.'

Bonnie put the coffee down, dropped the croissant and took hold of Will's hand. 'Will, Will, it's Bonnie, I'm here,' she said, brushing the hair back from his forehead. 'Can you speak to me, Will? Can you see me?'

His eyes were glassy and seemed slow to focus. He shifted his position slightly and finally gave her a weak smile. 'Bonnie?' he asked cautiously, as though testing how his mouth worked.

'Yes, Will; yes, it's me. Oh, it's so wonderful that you're awake.' She bent down and kissed him, holding her cheek close to his, stroking his face gently. 'You're all right, Will, you're going to be all right.'

Will nodded, swallowing hard.

'He'll be thirsty,' the nurse said, handing her a bowl of iced water and a small sponge on a stick, 'but he can't have anything to drink until the doctor's seen him. Just let him suck this if he needs it.'

Bonnie dipped the sponge in the water and held it close to Will's lips. He sucked it, swallowing cautiously. 'More?' she asked, offering it to him again, but he shook his head.

'Sylvia,' he said. 'Where's Sylvia?'

'Oh, she might pop in later,' Bonnie said, putting the bowl down on the table. 'But you don't have to see her. I've told her to stay away. She's the last person you need around you right now.'

'No,' Will said in a stronger voice. 'Sylvia, I want to see her, please, Bonnie . . .' And with unexpected force, he grabbed her wrist. 'I want Sylvia.'

'You can go back in now,' the doctor said a quarter of an hour later. 'It's looking good. We'll have to keep a close eye on him for a few days, but he doesn't seem to be suffering any memory loss. He keeps asking for Sylvia – that's your friend, isn't it?'

Bonnie twitched her shoulders. 'I've called her, she'll be here soon. She's just a friend, though. I'm his sister-in-law. He's going to be all right, then?'

'Yes, yes, I think so. I did a few cognitive tests and they were fine. All the signs are good now that he's come round. Take it easy, though. He needs to stay calm. Good to keep him talking for a while. The nurse'll keep an eye on him and tell you when he needs to rest.'

Bonnie went back into the room. Will was propped up now, and a little colour had returned to his face. 'Dear Will, thank goodness,' she said. 'You're looking so much better –'

'Sylvia?' he asked, interrupting her. 'I must talk to Sylvia.'

Bonnie felt like a balloon that had been pricked. 'She's on her way,' she said abruptly. 'Whatever happened to you, Will, do you remember?'

He nodded slightly. 'Most of it . . .'

'Best not to talk about it now,' she said, 'plenty of time for that later.'

'Sylvia!' he said as the door swung open, and Bonnie felt her skin prickle with resentment as Sylvia crossed to the other side of the bed and took Will's hand.

'Looking better, isn't he!' Bonnie said, feeling as though she had some ownership of the process of Will's improvement.

'Yes, yes, he is, much better,' Sylvia said, smiling down at him and leaning over to kiss his cheek. 'Welcome back, Will, it's so good to see you awake.'

Bonnie sniffed slightly and shifted her position in the chair. With some obvious discomfort, Will turned his head back to her.

'Bon,' he said, 'd'you mind . . . I need to talk to Sylvia . . .'

There was a moment of excruciating silence as she looked at him, and then at Sylvia. 'Oh well, I suppose . . . if that's what you want . . . I'll wait outside, just call if you need me.'

Unable to look at Sylvia, she walked out of the room and slumped down on the seat outside. Her heart was beating painfully fast, and she felt as though she might burst with the hurt and the outrage of it. Coiling her fingers into a fist she punched the square metal arm of the bench hard, very hard, over and over again until her knuckles began to bleed, and she began to weep bitter, wrenching sobs until a nurse, with a cup of tea and a box of tissues, sat down beside her explaining that it was quite common for people to cry with relief when someone regained consciousness.

THIRTY-SIX

The three weeks leading up to Christmas were tense and busy. Each day the Boathouse was attracting more business and the initial staffing plan was proving inadequate. A number of complimentary reviews of the restaurant, and a feature about the gallery, had brought the customers in droves and the turnover was considerably higher than any of them had anticipated.

'I need someone else in the gallery,' Sylvia said. 'We always planned on a third person anyway, and now it's essential.'

Bonnie tossed her head. 'After New Year maybe,' she said.

'No, now,' Sylvia insisted. 'We're relying on Caro's goodwill all the time, it's not fair. The gallery turnover is almost double what we predicted. It's only because you're angry with me, Bonnie, that you're hesitating about it.'

'She's right,' Fran said. 'We need a part-time person for the gallery, another part-time person for the kitchen and an extra waitperson for Saturdays and Sundays.'

Bonnie shuffled the papers on her desk. 'It's Christmas next week, can't it wait?'

'No,' Fran said, 'it can't. We need people in place for the crucial time between Christmas and New Year.'

'It all seems to be happening very quickly,' Bonnie said. 'I'm not convinced.'

Fran got up and marched irritably across to the window and back again. Bonnie was being impossible, missing most of the time, totally disengaged and uncooperative when she *was* there, and still barely speaking to Sylvia. For the last three weeks, Fran had been running the restaurant business herself, something she'd been promised she wouldn't have to do, but she didn't have the power to make the final decisions. She thought she might have felt differently if Will really needed care, but he was out of hospital making good progress. She strode back to the desk and stood in front of it leaning forward, her hands flat on the surface.

'Well, you *would* be convinced if you were ever here when we're open, but you only pop in for half an hour at closing time. Have a look at the figures, Bonnie, be the businesswoman you are and take some responsibility for what you've created here.' The silence was oppressive, and she and Sylvia exchanged an awkward glance.

Bonnie stared hard at the papers on her desk, flipping the edge of one with the end of a pen. 'Oh, do what you like,' she said suddenly, getting up from the desk without looking at either of them. 'I can't cope with this.' And she picked up her bag and walked out of the office.

Sylvia and Fran looked at each other in amazement as they listened to her heels clattering down the stairs, and out through the empty restaurant.

'What are we going to do?' Sylvia asked.

'Get on with it,' Fran said. 'Use our own judgment, run it our way until she gets herself together.'

'And then suppose she doesn't like what we've done?'

'Hard luck,' Fran said irritably. 'She'll just have to put up with it. I don't know what the hell she thinks she's doing.'

'She thinks she's looking after Will,' Sylvia said. 'She can't leave him alone. I popped into the house to see him yesterday and he told me he feels like he's being held hostage. She wants to be at the house all the time, and keeps looking in on him, asking if he's okay, offering him tea, coffee, meals, cushions, newspapers, you name it . . .'

Fran shook her head. 'She seems to have lost it completely. What about you guys, you and Will – is it okay?'

'It's awkward. He's still pretty devastated that it didn't work out. He hasn't really forgiven me.'

'What's to forgive?'

'He hasn't forgiven me for not being in love with him. He's a man who's used to getting his own way. You know, I keep thinking that if we'd told Bonnie the truth earlier that day, she'd have seen us as equally guilty. As it is, I'm cast as the guilty one and Will as the victim, and he vacillates between enjoying the role of victim and being terribly frustrated by her obsession with looking after him.'

'And Irene?'

Sylvia grinned. 'She and Hamish have gone to Singapore for a week at Raffles, back tomorrow.'

'Smart woman,' Fran said with a laugh. 'Well, I'm going to have a word with Sean, see if he knows anyone for the kitchen job before I ring the agency.'

Sylvia got up, straightening her skirt. 'Okay, look, I know we interviewed some possible people for the gallery, but what do you think about Caro? She's so good, far better than Linda, who's a bit of a disappointment. The customers love Caro, and Rebekah too.'

Fran stopped short and looked at her. 'Really? I hadn't thought about it – you're sure? You don't have to do it because of me.'

'I'm not. I'm doing it because she's just what we need – efficient, knows and loves the stock, and she and I get on really well.'

Fran nodded. 'Then . . . good,' she said. 'I think she'll jump at it.'

Bonnie let herself in through the back door, switched on the kettle and went straight through to the living room, where Will was sitting on the sofa, his laptop on his knees. She hesitated in the doorway, watching him; the way he tilted his head as he worked was just like Jeff. All the time she was away from the house, she was obsessed with the feeling that she would come back and find him as she had found Jeff, twisted and cold on the floor, beyond any hope of revival. Each time she returned and saw him there, upright, conscious, still alive, her terror subsided.

'Bonnie!' he said, glancing up. 'You're back. Good news, you're getting rid of me at last.'

'Getting rid of you, what d'you mean?'

'Tomorrow! Ryan's here in Melbourne for a meeting and he can chaperone me home. I'll have someone with me on the flight. Not that I really need it – the hospital has cleared me to fly. I was bloody lucky to get the seat so close to Christmas. So, tomorrow I'll be off your hands.'

She stood in the doorway swaying slightly, feeling as though reality was slipping away from her. 'But you can't go,' she said, stepping into the room. 'You're not well enough. Something might happen, you need to stay through Christmas and New Year at least. Aren't you comfortable here?'

Will shook his head. 'It's not that, Bon, you've treated me like a prince, but I don't want to impose on you any longer, and I'd like to be home for Christmas –'

'But this is home,' she cut in. 'Well, it *can* be home. I . . . I hoped you'd stay on . . .'

'But my home's in Perth, Bonnie,' Will said. 'My business, all my friends are there. I'll stay with Ryan and Tania for a few days, then go back to my flat after New Year.'

Bonnie stared at him for a moment, trying to understand. 'Of course,' she said at last. 'It's Sylvia. It must be terrible for you being here, near her, after what she did.'

'Er . . . sorry, I don't –'

'No,' she cut in. 'I should have done it before. How thoughtless of me. How could you bear to be here with her so close. I'll tell her to leave. You can have the cottage, you'll be much more comfortable in there, and I can still look after you.'

'Whoa!' said Will, holding up his hand. 'This is getting away from me, Bon – I don't know what you're talking about. Why should Sylvia leave?'

'Well, obviously, because of what she did,' Bonnie said. 'What she did to you.'

Will took a deep breath. 'Look, Bonnie, Sylvia didn't *do anything* to me. I fell in love, she didn't, and I was, still am, shattered. At the time I was hurt and angry, a bit mad, but you can't make someone love you if they don't feel it.'

Bonnie got up shaking her head. Why was he doing this?

Sylvia didn't deserve his generosity. 'No,' she said, 'of course she has to go. She . . . she . . .' She paused, hardly liking to say it. So far everyone had avoided talking about what had happened. They were all being polite, skirting around it, but it had to come out in the end. Will would need counselling. She hadn't mentioned it yet but she'd made some calls and found the right person – she just needed to pick the right time to suggest it.

'She drove you to attempt suicide, Will, you almost died. Of course she has to go.'

Will's mouth dropped open. He stared at her with a look of complete amazement on his face. Then, slowly, he began to laugh, shaking his head, bending forward to put the laptop on the side table. 'So *that's* what you think, that's what all this has been about.' He smiled and held out his hand to her. 'Come over here, Bon, come and sit here with me and let me explain. I wasn't up on that bridge trying to kill myself.'

She walked over to him and he took her hand, drawing her down beside him on the sofa.

'But you were, you were so upset about Sylvia that you threw yourself off the bridge.'

Will patted her hand and smiled at her. 'Nothing so romantic, I'm afraid. I was very angry and upset and very drunk, but I certainly wasn't suicidal.' He laughed. 'I'm sorry, Bonnie, I thought you knew, I thought Sylvia would have told you.'

She tossed her head a little. 'Oh she keeps trying to talk to me, but I know what happened, Will. I'm not listening to her excuses.'

'Bonnie, listen to me,' he said, his voice low now, and serious. He sounded so much like his brother it could have been Jeff talking to her. 'That night I drove out of here and went to a bar in town. I had quite a few drinks and met up with a bloke I knew years ago at uni. I cried on his shoulder for a couple of hours and he was just as pissed as me. Then he starts baiting me, and we got in this argument about some Prosh stunt years ago and he's insisting I chickened out of jumping off the bridge. So I'm right off my brain and I say, okay, mate, c'mon then, let's go and do it now. So off we stagger. Christ knows what happened to him, he must have passed out on the way, because I end up on the bridge on my own. So I think I'll just climb up there anyway – well, I'm not sure if I slipped or fell asleep or what, because the next thing I knew I was waking up in the hospital. I wasn't going to top myself, Bon.'

'But you were devastated . . . you said so.'

'Sure I was, still am, but I'm a survivor, Bonnie, just like you. We pick ourselves up, dust ourselves off and start all over again, just like the song says. Just like you did when Jeff died, coming back here, catching up with your friends, starting the Boathouse . . .'

But Bonnie didn't hear the rest of it. Shaking off his hand, she ran out of the room and up the stairs into her bedroom, slamming the door behind her.

THIRTY-SEVEN

Lila sat in the big armchair in the corner of Fran's living room. She'd always loved Christmas, even when she was a struggling single mother and could barely get together enough to buy Fran a simple gift. She had always clung to the magic, loved the festivities, and this year she felt they'd all turned a corner. Lila didn't know much about how the Boatshed was run but she could see that Fran was happier, and then there was Rebekah, here on her knee, gazing wide-eyed at the sparkling tree, the decorations, the piles of paper and ribbon. Lila felt quite proud that she was the oldest person there. She thought she might be a matriarch at last, and she liked that. It didn't really matter that she couldn't quite keep track of everyone.

There was Fran, of course; Caro and Caro's husband, although she couldn't remember his name; and David, who was looking very happy. He had a young woman with him who insisted that she often saw Lila, came to her house, even. Lila didn't know where the girl had got that idea, but she seemed a very nice friend for David. Sylvia was there and Irene, and her gentleman friend had called by earlier. There had been another couple who'd dropped in; they'd insisted they'd known her for years, a little Japanese woman and a man who said his name was Tony and that he used to be married to her – or was it Fran that he was married to? Lila thought he must have been drunk. Anyway, it didn't seem worth worrying about, they were all very friendly. Lila could feel the goodwill and that was really all that mattered. Rebekah lurched forward a little and clapped her hands together.

'Clap, darling, that's it,' Lila said. 'You clap your hands.'

'Look, Mike, look,' Caro said. 'She's clapping!' And it seemed as though the whole room turned to look in delight at the baby on Lila's lap, and in that moment she experienced sheer joy that everyone in her whole family was together in one room, and she couldn't remember the last time that had happened.

Fran brought her a glass of champagne and perched precariously on the arm of the chair.

'Here you are, Mum. D'you want me to hold her so you can have your drink?'

Lila handed Rebekah up to her and took the glass. 'Thank you, dear. Good as gold, isn't she? Just like you were, you were such a good little baby, Fran.' She looked around, her eyes settling on Caro. 'I wish I'd been to see Caro while she was in the hospital. You could have told me sooner, Fran, I could gone up there on my scooter.'

Fran, bouncing Rebekah on her knee, gave Lila a very strange look. 'Caro wasn't in the hospital, Mum, remember? Rebekah was born at home.'

'Nobody told me that!' Lila said, swinging round sharply to look up at her.

'But you were there,' Fran said. 'You and Irene, it was my birthday party, remember? We were all there, in Caro's house, and she went into labour.' Rebekah leaned towards Lila, hands outstretched in front of her, and Lila put her hands on the baby's cheeks and kissed her.

'Go on with you,' Lila said, laughing partly at the baby but also at Fran. 'You're having me on. My memory might be a bit rusty but I'm sure I'd remember that, wouldn't I, Bekky.' And she took the little hands and rubbed them between her own.

'You delivered her, Mum,' Fran said, looking hard at her. 'You and Irene delivered Rebekah in Caro's living room.'

Lila hated it when Fran got irritable with her. 'All right, all right, no need to get stroppy with me,' she said. 'But you're wrong. I can't understand how you could get in such a muddle.

I'd certainly remember something like that.' She reached up to take the baby back onto her knee. Fran was at it again now, insisting, saying it all over again. Lila couldn't comprehend what was the matter with her.

'Go on with you,' she said. 'Don't be so silly, you're spoiling a lovely day.'

David's friend broke away from him and came over to Fran. 'C'mon, Fran,' she said. 'You promised to show me the pots of lavender Lenore sent you.' She slipped a hand under Fran's elbow, drawing her away.

Lila was quite glad. Something had obviously gotten in to Fran – maybe she'd had too much champagne. A bit of fresh air out in the courtyard might do her good. 'That's right, dear,' Lila said, 'you get a bit of air and have a look at the plants. I can look after Caro, can't I, darling?' and she patted the baby's cheek.

'That's Rebekah, Mum,' Fran said, turning back .

'Oh Fran, for goodness sake,' Lila said. 'You always have to have the last word, don't you?'

'It's no good arguing with her, Fran,' Jodie said as they stood in the sunshine beside the two huge terracotta pots of Spanish lavender that had been a surprise delivery on Christmas Eve. 'All the facts and logic in the world aren't going to make any difference to what she believes.'

'I know, *you* keep telling me, the *doctor* keeps telling me, but it's so *hard*, Jodie. She keeps taking me by surprise. She'll go along making perfect sense for a while and I start to think I've imagined it all, and then something like this happens and it really rocks me.'

'It must be awful, but the only thing that upsets Lila is when you argue with her. You're not going to convince her, just try to go along with it.'

Fran nodded, annoyed with herself for handling it so badly. Recently she seemed to ricochet between thinking Lila was fine and maybe she herself was the one who'd lost it, then Lila's extraordinary unreality would swoop on her with chilling force. It was a difficult time in many ways. Aside from the worry about her mother, Bonnie, seriously depressed since Will left, had shut herself away, not coming near the Boatshed for several days. Fran had invited her along with Irene and Hamish for Christmas dinner, but Bonnie had refused. Irene and Hamish had called around earlier for a drink, but had decided to have a low-key Christmas at home, in the hope that Bonnie might be persuaded to join them.

'What are you two plotting?' David asked, coming out into the yard.

'We're just talking about Gran,' Fran said. 'I can't seem to stop myself arguing with her and upsetting both of us in the process.'

David rolled his eyes. 'It's hard, isn't it? It feels patronising when I let her go on with the fantasies, but at least it keeps her happy.'

Fran sighed. 'I must try to remember that that's the most important thing.'

'I'm so excited about working at the Boatshed,' Caro said, watching Rebekah on Lila's knee. She'd barely been able to believe her luck since Sylvia had called her three days earlier.

'I'm delighted. You've been doing such a good job there since we opened,' Sylvia said. 'You're sure it's okay for you to start the day after Boxing Day?'

'Perfect, can't wait. I've loved helping out.'

'You and I can sort out a roster between us next week,' Sylvia said. 'We'll make you assistant manager, and it will be great to have your help with the suppliers as well as just dealing with customers. We might also need another casual person.'

Caro nodded. 'It feels like my dream job. I'd made up my mind I wasn't going back to Desmond Records, but never thought I'd do something like this. By the way, I've been meaning to ask – who's working in that long narrow room at the back? I was poking my nose up there the other day – looks like some designer's rented it.'

'It's mine,' Sylvia said. 'I'm using it as a studio, hoping I'll get some time to make up some more of my designs, maybe try to sell them.'

'You mean that's your stuff?' Caro said. 'I thought Bonnie must've discovered some cool new designer . . . well, I suppose she has . . . I mean, you are . . . you know what I mean.'

Sylvia laughed. 'Yes, I do.'

'What do Mum and Bonnie think?'

'They haven't seen it yet. Irene's seen it, but otherwise we've all been so busy, and then Bonnie . . . well, you know what happened. I just unpacked all my things and I've hardly had time to look at it since. I'm dying to show it all to someone else.'

'You can show it to me,' Caro said, sipping her champagne. 'I'd love to have a proper look at what you're doing.'

'What are you doing tomorrow? Oh no, it's Boxing Day,' Sylvia said.

'Boxing Day's fine for me,' Caro said. 'Mike's working seven till four. I'm not doing anything at all.'

'Well, come down to the Boatshed if you like. I'll show you my stuff and we can have a chat about the gallery – that is, if you'd like to. I mean, it *is* a public holiday.'

'I'd love it,' Caro said, 'I'll be there.'

Bonnie lay curled up on her bed under the quilt. Despite the fact that it was a warm day, she felt quite chilly – or was it just that she felt shivery, nothing to do with the temperature? These days she woke in the mornings dragging herself out of a heavy sleep, as exhausted as if she had been awake all night. The whole business of getting up, taking a shower and getting dressed seemed to take ages, and the prospect of the Boatshed was a nightmare. Her overwhelming desire was to stay in her room, go nowhere, talk to no one. Her bed was a cocoon; her friends and the staff had assumed the proportions of fast moving, fast talking, noisy, threatening robots who might at any time flick her with their harsh fingers and cause her to crumble.

'I don't know . . . the world seems all wrong, frightening,' had been the best she could manage when Irene asked her if she could explain how she felt. She would have liked to talk about the loneliness, the grief and hopelessness that greeted her when she opened her eyes in the morning, but it was so vast and nebulous it seemed to defy description. At the hospital and during the time that Will had been at the house, she had been driven by anger and resentment, but that had burned out to be replaced by this leaden feeling that allowed her no relief.

'I feel as though I'm walking round and round the rim of a big black hole,' she'd said to Jeff in the night, 'as though any minute now I might slip down into it.'

'Black holes aren't just empty spaces, you know, Bon,' he'd told her. And she could hear a familiar edge to his voice, an edge that trimmed his words when he was trying to be supportive but was running out of patience. 'They're not just neutral empty spaces, they're great voids, vacuums that suck you in and swallow you. Don't let yourself get too close to the edge.'

So she'd thought about it a lot, thought about what he'd want her to do, and she'd made him a promise. She couldn't cope with Christmas Day, that was just too much, but on Boxing Day, when the Boatshed was closed, she'd venture down there. Let herself in, have a look at the figures, get the feel of it again, stay for an hour. Then the following day she would go there for a minimum of one hour while it was open, and the day after that, two hours. She'd written the promise on the back of one of her favourite photographs of Jeff, one she'd taken herself on a boat on Lake Geneva, with the shadowy outline of mountains in the background. She'd been adjusting the camera and he had turned to ask her something, and she had captured that characteristic quizzical expression. It was the picture she always carried with her.

'I'll keep you to it,' Jeff had told her on Christmas Eve, when she explained about the promise, and she knew he would.

But here it was, ten o'clock on Boxing Day and she had managed to get up, shower, dress, eat a piece of toast, drink some coffee, and then, instead of heading out the door, she had crept up here again and crawled back under the quilt.

'Didn't you say you were going out, Bonnie?' Irene asked, tapping gently on her door. Ever since Irene and Hamish had got back from Singapore, Bonnie had sensed her mother's concern. She dragged herself upright and reached for the photo. Just one hour, that was all she had to do.

'Yes, Mum,' she said, 'I'm going. I'm going right now.' And

inhaling deeply she pushed back the quilt, got off the bed and opened the bedroom door.

'I love this one,' Caro said, picking up a sleeveless dress in aubergine wool with the skirt cut at a slant.

'This jacket goes with it,' Sylvia said, lifting out another hanger. 'You see, it's cut on the reverse angle.' They had been at the Boatshed for a couple of hours, going through the stock for the gallery and then making their way up to Sylvia's studio.

'It's beautiful,' Caro said, holding it up against her in front of the mirror. 'What are you going to do with all this, Sylvia? It seems a shame you can't spend more time on designing.'

Sylvia shrugged. 'I guess I will eventually, especially now that you'll be here at the gallery. I thought I'd make up some more pieces, then maybe talk to Bonnie about trying them in the gallery, or take them somewhere else. It's just that I don't know if anyone would take me seriously.'

'I think they would,' said a voice behind her. Bonnie, in a pair of jeans and a white linen shirt, was leaning against the doorjamb. 'Happy Boxing Day! I came in here a couple of weeks ago, Sylvia. You're very talented.'

Sylvia flushed deeply at the sight of Bonnie and her throat constricted with an irrational fear. It was the first time since Will's fall that Bonnie had spoken to her in a tone that wasn't over-loaded with hurt, anger and disapproval.

'Bonnie,' she said. 'I didn't expect to see you . . .'

'It's a flying visit,' Bonnie said, and Sylvia could see the lines of tension across her forehead and around her mouth, and that her hands were trembling. 'Reacclimatisation.' She smiled weakly. 'Hello, Caro.'

'Hi, Bonnie,' Caro said. 'Look, I should get out of your way . . .'

Bonnie held up a hand to stop her. 'No, don't stop, please. I just came to have a look at the paperwork and try to get the feel of the place. You two carry on – looks as though we'll have to think about developing a Boatshed fashion label.' She turned to leave and then stopped.

'Sylvia, I . . . I can't talk about it yet,' she began, 'but I was wrong . . . I'm really sorry . . .'

Sylvia moved towards her and then paused, sensing that Bonnie wasn't yet ready for physical contact.

'I'm sorry too, Bon,' she said. 'I was very wrong.' They faced each other, both awkward but savouring the shift of energy between them.

'I'll get on then,' Bonnie said.

And as she turned to leave, Rebekah, tucked into a corner behind the door in her buggy, let out a sudden cry of pleasure and dropped her plastic teething ring on the wooden floor.

Bonnie jumped in shock and poked her head around the door. 'The baby!' she said, and the colour drained from her face. 'The baby's here. Er . . . yes. I'll go, then.' And without a second glance she turned on her heel and ran down the steps, and they heard her office door slam behind her.

Sylvia and Caro stared at each other in surprise. 'That was a bit weird,' Caro said. 'She seemed okay and then . . .'

'Yes,' Sylvia said, 'yes, she did. Fragile, but better than I've seen her for weeks.'

'Doesn't Bonnie like babies?' Caro asked. 'She avoided Bek like the plague when we went back to her place after the opening.'

'Don't take this personally, Caro,' Sylvia said. 'It's nothing to do with you or Rebekah, but I think you may have hit the nail right on the head.'

Bonnie closed her office door and leaned back against it, her heart pounding. She felt she might throw up at any minute. Slowly she made her way to her desk and sat down. The room seemed to have a life of its own, circling and dancing around her in and out of focus. She put her hands flat on the desk in an attempt to steady herself. She'd been doing quite well since she left the house. For a moment there, while she was talking to Sylvia, she'd felt almost normal. But then . . . she remembered about deep breathing, how good it was supposed to be for calming you down, and she sat back in her chair, closed her eyes and tried to concentrate. It helped a little, but not enough. How was she going to get through this if every tiny step forward led to a huge step back? Reaching for her bag, she drew out Jeff's photograph and stared into his face, as though by peering intently into his eyes she could make him come back. But he was forever frozen in time.

Laid out on the desk in front of her were the neat columns of figures that Fran had extracted from the restaurant and gallery returns. So Fran had mastered the accounts. Bonnie gave a small, tight smile, thinking of her friend struggling to manage the financial side, the thing she had promised her she would never have to do. What would that have cost her; that and being here, virtually alone, during those first difficult weeks?

Bonnie bit her lip as she went through the paperwork. While she had been struggling with her own grief there had been no space to think about what her absence had meant to her friends. There were the wages and salaries records, and then contracts for the new staff. She looked through them carefully, admiring Fran's efficiency, touched by the strength and loyalty she had shown in taking over the reins.

The last of the three contracts was Caro's. Bonnie paused, staring at it, resentment battling with common sense and fair play. Caro was, of course, the best person for the gallery, it was an entirely sound decision, one which Sylvia and Fran had no doubt discussed in her absence; one she could not argue with or reasonably change. She liked Caro, and knew she would do a good job, and she would simply have to cope with it. They could not, after all, be expected to understand how it felt for her to know that not only was there a baby in the Boatshed today, but that she would be there regularly in future.

THIRTY-EIGHT

'The thing to remember,' said Jodie, resting her hand on Fran's arm as she pressed the bell at the gate of the hostel, 'is that the facilities are less important than the environment itself.'

'What do you mean?" Fran asked, her anxiety increasing with confusion.

'Some places look really elegant, beautiful floral arrangements, mix and match soft furnishings, snazzy artwork on the walls. But what you need to watch for is the way the staff treat the residents while they're showing us around. You'll know it when you see it,' Jodie murmured as a middle-aged woman in a smart grey suit opened the door.

'Ms Whittaker,' she said with a reassuring smile. 'Do come in. I'm Janet Roberts, director of nursing,' and she reached out to shake Fran's hand.

Fran had woken that morning with a sense of dread at the prospect of the day's program. She had been putting this off since before Christmas and now it was nearly the end of January. Bonnie had slowly returned to work in recent weeks, taking control of things again, managing each day with a rather brittle air of goodwill. She seemed frail somehow, lacking in her old energy and decisiveness, but at least she was there, and her hostility to Sylvia was a thing of the past. Thankfully, Fran had been able to hand over the reins and get on with the book.

Lenore was due to arrive in mid-February to spend a couple of weeks working with her, and Fran had thrown herself into it with feverish energy, using the impending visit as an excuse to avoid confronting the issue of her mother's future. Lila was so cheerful, and although she was often totally out of touch with reality, she hadn't seemed to be any danger to herself or anyone else. Not, that is, until the preceding week, when Fran had found her in a frightening state of confusion, in her dressing gown at four in the afternoon, unsure what had happened to her. It seemed that, forgetting which day it was, she had decided on Friday, but finding that the tablets for Thursday were still in the Webster pack, she had taken two days' drugs instead of one. The following day, she had got lost on the way back from the village office and Ray Barton had found her in tears trying to get into the wrong house. There was no real harm done, but it was a warning that time was running out and she would not be able to live alone much longer.

'I can help, Fran,' Jodie had said. 'I go to heaps of places in my job. If you want, I could suggest some of the nicer ones and I'll go with you to look at them . . . that is, if you wouldn't think I was interfering.'

'Interfering? I'd think you were saving my life,' Fran said. 'Honestly, I don't know where to start.'

So here they were on a guided tour around the first of seven retirement centres that had secure facilities for people with Alzheimer's.

'This is a typical room,' Janet Roberts said, throwing open the door of a sunny room containing two chintz covered beds and Queen Anne style chests of drawers and wardrobes. 'We find our residents are happier sharing – it provides them with both company and reassurance.'

Fran's stomach churned nervously. Having read horror stories about these places she was relieved to see that although it did have an institutional air, it also had a certain graciousness of décor. They moved on down the passage to a bathroom that was shared between two rooms, each accommodating four people.

'It works well,' Jan continued, 'although sometimes people do lose their way and end up in the wrong bedroom or bathroom.' She turned back to them smiling. 'You'll see the names of each occupant on the door along with a flower that matches a flower on the door of the corresponding bathroom. We hope they make the connection but it doesn't always happen. In the gentlemen's wing, there are tree motifs on the doors.' She stopped briefly and looked hard at Fran. 'This is such a difficult time for families,' she said. 'We do understand what you're going through.'

Fran, who was feeling so unbelievably awful that she was sure no one could possibly understand how it felt, smiled weakly in appreciation. 'She's very nice,' she whispered to Jodie as they were borne off to visit the residents' lounge and the television room.

'Yes, but this will be the telling moment,' Jodie whispered.

A couple of elderly women were wandering from side to side along the passage ahead of them, occasionally grasping the rail to steady themselves.

'Come along now, you two,' Janet said imperiously, 'make way, make way.' And the women stopped and pressed themselves back against the wall, staring in confusion as Janet steamed ahead with Fran and Jodie behind her.

Jodie turned to Fran and raised her eyebrows. 'See what I mean?' she whispered.

'I can't imagine how I'm going to do this,' Fran said that evening as she and Jodie sat facing each other exhausted. 'She's going to be devastated. If only there was some other way. Maybe I *could* manage here . . .'

'No, Mum,' David said. 'We've talked this through before. I know it's terrible, but Gran needs to be somewhere safe, for her own sake. You have to be at the Boatshed, you have to have a life. You can't do this.'

Jodie nodded, sipping her tea. 'David's right, Fran. I've seen people give up everything to look after someone with Alzheimer's, and it destroys them. Honestly, Lila will be better somewhere that's safe and friendly. You can't be here all the time – suppose she just let herself out and wandered off? And she may deteriorate quite rapidly and then you'd have to move her again. Another upheaval at that stage would be really bad.'

'It feels so selfish,' Fran said, feeling her eyes fill with tears. 'She looked after me all alone, it was a real struggle, I owe it to her . . .'

'No,' David said again. 'You don't, Gran did that because she had to and she chose to. This is different. Do you think if she was really herself again she'd want you to give up everything to spend the next few years looking after her?'

Fran sighed and wiped her eyes on a handful of tissues. 'No, no, I know she wouldn't, but she's different now, and it's so sudden and so sad . . . and I just don't know how I'm going to tell her. And I need to stop her riding her lovely scooter . . .'

David sat down on the arm of her chair. 'You don't have to do it alone,' he said putting his arm around her shoulders. 'Caro and I will go with you. Honestly, Mum, you have to do this, for Gran and for yourself.'

Later that night Fran wandered aimlessly around the house, tidying things that didn't need to be tidied. How was she to tell Lila that she was no longer capable of living alone? How to explain that she must give up her own home, so lovingly refurbished in varying shades of purple, and live in a place not even of her own choosing where everything would be determined for her by someone else?

Flicking through the TV channels for a distraction she discarded serious current affairs on the ABC, a Japanese film on SBS, and a lot of half-clad youthful bodies on a reality show, and settled finally on a gruesome cosmetic surgery makeover. The woman looked perfectly okay until the surgeon, his own face tightened into an unnatural permanent smile, started to highlight with a purple marker the areas that 'needed work'. Fran shifted restlessly on the couch. In the last few months she had got on top of her craving for sugar, but tonight it had started to bug her again.

'If you eat plenty of protein and vegetables you'll beat the sugar cravings,' Bonnie had told her a few months earlier. And she had; she'd lost a little weight and stopped obsessing about Twix bars, and KitKats, and other sinful indulgences. Now they were back inside her head again, and not only in her head but on the screen in front of her – KitKats, closely followed by a picture of a Big Mac dripping with yellow plastic-looking cheese. Fran stared intently at the screen, wondering why someone with a flare for the creation of fine food was such a sucker for junk. She could just slip out and get some. What was that about the calories not counting if no one saw you eat it? It would make her feel terrible, of course: heartburn, headache, increased heart rate, bloating, raging thirst, guilt, inadequacy, more guilt and more inadequacy. On the other hand . . . Within minutes she was on her way to McDonald's and then to the all-night petrol station for the chocolate.

By the time she got home, the made-over woman, her face in a cloned smile, was revealing ridiculously taut breasts and thighs to her adoring friends and family. Fran flicked the channels again and settled for Frank Sinatra and Ava Gardner, feeling the perceptible mood lift as the burger, fries, two KitKats and a Mars Bar delivered the brief anaesthetic interlude. An hour later, having passed the chemically induced peak and heading for the trough, her heart beating uncomfortably fast and nausea threatening, she slumped into the inevitable mood change. Seventeen years alone. What was wrong with her that she had no one in her life? At any other time Fran might have reminded herself that her single status was largely her own choice. But she couldn't feel that, not tonight.

The next morning, with a thumping headache, she reluctantly called the two places she and Jodie had felt stood out above the others; hostels where the staff very obviously treated the residents with respect and affection. There were endless forms to complete and photocopies of other documents to assemble, but by midday Lila's name was on the waiting lists and her needs assessment placed her quite near the top. Fran swayed back and forth between anxiety about Lila's safety and relief that the waiting list bought her a few more weeks or months of independence. With a growing sense of loneliness she slipped the documents into envelopes to mail to the hostels, feeling she was committing an act of treachery against the mother she loved and who was so rapidly disappearing.

*

Will picked up the phone and put it down again. He'd done that half a dozen times but hadn't managed to sum up the courage to dial the number. It wasn't that he didn't want to speak to Sylvia, he really did. He needed a conversation that would file down the raw edges. He'd left Melbourne quite suddenly, which was probably a good thing, but in the rush of organising it and of Ryan collecting him, and Bonnie wandering around like a stunned mullet, he hadn't had a chance to talk to Sylvia.

'Take care, Will,' she'd said, holding out both her hands as he left. 'I'll be thinking of you.'

He'd taken her hands and mumbled something incomprehensible because he'd felt like crying.

'I could come to the airport,' Bonnie had said, tears bright in her eyes. 'You might need a hand.'

Ryan, primed by Will to expect this, had graciously and efficiently deterred her with an assurance that he could manage Will single-handed. At the time Bonnie had been barely speaking to Sylvia and the tension was palpable. He had tried to explain that the responsibility for the secrecy rested with him but Bonnie hadn't wanted to hear it. Since then, things seemed to have improved. She had called him a couple of times, apologising for overreacting, trying to explain how he and his accident had become so closely linked to losing Jeff that it had knocked her off balance. Her friendship with Sylvia now seemed to be restored, but it was all a bit too complicated for Will. He had listened and tried to understand but he couldn't quite get where Bonnie was coming from. And now it was almost the end of January and he still hadn't had this important conversation he needed to have with Sylvia.

'I don't know what to say,' he said to Tania, tossing the phone restlessly between one hand and the other. 'I want to talk to her, but I want to make it right, not stuff it up.'

'What would make it right?' Tania asked, taking a bottle of Verdelho from the fridge bag she and Ryan had brought with them, and motioning to him to open it. Ryan, who had walked straight in and put on the television to watch the cricket, glanced back over his shoulder.

'Leave well alone for a while,' he said, dropping into a chair.

Will ignored him. 'I don't know, really,' he said to Tania. 'I suppose I want to tell her it's all right; that I'm all right. That I realise I went . . . well, I lost the plot.'

'In wanting to marry her, or in getting pissed and falling off the bridge?' Tania asked. She'd also brought a baguette and cheeses, knowing Will wouldn't have anything in his fridge for lunch, and she started unwrapping the food and setting it out on the benchtop.

'Both, but mostly the former.'

'But you *did* really want to marry her,' Tania said. 'When you told us in the restaurant, you weren't in any doubt.'

'I know. I don't know what came over me, really. She was so strong, so . . . so sort of complete. Don't really know how to explain it, but she didn't play games, she was just herself, and I did . . . still do . . . love her, but I can see it would never have worked.'

'Because?'

'Because we both want different things from life, we're at different stages. Because of the age thing . . . I thought it didn't matter, but . . .'

Tania walked around the benchtop, took the bottle and the corkscrew from Will, put her hands on his shoulders and pressed him downward so he was perched on a stool. 'Look, Will,' she said, 'I can tell you why it wouldn't have worked but you won't like it.'

He stared at her. She knew him better than anyone and he knew she was about to deliver some horrible home truth.

'Okay, tell me, I can take it.'

'It's not the age that matters, it's what you do with it. I love you to bits, Will, but sometimes I wonder if you're ever going to grow up. You have the tenacity of a butterfly when it comes to relationships. You're a hit and run man. Oh, I know that suits some women who are as scared of attachment as you are, but it's not very mature. You haven't got a clue about what it takes to build a relationship that'll last. The reason it could never work for you and Sylvia is that she's obviously very grown up, and you're still behaving like an overgrown teenager.'

'But –' he began before Tania held up her hand to stop him.

'I told you you wouldn't like it but it's true. You're forty-three, Will. If you want a mature relationship, then you have to change yourself, not just find someone who's mature herself and hope she'll do it all for you. There's a lot of years ahead – it's time to learn another way. You don't have relationships, you take hostages, and then, after you've kept them in benevolent emotional captivity for a few months, you kick them out. It's no way to live, Will, and it's certainly no way to grow old.'

That evening Will sat alone on his balcony, watching the sun set over the river, considering what she had said, trying to understand how he could be different, and how, had he *been* different, it might possibly have worked. He thought Tania was probably right. The old way didn't seem very attractive anymore. This experience with Sylvia had opened him to risk, made him emotionally vulnerable. It was a new feeling and it scared him horribly.

The sun sank behind the dark silhouette of the city skyline across the river and the myriad colours of the lights in the buildings were reflected in the still water. Perhaps that's what he wanted to tell her; that while it still hurt like hell, he knew that she was right. She had changed him and he was grateful. Yes, he was grateful for that. He picked up the phone again and this time he dialled the number.

Sylvia put the phone down and lay in the darkness, looking out through the half-open curtains at the shadowy shapes of the trees. Having lived so long with Colin, whose life and emotions had always been focused elsewhere, Will's sudden and devouring attention had at first been seductive and later smothering. There must, she thought, be a happy medium, but perhaps it was not something she would ever experience. She lay absolutely still, feeling the tears on her cheeks, making no attempt to stop them.

His phone call provided a resolution of sorts but now, strangely, she felt the loss of him in a way that she had not allowed herself to feel before. Now she knew he had shifted, and it was safe to feel her own grief; to feel the ache of longing for his warmth, for the tenderness, for the liberation of sex with someone who wanted her as much as she wanted him. She let herself dwell on the memories; how it felt to rest her cheek against his chest, to wrap her legs around his waist, to feel his mouth travelling across her body, to hold his hand in the darkness and feel his breath on her neck. She remembered how it felt to be wanted, and to want, to be driven by desire and to satisfy it, and then to be able to laugh about it.

'You are a fantastic lover, Sylvia,' he'd said, lying back on the rumpled bed in Hong Kong. 'You knock my socks off.'

'You weren't wearing socks,' she'd laughed, drawing the sheet over her.

'Sorry, I meant rocks,' he said, and they had rolled around on the bed together laughing.

'I didn't know I could be like this,' she'd said, kissing him, and he'd grasped her and pulled her on top of him again.

'I always knew it,' he said, 'the moment I first saw you, I thought, married to a vicar, my arse – that woman's a sex maniac if ever I saw one.'

In the darkness Sylvia laughed through her tears and turned onto her side, wondering whether she would ever be that way again, whether she had discovered that abandoned, sensual side of herself only to let it wither. At fifty-six it didn't look hopeful, but this itself had been the most unlikely adventure, an indication surely that anything was possible. And anyway, did it really matter? At this time of life there were other compensations, her friends, her creative work, mending her relationship with Kim, the spiritual life that she had neglected at a time when she should surely have turned to it for reassurance. The single life was very attractive.

'The trouble with Bonnie,' Irene had said recently, 'is that she really thinks that no one could be alone by choice. But it really is the right choice at certain times in our lives.'

'I know what you mean,' Sylvia had said. 'Leaving Colin seemed to open up my life in an incredibly exciting way. Will was part of that . . . at least, until he wanted to turn it into something different. Now, being single seems to have a lot going for it.'

And while she still felt that way, she thought she was better able to understand Bonnie. Her relationship with Jeff had become her purpose in life; losing him had robbed her not just of the man she loved but of a whole way of being herself, and somehow Sylvia's relationship with Will and his accident had become a part of that.

'You had no obligation to tell me, Sylvia,' Bonnie had said recently, 'and I had no right to behave as I did. I just wish you'd told me right from the start.'

'I wish I'd told you too,' Sylvia replied. 'I wish I'd done it all differently, but I don't wish that this thing with Will and I hadn't happened.'

She knew her grief tonight was natural; healthy, even. But Bonnie still had a long way to travel, that was apparent in her cautious, sometimes brittle manner. It was about Jeff, and about being alone and frightened of the future, but it was also, Sylvia was sure, about the child who had died, a tragedy still raw after all those years, and still lurking beneath the surface.

THIRTY-NINE

'They've made a damn good job of this place,' Marjorie said, swallowing the last mouthful of lemon pancake. 'Food's consistently good, nice friendly staff and service. I've brought quite a few people here, and I managed to get all my Christmas presents in the gallery. Bonnie should be really proud of it.'

'I'm sure she is,' Irene said, 'but I'm still worried about her.'

They had stopped off at the Boatshed on their way home from art class, and were sitting outside at a shady table on the deck. Hamish, who was to play in a golf tournament the following week, was on the course, working on his handicap. He was endlessly patient and considerate, but there were, Irene felt, some aspects of life that men simply didn't understand, and certain subtleties of meaning and emotion were among them. Hamish was better than most, but it wasn't like talking to another woman. Not that Marjorie was the mistress of the subtle nuance, Sylvia or Fran might have been a better bet, but in view of everything that had happened, Irene didn't think it fair to expect them to leap into this emotional space.

'When are you *not* worried about her?' Marjorie said abruptly. 'Ever since Jeff died and Bonnie came home you've been worried, and you've bent over backwards to help and support her.' She paused, holding up her hand to stop Irene's protests. 'Yes, you have. No one was around to help you through the loss of Dennis, and you managed it and made a wonderful life for yourself. Bonnie will do the same given time. Look what she's done with this place. You can't do the grief and loss stuff *for* her Irene, she has to do that for herself, and for some people that takes a very long time.'

Irene sipped her coffee and looked out across the water where windsurfers were struggling to stay upright in the choppy waves. 'The Will and Sylvia thing really upset her –' she began.

'I know! I know all that, and while it was, in some ways, unreasonable it was also understandable. But that's over. She and Sylvia and Will are sorted out now. Bonnie's still a bit fragile, but that's understandable too.'

'Tomorrow is the anniversary of Jeff's death,' Irene said. 'I'm not sure how she's going to get through it. She hasn't mentioned it, and I don't know whether I should or not.'

'Course you should,' Marjorie said, peering into her coffee cup and registering disappointment that it was empty. 'Suggest that you do something together, some little ritual. You can't ignore it.'

Irene remembered the first anniversary of Dennis's death when she'd had no one to talk to. Bonnie and Jeff were in Zurich and friends who had rallied round a year earlier were caught up in their own lives. She'd gone to the crematorium alone, placed flowers by the plaque and carried on a silent conversation with Dennis about how much she missed him, and how she hoped he'd always known how much she'd loved him. It still brought her to the brink of tears to remember the loneliness, how contained she had tried to be in the renewal of her grief. She wanted to help Bonnie pass this milestone but she knew that it was complicated by another grief that ran even deeper.

'There's another thing,' she said. 'I think Caro's baby is stirring up some old stuff for her about Lucy dying. Having the baby around may not be a good thing.'

Marjorie peered at her intensely and then put her hand across the table, on top of Irene's.

'If, after all these years, Bonnie is disturbed by the presence of a baby she needs to do something about it.'

'Okay, but what?' Irene said. 'She can't tell Caro not to bring the baby, it wouldn't be fair. That was part of the deal when they gave her the job.'

'No, no, and that wouldn't be doing anything about it, it would just be avoiding it again. That's what I mean, she can't go on avoiding the issue. She needs to come out and talk about it, work her way through it, get some help – counselling, perhaps. She can't spend the next thirty years freaking out over babies, for heaven's sake.'

'God, you're brutal. I don't know why I talk to you,' Irene said.

'Sometimes,' Marjorie said, shaking the crumbs from her napkin and laying it on the table, 'brutal is what's needed. And anyway, I'm not only brutal, I'm right. In this instance at least, I'm absolutely right.'

On the floor above where Irene and Marjorie sat, Bonnie was at her desk studying a business proposal Jack Bannister had sent her. He had mailed it to her a couple of weeks earlier but what with the emotional struggle of getting herself back to work at the Boatshed, this was the first chance she'd had to look at it, and even now the desk calendar he'd sent her for Christmas kept demanding her attention. It was an elegant piece of solid glass and stainless steel that showed the month, the date and the time and, if you pressed a series of small arrows on the side, you could get the time in other parts of the world. Bonnie had been surprised to get a Christmas gift from Jack, and surprised by how much she liked it. Several times a day she would glance at it, pleased not only by the sophisticated design, but by what it told her about Jack. Somehow he must have realised that time was important to her, as was a feeling for time in other places.

Bonnie disapproved of the growing trend not to worry about time, the discarding of watches, and people's willingness to trust that there was always a clock somewhere nearby should they need it. She thought it a silly affectation, an attempt to appear free thinking and unfettered by responsibility. Fine, she thought, for people who *did* live an unfettered life, but simply silly and irresponsible for those who were still fettered. There weren't always clocks close by and as a result, people were late for appointments and constantly stopped strangers to ask the time. Only someone who appreciated all the values inherent in knowing the time would pick a gift like this. She'd liked Jack from the first day they met and this gift had made her warm to him on a more personal level. He was the sort of man she was used to.

But today the calendar was diverting her attention for another reason. On this day a year ago, she and Jeff had gone out for dinner with friends from London, who were in Zurich for a long weekend break.

'Where can I buy great shoes, Bonnie?' Anna had asked as the waiter poured the liqueurs. 'Tomorrow is shoe-shopping day.'

'I'll take you if you like,' Bonnie had offered. 'There's a fabulous place I go to. They have the best selection and you'll never find it on your own.'

'She's right, Anna,' Jeff had said. 'Let Imelda here be your guide, but you'll need the platinum credit card!'

The next morning Bonnie was up early to meet Anna, and Jeff, who had woken feeling seedy, was sitting up in bed reading the paper when she bent to kiss him goodbye. Why hadn't she known that this was really goodbye, that they had eaten their last meal together, made love and shared a bed for the last time?

'I think I could do with a walk later,' he said, holding her wrist gently to draw her back to return her kiss. 'It looks like snow out there, and I need to shake off last night's meal.'

Bonnie smoothed the edge of the sheet. 'Me too. I had far too much wine. Okay, darling, I'll see you later and we'll walk.' She still didn't understand how she could not have known then that the last few hours of Jeff's life were expiring, how she could have been helping Anna choose some Bally shoes while he was struggling to maintain his grip on life, perhaps calling out to her.

The apartment had seemed unusually silent when Bonnie returned just after midday. She popped her head around the bedroom door and saw that he had made the bed in his usual haphazard male way and, with a minor flash of irritation, she went in, straightened the quilt and patted the pillows smooth. Then, calling out to him, she went back into the hall, through the lounge to his study, and there she found him, not sitting at the desk in his swivel chair, but lying on the floor, his body twisted awkwardly, his face contorted in a grimace of pain . . . or was it fear?

Head reeling, she bent down beside him and touched his face. He was quite cold. Gone – ripped away from her without warning, without a chance to say goodbye or to tell him how much she loved him, without the chance to draw from him the instructions she needed for life alone.

A year. What was she supposed to do now? Something to mark her remembrance? But everyone knew she remembered; everyone was sick of her remembering, although they were too kind to say so. Perhaps the best thing she could do would be to show him that she was getting on with life, that she had kept the promises written on the back of the photo. Now, perhaps, she needed to make another promise – to break out of this half-life. But how was she to do it?

'We're making fantastic progress,' Lenore said. 'It's really coming together.'

Fran got up from the table and stretched. 'I know. It's exciting, isn't it? I can hardly believe that before long it'll be a real book on the shelves with my name on it.'

Lenore grinned, pushing the paperwork aside. 'Enough for today, I think. Are we going to pop across and see Lila this evening?'

Fran shook her head. 'No, I went this morning while you were at that meeting in town, and Caro and Mike are going this evening. We've got quite a good roster now. Jodie's turn in the morning, and then I'll go tomorrow evening.'

They closed the office door and made their way out through the empty restaurant and onto the boardwalk into the welcome chill of the sea breeze. Lenore had arrived a week earlier and although Fran's initial ambivalence about her had been resolved during the visit to Sydney, she had still been anxious at the prospect of working closely with her for a couple of weeks. Even with her new-found confidence she had feared Lenore's strong opinions, and worried that she might find herself pushed into accepting changes that she didn't really like. That apprehension and the prospect of Lenore's presence as a guest in her home had sent Fran out in a late-night search for junk food on the three evenings prior to her arrival. And the batch of brownies knocked up early in the morning was only half a batch by the time she left the house to meet Lenore's flight. But from the moment they sat down together to begin work, Fran's fears had evaporated.

'I wouldn't mind a walk,' Lenore said, 'along the water. I could do with the fresh air.'

Fran grinned, 'You and your walks.'

'Don't say you don't feel better for it,' Lenore said with a laugh. 'You wouldn't have been going every morning if it wasn't working for you.'

'Okay, okay, I give in, yes, you changed my life,' Fran said. 'Instead of lying in bed till the last minute I'm up at dawn marching around St Kilda like a madwoman. And I *do* feel better for it. I never thought the day would come when I would actually look forward to going for a walk at first light.'

They walked on through the dusk in companionable silence, watching the sun sink below the horizon and its last rays wash the sky with a pale peach glow.

'Sylvia showed me her studio and designs today,' Lenore said. 'I don't think she has any idea how good she is.'

'I know,' Fran agreed. 'Bonnie's thinking about the possibility of developing a label for her.'

Lenore paused, turning to look at her. 'There's huge potential there. I know some people in the rag trade who would be bowled over by what Sylvia has in that studio, but she needs to get serious about it. I could suggest a few contacts and so on, but I don't want to be pushy.'

Fran laughed as they turned back to the path. 'That doesn't sound like you.'

Lenore pulled a face. 'I know I can be a bit overbearing but it's just a mask.'

'What do you mean?'

'It's an act I put on when I'm feeling particularly intimidated.'

'You? Intimidated?' Fran said. 'You're the intimidating one.'

'It's all bluster,' Lenore said, stuffing her hands into the pockets of her jacket. 'I'm constantly terrified that I'll be revealed as knowing absolutely nothing.'

They were near a seat and Fran paused and sat at the end, looking up at her.

'You're kidding?'

'No! I'm terrified of everything and everyone, honestly. When I was young I used to be really confident. I was a bossy, domineering teenager determined to get my way about everything.'

'And now?'

Lenore shrugged. 'I'm a dithering mass of anxiety and indecision. I just manage to hide it quite well.'

'You certainly do,' Fran said. 'It's hard to believe. What happened?'

Lenore took a deep breath and joined her on the seat. 'You know what happened. I stuffed up my life. I was desperate to get away from home and I grabbed the first bloke who showed a serious interest. So there I was in this terrible marriage with two tiny babies and I realised that all my teenage urges towards other girls hadn't just been a stage I was going through, they were an indication of who I really was. I fell in love with a wonderful older woman . . . and you know what happened after that. The price I paid for being myself was the loss of my children. Being labelled an unfit mother and constantly being knocked back in my efforts to see them isn't great for self-esteem.'

'It must have been terrible,' Fran said. 'I suppose it's obvious that something like that would change you.'

'I spent a very long time in a very dark tunnel thinking I might never come out the other end,' Lenore said, 'but of course eventually I did, and I was different. I was a jittery, frightened person, always covering my inadequacy with bluster. What you see these days, Fran, is not at all what you get. It's there to protect me, and often it wears very thin. People like you trigger my insecurity. I was terrified that day we met. I'd been dreading meeting you.'

Fran stared at Lenore seeing, for the first time, the vulnerability in her face, the nervous way she ran her hand through her thick hair, the flicker of her eyes as they scanned Fran's face. Everything, the vivid turquoise contact lenses, the beautifully cut hair, the dramatically simple black and purple clothes she always wore, the bold silver and turquoise jewellery, suddenly looked like a disguise – impressive, strong, but still a disguise.

'*I* was terrified of *you* that day,' Fran said, still staring at her. 'You were so confident, and so strong.'

Lenore shook her head. 'Not me! Going to meet this brilliant food writer, full of wonderful innovative ideas, bursting with talent, running her own business! Scary stuff. I didn't want to be there, I can tell you, but Jack insisted.'

'It's hard to believe,' Fran said. 'I mean, I can understand everything you said about the effect of the past, but how could you be scared about me? Bonnie, yes, she's impressive, but me . . . ?'

Lenore laughed. 'Bonnie, I could cope with. She's a businesswoman, she was there to do a deal and so was I. She's good, no doubt about that, but you, Fran, you're another story entirely. Competent, self-possessed, talented and you didn't say much, and the less you said the more terrified I became.'

'I didn't say much because I was so intimidated by *you*,' Fran said, smiling at the irony of it. 'You were so full-on, Lenore, that mask is one hundred per cent effective. I came out of that meeting needing artificial respiration. It's really only since you arrived here that I've stopped being scared of you.'

They stared at each other in the half-light. 'Well,' said Lenore, 'I still have a way to go with that.' She laughed. 'Hey, can you imagine two blokes doing this, talking to each other, admitting their insecurities?'

Fran shook her head. 'No way. But I gave up trying to understand men years ago. Even the ones I like and love are like another species. Aren't you glad you aren't one?'

'Ha!' said Lenore, throwing back her head, the depth of her laughter caught in the wind. 'Aren't I just. Although I do envy the head start they seem to have with other women!'

FORTY

Lila was confused and rather irritated. This was the third – or was it the fourth? – time she had found herself in the garden in her night-dress in the middle of the night. She had no idea how long she'd been there. It was a bit of a worry, really: if you could wake up to find yourself in the garden you could, presumably, wake up and find yourself more or less anywhere. At the shops perhaps, or wait-ing at the bus stop. She sighed, looked around, noticed that she was holding an egg whisk. Now, why on earth . . . ? Oh well, maybe it didn't matter too much. Good thing no one knew about it or they'd really think she'd lost it. There were a lot of funny things going on at the moment and Lila felt she needed to keep her wits about her. The family was all over the place, obviously; was it the Boatshed or the baby that had made everyone so odd and confused?

'You remember Lenore, Mum,' Fran had said a few days earlier, and this woman that Lila had never seen before waltzed in and gave her a red hat.

'It's smaller than your other one,' the woman had said. 'This might be better for the cooler weather, but I thought you'd like the net and the feathers.' And she'd given Lila this very nice hat, a little red pillbox, not unlike the one she'd worn at Fran's wedding, except that one had been pale blue. This one had a veil of speckled net at the front and three red feathers curled around the side. A very nice hat, but what sort of behaviour was that, giving a red hat to a perfect stranger and saying that it was smaller than the one they already had?

Lila had pointed out, politely of course, that she didn't own a red hat, and then Fran got all hot and bothered and made her go and look on the top shelf of her wardrobe, and there, to Lila's great surprise, was a big red hat with a lot of chiffon on it. Gremlins, she thought, but Fran and the other woman had just smiled and asked her to try on the pillbox hat. Suddenly, family responsibility seemed to weigh heavy on Lila. She loved them all so much, but really – you sorted out one problem and then there'd be something else. Didn't it ever stop?

Over in the corner of the garden, her scooter sat hunched and broody under its waterproof cover. Lila pulled off the cover and, putting the egg whisk in the basket, she climbed on. It was a beautiful clear night and quite mild now. Perhaps it wasn't so bad being out here, after all, no harm in it. Lila leaned back in the comfortable circle of the seat and closed her eyes. It was nearly two weeks since she'd been out on the scooter. David had said there was something wrong with one of the tyres, and he'd taken it off and promised to get a new one. But it had happened the day after she lost her way back to the unit, and Lila had a sneaking suspicion that it was a plot hatched by Fran to stop her riding it at all.

She stood up for a moment, lifting the seat to get to the storage compartment, and took out a thing called a Walkman that David had given her for Christmas. He'd put in a cassette that had Marianne Faithfull on it singing the Lucy whatsit song; he'd recorded it for her, over and over again.

'You can put the little earphones on and play it while you're riding, Gran,' he'd said.

And Fran had said, 'Oh, for goodness sake, how will she hear the traffic, David? She might have an accident.'

'I think she'll be all right, Mum,' David had said. 'You'll be all right, won't you, Gran?'

'Of course I will,' Lila had said, putting on the earphones and waiting for David to show her how to switch on the music.

She put it on now and sat back in the delicious silence and stillness of the night, watching a shooting star flash across the sky, humming along with the cassette. In the past Lila hadn't thought much of Lucy Jordan, believed she was a bit of a quitter. Now she could understand how Lucy might have felt. There was so much to do keeping everybody going, especially when they kept getting things mixed up. These days Lila sometimes thought it wouldn't be too bad to climb up somewhere and be whisked off by the man in the big white car, or on a scooter even. It sounded rather liberating.

David pulled on his leather jacket and opened the front door, waiting for Jodie, who was searching for her phone.

'C'mon, Jode,' he called. 'Let's go.'

She emerged from the bedroom checking her battery and put the phone in her bag. 'I don't think I'll stop for coffee this morning,' she said, reaching up to kiss him. 'My turn to go to Hawthorn.'

David glanced at his watch. 'I can come with you, if you like. My first class isn't till nine-thirty. You can drop me off at the tram on the way back.' They made their way through the early traffic in the fine drizzle that had come with the dawn. Now the sun was breaking through with an almost blinding intensity.

'She might remember you today,' David said hopefully.

'Don't worry about it,' Jodie said. 'The main thing is that she always remembers you and Fran and Caro . . .'

'And Rebekah, of course,' he added. 'She remembers Mike too, although she calls him Nick and thinks he's a lawyer.'

Jodie shrugged. 'Recent memory is always the first thing to go, Dave, she can't help it. She and I got on well for a long time; you don't have to feel offended for me, I'm not taking it personally.'

They parked in the drive and it was just turning eight o'clock when David knocked on the front door. Lila was always an early riser, awake by five and up and dressed by six, but there was no answer and the bedroom curtains were closed.

David felt a twinge of anxiety. 'Round the back?' he suggested, and went to the side gate, only to find it locked.

Jodie bent and peered through the letter box. 'Hello, Mrs Whittaker,' she called. 'It's David and Jodie.'

They stood side by side at the door, listening for sounds of movement within. David pulled a face and got out his key. Fran had given them all keys for use in an emergency and using his for the first time seemed like a horribly significant step.

'Gran,' he called, opening the door slightly. 'Hi, Gran, are you there?'

'Let me go first, Dave,' Jodie said gently but firmly, moving past him into the house and making for the bedroom. He followed her cautiously, dreading what they might find, but the bed, which had obviously been slept in, was empty.

'Must be out the back,' he said with relief, looking through to the kitchen where the back door to the garden stood open. 'Hey, Gran,' he called, as he reached the open door, 'it's us, David and Jodie –' He stopped suddenly, captivated by the sight of Lila in her nightdress, sitting on the scooter, the Walkman in her lap, headphones on her ears, an egg whisk in the basket. 'Ah, look Jode,' he said, putting his hand on her shoulder. 'There she is, she's fine, she's listening to her song.' He made to cross the lawn but Jodie put her hand on his arm.

'Let me go,' she said.

He looked at her and then back again at Lila, and this time he saw the unnatural stillness, the rigid smile and the awkward tilt of her head. 'No,' he said firmly, holding up his hand to stop her, goose bumps rising on his skin. His shoes left flat dark prints on the silvery damp surface of the grass as he made his way towards her, and he reached out to touch her arm. Lila's skin was cold, the sleeve of the nightdress soaked. 'Gran,' he whispered. 'Oh no, Gran, please no.' Her face and hair were coated with a misty glow of moisture that seemed suddenly to blaze with light as the sun emerged from the shadow of a cloud.

Leaning forward, David took the headphones from Lila's ears and put the Walkman into the basket. Standing on the running board of the scooter, he bent over and kissed the cold, wrinkled cheek. 'Oh, Gran,' he whispered, 'I'm so sorry. We should have been with you.' He paused as the first tears began. 'I love you. I don't know if I ever told you that.'

'She knew,' Jodie said, gently touching his arm. 'And she was so proud of you.'

He nodded, reaching out for her, sobs rising in his throat. 'But I didn't do enough. I wasn't here, I was always going to spend more time with her, ask her things. But I just never did.'

'We never do,' Jodie said, holding him. 'But she knew, just the same, she knew.'

As the organist began the first bars of the Twenty-third Psalm they rose to their feet, voices wavering at first then gradually coming together in greater harmony. Irene glanced at Bonnie, who was standing quietly beside her, hymn sheet in one hand but not singing, just staring ahead in silence. Three weeks earlier they had gone together to mass at the convent chapel, something they hadn't done for decades. Bonnie had felt it was what she wanted and needed to do on the anniversary of Jeff's death. It had surprised Irene; she couldn't remember the last time she'd been to mass and she had found it profoundly moving.

She had been brought up a Catholic and for many years her faith had been central to her life, and part of the structure of her marriage to Dennis. But in the years since his death she had come to feel that it was ritual without substance. She wasn't sure what she believed these days; sometimes she felt she had a simplistic, childlike faith, and sometimes none at all. But she was thankful that Bonnie had found some sort of solace in the service and the peaceful sacred space of the chapel. They had sat in silence after the mass, mourning lost husbands, allowing themselves to feel their absence, and Irene had felt closer to her daughter than she had for years. Bonnie had seemed a little different after that, as though she was putting something behind her, but now Irene was anxious that Lila's death, following so soon on that anniversary, might disrupt this new equilibrium.

She stared ahead to where Lila's coffin, draped in deep purple brocade and topped with a simple bouquet of white roses, stood at the altar steps. The voices around her soared as the mourners joined in the familiar words. 'In pastures green he leadeth me, the quiet waters by,' sang Hamish, in what had once been a striking baritone. A tear escaped from Irene's eye and she reached for his hand. Hamish gripped it firmly, smiled at her, and continued singing. Quite suddenly she was reminded of a party fifty years ago, Hamish and Dennis singing 'Bye Bye Blackbird'. He'd had rather a good voice. How strange that she should only recall it now, how much they still had to learn about each other. On Hamish's other side, Sylvia sang confidently without a hymn sheet, watching Fran, who was in the front pew flanked by Caro and Mike, and David and Jodie.

'Such a peaceful way to go,' Irene had said to Bonnie when Caro phoned to tell them the news. 'She just loved that scooter. Imagine her there, listening to her music like that.' And as the tears poured down her face she was struck with the terrifying reality of her own and Hamish's ages, and fear of her own mortality intruded ruthlessly on her grief.

'Apparently the doctor said she wouldn't have known any-thing,' she went on, hugging Bonnie. 'It would have happened quickly. I'm glad she was still in her own place. Poor Fran, she was so dreading having to move her. She'll be thankful for that, at least.'

Fran was indeed thankful that she had been spared the awful task of moving Lila to a hostel, but she was also bereft. For as long as she could remember, Lila had been the strong and guiding presence in her life, always supportive, often wise, sometimes caustic and uncompromising, but always loving and, most of all, always there.

The crematorium chapel was packed. It was strange, she thought, how people turned up at funerals, people you didn't expect, people you didn't even know. There were residents and staff from the retirement village, a few old familiar faces from Lila's days at the post office, some neighbours from fifteen years ago. But there were others she'd never seen before, strangers from corners of Lila's life of which she knew nothing. And at the back of the chapel, a small cluster of women in purple with red hats.

Since the moment that David had appeared at the Boatshed to break the news, Fran had felt as though the solid block on which her life had been built had been kicked from under her and that she was now swaying perilously above a great void. To those around her, Fran's behaviour seemed natural. She wept long and often and, with her children and friends around her, made decisions about death notices, the funeral and the flowers. She was clearly devastated, but she was freely expressing her grief, not bottling it up in an effort to be brave. But what they couldn't see was the agonising combination of grief and fear, the sense that without Lila she would not know who or what she was. While she grieved for Lila, Fran feared for herself and doubted her ability to respond to the challenge of this loss.

She looked around the chapel. There would not be one person there who had not suffered the loss of a loved one, and probably been changed by it. Many, like her, would have felt suddenly orphaned by the death of a parent, a feeling so intensely disturbing that she could not describe it without embarrassment. If others managed it, Fran supposed she too would adjust in time. Meanwhile, she felt that Lila's dementia had robbed them of precious time, and she was crushed by guilt about all the times that she had not done enough, had spoken harshly, or simply not bothered to understand.

FORTY-ONE

'Lenore tells me she's staying on for a while,' Bonnie said, perching on the edge of Fran's desk. 'Is that okay with you? She can stay with Mum and me if you prefer.'

'It's fine,' Fran said, shaking her head. 'We're getting along very well. Having her there has really helped since Mum died.'

The phone rang and she signalled Bonnie not to leave while she answered it. Bonnie slipped off the desk into a chair, watching Fran as she talked. It was three weeks since the funeral and Bonnie thought she detected more than grief. Fran was afraid, and Bonnie knew that feeling inside out.

'So how are you going?' she asked as Fran put down the phone.

'Okay, I suppose,' Fran said thoughtfully. 'Sad, terribly sad, but grateful that Mum died without knowing what was happening, that she didn't have to go into care. But I miss her terribly.' She shrugged. 'I spent so much of my life responding to her or reacting against her. Now it's hard to know who I am without her as a reference point.'

'But she's still your reference point,' Bonnie said, 'if you want her to be. I felt the same when I lost Jeff. Who am I without him around? I'm still struggling to find out, and he's still the reference point; too much so, really, although you probably already know that.'

Fran smiled. 'It must be harder for you, because it was so unexpected. Jeff was young – it always seems worse.'

Bonnie pleated the fabric of her skirt between her fingers. 'It's hard, isn't it, all this change just at the time when you expect to be sitting back and taking things a little more easily.' She paused, looking up. 'Sylvia says we have to be our own reference point, that's the battle . . . the challenge is to become central in our own lives.'

'I said it, but I didn't say it was easy,' said Sylvia from the doorway. 'Can I join in?'

'Sure.' Fran gestured towards the other chair. 'All our upbringing as good Catholic girls was focused on not being selfish,' she said. 'It was always about someone else being central, deferring to others. Parents, husband, then children –'

'And God,' Sylvia cut in. 'God, most of all. Remember the Princess Diana interview when she said, "There were three people in this marriage"? I was sitting watching it with Colin, and I just wanted to yell out welcome to the club, darling, there are three of us in this one too, and Himself is a far more terrifying third party than poor old Camilla.'

Bonnie nodded in agreement. 'That must be so hard. Jeff was a humanist and so I just took on his views – not that it bothered me. But it's like you giving up your Catholicism to marry Colin. We're so willing to do as we're told to please men. Or, at least, we were.'

'Fran wasn't,' Sylvia said, looking at her. 'You made what you wanted for yourself.'

'In a chaotic sort of way,' Fran said. 'I couldn't cope with Tony's assumptions that his opinions, his needs, his everything came first. And Mum was the example that women can do fine on their own. But she was always in my head, the Lila-filter. What would she do? How would she do it? What would she think?'

'What a year,' Bonnie said with a sigh. 'This time last year we hadn't met, we didn't even know we would . . . deaths, a birth, a divorce, a business . . .'

'You just never know what's around the corner,' Fran said, glancing out across the car park where Lenore was rummaging for something in the boot of her car. 'And there's Lenore too,' she said, 'what a surprise gift she's turned out to be.'

Bonnie laughed. 'That wasn't what you said the first time you met her!'

'No, strange how things happen, isn't it?' She sighed. 'And David and Caro, I got them back in very different ways, and Rebekah.' She picked up the framed photo on her desk. 'When I get bogged down in grief about Mum, I keep thinking about Rebekah and how lucky I am . . .'

'Yes,' Bonnie said, suddenly brisk, standing up and straightening her skirt. 'We've all had our dramas this year but we all have things to be thankful for. Must get on now.' And she whisked out of Fran's office and disappeared down the passage into her own.

'Whoops!' Fran said, looking at Sylvia in amazement. 'What happened there? What did I say?'

Sylvia raised her eyebrows. 'I think you pressed a few buttons without even knowing it,' she said, and she got up to close the door. 'There's something I think I should tell you.'

Fran lay awake in the darkness listening for something, anything. She felt restless, nervous. It was just after two. She hated waking up at night, always had done, and it was worse now; grief, like every other emotion, was so much more extreme in the wee small hours. It had been a strange sort of day, the Boathouse had been very busy, and she and Lenore had been completing the final checks on the manuscript.

'I've organised to meet the designer and the photographer the day after tomorrow,' Lenore had said that afternoon. 'They'll start on it straight away, then we'll be ready to go.' She packed the manuscript pages into her briefcase and began to lay some of Sylvia's designs into the large portfolio along with sketches for the book cover. 'All ready now.'

'It's going to be weird without you,' Sylvia said. 'We've got used to having you around.'

Lenore laughed. 'The original guest from hell – came for a fortnight and ended up staying five weeks. But it's been so good being here, and I guess I'll be back again fairly soon. And if you're sure you're happy about it, Sylvia, I'll take these designs to a couple of people in Sydney.'

Bonnie had cooked a farewell dinner for Lenore, and by the time she and Fran got home it was after ten. A strange sort of tension seemed to have developed between them during this final day. Fran had drawn on Lenore's strength and they had grown closer in the weeks since Lila's death, and she was dreading her departure the next morning. Lenore pottered around gathering up her things while Fran made tea, which they drank in an uneasy silence, broken only by desultory fragments of awkward conversation. They had spent almost every evening for the last month together talking, laughing, watching old movies. There had been no late-night hunts for junk food, not even the desire for it, but now it seemed that something special had evaporated as Lenore's leave-taking approached.

Fran sat up and stared out of the bedroom window across the dark rooftops of the houses to the tops of the tall trees in the nearby park. She listened to the silence, wondering if Lenore was awake or sleeping soundly, happy at the prospect that tomorrow night she would be home in her own bed. Breathing deeply, Fran waited for the spasm of loneliness to pass. Was she imagining it or had she been feeling something genuinely different since her trip to Sydney? Were these feelings authentic or was she simply lonely, reacting to a series of changes, capped by the pain of losing her mother? Fran had always been an emotionally cautious person, her father's desertion had made her wary. She often wondered how she and Tony had ever got it together, and since then she had avoided involvement; she was good at friendship but intimacy was terrifying. And anyway, suppose she was wrong?

She got up and walked over to the window. She could follow her instinct and take this chance, or she could ignore it, discount it as a side-effect of grief, but maybe then she would lose the opportunity of finding something precious. Lenore's door was open slightly and Fran paused outside it, her heart beating furiously.

'Lenore,' she whispered, her feet moving silently over the soft cream rug. Lenore was asleep, one arm flung above her head, the other on top of the covers, her breathing soft and steady as a child's. Fran crept to the side of the bed and put her hand cautiously on Lenore's arm.

'Lenore,' she whispered again, and Lenore's eyes flew open. She hitched herself up on her elbow, blinking and rubbing her eyes.

'Fran?'

'Lenore, I . . .'

'Fran? Are you okay?'

Fran hesitated. 'I wondered . . . I felt . . . I don't know how to say this . . .'

Lenore turned back the bedclothes and reached out for Fran's hand, drawing her closer to the side of the bed, and Fran slipped in beside her.

'Lenore, is this . . . well . . . is it okay? I . . .'

Lenore stroked her cheek. 'Okay? Darling Fran, every night I've lain awake hoping this would happen. Now tonight when I finally gave up and fell asleep, here you are. So it's very definitely okay with me. I just hope that you'll think it's okay in the morning.'

The Boatshed trading figures for the period to the end of March had outstripped Bonnie's predictions. In addition to their paid advertising, Fran's regular columns in two Melbourne newspapers, an in-flight magazine and a food and tourism e-zine were the sort of publicity that money could not buy. In the first days of April, Bonnie completed a project assessment and mailed a copy to Will. He had a financial and an emotional investment in the Boatshed and she was glad to be able to send him such positive figures and predictions.

She was also pleased to have grounds for re-establishing regular contact. In January she had called him twice in an attempt to explain the emotional state that had driven her earlier behaviour, but from those brief, though amiable, conversations, she had realised that while he sympathised with her grief and fear, their effect was not something he could really understand.

Bonnie knew he had been in Melbourne in January. She had caught sight of him in the city, getting out of a taxi on Southbank, and she had been about to duck through the traffic to catch up with him but stopped in her tracks. He needed space, they all did. Will ran up the steps of a building and, mildly disappointed but thankful she had held back, Bonnie watched him go. She'd wondered whether or not to tell Sylvia and eventually decided against it. Will would be back in touch again in his own time and she didn't want to rake over those coals again. Besides, now that it was all over, she recognised her own voyeuristic interest in what had happened between Sylvia and Will.

'I can't imagine how she could have done it,' Bonnie had said to Fran. 'I wouldn't have had the confidence.'

Fran laughed. 'You certainly had it when you were younger, Bon.'

'I know, I know – the banker,' said Bonnie, having the grace to blush. 'But not now. I suppose it's the effect of being married so long I can't imagine . . . but then, Sylvia had been married for that long too. It's just so extraordinary. I mean, he's so much younger and so youthful and handsome. It's such a reversal of the usual younger woman, older man thing. I'd have been so conscious of my age . . . my body . . .'

'Sylvia's a very beautiful woman,' Fran said.

'Yes, but it's not as though she looks particularly young for her age,' Bonnie said. 'You can't say she's unmarked by time.'

'Remember the movie *Calendar Girls*?' Fran asked. 'Those women were our age and older and they looked wonderful because of who they were. It came from within. Mind you, here I am saying this and I've got more body image hang-ups than anyone. But it would be nice to think Will responded to Sylvia's inner beauty, rather than the sort of instincts that motivated him in the past.'

'You don't like him much, do you?' Bonnie asked.

Fran sighed. 'Not a lot. I mean, I don't actively dislike him, I just think he's a bit . . . he's such a boy. He's obviously brilliant at what he does, and he's very good looking, but he's in his mid-forties and he doesn't really seem grown up. But that's me, my patience with the male of the species is limited and I'm probably not always fair.'

'I still think it's amazing,' Bonnie said. 'All those years of monogamy and a sex life that was virtually nonexistent, and yet she was able to be so . . .'

'So what?'

'Well, so adventurous, so confident, I suppose.' She was hedging, unable to articulate what might sound judgmental, which was that Sylvia had behaved like a man, indulging in a casual affair with no hope of, or desire for, a future. It was this that Bonnie found so breathtaking – something that had seemed so easy in youth now bore a patina of daring self-indulgence that shocked and delighted her in equal proportions, and made her feel more conservative than ever.

Bonnie put the papers in an envelope and addressed it. She would catch up with Will before long; he was family, after all. She had decided to send a copy of the assessment to Jack Bannister, who, unlike Will, had been in constant contact. He was, he had told her tongue-in-cheek, having a midlife crisis which manifested itself in a desire to branch out into new areas. He was pressing her to agree to a partnership in another Boatshed or, as he called it, 'another Fran Whittaker restaurant'.

'Her name's getting known,' he told Bonnie, 'she's not just a Melbourne identity now. I think it would work, and if we're going to do it it would be ideal to announce it when we launch the book.' Fran's book, *Food, Love and Duty*, was to be released in early October for the Christmas market.

'It might work but not as a central city thing,' Bonnie had argued. 'I don't think that would work at all.'

'No way, that's not what I had in mind,' Jack said. 'There's a place in Manly by the water, a lovely old building. I'd like you to come up and see it, Bonnie. And we could probably get that column of Fran's syndicated in some papers here too, that would help.'

Bonnie was undecided. Despite the success of the Boatshed she was nervous about branching out so soon and, remembering Fran's original resistance, she feared expansion might also be met with reluctance. And then there was Sylvia. The gallery was a big part of the Boatshed's success.

'Surely we could get Sylvia or Caro up here for a few weeks to sniff out the stock for us and get it up and running,' Jack had suggested, but Bonnie was not so sure. Caro was obviously fully committed with the gallery and Rebekah, and although Sylvia had abandoned the idea of a move to England, Bonnie recognised that if there was anything that would keep her involved in the Boatshed it was the chance to expand her own creative work. Packing her off to Sydney for several weeks to start another gallery might be a bad idea. Bonnie's instincts told her that the right move would be to take on more staff at the gallery to free up time for Sylvia, to build on her design work and follow up some of Lenore's contacts. If Jack wanted a gallery in Sydney he might just have to find the right person there himself.

She leaned back in her swivel chair, staring at the papers on her desk, mulling over the pros and cons of expansion. It wasn't only the others; she was still struggling to cope with things one day at a time. She would wake early and get up immediately, make coffee, take it back to bed, and talk herself into the day and out of the morass of depression. Once she arrived at work she usually felt better, but nights and early mornings were a battle, and she still felt she was poised on an emotional knife-edge.

Bonnie had never taken drugs. The occasional aspirin for a headache, an antibiotic for an infection, but nothing mood altering, with the exception of alcohol, and that almost always in moderation. Even as a child of the sixties she had never smoked a joint, experimented with acid, or taken amphetamines. But during the Will crisis, she had paid a frantic visit to her doctor.

'I'm going to give you a prescription for Valium, Bonnie,' the doctor had said. 'Just a little helper to get you through this difficult time. Come back in three weeks and we'll see how you are then.'

When Bonnie returned three weeks later her own doctor was on holiday, and the locum, who looked as though she was no more than twelve years old, had prescribed antidepressants. Unfortunately, the twelve year old had failed to mention that it would take several weeks before Bonnie felt the effect of the antidepressants, so Bonnie, with a naïve faith in the authority of the medical profession and the pharmaceutical industry, kept taking the tablets for a while and, then, feeling no improvement, stopped. What she did feel was that she was not quite herself but, she rationalised, that might be a good thing. Was this the right state of mind in which to launch into another business? To her own surprise she found herself discussing it with Hamish, of all people, having first sworn him to secrecy.

'Weren't you on an emotional knife-edge when you came up with the Boatshed project?' Hamish asked. 'If that energy kick-started you the first time it could well do so again.' But then, Hamish didn't know about the effort it cost her to keep going every day.

Bonnie stopped fiddling with her pen. Too much, she thought, too many decisions, too much pressure. She wandered down into the restaurant and sat at one of the tables by the window.

'Cup of coffee, Bonnie?' Tan asked, appearing immediately at her side.

'Camomile tea, I think,' she said. 'And one of those new orange and almond thingos that Fran and Sean were trying out.' Perhaps a few calming herbs, and some comforting sugar would help her with the decision-making.

'I've made up my mind to go back to England,' Sylvia said. 'Only for a holiday, of course. I think Kim's starting to forgive me. She's got a job and a woman to look after Charlie and James. She sounds like a reverse edition of me, her daughter and grand-children live in Perth.'

'That sounds splendid,' Veronica said. 'When will you go?'

Sylvia put her cup down on Veronica's coffee table. 'Not for a while yet. It depends on the gallery, and what we decide about the fashion label idea, but September or October would suit me best.' She looked around wondering if she was doing the right thing, wondering whether Veronica would like what she had in mind, or if she might even be offended by it.

'The thing is,' she began, 'there's a lot happening at the moment. The gallery's very busy and we need to take on another part-time person.'

Veronica nodded. 'I can see how well it's going,' she said. 'The times I've been in to see you, or to have lunch there with my friend, it's always busy.'

'Well, we do need another part-timer, someone who'd also be prepared to do extra hours from time to time if Caro or I were away,' she said. 'I was wondering . . . I hope you don't think this is a cheek, but would you be interested?'

'Me?' Veronica said, straightening up in surprise. 'Work at the gallery?'

'Oh look, I didn't mean to offend you, I –'

'But, my dear, I'd love to. I'd simply love it,' Veronica said, clasping her hands together. 'But don't you want someone younger?'

'We want someone who loves the place and can do the job,' Sylvia said. 'Age isn't important.'

Veronica pulled a tissue from her pocket and Sylvia saw tears in her eyes. 'This has come at such a time . . . a time when I needed something,' Veronica said. 'I really can't tolerate the new Canon and his wife. Talk about testing my Christian spirit. I've given up on them. I told him last week I wouldn't be doing any more work for the church. God's not my problem, you understand, just him. So, yes please, Sylvia, I'd love it. When can I start?' They worked out the details over a second pot of coffee.

'Bonnie will draw up the contract and mail it to you in the next couple of days,' Sylvia said. 'I'm so glad, Veronica, and I'm sorry about the new Canon. You've put so much into the church community.'

Veronica shrugged. 'It's not only me. A few of the other stalwarts have fallen by the wayside. He's a strange combination of that happy-clappy Christian practice and an almost Victorian attitude to the way things are run. One feels . . . I feel . . . that my contribution is no longer valued.' She paused. 'Of course, I know from what you've told me that Colin had his shortcomings as a husband, but he was a very good pastor. Open minded, inclusive and very supportive. I miss that, and I miss you being there. Anyway, before you go, come out into the garden. I want to cut you some roses to take home.'

'Have you seen Colin at all?' Sylvia asked as they strolled between the rose bushes.

'I have,' Veronica said, clipping perfect Albertine buds and then moving on to an Iceberg. 'He came to see me a couple of weeks ago. He'd discovered he'd got a couple of my books and wanted to return them, or so he said. Actually, I think he wanted to talk, find out if I'd seen you.'

Sylvia swallowed hard. It was eight, almost nine, months since she had left him, and apart from a few polite telephone conversations about money, possessions and the divorce papers, he had simply dropped out of her life, and while his presence in her memory was unavoidable, it was not charged with any emotion. It was as though he had slipped into quicksand which had closed over him.

'How is he?' she asked.

'Rather low,' Veronica said, turning to her. 'The church has found him an administrative job, but his friend has left him. I gather there was something of a confrontation; things hadn't been going well since you split up and he left the church. She told him that she felt he was using her as a crutch. She said she was a social worker but didn't want a partner who wanted to be part of her case work.'

Sylvia raised her eyebrows and reached out to take the roses. 'Did she really?' she said. 'That was quick. It took me more than thirty years.'

'Young women,' Veronica said with a smile, 'they know what they want these days, and they don't hold back from telling it how it is. Not like our generation, Sylvia. We all wasted a lot of time and a lot of energy trying to make ourselves into what the men wanted, usually at high cost to ourselves. It's different now.'

Sylvia realised she had driven home from Box Hill without being aware of the journey. She had been thinking about Colin, she was still thinking about him, thinking of his sadness, his loneliness, and how incapable he would be of managing life on his own. She had seen it so often, men, especially older men, who seemed so totally unprepared both emotionally and practically to cope with life after a relationship breakdown. For her the separation had opened the door to new opportunities. Her early anxiety about where she would live and work had soon evaporated. The tension with Kim had been painful, a battle of wills almost, in which Sylvia had had to stand her ground, refusing to buy into the emotional blackmail which, she suspected, Kim probably didn't even realise she was exerting. But finally, her daughter had stepped back.

'I think I've been really unfair,' she had said, calling one evening when Sylvia was on the point of going to bed. 'I so much wanted you here, wanted to go back to work, and wanted you to be the one who looked after the kids. Even when you talked about it, I still didn't think about what it would really be like for you.'

'What changed it, then?' Sylvia asked.

'Dad did,' Kim said. 'He kept talking about coming here to stay with us, bringing his girlfriend and how important it was to him that I should accept her, have her to stay at the house. All that. He didn't seem to give a thought to what that might be like for me, it was just about what he wanted. I realised I was doing the same thing.'

By comparison, Sylvia reflected, Colin had lost so much, his faith, a successful career in the ministry, respect, status, a dutiful wife and now his lover, even his relationship with Kim had been damaged. She let herself in to the cottage overwhelmed suddenly with the feeling that she should call him, ask if there was anything she could do to help. She had so much now, it even looked as though her aspirations in design might be met. Surely she could afford to be generous? Perhaps he'd like a cup of coffee, a shoulder to cry on, someone to talk to. Even so, her hand trembled as she dialled his number.

'Hello,' he said, 'Colin Fleming.'

And Sylvia was paralysed by the sound of his voice. She stood there, rigid, as he repeated his name. His very tone exuded the sulky self-absorption that she had come to detest. She could see him so clearly – in these different, straitened circumstances, but in the same old pattern of being – and it transported her back to the emotional desert of their life together. This was something she couldn't do again, not with him, not for him. For thirty years she had found her own way through his chosen life, now he must find his own. Slowly she put down the receiver, shivering with relief as it clicked back into place.

FORTY-TWO

Mike was cooking steak and chicken breasts on the barbecue for Caro, Jodie and David. They sat at the table on the deck watching him as he turned the steaks and the fat splashed and hissed on the charcoal. There was a big salad in the middle of the table, a pot of hummus that Jodie had made, and some warm Turkish bread. David broke off a large piece of bread and dipped it in the hummus.

'I was going to be in Turkey by now,' he said, grinning at Jodie, 'but I changed my mind, so I might as well just eat the Turkish bread instead.'

'Turkey,' said Caro. 'Huh – that was very smart.'

'You gotta stay now, man,' Mike called from the barbecue. 'You're an uncle.'

'Indeed I am, and I also have a new job.'

Jodie smiled and put a hand on his. 'He's insufferably pleased with himself, but it is a rather good one.'

David took her hand and held on to it. He was unbelievably happy.

'Director of studies,' he said with a grin. 'At the Rosenthal Language School, in the city. They've got branches all over the place, Australia, New Zealand, Europe.'

'Turkey?' Caro asked, smothering a laugh.

'Shut up, you.'

'Joking, joking,' she said. 'Congratulations, Uncle David, let's drink to your success. When do you start?' She got up to pour more wine into three glasses and topped up David's with mineral water. 'Sure you don't want a little wine to celebrate?'

He shook his head. 'No thanks. Next month.'

'To the director of studies,' Caro said, raising her glass. 'Does this mean you'll have to wear a suit?'

'From time to time, I'm afraid,' David said. 'But as far as I can see, that's the only drawback.'

Mike piled the meat onto a serving plate and turned down the heat on the barbecue. 'Very good news,' he said, raising his glass. 'Cheers, mate! Congratulations.'

David looked at his brother-in-law, remembering his rage at him in the days after Rebekah's birth. Sometime in the last few months it had burned out without him even noticing it. Perhaps it had just been the overbearing self-righteousness of the non-drinker – or more likely, he thought, it was having someone precious of his own whose love had sweetened the bitterness of jealousy, and pointed the way out of victimhood.

'You have to stop looking so smug,' Jodie teased him. 'It's not dignified!'

'Speaking of smug,' Caro cut in. 'Have you noticed that Mum's been looking a bit smug recently?'

'No, babes,' Mike said, cutting into his steak. 'I haven't noticed anything.'

'Well, no, *you wouldn't*, would you?' Caro said. 'You didn't even notice when Rebekah got her first tooth. Good thing you're not a surgeon – you wouldn't notice if you were cutting up the wrong person.'

'Don't think so,' David said. 'Why?'

'Yes,' said Jodie. 'There's something different about her.'

'She's probably still upset about Gran,' David said. 'It's not very long, after all.'

'Of course she is,' said Caro, 'we all are, but this is different, don't you think, Jode?'

Jodie nodded. 'Yep, a bit as though she's got something up her sleeve.'

'Exactly. You see? It takes a woman to notice things like that. You don't think she's got a lover, do you?'

'Mum?' David's head shot up in shock. 'A lover? Nah! No way.' He shook his head and helped himself to salad. 'Absolutely no way, not Mum.'

'Why not?' Jodie asked.

'Well,' he shrugged, 'she's . . . she's Mum, she's just not into that sort of thing.'

'What sort of thing? Sex? Men? Love? Romance? Relationships?'

'Yeah, all that. Gave it up years ago.'

'We don't actually *know* that,' Caro said, grinning. 'And I'm sure she's up to *something.*'

'Would you mind if she was?' Jodie asked her.

'Not at all, I'd be happy for her, but I'm a very nosy person, I'd just like to know. What about you, Dave?'

'Never thought about it, really. Mum with a bloke? Okay, I suppose, if it made her happy.'

'Think laterally,' Jodie said with a smile. 'It might be a woman.'

David paused, a forkful of chicken halfway to his mouth. 'No,' he said. 'Definitely not Mum, not her style at all. Caro?'

'No,' Caro said, 'not a woman, that'd be far too daring for Mum. If there is someone, it's a man. No doubt about that.'

It was bound to happen, of course. Irene had always known it, Sylvia had long suspected it, and in the few weeks since Sylvia told her about it Fran had expected it; something would trigger a reaction, Bonnie would crack and all hell would break loose again. Now it had happened and Irene cursed herself. It was a stupid thing, really, but she'd gone into the gallery to say hello to Caro, and there were several customers waiting to pay for their purchases. Rebekah, who had been sleeping peacefully in her pusher, woke suddenly and began to cry, and Caro looked hopefully at Irene.

'Shall I take her on the deck?'

'Please,' Caro said, 'if you've got time. You could give her a drink of water, there's a bottle in her bag.'

And Irene had wheeled the pusher out into the sunlight on the deck, got out the bottle, and lifted Rebekah onto her knee. The baby stopped crying immediately and reached for the bottle with a big grin.

'That's it, darling,' Irene murmured, 'have a lovely drink,' and she sat there watching Rebekah's little hands clutching at the bottle, thinking how sad it was that Lila was not here to enjoy her great granddaughter. Rebekah finished guzzling the water, and Irene sat her up straight and rubbed her back until she gave a loud burp. 'Well done,' Irene laughed, 'well done. Shall we have a little walk along the deck and look at the gulls?'

And as she stood up and gathered Rebekah to her, she saw Bonnie standing in the doorway, and Irene knew by the way she turned, ran back up the stairs to her office and slammed the door, that this was the moment she'd been dreading for years. What she didn't know and couldn't bear to think about was just how it would all be played out.

'Well, Irene, you couldn't *not* hold the baby in case Bonnie saw you,' Hamish said when she told him later. 'I can't believe that she's gone all these years and it's only upsetting her now.'

'It's not only now,' Irene said, 'it's always been there, but Jeff's death brought it to the surface.'

'She can't have been avoiding babies for twenty-five years, surely?' Hamish said, pouring her a gin and tonic. 'Babies are everywhere.'

'Not really. Not in the sort of social circle they were involved with. They were living in Montreux at the time and they moved to Zurich quite soon after that. Jeff wanted them to put it all behind them and the friends they made in Zurich were older, and usually with lots of money, so they employed nannies and au pairs. I suppose there was a baby or two among them, but it would have been easy for Bonnie to avoid them. Oh dear, Hamish, whatever am I going to do?'

'Absolutely nothing,' Hamish said. 'You said Bonnie's gone home, and she knew you were staying here with me tonight. She knows where you are if she needs you. She might be very glad of some time alone, to think things through.'

'Thinking, huh!' Irene said. 'That's the trouble, if you ask me. Too much thinking, not enough talking. Jeff made sure of that.

It was a taboo subject as far as he was concerned. Sometimes, Hamish, I feel you've got in touch with your feminine side and then you come out with something like this. Thinking, indeed!'

Bonnie was packing a suitcase. It was a fairly small one but she was having difficulty deciding what to put in it because she couldn't concentrate. Why on earth had she packed bathers? She took them out and put in a few pairs of knickers, a couple of bras, and two silk shirts. Then she stopped and sat down on the side of the bed. The flight left at ten-thirty in the morning. She thought she'd get a taxi to the airport rather than leave her car in the car park. She folded a pair of black pants and a skirt, put them in and then took the skirt out. It took her an hour to pack the bag and even then she wasn't sure she'd packed what she'd need.

From the moment she'd walked out on to the deck and seen her mother with the baby, Bonnie had known that she had to get away, just get out of there for a few days, give herself some space. And she'd known immediately and exactly where she was going to go. She'd run up the stairs to the office, called Qantas, booked the flight, and then sat there in relief like a junkie who'd just got a fix. She hadn't called him to let him know, but she was sure he wouldn't mind – she'd call from the airport. She was glad she had the house to herself this evening; she couldn't have handled having to talk to anyone, even her mother. Most of all her mother.

Very effectively and with a resolve born of desperation, she managed not to think about it all. She thought instead about the Boatshed, about whether they needed to change the menu, about whether Sean and Tan should get bonuses – maybe all the staff should get them, they'd worked so hard. She thought of simple, comparatively trivial things, and at half-past eight she took some Valium and went to bed, where she slept heavily until the alarm woke her. Then she dragged herself out of bed, showered, put on the Chanel suit, drank a cup of coffee and called a taxi to take her to the airport.

*

'I've no idea where she is, Fran,' Irene said when she came home later that morning to find a frantic message from Fran on the answering machine. 'There's just a note here that says, "Gone away for a couple of days, will call later". It doesn't say where, but her car's here, so she can't have gone far, unless she went in a taxi.'

Fran put the phone down and tried Bonnie's mobile again. It was still switched off. This she did not need. They had a meeting in fifteen minutes, something she really didn't want to do alone.

'God knows where she's gone,' she said to Sylvia. 'I may have to kill her when she gets back. A few months ago she was the one lecturing me about being businesslike. Huh! Anyway, I hope she's okay. D'you think she's on her own?'

Sylvia thought for a moment. 'Unlikely. She's used to having a man to lean on, that's the sort of support she'll be looking for.'

'She's left her car behind so either she's gone *with* someone, or *to* someone. You don't think . . . ?'

'To Perth, you mean? To Will? Surely not, not after everything . . .'

'He *is* Jeff's brother, and who else is there?'

'I don't know. Oh Lord, I hope not. The last thing we need is all that stirred up again. Have you tried her mobile?'

Fran nodded. 'Many times. It's switched off. Consistent, of course, with a four and a half hour flight to Perth, don't you think?'

Sylvia sank her head in her hands. 'Shit, shit, shit. She'll regret it. This is not a Will thing, he'll have no idea what to do with her. Should I ring him, do you think?'

'I think you should stay out of it, Sylvia,' Fran said. 'If she *has* gone to Perth there's nothing we can do about it anyway. You getting involved will only make it worse. We just have to wait until we know for sure. Meanwhile, I have to go to this meeting.'

Bonnie pulled her bag off the carousel and looked out at the taxis lining up in front of the arrivals hall. For one moment during the flight she'd had a flicker of doubt about what she was doing, but a double brandy had sorted that out. She wasn't really sure why she'd come, what she expected, but he was a man she could talk to, and anyway, they had plenty of other things to discuss. She stopped herself from thinking about it, fearful of undermining her own confidence, and dialled his number.

'Jack, hi, it's Bonnie. Look, I'm in Sydney, just got to the airport. I thought we might go and take a look at the place in Manly.'

There was a brief silence at the other end.

'Um . . . yes, of course,' he said eventually. 'I didn't realise you were planning on coming up today. I'll have to try and shift a couple of appointments.' He took a deep breath and his tone changed to something more welcoming. 'Look, why don't you just take a cab over here to the office, and I'll sort things out and arrange to get the keys for the Manly place.'

'Terrific,' Bonnie said, thinking she sounded a little loud and brittle. 'And I wonder . . . I could get a hotel, of course, but maybe you . . .'

There was another awkward pause. 'Er . . . yes, sure, Bonnie,' he said. 'No worries, we'll fix you up.'

She slipped the phone back into her bag, stepped through the automatic doors and joined the taxi queue. Obviously this had been the right thing to do – be decisive, don't stand still. That was Jeff's theory, so he'd think she was doing the right thing.

A cab drew up alongside her and she slipped into the back seat, gave the driver the address and they moved slowly out into the stream of traffic. She did get another little flash then, a nudge that perhaps Jeff might *not* think this was such a good idea after all, but she dismissed it. Jeff and Jack were alike in many ways. She needed that sort of male energy to get her through this crisis, and anyway, he'd been urging her to take a look at Manly.

She glanced at her watch, thinking perhaps she should call the Boatshed and let them know where she was, but it was pleasant being away on her own, not having to think about anything else. She would take Jack to lunch, a nice meal, some good wine and conversation, the sort of conversations she hadn't had for a long time – the harmlessly flirtatious conversations that you couldn't have with women.

*

'Lovely views, of course,' Jack said, wandering down the length of the building. 'It's an old factory. What really grabs me is the scale. Some of these old buildings are just too big, like barns. The scale of the Boatshed is perfect, the height and the floor space, big enough to take plenty of tables but not so big it's intimidating.'

'Yes,' Bonnie said, feeling vague and disoriented. 'I see what you mean . . .'

'We could create the Boatshed atmosphere here using the same design techniques, same colour scheme and so on. That courtyard would be a great alfresco dining area, and if you come through here you can see what could be the gallery.'

Bonnie followed him, trying to match his enthusiasm. If there was going to be another restaurant, both the location and the building were ideal but she wasn't in the mood for it right now. She wanted something more personal, more . . . affectionate.

Lunch had been a disappointment. When she'd arrived at the office it hadn't been at all as she'd expected. She could see now that it was foolish of her to have anticipated something like Jeff's office: tall building, marble entrance foyer, lifts, elegance, luxury, the very latest technology everywhere. Bannister Books' office on the other hand, was an old warehouse, the entrance tucked away in a narrow side street. The warehouse had been converted into a huge, open plan office with a few private offices along one side. Raw brick, rafters, walls of books, posters, and quite a lot of glass and iron: cool, functional design, and so casual.

The receptionist had green hair and a nose ring and when Bonnie gave her a card and asked for Jack, she yelled across the vast open expanse of the main office, and Jack, who was standing by a white-board talking with a couple of other people, waved and made his way across to her. It was totally unlike the hushed elegance of Jeff's office, where pale carpets, massive desks, leather sofas and original works by significant artists stretched in every direction.

Jack led her to his small glass-enclosed office which was stacked high with books and files, and where colour negatives of food were lying on the light table.

'Look at these, Bonnie,' he'd said. 'Some of the plates for Fran's book. Have a look through them while I make a call.'

Bonnie stared at the negatives of glistening salad leaves, chick-pea patties, soups, pancakes and something she couldn't identify – tofu, maybe? Eventually, she moved some books from a chair and sat down. As soon as Jack finished his call she'd take him to lunch.

'I've sent out for some sandwiches and fruit,' Jack said, putting down the phone. 'I'd love to take you to lunch, Bonnie, but I have to hang on here. I wasn't able to cancel everything. One of our authors is on his way here from Wollongong. So we'll have a sandwich, and I'll see him and then we can pop out to Manly.'

Bonnie's disappointment was such that when the sandwiches arrived she couldn't eat a thing.

So here they were, inspecting the property, and she could see Jack checking his watch. Why had she imagined it would be like going to Jeff's office? Why had she assumed that it would be like the times she turned up there, greeted by the charming concierge in his gold-trimmed uniform, whisked in by the discreet, softly spoken Frau Trautmann, who had worked for him for years, and then later escorted out by Jeff to some small, delightful restaurant? Perhaps she hadn't made the right decision, after all. She began to feel a little light-headed and nauseous.

'Now, Lenore's delighted for you to stay with her,' Jack said as he drove out of Manly. 'So I'll drop you off there. She's out of town but she'll be back tonight. I've got a good bit to get through this afternoon, so I'll give you a key. It's handy for the city, or anywhere else you want to go. If you're free tonight, perhaps I could take you to dinner?'

Bonnie hadn't factored Lenore into this visit. She'd assumed Jack would put her up, assumed that once she arrived he'd look after her, just as Jeff would have done, getting her from place to place, organising things for her. Well, of course he had done just that, but it was all so different.

'Make yourself comfortable,' Jack said when he'd shown her around Lenore's house. 'Help yourself to tea and coffee, food . . . whatever.' He glanced at his watch again. 'I must get back to work. It's twenty past three – is seven-thirty all right for dinner? I'll pick you up.'

'Fine,' she said. 'Thanks, Jack, I'll be ready.' And with a terrible sinking feeling she watched him drive away.

'She's in Sydney,' Sylvia said under her breath so that the two women examining scarves in the gallery couldn't overhear her. 'Lenore called while you were at the meeting.'

'Sydney? Why Sydney, what's she gone there for? Oh, don't tell me – Jack Bannister?'

'Yes. Bonnie just turned up, rang Jack from the airport. Very odd.'

'Odd – you're not kidding!' Fran said. 'Oh, I hope she's not going to make a fool of herself.'

'Well, apparently he's got a monstrous sort of day, but he took her off somewhere to look at a property, and then dropped her at Lenore's place. She's up in Newcastle, back later tonight, and Bonnie's staying there. She asked Jack if she could stay with him.'

'You don't mean she propositioned him?'

'No, nothing like that. Just sort of assumed he'd look after her. It seems he thought she was sounding pretty strange on the phone and he rang Lenore and arranged for her to stay there.'

'Smart man. Did Lenore say how Bonnie is?'

Sylvia shrugged and shook her head. 'She just said that Jack said Bonnie was very strange, like she was on drugs – animated one minute, but then seeming not really with it.'

'You told her about the baby crisis?'

'I did. She'll talk to her tonight and call us in the morning.'

Fran waited as Sylvia gift-wrapped the women's scarves and took their money. 'She is so much going to wish she hadn't done this. I was so cross with her this morning, and now I can only think about how fragile she is.'

'I know,' Sylvia said. 'Thank goodness Lenore will be back tonight. Let's just hope Bonnie doesn't make a complete fool of herself in the meantime.'

*

Bonnie peered at herself in the mirror and thought she looked a bit odd, wobbly. Perhaps the mirror was slightly distorted – probably a cheap mirror. She was glad she'd worn the Chanel suit, it was more than a year since it had had an airing, but her hair didn't really go with it. Until now she had liked her very short, spiky cut, it seemed to fit with her life in Melbourne, with the woman she had become, the woman who had started the Boatshed. But tonight she hated it, she wanted her old hair back again, the shiny, blunt, mahogany bob that Jeff had loved, as he loved this suit.

Sighing, she rinsed her hands at the basin and waved them in front of the irritating hot air dryer and then made her way back into the restaurant, wondering if she'd had too much to drink. Her legs felt a bit funny. It was only nine-thirty but she felt quite light-headed and a little dizzy.

When Jack had left her at Lenore's that afternoon, the depression had closed in and she wandered restlessly around the empty house pushing away the urge to scream or smash something. Eventually she ran upstairs to the room where Jack had put her bag, took some of her pills and threw herself on the bed. Wiping out the rest of the afternoon with sleep seemed the only way to cope, and setting the alarm to wake her at six-thirty, she lay back waiting for merciful oblivion. When she woke three hours later she felt decidedly groggy, but a shower helped, as did a couple of large gins at the bar with Jack, and some excellent wine. The food looked delicious but she could barely touch it. She made her way cautiously back to the table, just as the waiter arrived with their coffee and two large brandies.

'So what did you think of the Manly property?' Jack asked, swirling the brandy in his glass.

Bonnie took a sip of hers and thrilled to its fire as she swallowed it. 'I liked it. I think it would work,' she said.

'Good,' he said. 'Have you sounded Fran out?'

'Only in terms of a future possibility, nothing specific.' She didn't want to start talking business. They'd talked books and movies earlier, and she'd told him a bit about life in Switzerland. Tonight she'd wanted something different and it had felt good, like dinners in Zurich with Jeff.

Jack nodded. 'Of course, but we shouldn't leave it too long or we may lose the chance of a lease. When you get back, perhaps you can talk to her in more specific terms. She doesn't need to be hugely involved, of course, but she does need to be on board, and we need to discuss some sort of partnership arrangement. I'll get –'

'Sure, Jack,' Bonnie interrupted. 'But let's not talk about it tonight. There are so many nicer things to discuss. I've been telling you all about my life, time for you to tell me about yours. You never talk about yourself, and that makes me feel you must have all sorts of secrets.' She reached across the table and put her hand on top of his. She thought he looked a little shaken. He wasn't a man who constantly talked about himself and expected women to sit by in admiring silence; he was like Jeff in that way too, interested, inclusive. She squeezed his hand gently just before he eased it away and folded his napkin.

'Not really,' he said awkwardly. 'Just pretty ordinary – the army, work, marriage, divorce. Pretty average for a bloke my age, I think. Maybe we should be making a move, Bonnie. I'll get the bill.'

She waved her hand to stop him. 'It's early yet,' she said. 'Let's have another brandy and you can tell me about the army.' The table seemed to move slightly and as her elbow slipped off the edge, she knocked her cup, splashing coffee onto the tablecloth.

'Are you sure you want another drink?' Jack asked.

'Absolutely sure,' she smiled. 'The night is young.'

'Hmm,' he said, nodding to the waiter. 'The night may be but I'm not. If you'd like it, perhaps just one more, and then we must get going. I've got an early meeting in the morning.'

FORTY-THREE

Fran sat in the moonlit courtyard at the back of the house in a towelling dressing gown, her feet on the lower rung of the table, drinking a cup of tea and staring at an old shoebox full of letters. She was exhausted, but too wide awake to sleep.

'You'd better see if you want these, Fran,' Sylvia had said earlier that evening. They were at Lila's unit, sorting and packing her possessions with Caro and Jodie. 'They're airmail letters.'

'Not more, surely,' Fran said. 'I'm beginning to wonder if Mum ever threw anything away.'

'Well, these seem to be from you,' Sylvia said, handing her the box.

They were her letters home from England in the sixties, her own voice speaking across the decades, the voice of the person she used to be.

'Oh, can I read them, please, Mum,' Caro had begged.

'Okay,' Fran had agreed, 'but not yet. I want to read them first.'

She had brought them home intending to look at them another time, but the pull of the past was irresistible and in surrendering to the temptation to read just one she had been unable to stop. It was a relief to find that she didn't dislike the young Fran, but it was surprising to feel as though she was listening to a stranger; the enthusiasm and naïveté left her feeling exposed, naked almost.

She could remember writing them, could picture herself at the table by the window in the shared house near Paddington Station, or in the café where she stopped for a bacon sandwich on her way to the job in the record shop in Edgware Road. She could even see herself sitting on a seat in Kensington Gardens near the Peter Pan statue, an airmail pad on her knee, her backpack on the grass beside her, filling in a free half-hour with a letter to Lila. The connection with home had been vital and she had hung on to her mother's letters, which arrived regularly once a week making her feel safe enough, loved enough, to stay away. If only she had kept Lila's letters to her, how she would have loved to read them now.

'I'm dying to know what you sound like,' Caro had said. 'Did you tell Gran everything – I mean, boyfriends, wild parties, getting drunk, drugs, everything?'

'Not everything,' Fran had said with a laugh. 'Probably a bit about boyfriends, a few parties, definitely not about getting drunk, and certainly nothing about smoking the occasional joint.'

What *had* she sounded like? Excited, a bit scared, high on possibilities, thrilled by London and everything it symbolised, a present packed with action, a future throbbing with opportunity. What had she done with all that? Had she wasted the enthusiasm, the experience, the opportunities? Frittered them away? There was so much she wished she'd done or done better, but the greatest satisfaction of her life – her children – made it impossible to wish certain things undone. She was fifty-six, a mother, a grandmother, and now a reasonably successful businesswoman, although the latter title still sat uneasily with her. The truth was that right now she wouldn't change anything.

In England, aged twenty, she had fallen in love with Daniel, a law student from Jamaica, and tonight she had been reminded how, in letters home, she told Lila quite a bit about him except for the fact that he was Jamaican. Thirty-six years on, she knew that the censorship was unnecessary. Lila was the most open-minded, least judgmental person Fran had ever known. She would have welcomed Daniel, irrespective of colour or ethnicity. So what would she feel if she was here now, if she knew about Lenore?

Fran had never imagined that she would be attracted to another woman, let alone make love with one. Her closest friends were women, some of them in same-sex relationships, but she had never felt this sort of chemistry before. Even in her mounting desire she had felt strange and a little uneasy exploring another woman's body, so familiar and, at the same time, so thrillingly different. But for the first time in her life she had felt she was making love rather than just having sex, and the moment she abandoned herself to the bliss of it, let go of the feeling that she must satisfy and be satisfied, she knew she was tasting an intimacy that had, until now, eluded her. Even with Tony, sex had seemed more about lust structured into ritual than an intimate expression of love and sexuality. She wondered now if she had always been a lesbian without knowing it, or was she just one of a growing number of women who had found same-sex love and sexual pleasure after half a lifetime of heterosexual relationships?

'You know what they say about lesbians and how it all happens so quickly?' Lenore had whispered that first night. 'Meet in the morning, move in together in the afternoon, get married that night.'

'Do you think it's true?' Fran asked, thinking her question sounded terribly childish.

'Not always, but it's not uncommon.'

'Well, if I could keep you here forever, I would,' she said. But she had sensed that Lenore was holding back, cautious still, anxious to protect her, or perhaps to protect herself.

'In a few days' time,' Lenore had said the next morning, catching hold of Fran's arm as she got out of bed, 'if this doesn't feel right, promise you'll tell me the truth – you won't just run and hide?' And in the weeks since they parted, Lenore's anxiety seemed to have grown. 'I know what I want, Fran,' Lenore had said to her at the airport. 'And I don't want to sound patronising but this *is* new for you.'

'You think I'm just experimenting,' Fran had said. 'I promise you I'm not. I mean, surely the first time you sleep with anyone you're attracted to it's something of an experiment.'

Lenore put a hand on her cheek. 'But it's more than that and you need to be sure not just for yourself but for me too. I loved you from that first day when you frightened the life out of me, and I'd trained myself to accept that we could only be

405

friends. Now I'm scared that in a week or two you'll get cold feet, wake one morning in a panic and turn away from me. It's happened before and I'm not in the habit of seducing straight women.'

'It was me who came to your bed,' Fran said, biting her lip to hold back the tears.

'I know, but even so you need to take time. I'm still scared that this is a reaction to loss and loneliness.' Lenore paused and turned away briefly. 'I'm sorry, Fran, I must sound like the most awful fascist,' she said, and for the first time Fran saw tears in her eyes. 'But I'd reached a time of my life where I'd sworn off relationships for fear of getting hurt again. I'm sixty-two, and I thought I was done with love and all its terrifying emotional peaks and troughs. I don't want to get dropped when your children or your friends disapprove, or you discover you're embarrassed to be seen with me in public. I've been through all that, Fran; I don't want to do it again. Take time. I'm a coward, I know, but I won't come back until I'm sure it's safe.'

Fran sighed and put down her empty cup. Every day since then they had talked on the phone, every day the emails hummed through cyberspace, her own loving and emotional, Lenore's more cautious. She thought of Lenore tonight, coping with Bonnie, and wondered what was happening in the little house in Surry Hills. Whatever would Bonnie say when she found out about this? What would Lila have said? Fran stretched her arms above her head, looking up at the fragments of moonlit sky showing through the vines that spread across the lattice.

'Well, why not, Fran? Who you love is your own business and no one else's.' She could almost hear her mother's voice. 'You have to be true to yourself or life's not worth anything.'

'Thanks, Mum,' Fran whispered into the darkness, 'that's what I thought you'd say.'

Bonnie slipped into the back seat of the taxi and slid across to make room for Jack.

'This was such a lovely evening,' she said, resting her hand on his thigh, her head dropping onto his shoulder as the cab pulled away. 'It feels like, well . . . like old times, like I used to be.'

'I'm glad you enjoyed it, Bonnie,' Jack said, lifting her hand off his leg and, as it started to stray back, taking it firmly in his and holding it. 'You must be very tired.'

The cab seemed to sway a lot but it felt good, as though she was on her favourite train ride, the one that meandered up a steep single track, through pastures filled with wildflowers and grazing cattle, and the higher wooded slopes to the snow-capped peaks of the mountains. It was a journey from warm spring sunshine to blinding whiteness, where you could stand surrounded by snow without a jacket, breathing the sharp, pure air at the summit.

'Dear Jack,' she said, lifting her head to kiss the line of his jaw. 'You didn't tell me about your life, but you can do that when we get home.' Her head spun a little as she rested it back on his shoulder.

Jack cleared his throat and kept looking straight ahead. Lenore's house was still in darkness when they drew up outside.

'Hang on for me, will you?' Jack said to the driver. 'I'll just be a couple of minutes, and I'll get you to run me back to Elizabeth Bay.' And he helped Bonnie out of the car and attempted to steer her up the front path. 'I'll see you in, Bonnie,' he said. 'Lenore will be back soon.'

'You aren't going, are you, Jack?' she said, plaintive suddenly. 'I'll make coffee, we can talk some more. I want to hear all about you.'

'It's late, Bonnie,' he said, guiding her up the path, his arm around her waist to steady her. 'I've got an early start.' He slipped the key in the door and snapped on the light in the hall. Immediately, Bonnie reached behind him and snapped it off again, laughing.

'No, no, too much light, it's much more fun in the dark. Always leave the light off, more intimate, you see.' And she turned towards him, slipped her arms around his neck, drew his head down towards her and kissed him. He was stiff and unresponsive at first, so she moved closer, pressing herself against him, sliding her fingers into his hair. As his arms closed around her, Bonnie felt she was melting back into a familiar and blissful cushion of safety. Blood surged through her veins as Jack responded to her kiss, holding her closer now, his mouth controlling hers, his erection hardening against her belly. She was lost in the sheer relief and joy of feeling needed and wanted. She pulled at his shirt buttons and slid her hand onto his bare chest but at the touch of her fingers, Jack pulled away suddenly, grasping her wrists and holding her at a distance, breathing deeply to regain his composure.

'Bonnie,' he said, 'Bonnie, this is not a good idea . . .' He stepped back slightly and she could see him outlined in the doorway against the light from the street. 'You're upset, Bonnie, and you've had a lot to drink. I don't think . . .'

She moved towards him again, driven by the longing to be held, but he managed to keep her at arm's length.

'I'm going now, Bonnie,' he said. 'Lenore'll be back soon.'

'No, Jack,' she cried, encircling his neck again. 'Stay, please stay, I need you. Stay with me, please, Jack.' She was clinging to him now, grasping at his hair, his jacket, his face.

'Don't go,' she pleaded. 'Stay with me, please stay.' Panic rose in waves that broke into shuddering sobs. She clawed at his face, trying to drag him closer, her nails tearing into his neck and cheek. 'Don't leave,' she cried, 'I can't . . . don't leave me, hold me . . . please, Jack, hold me . . .'

'Bonnie, please,' Jack cried, trying to grip her wrists again. 'Please stop. I'll wait if you want but stop, please stop –' The hall light snapped on suddenly.

'Whatever's going on in here?' Lenore asked, standing in the doorway, glancing from the misery etched into Bonnie's face to the streaks of blood running down her brother's cheek. 'Seems I got back just in time. Now, which one of you am I supposed to be rescuing?'

FORTY-FOUR

It was one of those humid Sydney mornings when the light is a painfully white blanket of cloud. Lenore put a large glass of water and a cup of tea on the bedside table and opened the window slightly.

'It's after eleven, Bonnie,' she said softly. 'How are you feeling this morning?'

Bonnie struggled upright, dragging a pillow behind her, and leaned back against it. 'Like death,' she murmured, shaking her head and then stopping suddenly. 'Shit! That felt like a load of crockery slipped off the shelves in my head and crashed.'

'Drink some water,' Lenore said, settling cross-legged on the end of the double bed and leaning back against the brass rail.

Bonnie gulped the water, wondering how much of what was in her throbbing head was memory and how much imagination. Her body felt leaden, with the exception of her stomach, which was distinctly volatile. Her eyes were sore and scratchy, and the room seemed to be swaying like the cabin of a ship. She had difficulty staying upright.

'I'm sorry . . .' she began, and Lenore held up a hand to stop her.

'No need for apologies. We just want to know that you're okay.'

Bonnie closed her eyes and took a deep breath. 'What happened, Lenore? I think it was awful, but it's such a muddle. I dreamt, or maybe I didn't dream it, that I tried to seduce Jack.' She opened her eyes. 'And I think I hurt him.'

Lenore nodded. 'You scratched his face and neck. It did bleed a bit.'

Bonnie's hand shot to her mouth and she put down the cup. 'What was wrong with me? I was like a madwoman. All day and the day before . . . since . . . since . . .'

'Since you saw Irene with the baby?'

Bonnie nodded.

'How much Valium did you take?' Lenore asked.

'No idea,' Bonnie shrugged. 'I remember packing my bag and taking something to make me sleep, going to the airport, going to Manly with Jack, then coming back here.' She shook her head and winced again. 'I think I took some more then. Then Jack and I were in a restaurant – drinks, maybe? Then what . . . ?' She looked up in confusion.

'You really want the details?'

Bonnie nodded.

'All of it?'

'Yes.'

Lenore told her the story from the moment of her call from the airport until she had arrived home to find them in the hall, Bonnie sobbing and screaming, Jack with blood running down his face, trying desperately to restrain her.

'You had quite a lot to drink at the restaurant,' Lenore said. 'And Jack says you ate nothing at lunch and hardly anything at dinner. He blames himself. He says he should have seen what was happening and insisted on bringing you back here earlier in the evening.'

Bonnie sank her face into her hands. 'And that was the end of it?' she asked. 'When you came back?'

'More or less,' Lenore said. 'I put the light on and it seemed to shock you, and the taxi driver came running in to see what was happening. You staggered around a bit, bumping into walls, but . . .' she paused, grinning. 'You were quite aggressive and wouldn't let us get hold of you. Then you crashed into the wall and fell. When we sat you up, you were sick and then you passed out. My neighbour heard the noise and came out; he's a doctor. Jack told him you'd been acting strangely all day, hardly eaten anything but had quite a lot to drink, then we had a look in your bag and found the Valium. We weren't sure how many you'd taken but then you came round and he thought you'd be okay. You seemed to be through the worst of it. You weren't making much sense, but you obviously weren't in a critical state, so we just brought you up here and I put you to bed. You've been sleeping for nearly twelve hours.'

Bonnie put her hand up to brush away the tears, and winced at the tenderness of her right cheekbone.

'You hit your face on the corner of the hall table,' Lenore said. 'You're going to have a lovely bruise there, I'm afraid.'

'Oh, Lenore,' Bonnie said, burying her face in her hands again. 'I'm so sorry.'

Lenore put a steadying hand on her arm. 'Don't be. You were terribly upset, you couldn't eat, it was understandable.'

'I was terrible,' she said. 'And poor Jack – whatever must he think of me? How will I face him again?'

'Jack's fine,' Lenore said gently. 'He's not the best in an emotional crisis, he's a real bloke in that way. But he does understand, honestly. You don't need to worry about Jack.'

'But it's so embarrassing,' Bonnie sobbed. 'Humiliating. I virtually propositioned him and I scratched him and drew blood, and all the trouble I've caused you . . . and I embarrassed you in front of your neighbour.'

Lenore hoisted herself up to sit beside Bonnie on the bed and put an arm around her shoulders, holding her firmly until the worst of the weeping had passed. 'Bonnie, it really is okay,' she said gently. 'We're just glad you were here with us, not with strangers. Jack and I are fine, and we want you to be fine too.'

'I must go,' Bonnie said suddenly, straightening up. 'Get out of your hair, leave you in peace. This isn't fair at all.'

Lenore took her hands again and held them firmly in her own. 'It's too soon,' she said. 'You need to rest some more, drink lots of water, sleep a bit more. Then you and I have things to do.'

Bonnie blinked. 'What things? I have to go back to the Boatshed. You must want to see the back of me as soon as possible.'

Lenore shook her head. 'Not at all. I've talked to Fran and

Sylvia, everything's fine at the Boatshed, and I've told Irene you're here with me, and you're staying on for a day or two. I mean it, Bonnie, you and I have things to talk about.'

'We do?' Bonnie slumped back against the pillow. 'If I start talking, I might never stop,' she said.

'Exactly.'

'I want him back, Lenore,' she said. 'I want Jeff back.'

'I know you do, but he's gone, Bonnie, and you have to leave him in peace.'

Bonnie nodded. 'But it isn't only Jeff.' she paused, looking up. 'You know, don't you? Mum's told you, or Sylvia has.'

Lenore nodded and took her hand. 'I know.'

'Oh Lenore, I want Lucy, I want my baby back.' It was the first time she'd said it. The first time since she had stood and watched that tiny white coffin lowered into the ground. Holding Jeff's hand, she had walked back to the car feeling as though some vital organ had been ripped from her body. 'I want her back, Jeff,' she had wept, leaning against him as they made their way to the car.

'I know, darling,' he'd said. 'So do I, but she's gone and talking about it won't help.'

'I want my baby back,' she said again now, and speaking it at last she could hear the pain trapped in her own voice.

Lenore reached out and hugged her. 'I know, Bon, I know how that feels, I really do.'

'He would never talk about it,' Bonnie said, the tears flowing freely again now. 'He wouldn't let anyone else come to the funeral because he couldn't bear it. There was just us, and when it was over he never let me talk about it again. He buried it, like we buried her. We had to move away, start again, he said, no one to remind us with their sympathy, with their concern. I wanted to talk about her, I begged and begged, but he'd just go and shut himself away.' She paused to blow her nose. 'I never stopped longing for her, Lenore. Not talking, pretending it hadn't happened, just made it worse. In the end I didn't even know how to talk about it. When Sylvia asked me, I felt as though I was acting a part . . . I want her back so much, and I still think about her every single day.'

412

The tears were burning her eyes now, and every ounce of strength had drained away. It was such a relief to say it after all those years, to say it without risk of disapproval or reprimand, without watching as the door was closed on her.

Lenore handed her some more tissues and looked closely into her face. 'That's what we have to do, you see, talk about it. You're going to rest a bit more now, then get up and have a shower and I'll make you something to eat. Then, I think, we might get in the car and drive somewhere near the water, find ourselves a beautiful spot to sit in the fresh air, and we're going to talk, you and I, about our lost children, and about being frightened of being ourselves, and we're going to cry buckets. We're going to do that quite a lot in the next few days, and you'll start to feel just a little bit better every day. And one day, probably quite soon, you'll be able to look at Rebekah, and pick her up and cuddle her. It's hard emotional work, Bonnie, work that should have been done years ago. The pain, the longing, well . . . they never go away, but it will feel different after this, I promise you, really different.'

'I think we should take the decision now,' Sylvia said. 'Bonnie's been gone a week and she won't be back until Sunday. It's only three weeks away and either we need to plan and advertise a Mother's Day lunch now, or we decide to close and let the staff have the day off. We can't wait any longer.'

'Okay,' Fran said. 'I vote we close. I don't want to be part of that horrible commercial Mother's Day thing. If we close we can have a picnic, same as last year.'

They were sitting with a pot of tea at a corner table in the restaurant, which had closed an hour earlier. In the kitchen, Sean and the staff were cleaning and setting up for the next morning. Tan and the waitstaff were laying the tables for breakfast.

'Bonnie may not approve,' Sylvia warned. 'She'll say it's not good business practice.'

'And she'll be right but I don't care,' Fran said. 'It's important to us, to me especially, for Mum's sake, a memorial picnic. And the staff deserves the chance to be with their families. We could invite Sean and Graeme – their mums are in Ireland and New Zealand.'

'And Tan,' Sylvia added. 'Her mother's in Vietnam, and I'd like to ask Veronica.'

'Okay then,' Fran said with a grin, 'that's settled, executive decision.' She pushed the files aside and leaned on her elbows. 'What have you decided about the fashion label?'

'I want to go ahead. Bonnie's prepared to back it, so it's an incredible opportunity. It's what I always wanted. I'll do as Bonnie and Lenore suggested, go to Sydney and meet a couple of Lenore's people, get some advice and some feedback. After that I'll trust my design instincts and Bonnie's business sense.' She leaned back in satisfaction. 'It's so exciting, Fran. When we first started here I felt strange, a bit out of it. You had the central involvement, trading on your name and reputation, all your creativity. Bonnie had the ownership and the organisation of everything. Now I know it'll be different, that I can contribute something creative, build up my own work as part of it.'

'I'm so glad,' Fran said. 'It's selfish of me, but I kept hoping Kim wouldn't persuade you to go to England. This will be wonderful for you, Syl, so exciting.' She leaned forward, glancing around, lowering her voice a little: 'Poor Bon. I hope she gets through this all right. So much for the saintly Jeff. I can't imagine how she survived not talking about it all those years.'

Sylvia nodded. 'It's a relief to know that he wasn't entirely perfect,' she said. 'It would have been terrible for him too, but just think how crippling it was for both of them. I know this sounds horrible but I can't help wondering if her desperation about losing the child was what made her cling to him so much. Blinded her to his faults. Irene says he was a very lovely man and a good husband, but terribly uptight about a lot of things.'

'Yes, she told me that too,' Fran agreed. 'Bonnie always makes him sound so perfect, but I actually like him better now I know he had some faults.'

'Me too. I suspect there are lots of men of our generation like that; totally unable to confront their emotions. Colin was the same. It must be terrible for them, but it's not much fun for the women who marry them either. D'you think she'll be able to handle working with Jack after the other night?'

Fran poured the last of the tea. 'Lenore says Jack's really cool about it. She's told Bonnie to just face it head on when she sees him. Make a joke of it and he'll respond to that. It sounds like good advice, if she can manage it.'

'So, what're you two dames plotting now?' Sean asked, ambling over to their table.

'Mother's Day,' Fran said with a smile, gesturing to him to join them.

'Ugh!' he said, pulling out a chair and sinking his head in his hands. 'Don't talk to me about it. I know, I know I have to come up with some special menu.'

'How about sandwiches of sliced bread and tinned ham,' Fran said, 'with a Thermos flask of sweet tea?'

'Heaven!' he said. 'Sounds like when I was a kid and we used to go to the beach in Galway, and sit on a rug.'

'Exactly,' Fran said. 'And that's what we're going to do this year, all of us, only not in Galway. A day off, a picnic, plastic plates, sand in our food.'

'A day off?'

'A day off. All of us. We'll close for the day.'

'Lord! What'll Bonnie say? She won't like it.'

'She'll love it,' Fran said decisively. 'At least, by the time I've finished with her, she will.'

FORTY-FIVE

Sylvia lay on the same tartan rug in almost exactly the same place as last year, remembering how she had felt that day. She had been numb with the shock discovery of Colin's deception. Telling Fran and Bonnie that night had been the defining moment. Would she have been able to do it without them? Their friendship had given her courage, a place to go, the chance of another life. It was hard to imagine that she could have coped without all that. A shadow fell across her face and Irene settled into the canvas chair that Lila had occupied last year.

'I wondered if you'd fallen asleep, Sylvia,' she said.

'No, just thinking,' Sylvia said, sitting up. 'Thinking about all that's happened since we were last here.'

Irene smiled, looking out to where Mike and Hamish stood talking, ankle deep in the shallow water. 'You were a married woman this time last year,' she said.

'And you were a single one,' Sylvia countered.

'A great and surprising change for both of us,' Irene said with a laugh. 'A reminder that anything is possible. Dear Hamish, who would have thought it? I gained a partner, and I also feel I gained a second daughter, Sylvia. I can't quite tell you what it's meant to me having you around. I hope you've finally made up your mind to stay put in the cottage.'

'I'd love to,' Sylvia said, 'although I still can't get past the feeling that I'm taking advantage of you.'

Irene shook her head. 'It's a two-way thing. I have the pleasure of your presence, which is also a safety net for me, and the cottage is being used. I'm really enjoying all the comings and goings – with Bonnie, you, visits from Fran, Caro and Rebekah, and occasionally Jodie. Even Marjorie seems to be trying to get in on it. You've all made that great big house come alive again, just as you did when you were teenagers.'

'And we're just as much trouble,' Sylvia said with a smile. 'I don't know how I'd have got through this year without you all.'

'Oh, you would, dear,' Irene said. 'It's amazing how tough and resilient we women are when we have to be. But loving friends help to take the edge off it all. As, I believe, you very wisely said to Bonnie at one point, in the end we're always alone, but there's no doubt the company along the way makes a big difference.'

A few feet away, Bonnie sat on another rug, listening to Tan telling Veronica about her family in Vietnam. Their voices were pleasant, melodious; she wasn't listening to the words, just the rise and fall of the sound. Last year she had felt a pain so sharp it was like a knife turning inside her, and while she had focused on losing Jeff, it was much more than that. It was about Lucy, and Jeff's death had felt like acid poured onto the old wound. Once he was gone she was free to talk about it but didn't know how to break her silence. She lay back on the rug and stretched her arms above her head. It still hurt, of course, but just as Lenore had promised, it was different, softer, more textured, something she could acknowledge, talk about, explore. They had all been right, her mother, Fran and Sylvia, when they told her it was time to let go, start a new life; she had tried and she had the Boatshed to show for it. But in the end it had been those days with Lenore that had taken her to a place where she knew it was all right to be alone.

'I always thought that Jeff knew best,' she had told Lenore, 'that men knew best about everything, really. That's what we were brought up to believe, and it's hard to shake that off. I thought he would always do what was best for both of us and that I had to live up to that.'

'He was just a man, Bonnie,' Lenore said. 'A man devastated

by the loss of his child. He probably did think he was doing the best thing for both of you. But he got it terribly wrong.'

It seemed all right to admit that now. It wasn't a betrayal, just an acknowledgment of the truth. It didn't mean she loved him any less, just that now she knew she should trust her own instincts to guide her.

'What d'you think, Bonnie?' David said, sitting down cross-legged beside her. 'Good picnic, bad business decision?'

'Both,' she smiled. 'But the first is what matters.'

He nodded, and sipped his glass of soda. 'I wish Gran was here. I miss her so much. It wasn't till she'd gone that I realised all the things I wished I done. I just took it for granted that she'd always be there. Like Mum, constant, unchanging to the last – well, almost the last.'

'But Fran's changed a lot this year.'

'Yes,' he said. 'Yes, she has, the Boatshed's done wonders for her.'

'It's not just a one-way thing, David,' Bonnie said. 'All her work over the years has led to this. It would be a very different place without her.' She looked across to where Fran sat in a folding chair with Rebekah on her knee, chatting to Sean and Jodie, and she remembered how Fran looked when she walked into the restaurant a year ago. She seemed more comfortable with herself now. They were business partners as well as friends, and she and Sylvia had more than proved themselves in that respect. It was all so different from that first ambivalent discussion at the Boatshed. 'She's an amazing woman, your mother,' Bonnie said. 'You know we're planning another restaurant in Manly? From now on, nothing will surprise me. She's grown in so many ways. Who knows what next?'

David finished his soda and stretched his legs out in front of him. 'I think she's there now,' he said. 'I don't think there'll be many more surprises for a good while yet.'

Bonnie smiled at him. 'Don't you be so sure. I thought that about my mother and look at her now.'

*

'I'll take her, Mum, give you a break,' Caro said, reaching out for Rebekah. 'Anything wrong? You look a bit fed up.'

'No, nothing,' Fran said, standing up and brushing grass off her skirt. 'Yes, you take her now, I could do with stretching my legs.' The picnic had been a good decision, something they all needed. Sean and Graeme, hand in hand, were down by the water now, David and Jodie following them. She remembered David and Lila last year, dancing on the sand, Lila in her purple, so completely absorbed in the dance. Back then she had thought David looked fragile and sometimes she could still see it, but there was more to him now, he had built an inner strength. Jodie had been good for him, good for all of them.

Bonnie looked up and smiled at her. 'The right decision, Fran,' she called. 'Absolutely right!'

Fran waved in acknowledgment. 'Wait until I bring out the tinned ham sandwiches,' she said. 'Everyone has to eat one in honour of Mum.' How Lila would have enjoyed this big crowd of people, different families, different lives, bound by love and friendship. She struggled against the tears, reminding herself to count her blessings, but it was hard when someone who figured so strongly among those blessings was missing.

'I don't think I can cope with it,' Lenore had said over the phone.

'It's just a picnic,' Fran said. 'It's not like we're announcing anything to them, just letting them see us together. They'll work it out in their own time.'

'And what if they work it out and don't like it?'

'Lenore, it'll be all right; trust me, please, trust them, my children, my friends. This is how Mum would have done it. She would have let them watch it unfold, expected the best of everyone; expected them to care enough to be happy for us.'

But still Lenore had demurred, wanting more time, anxious about Fran's commitment as well as the reactions of the others. Fran sighed and swallowed the lump in her throat, wondering how long it would take for Lenore to feel safe.

David was circulating with another bottle of champagne, topping up the glasses. 'Time for a toast,' he said. 'Come on, Mum, where's your glass?'

She held it out and the stream of champagne sparkled gold in the sunlight.

'To mothers,' David said, holding up his glass, 'and their daughters.'

'And their sons,' Sylvia called.

'And grandmothers,' he said, 'and in memory of one special great grandmother – to Lila.'

They raised their glasses, chorusing the toast, pausing to savour their memories of Lila before the conversation began again.

'She would have loved it, wouldn't she, Mum?' Caro said, hugging her with tears in her eyes. 'She would have been here in her purple with that lovely little red hat Lenore gave her and – oh look, there *is* Lenore. You didn't say she was coming.'

Fran swung round, her skin prickling with shock. Lenore was walking towards them, her usual brisk and confident manner slower now, more cautious, sunglasses hiding her eyes, hands pushed down into the pockets of her black leather jacket. The disguise was in place but Lenore's occupation of it was tentative.

'I can't come,' she'd said, 'because they'll see me as I am – your kids, Bonnie, Sylvia, Irene . . . what'll they think? It's safe just being Lenore, but now I'll be the lesbian who seduced their mother, their friend. And I'm scared that you'll run away.'

'Hey, Lenore,' David said, walking over to greet her. 'Just in time for the ham sandwich ceremony.' He bent to kiss her and took her hand, leading her over to the group. Fran watched them close in around Lenore, Caro hugging her, Bonnie struggling to her feet to kiss her, Sylvia stroking her shoulders, handing her a glass of champagne. Lenore's eyes were hidden still behind the dark glasses as she edged towards Fran.

'You came,' Fran said, holding out both hands to her.

Lenore nodded. 'Obviously,' she said, and taking Fran's hands she stepped forward and kissed her on the lips. 'But in terror.' She took off her sunglasses.

'It'll be all right,' Fran said. 'You can feel that, can't you, now you're here?'

Lenore looked around. 'Yes,' she said. 'I can, you were right. And you're not going to run away?'

Fran shook her head. 'No way, not ever, there's no escape now . . .' She paused, glancing over Lenore's shoulder. 'Oh my goodness, look what's happening over there.'

Bonnie, sitting beside Caro, was reaching out her arms towards Rebekah. 'My turn now, I think,' she said. And Caro, looking up in surprise, handed the baby to her with a nervous glance at Irene.

'You really are gorgeous, you know,' Bonnie said, and Rebekah chuckled and reached up a hand to touch her face. Bonnie turned to them with a smile. 'Now, what do you think about designer baby wear?'

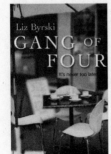